PRODIGAL

DEAD HOLLOW TRILOGY (BOOK ONE)

JUDY K. WALKER

Titles by Judy K. Walker

THE DEAD HOLLOW TRILOGY
Prodigal
Founder
Heir

THE SYDNEY BRENNAN MYSTERIES
(IN ORDER OF PUBLICATION)
Back to Lazarus (A Sydney Brennan Novel)
Secrets in Stockbridge (A Sydney Brennan Novella)
The Perils of Panacea (A Sydney Brennan Novel)
No Safe Winterport (A Sydney Brennan Novella)
Braving the Boneyard (A Sydney Brennan Novel)
River Bound (A Sydney Brennan Novella)

Cover design by Robin Ludwig Design Inc. http://www.gobookcoverdesign.com/

ISBN: 978-1-946720-00-9

For my Wild and Wonderful Kith and Kin—I hope the love comes through

_1_

Traitor, _she thought._

The school bus slowed, and a young girl stood and lurched down the aisle. Her heavy backpack swung wide with every step, swaying into alternating seats. There was no one left to clobber (hers was the last stop), but today she wouldn't have cared anyway. She gave an extra stutter-step and grabbed a seat's metal frame to keep from stumbling when the bus finally stopped.

"Have a good weekend, Rachel," the bus driver said, opening the accordion door with a screech that cut through the rumble of the diesel engine.

The girl stared down at the treads of the steps as she exited, staying to the right to avoid stepping on gum. "Goodbye, Mr. Dewey."

At the bottom, she took the final long step to the ground in a big hop, landing decisively on both feet. It was, after all, Friday. Even if Evie had betrayed her.

Rachel paused just long enough to free her long, dark hair from a backpack strap, then started up the hill, hunched forward like a turtle. There were three homes on the dirt road—a trailer, followed by Evie's house and Rachel's house—then a long stretch of nothing but vegetation until the route looped around and joined up with another back road. The steep incline and the few leaves remaining on the trees (some orange and yellow *and red, but mostly brown) still shielded Rachel's house from sight. She kicked stray bits of gravel from the road as if they'd insulted her, until the breeze caught a cloud of the roused dust and sent it toward her eyes.*

Well, booger butt.

Rachel didn't stop, just ducked her head even more as she rubbed at her eyes. Would she have gone to Melanie's sleepover—without Evie—if Melanie had invited her instead? No. *Because Rachel and Evie were best friends, and best friends don't do that to each other.*

Except... if Rachel were honest with herself, she knew she would have gone, too. And she knew Evie would tell her all about it tomorrow, with funny stories of who said and did what, stories that would make Rachel feel better, that would remind her that she was better off with Evie than with Melanie and her friends any day.

Rachel also knew that she'd be lost without Evie. She'd be eating lunch alone, sitting—

Evie's dog was barking. A lot.

Rachel opened her mouth to yell at Trooper to stop (he listened to commands), but when she lifted her head, there was a man. Standing right in front of her.

Tall and old like her teachers, he didn't speak. Just stared at her with a funny expression that wasn't quite a smile.

Rachel tried to smile at him, but she couldn't get her face to move. She couldn't speak either. She knew she should, that there was something wrong, but she was so scared, she couldn't make a sound. Except the noise of her breath starting to whistle in her chest. She reached toward her jacket pocket.

Suddenly the man moved in a blur, slapping a hand over Rachel's mouth and throwing her under his arm in one quick movement, as if she were a football. An eleven-year-old football.

Rachel's backpack bounced painfully. She wanted to scream for help, to bite his hand or kick him, but more than that she wanted to breathe. She needed to breathe.

The man was in no particular hurry now that he had her in hand, but spots appeared in front of her eyes and she couldn't see where he was going. Was there a car? Her chest grew tighter.

I can't breathe! *she screamed inside her head.*

Trooper was going crazy. She couldn't see him either, but she could hear him snarling, lunging against his chain and pawing at the ground.

Help me, Trooper.

Then the spots in front of Rachel's eyes disappeared in blackness and a roaring sound filled her ears, so loud she could barely make out the man's voice when he spoke.

"Well, that was easy," he said, bruising Rachel's ribs as he hitched her higher on his hip. "And so it begins again."

2

The girl looked at him with wide, scared eyes, the white sclera visible even in the fading light.

He twisted in his seat, his sleeve making a synthetic whisper against the seat cover's cheap, gray fabric as he stretched past the girl for her backpack. She recoiled from him, curling into a fetal position as best she could with her hands and feet secured, while whimpering through the gag.

"Relax," the man said.

Not that it made a difference.

There was no one to see her, or hear her, for miles. Nothing but silent trees, as far as the eye could see. Well, almost nothing.

He reached into the girl's backpack, only to quickly jerk his hand back with a gasp.

He carefully pulled out the offending item—a spiral notebook. The sharp, bent end of its coiled wire had caught his finger. With everything else they were paranoid about, how was it that parents never saw the dangers in front of them?

He emptied the rest of the pack on the bench seat next to him —a couple of thin, hardcover textbooks and a zipper pouch full of goodies. There were the usual pens and pencils, a plastic compass she might use once all year, a tiny ruler, a key ring, and some kind of school ID card. He looked at the ID card... twisted to look at her... closed his eyes... looked at the ID card again.

And then he howled.

No other word could describe the inhuman, snarling frustration that tore from his throat while the girl trembled in the seat behind him, unnoticed. He slammed his hands into the steering wheel, then squeezed it hard, imagining it was someone's throat. Imagining it was *his* throat. But *he* would come later.

The man took a deep breath, then sighed it out. It didn't matter. Who the kid was didn't matter. What mattered was that he had her. He returned the girl's belongings to her pack, except for a couple of items. These he took outside, and placed strategically in the spot he'd chosen earlier. The echo from his slamming door had barely faded when he finished.

Perfect.

Back in the vehicle, he hardly spared a glance for the girl, except to wonder how much she weighed. They had a long way to go. The engine started on the first try, as he'd known it would, and he reversed until he felt his tires hit asphalt again.

A long way to go, indeed.

3

A dam Rutledge was cold.

He leaned forward, peering into the narrow tunnel his headlights cut through the dark. The forest crowded the two-lane road, helping to disguise the rise of the mountain on one side and the occasional precipitous drop on the other. Branches of the mostly leafless deciduous trees crept toward the center line from above, while the conifers kept their distance, upright sentinels. Adam squeezed the steering wheel hard to quell the trembling in his hands.

It was just so cold, too cold for this time of year.

Yeah, right. That's why my hands are shaking.

By now, Ruthie would have found the note on the register. She'd be cursing, probably taking out her frustration on whoever she'd found to cover Adam's Friday night shift. Maybe she'd fire Adam. He'd grabbed his duffle bag and blanket from the back room, just in case. And because he didn't know how long he'd be gone. Or, let's be honest, if he'd be back. He'd lasted longer at Ruthie's than he'd ever have thought he would, but it was probably time.

What the hell do you think you're doing?

That's what Ruthie would have asked—yelled at him—if she could have.

And Adam wasn't sure how to answer.

He felt wide awake for the first time in... well, a long time. A very long time.

It must have rained recently. The asphalt reflected shiny black in his headlights. Adam braked more suddenly than he should have, approaching the familiar sharp turn alongside Dead Hollow. The metal guardrail there was deeply dented, but still technically intact. He held his breath until he'd made it through to the other side without sliding on his bald tires. Thank God the road wasn't yet cold enough to freeze.

Adam geared down as he approached the next steep incline, and the car's engine whined. His beater hatchback got good gas mileage and was handy for sleeping rough, but it definitely was not made for mountain roads. The last hill before JJ's house was going to be a doozy. Worst-case scenario, he could pull over and walk it.

Adam felt as though he had been to the Tulley house as many times as he'd taken breath, and he was shocked to suddenly realize that he'd never driven there. Hopefully, Mr. Tulley wouldn't shoot him before he could identify himself. Eighteen years was a long time.

The lights from the car's console seemed too bright, and Adam squinted at the road, wondering if he'd missed his turn already. The high, bright headlights of a large pickup in his rearview mirror didn't help, reflecting in his eyes even with the mirror flipped up. A glint of red appeared ahead to the left, and Adam tapped his brakes. The glint wasn't eyes shining—just a simple bike reflector mounted on a pole—but Adam's relief was tinged with anticipation, and more complicated emotions he didn't have time to consider.

The little car bounced as Adam made the turn onto the dirt road over uneven ground. He blinked as the pickup turned left as well, its lights a blinding, mad strobe. Not many people lived up this way. Adam felt a prickle on the back of his neck: was he being followed?

Adam downshifted even more, but his hatchback still crept up the hill. Maybe the truck could give him a push. He flipped his rearview mirror back down to get a sense of how close the truck was, just in time to see a second pickup following the first. Wait... a third pickup.

Frick. Why were they following him? Did they know who he was?

The pickup on his tail laid on the horn. *Beeeeeeeep... beep-beep*.

There was nowhere to pull over—the road was little more than a single lane—and it should be obvious that Adam was driving as fast as he could. What did they want from him?

The truck behind him accelerated, its engine roaring and its headlights looming larger until they filled the back windshield. Adam weaved the car as best he could on the narrow road and braced himself for impact.

I never should have come back.

The truck fell back for a moment, until a couple of car lengths separated them. It paused, then sped forward again just as the first residence appeared on the right—a trailer with lights shining from every window. Adam veered toward its driveway and felt the barest tap against his bumper when his car lurched back to the center. He struggled to bring the vehicle under control.

His heart pounded as the truck slowed again. The world was a kaleidoscope of harsh white light and black sky, with tree trunks flashing gray between, but he knew JJ's house was coming up next. Or at least, where JJ's family lived two decades ago. For the first time, it occurred to Adam that they might not live there anymore. What if it was a house full of strangers? Or worse, what if it was empty?

Adam goosed the gas pedal until his tires spun on the dirt road. The hill leveled out a bit and he sped ahead, catching sight of JJ's driveway.

The pickup behind him accelerated, too, and Adam's stomach

rolled as the truck blasted its horn again. The hatchback fishtailed as Adam swung into JJ's driveway. A porch light flashed on about a tenth of a mile ahead, and he raced toward it like a beacon, gaining a little ground on the trucks when they slowed for the turn. The house was smaller than Adam remembered and oddly silhouetted, front-lit by the porch light with the slightest glow of sky above and behind. The car slid toward an old oak tree, stopping well short of the front steps.

Adam yanked the emergency brake, threw the car door open and bolted toward the house, just as the first pickup rolled to a stop behind him, blocking his car in. The other two followed suit, spreading lengthways to form a barricade as far as the trees on either side. The porch light reflected from a picture window to the right of the house's entrance, making a glassy mirror that showed a man with a rifle climbing from the first truck. Adam slowed, now afraid to run, as if he were sneaking past a predator.

He made it as far as the first step when a deep voice rang out behind him, cutting through the sound of a dog barking, "Stop right there! Where the hell do you think you're going?"

It wasn't the words that stopped Adam, but rather the tone of voice, the arrogant confidence that came from holding a gun on someone. Adam slowly raised his hands, but didn't turn around. Out of the corner of his eye, he saw a couple more men rolling out of the last pickup, pulling rifles from the rack in the back window as they did.

The air rang with silence as a dog abruptly stopped barking, followed by the sound of protesting springs on the screen door of the house. The squawk was as reassuring as it had been all through his childhood.

A woman stepped through the door, letting it bang shut behind her. She wore jeans and a hooded sweatshirt. Her long, dark hair hung loose, bits of it caught up in the hood. Taller than Adam expected, shadows hid her face, but the shotgun in her hands was clear enough.

Despite everything, Adam felt a grin sneaking in as it always did, pulling up the corner of his mouth, even though it was the last thing he wanted to do.

"What the hell are *you* doing here?" she asked, her breath clouding the cold air.

He wished he could say.

4

———

Jennifer Jane Tulley looked out at the half dozen or so armed men in her yard before returning her gaze to Adam. Tall and broad-shouldered, dark-haired with heavy brows that emphasized the deep shadows the porch light left beneath his eyes. Was the little punk smiling? He still had that damn dimple, peeking through the scruff on his face. She struggled not to smile back, to keep the steel in her voice and her spine. Some days it just didn't pay to get up in the morning, and this seemed to be one of those days.

"I asked," she continued, looking past Adam at the other assorted men in her yard, "what the hell you think you're doing here? Leslie, you want to speak to that?"

A man in a heavy flannel shirt spoke from the driver's side of the first pickup to arrive. "You know what we're doing, JJ. Now put the goddamn shotgun down."

Instead of relaxing her grip, JJ lifted her arms higher to sight along the barrel at him. Not that she needed to at this distance. She watched Adam take a slow step sideways, just to be safe.

"What do you think my daddy would've done if you showed up

on his own property and told him to put his goddamned gun down?" JJ asked.

He would've blown your balls off. Everyone knew it, but sometimes they needed a reminder that she was her father's daughter. Trooper let out a low yip of solidarity from his tie-out.

Leslie didn't speak, but he did lower his rifle. The man who'd driven the second pickup—wearing a camouflage jacket and rendered almost unrecognizable by the trucker cap pulled down to his eyebrows—set his own weapon on his seat and stepped away from the pickup, raising his hands. A long-eared hound in the back stood and looked around the cab, only mildly curious.

"Easy, JJ," the man said. "It's nothing to get riled up about. We'd just finished searching the hollow when we saw this guy driving by in a strange car. You can understand why we'd want to check him out."

JJ stared at Adam. He took the hint, pulling his baseball cap down, and climbed the rest of the steps in a hurry. Too much of a hurry, in fact. A sneakered toe caught the edge at the top, and he narrowly missed bumping against JJ. She had a sudden flash of Adam slipping while they were climbing a clump of sugar maples as kids, hanging upside down—literally red-faced—until she and Danny got an adult to pry his ankle loose. Good to know some things never changed. Adam moved behind her, and she turned her attention back to the trespassers in her yard.

"I appreciate that, Malcolm," JJ said, lowering the barrel of her gun a few inches. The damn thing was getting heavy. "Now that you know everything's okay, you can get back to your family. That's where everybody should be tonight, at home with their families."

Malcolm nodded and moved his rifle to the rack in back so he could climb in. "All right, JJ. You take care, and let us know if you need anything."

JJ nodded back, finally letting her gun barrel point at the ground. "Thanks, Malcolm. Give Marlene my best."

JJ watched the men return to their vehicles, but really her

attention was focused on Leslie. He'd been a bully when they were kids, and wasn't much better as an adult. The only thing you could count on was his unpredictability. Leslie leaned in to the pickup next to him and said something to the man inside that JJ couldn't hear. The other man's foot came back out to rest on the ground, and he hovered, half in and half out of the truck.

Damn. She should've known it wouldn't be that easy.

"JJ," Leslie called out, "no offense, but how do we know that's not Marcus hiding behind you? I mean, we wouldn't want him sneaking his way back into your house and doing something. I hear he's a pretty mean drunk."

"You know damn well it's not Marcus," JJ said.

Leslie shifted so he could grin at the man next to him. "Maybe I should come inside and check your house for you, just in case."

JJ felt her father's temper roll through her. She'd never admit it to anyone—least of all to her daughter—but JJ occasionally wished she were a man, so her physical power could match her fury. But then she'd probably just end up in jail, like most of her cousins on her dad's side. Instead, JJ turned to her most powerful weapon —her mouth.

"Thanks, but no thanks, Leslie. If you're so hard up for company, why don't you head over to Old Man Prior's. I hear he's got some new ewes you could break in."

JJ heard appreciative snickers in the dark. Leslie looked around, trying to gauge the source of the sounds, then stepped toward the house, pointing at JJ as if his index finger were loaded.

"Fuck you, JJ."

"Nope. Sorry. I don't have sex with sheep, even by the transitive property. Now get off my land, before you put me in a bad mood."

Leslie pointed again, but before he could speak, a deep growling rolled from the dark. Les jerked, glancing in the direction of the sound, where Trooper's four-legged silhouette stood, immobile. Then he ran a hand through his wavy dark hair, before swatting dismissively in JJ's general direction and heading back to his pickup.

JJ watched while the three vehicles began five-point ballets, trying to turn around in the now-snug quarters. She felt Adam move closer, head near her shoulder.

"The transitive property?" he asked. "Where did that come from?"

"I didn't sleep through math class," JJ said. "Did anyone recognize you?"

"I don't think so," Adam replied, so close she felt his warm breath stir her hair.

"You'd better hope Leslie didn't."

She waited until the last of the taillights winked down the driveway, then headed down into the yard. Adam stumbled after her. A large German shepherd mix tied to a doghouse wagged his tail and woofed as JJ approached. Adam flinched next to her. She looked at him, but his face was in shadows.

"I never knew you to be afraid of a dog," JJ said.

"He startled me."

JJ didn't believe him, but didn't push it. She squatted down and rubbed the dog's face, back and forth on both sides. She couldn't see his doggie grin, but she could feel it.

"Sorry, Trooper," she whispered, dropping her head next to the dog's. She ignored the itch of his hair against her face and took pleasure in its warmth. "I hate having you out here, too, but it's just for a little longer."

JJ felt a sudden pressure in her eyes and sinuses. Putting dogs on tie-outs was one of the few things she'd ever fought with her father about. It was ridiculous that seeing her dog on her dad's old chain could almost reduce her to tears now, when there were so many things in the world—in Beecham County—that were so much worse. But then, she didn't have control over those things, and she did control how she treated her dog.

Unfortunately, Trooper was a much better watchdog outside

than inside, where he tended to sleep like the dead. On the couch if no one was watching. She hugged him to her leg one last time, then stood to confront everything else, all the bad crap. Maybe there was something she could do about that after all.

"So you heard about the girl?" she asked.

Adam was still backlit from the porch, and JJ wished she could see his face, but she didn't very well have the time to take him inside and interrogate him about where he'd been and what had brought him back. She heard Adam let out a breath before he said, "Yeah."

"Well, then, let's go," JJ said, striding back toward the house.

"Go where?" Adam asked, struggling to keep up as they crossed the unfamiliar yard.

Out of the corner of her eye, JJ saw him make a last-minute, wild leap over Evie's prone bicycle. She wished she could laugh. "Down the road to see her parents."

Adam stopped following her.

JJ slipped inside to grab her keys from the dining table. She didn't always lock up, but she'd been more diligent about it lately, even though she suspected one determined run at the front door with a strong shoulder would be enough to bring it down.

Adam was still standing at the bottom of the steps when she came out. "Are you sure that's a good idea?" he asked. "Don't you think maybe the parents want to be left alone?"

The key stuck in the door, and JJ cursed under her breath as she yanked it free. "No, I don't. I think they want their daughter back. And we're going to find her."

Adam blinked in the glare of the porch light. His eyes glistened, and his nose was pink with the cold. He looked twelve years old again. Okay, maybe fourteen. JJ felt a thickness in her throat.

"Do you really think so?" Adam asked. "Do you think we can find her?"

JJ put her hands firmly on his shoulders. She could feel her lips pressing together, hear the branches tickle each other in the breeze. She had the sensation that time had stopped, and something was waiting for her answer.

"Yes, we will," she said. "This time, we will."

Adam dropped his eyes to the ground.

JJ leaned forward, kissing him on the cheek. "Welcome home."

5

———

JJ led Adam to an old Bronco, color indistinguishable in the porch light she'd left on. The passenger seat was patched with a strip of duct tape, but it seemed to be holding, so Adam flopped down, suddenly exhausted. No, that wasn't quite true. Part of him was still wired, too. It was just hard to tell where one part left off and the other picked up.

"Sorry, Janie—what?" He'd missed whatever she said. It must have been directed at the exhausted part.

"I said, how'd you find out about the girl so fast?"

Excellent question, but one he couldn't answer, at least not in a way JJ could understand. Not yet and maybe not ever. "Does it matter?" he asked.

Adam shivered. JJ didn't bother with the heat, either because the SUV hadn't had time to warm up or because the heater didn't work. His money was on the latter. Adam leaned his head against the window and felt the chill radiating through his cap. He stared into the dark, but couldn't see anything except his breath fogging the glass. JJ switched on the headlights, and as she turned her vehicle in the driveway, the high beams spotlighted a familiar poplar tree. Mr. Tulley once caught him and Danny and JJ carving their initials in it with Danny's pocketknife. He'd threatened to tan their hides if they ever so much as breathed on that tree again. Adam had never been so scared in his life. But that was a few months before Adam, and everyone else in Beecham County, learned what real fear was. Sometimes, he felt like he'd never forgotten it.

They reached the bottom of the driveway, and JJ turned left, drove about fifty yards, and turned left again at another nearly hidden driveway. This house sat closer to the road than JJ's, and it was lit up like a Christmas tree, with most if not all of the interior and exterior lights turned on.

"You didn't mention they were your neighbors," Adam said.

JJ slowed, keeping her eyes locked on the short, steep drive ahead. It had a few gullies that took swerving around, but surely JJ knew them by heart.

"Their girl is best friends with my daughter," she said.

"You have a daughter?" Adam asked, incredulous. He shouldn't be, but he couldn't help it.

Now JJ glanced at him, grinning. "Yes, I have a daughter. Evelyn. Evie for short. Almost twelve years old. She's at a sleepover tonight."

"Wow," Adam said. JJ Tulley, a mom. Adam found himself grinning, too. He thought of all the times JJ had gotten him and Danny out of trouble, usually with her smart mouth, but with her fists if necessary. He wouldn't exactly have thought of JJ as maternal, but she had been a Protector, just like her dad. "I'll bet she's an amazing kid. Do I know her dad?"

JJ's grin disappeared as she pulled her Bronco off to the side of the driveway, mashing down some high grass. "*She* barely knows her dad."

"So you're not married?" Adam asked.

"Not anymore," JJ said, with a that's-the-end-of-the-conversation tone. Then she cut the engine and reached for her door, ready to bolt from the SUV, but Adam grabbed her arm.

"Wait," he said. "Give me a minute."

JJ turned to him, and Adam found himself lost in her face. He couldn't make out details, but the light from the car's interior and the house's exterior gave him the broad strokes, a blurred version of the adult that his mind overlaid on his memories of the child. It wasn't that JJ's face had changed with age, so much as time had refined what was already there. Her cheeks were less full, brows sharper. She still had that deep divot beneath her nose and above her lip. Was there a word for that? Same shape to her eyes, same determined set to her mouth. But now there was another child that wore her face, nearly the same age that they had been when everything fell apart. Adam was shocked when he felt his own eyes start to tear, and quickly looked away.

"What's the family's name?" he asked.

"Nicholson—Dorothy and Otto. I doubt you know them. Dorothy was a couple of years behind us, and Otto's from somewhere over toward Kentucky. Their daughter's name—"

Adam heard JJ hesitate, stumbling over the verb tense.

"Their daughter's name is Rachel. Just let me do the talking."

"Okay," Adam said, and they climbed out of the Bronco into a night that felt even colder than it had a few moments ago. Adam rubbed his arms and almost complained, but JJ was halfway to the front door already. And she was probably wearing less than he was.

The Nicholson house was a simple, two-story affair with white siding and black shutters. A gray-painted concrete slab served as an entryway, topped with an overhang supported by slim, white pillars and a strip of decorative, black-painted metal scrollwork on either side. There was a doorbell, but JJ didn't bother, banging on the screen door instead.

A bearded man in jeans and a Washington Redskins sweatshirt opened the main door, pausing just a moment before unlatching the screen.

"Hey, JJ," he said. His bulk filled the doorway, but he was the kind of fit that came from a lifetime of hard chores, not from going to the gym every morning.

"Any word?" JJ asked.

He shook his head and stepped aside. "Grant's coming by again later tonight. Come on in. Dorothy will be glad to see you."

JJ squeezed through, trying not to let the heat out, and Adam followed suit, closing the door behind him. Otto led them through a mudroom and kitchen into a living room where a woman sat on a flower-patterned sofa. She leaned forward so her long, brown hair curtained her face, and stared down at the cordless telephone clutched in her hands. The two men stood awkwardly while JJ negotiated around the coffee table to sit on the cushion next to her.

"Dorothy," JJ said softly, reaching out to take her closest hand. "How are you holding up?"

Dorothy lifted her head and nodded, as if that were an answer to the question, but didn't speak. Her face was tear-streaked, and her eyes and lips were deep pink and puffy. She looked barely out of high school herself—too young to have a daughter in middle school—but Adam suspected Dorothy was one of those people who appeared even more vulnerable in times of trouble. Sitting next to JJ, the woman was a thin-limbed, spring-blooming dogwood sheltering alongside a solid, straight-trunked red oak. Something about Dorothy—the high, even cheekbones, the deep brown eyes and skin that was just a shade or two darker than most people in Beecham County—looked vaguely familiar.

"You used to love Smarties," Adam said, the words out before he knew they were there.

Dorothy looked up at him, surprise snapping her out of her lethargic confusion for a moment. "Do I know you?"

"I remember how Mrs. Mitchell from the corner store would pull a roll of Smarties from a dish behind the counter to give to the kids before we left with a loaf of bread or whatever. But you couldn't wait until you got home. You'd sit outside on the sidewalk and peel back the wrapper," Adam said, demonstrating with his hands, "and you'd examine each little individual candy pellet before you ate it, like you were trying to figure out what flavor it was."

Dorothy's head tilted and her eyes lost their focus. Her

husband, Otto, went so rigid next to him that Adam could feel the man's stillness as if it were movement.

"Did they actually have different flavors, or were they all just sour?" Adam asked.

A ghost of a smile appeared on Dorothy's lips. "That's what I was trying to figure out, but I don't think I ever did." She paused, staring at him. "You're Adam, aren't you? You were JJ's best friend."

Dorothy's head swung to JJ for confirmation.

"Best instigator," JJ said. "He was always getting me into trouble."

JJ quickly glanced at Adam, but he knew not to challenge her. "I haven't thought about Mrs. Mitchell in years," JJ continued. "She moved to North Carolina to be near her grandkids when Mr. Mitchell died and the 7-11 people bought her store. I wonder what ever happened to her."

Adam bumped his elbow on the entertainment center behind him. The top shelf held photographs, the bottom one video games and DVDs and other miscellaneous, stackable entertainments. Adam picked up a photo from the top shelf.

"Is this Rachel?" he asked.

Dorothy nodded without speaking, her eyes filling with tears again.

The girl looking sideways at the camera seemed a little small for her age, a little unsure, but healthy. Maybe she just hadn't hit her growth spurt yet. She had her mother's dark hair and full lips, but her father's pale complexion and vivid blue eyes that stared out at the world.

"She's beautiful. She has your eyes," Adam said, meeting Otto's intense stare. Adam was suddenly seized by nausea and a sense of falling. He swallowed, afraid to blink, and in a moment the vertigo was gone. The last time he'd slept was this afternoon before his shift, but when was the last time he'd eaten?

Adam turned to carefully place the picture back on the crowded shelf. His eyes were drawn to a photo of a nicely dressed

Dorothy and Otto (wedding?), and a picture of a boy in a baseball uniform, with a smaller candid of him and Rachel tucked into the frame. The boy looked a couple of years older than her.

"How's Jacob doing?" JJ asked.

Dorothy mashed her lips together until she could speak. "He's been in his room all evening. I think he feels guilty. Like if he'd been here, she wouldn't have wandered off."

Wandered off. So that's what she was telling herself. Adam thought that was probably a good thing, for now, although a quick glance at Otto's grim face indicated the girl's father harbored no such illusions.

Dorothy looked at Adam again, then back at JJ before shaking her head. "Adam Rutledge," she confirmed to herself, obviously pleased her brain was still functional enough to bring his full name to mind. "You were always hanging around outside Mrs. Mitchell's, waiting for JJ."

"Never helped me carry anything home," JJ groused.

Like you'd have let me, Adam thought, but he just smiled.

"You'd lean up against the ice box," Dorothy said, "like the world was too heavy to stand up straight anymore. You and that fidgety boy, the one who couldn't stop flipping the little metal door open, until Mr. Mitchell would finally come out and yell at him for melting the ice."

Crap. Adam should have listened to JJ and kept his mouth shut. JJ glared at him, and he saw the same thought running through her mind.

"Dorothy, we're gonna go now, but you know I'm right next door if you need anything," JJ said, standing quickly. But it was too late.

Dorothy's brow furrowed. "That boy... that other boy..." Then her mouth dropped and her eyes opened wide in comprehension.

"Danny," Dorothy said.

And she started to scream.

6

"Dorothy, calm down," JJ said, placing her hands on the woman's shoulders.

But her screams continued, and it was all JJ could do not to cover her own ears. Otto momentarily froze, and Adam stood rooted to the spot, face pale and mouth open. For just an instant, JJ feared Adam would start screaming as well.

"Adam," JJ barked, pointing toward the front door, "get out of here. Now."

The sound of JJ's voice spurred Otto into action. He moved to the cushion on the other side of Dorothy, putting one hand on her shoulder and the other on her thigh while murmuring reassuringly. Adam finally closed his mouth, but his eyes were still too wide as he turned and left the room, his legs awkward as though he'd forgotten how to walk. JJ heard the front door close behind him when Dorothy paused. The woman's face was pink with effort, and she sucked air in great, heaving gasps.

At least if she hyperventilates, she can't scream. JJ felt a twinge of guilt at the thought—briefly—before flinching as Dorothy began wailing, a long, drawn-out extension of the sobs that racked her small body. JJ was suddenly aware of how cold her hands were as she took Dorothy's warm cheeks between them. "Hey, Dorothy, you need to calm down."

Tears streamed down Dorothy's face from eyes that had squeezed shut against the world, and she continued to keen for her daughter.

"Dorothy," JJ said, gripping the woman's cheeks more firmly with her fingers, "if you don't calm down, I'm going to slap you. Hard."

JJ squeezed for emphasis, and Dorothy opened red eyes. Her breath continued to wheeze, but without the previous moaning exhales.

"Good girl," JJ said, gently massaging the back of Dorothy's head as she rested her forehead against Dorothy's.

"JJ," Dorothy whispered, "where's my little girl?"

JJ's voice was strong as she said, "We're going to find her, sweetie. I promise. But you have to hold it together." She squeezed Dorothy's shoulders and smiled. "Now why don't you go wash your face?"

Dorothy looked at Otto. The big man nodded and touched her hair. "Go on, honey. It's okay."

JJ and Otto leaned over the back of the couch, watching until Dorothy shut the bathroom door behind her. JJ sighed and closed her eyes for a moment, letting the emotions wash over her. What the hell was she thinking, making a promise like that? It was the same promise she'd made to Danny in her heart, but never shared out loud. Even as a child, she'd had more sense than that. So what had gotten into her tonight?

"You might want to give Doc Hammond a call," JJ said. As time went by, it would become more and more difficult to calm Dorothy —or get her to sleep—without pharmaceutical help.

"I will," Otto said. Already standing, he towered over her.

JJ pushed herself reluctantly from the couch and headed toward the front door. She made it as far as the kitchen when she felt Otto's hand on her elbow.

"Why is *he* here?" Otto asked, flicking his eyes toward Adam waiting outside.

"He grew up in Cold Springs. Why wouldn't he be here?"

Otto stared at JJ, unspeaking, mouth set and the slightest quiver in his jaw. JJ instinctively looked at his hands; they weren't clenched into fists. Yet. She tucked one hand behind her and reached for the kitchen table with the other, gripping the tabletop.

"So you know what happened when we were kids?" JJ asked. Otto didn't answer, but he didn't have to. "Who told you?"

Otto shrugged. "People talk."

JJ narrowed her eyes. People do talk, but she found it hard to believe someone had been callous enough to tell the man about a twenty-year-old unsolved kidnapping the day his own daughter disappeared. Otto must have known about Danny prior to today.

"Why is he here now?" Otto reiterated, crossing his arms.

"For God's sake, Otto, Adam was a child, too, when it—"

"*Why?*"

JJ forced herself not to flinch when he yelled, to hold her position. "I called Adam," she lied, effortlessly. She lifted her chin, almost begging Otto to challenge her. "I wanted him here."

Dorothy's voice called out from the living room, looking for the two of them, asking if everything was all right. Otto's face softened, and JJ could almost believe she'd imagined his hostility just moments ago. Almost.

"Thanks, JJ," he said. "I know it means a lot to Dorothy having you here."

JJ nodded. "I'll drop by again in the morning."

Otto returned her nod and patted JJ's arm as he passed. She watched him follow his wife's voice into the other room, as if nothing had happened. And it hadn't, not really. Except that was the first time in the five years she'd known him that she'd ever heard Otto Nicholson raise his voice.

JJ gazed out the kitchen window at her car, her anxiety for the man inside it turning to anger, as her anxiety usually did. If even-tempered transplant Otto was suspicious of Adam, what chance did the damned fool have with the people who'd actually lived here twenty years ago?

7

A dam sat in JJ's Bronco, shivering. His teeth had begun chattering right about the time Dorothy's screams stopped inside the house. Not that there was exactly a connection between the two, but the silence did make his skin crawl. He rocked in his seat, trying to warm up, trying to make the creeping sensation go away. But it wouldn't. Adam set his feet on the dash and tucked his knees into his chest, trying to help his mind and body relax. When that didn't make him still, he pinched the bridge of his nose until his fingers ached and his eyes watered.

Please forgive me, Danny.

The sense of familiar and utterly freaking crazy were at war in Adam's mind. He tried to sort through some of what he'd heard this evening. Twenty years of catching up in twenty seconds. That's what it felt like. Otto Nicholson had said *Grant* was coming over later. Grant Mason had been a couple of years ahead of them in school, and his father was the Beecham County Sheriff when Adam and JJ were kids. Grant must have followed in his dad's footsteps.

Adam had tried to block out the details of what happened back then, when Danny was taken, including the many times Sheriff

Mason had questioned him. As a child, Adam was sure he knew *something*, something that would save his friend Danny, that would help them find him. The Sheriff was sure, too. But neither of them knew what it was. No matter how many times and how many ways Sheriff Mason asked him, they couldn't tease the key from Adam's mind. And then Adam started having difficulties figuring out what was real and what was... well, something else. All in his mind.

Maybe it—the key—was never there. Or maybe it was still waiting for Adam to find it. And so was Danny. And everyone else who couldn't let go.

Jesus, Danny, I'm sorry.

Adam sighed. *And yet here I am, freezing my buttkus off.*

He wasn't wearing a watch. Adam wondered how long he'd been waiting for JJ—fifteen minutes? He squeezed between the seats to the back of the vehicle and rummaged around in the storage space behind the back seat. If he knew JJ... *yes*. He found two gallons of distilled water, a set of jumper cables, a first aid kit, and a paper grocery bag with a flashlight and a musty wool blanket.

Climbing back into the front with the blanket, Adam banged his head on the roof and narrowly missed knocking the vehicle out of park. *Focus*. He pulled the blanket tightly around himself. Good Lord, he was hungry. Normally, he would've grabbed something right before his shift at the bar, but he hadn't given a thought to food when he'd jumped in his car and started driving.

The SUV's cup holders and storage trays were filled with random keys and bits and bobs, but nothing edible. Adam tried the glovebox and found it locked. It had been a while since he'd picked a lock—

JJ flung the driver's side door open. "What are you doing?"

"Looking for something to eat. Why's the glovebox locked?" Adam asked.

"Not to keep people out of my Twinkies." JJ slammed the door behind her and reached for her seat belt. "I have a child. I'm not about to carry a handgun in my vehicle without locking it up."

Adam blinked hard. "You carry a handgun?"

There was a whining sound when JJ turned the ignition, and for a moment Adam thought they'd be getting the jumper cables from the back. As soon as the engine caught, JJ threw the SUV in reverse and said, "Why are you surprised? You just saw me point a shotgun at a passel of people on my front porch."

"Well, yeah," Adam admitted, struggling to get his own seat belt on as the vehicle spun in a wide arc, throwing him sideways against the window. "But that was a shotgun, from your house, on your own property. That's different. Is everything okay?"

Adam clutched the door handle as JJ veered around a rut, but he pressed on. "Janie? What's going on with you?"

"That's right—you don't live here anymore, so you wouldn't know what's going on with me." JJ shook her head. "My daughter's best friend disappeared today. That's what's going on, and that's *all* that's going on. I didn't think we'd ever get Dorothy calmed down. And you... what the hell were you thinking?"

"I didn't say anything," Adam said, trying to keep his voice even.

JJ snorted. "You didn't have to."

"Exactly." Adam gripped the dash as JJ swung the vehicle around, from the Nicholson driveway onto the road and into her own driveway, without so much as a rolling stop. "You stayed in Beecham County—lived here your whole life—so people don't automatically think of Danny when they see you. Once they recognize me, it's hard for them to think of anything else."

"No shit, Sherlock," JJ said, dripping sarcasm. "Why do you think I told you to keep your mouth shut?"

"You use that language with your kid?" Adam snapped.

He could feel the anger radiating from JJ as she held her tongue. JJ always had been the one with the "potty mouth." That was Iris's term, the first and only time she'd laid down the law with Adam about bad language. They'd been in kindergarten at the time, and JJ had gotten in trouble for calling Leslie Beck an "ath-hole." Subsequently, her adult front teeth filling in did wonders for her swearing abilities.

JJ parked next to her house and shut off the engine before answering. "No, as a matter of fact, I don't swear in front of my daughter." Her voice softened. "I guess you still bring out the best in me."

Adam's breath caught in his throat.

She doesn't hate me.

Not that he'd really thought she would, at least not rationally, but that nagging doubt had hung over Adam for years. It was the main reason Adam didn't leave the house on the rare occasions that he returned to visit Iris. But knowing that he and JJ were still okay, that was *something*. Adam felt a rush of uncharacteristic—not optimism exactly—contentment. Like one less piece of him was missing, and he was one step closer to being whole.

"Then I guess it's a good thing I came back," Adam said.

"I guess it is," JJ said, reaching over to tug the bill of his baseball cap down over his eyes. "Come on in. Let's make a game plan."

But first she headed toward the doghouse, cooing to her furry friend. After a quick pat, JJ unclipped his collar from the tie-out. The big dog followed them to the house and shoved a cold nose in Adam's hand while JJ swore at the front door key. Adam's heart pounded faster and his mouth grew dry and sticky.

"His name is Trooper," JJ said, finally shoving the door open.

Adam squatted next to Trooper to get acquainted while JJ wandered around flipping on lights. JJ was right; Adam wasn't afraid of dogs as a rule, and he wasn't sure what it was about this one that had made him so uneasy. Trooper was calm and affectionate, giving a measured lick when Adam rubbed behind one crooked ear. The other ear stood at attention.

"You're a handsome boy, aren't you?" Adam whispered, putting his face close enough for one last lick before standing.

Looking around the Tulley house, Adam experienced a disorientation that was becoming familiar. The basic layout of the entry appeared the same. A bench sat next to the door with pairs of boots beneath it. There was a small, functional kitchen to the left off the otherwise open floor plan, but the bare subfloor he remembered from their youth had finally been covered by wood laminate. A twelve-point buck still watched from above the mantle, but the adjacent wall sported school papers on a cork board, hanging above a small desk. The sofa looked like it had been purchased in the past decade, but the dining table... Adam walked over for a closer look. There were two place settings, and the rest of the surface was covered with bags of chips, mail, and a permission slip. Adam went to the chair that faced the windows and slipped his fingers under the edge of the table. Nothing.

"Try the next seat," JJ said, with a hint of a smile that looked almost embarrassed.

Adam reached beneath the table and felt imperfections in the underside surface. He got down on one knee and looked up at his initials in the wood, rubbing his index finger over the evidence of the past. It was real. He was here. Even if everyone else wasn't anymore.

"I'm sorry about your dad," he spoke from the floor. "When did he pass away?"

JJ folded her arms over her chest. "Last year. It was quick."

Adam looked at her angry, challenging eyes. She was lying. Cancer, maybe? Whatever, she was still raw. At least, as raw as JJ ever got. Adam kneed up into a chair. "He was a good man. Closest thing to a father I ever had. How's your mom? And your brother?"

"Mom's still married to The Dweeb." JJ rolled her eyes and Adam grinned at their childhood name for JJ's stepfather. "But she loves Evie and makes a great grandma. My brother moved out west. Haven't seen him in years. You eat dinner?"

"Yeah," he lied. He'd been starving a few minutes ago, but seeing Trooper again had thrown his stomach off, and it hadn't quite settled yet. Plus, Adam didn't want them to get sidetracked. "Why don't you tell me what happened today?"

"Okay." JJ joined him at the table, took the clip off a bag of cheese popcorn, and set it between them. "Here's what we know. Rachel and her brother Jacob and my daughter Evie are the last kids off the bus. It's hard for the bus to get turned around on our road, so the driver just drops them at the bottom of the hill. Jacob had football practice and Evie had a sleepover that Rachel wasn't invited to, so Rachel was walking by herself. Bus driver dropped her off at the usual time—just before four o'clock because it's a long route—and didn't see anything unusual."

"But he wouldn't," Adam said. Despite his lingering queasiness, he found his hand reaching for the popcorn once the smell hit him.

JJ shook her head, but she was agreeing with him. "No line of sight. Dorothy was a little late getting home from work—she waitresses part-time at the River Lounge—and didn't see Rachel, but she wanted to get dinner started and just figured the girl was playing outside. Rachel had been in a little bit of a funk over this sleepover thing, and Dorothy thought she might need the space. Dorothy didn't get worried until Otto came home and they couldn't find her. They went ahead and called the law—"

"That's Grant Mason?" Adam interrupted.

JJ nodded. "He's the Sheriff now, and Luther Beck's one of his deputies. I can't remember the other one—somebody from Plattsville, and then there's a new woman, too. Anyway, there was only an hour or two of light left, but they used the volunteer fire department to get a bunch of people out searching as soon as they could. Even with Malcolm's best tracking dog, nobody found hide nor hair of her."

The powdered cheese left a nasty taste in Adam's mouth, and he coughed a random kernel loose from his esophagus. "So how do we find her?" he asked.

"I don't know," JJ admitted. "I was hoping you would."

8

———

Deputy Luther Beck stumbled through the front door of the Sheriff's Department to the smell of coffee hours past its prime. He shook the water from his coat by the door and hung it on the coat rack the new girl had improvised. Then Luther put half a sandwich in the fridge and made his way back to Grant's office.

The Sheriff's door was open, and Grant sat behind his spotless desk. Luther knocked on the doorframe to get his boss's attention before entering.

"I take it you're not planning on going home tonight?" Luther asked.

No doubt Grant had shaved this morning before work, but that must have been sixteen hours ago or more. His face was shaded with auburn stubble, and he looked exhausted. Luther reached up to check his own dark mustache, but nothing felt out of place. His burgeoning beard was a whole other story. Luther couldn't quite seem to figure out where it was supposed to grow and where it wasn't.

Grant sighed and rubbed his hands over his face. "Maybe in an hour or two."

Luther waited, but Grant didn't say anything else. In addition to being a neat freak, his boss was not the most chatty bastard he'd ever met. "That coffee recent?" Luther asked.

"Maybe an hour or two—"

The two men looked at each other, caught in a moment of déjà vu, and chuckled.

"I'm gonna make a fresh pot," Luther said. "Why don't you do some jumping jacks or something? Don't worry—you won't scare the new girl. She must've gone home already."

Grant rose and followed Luther. "Beth's over at the Command Center. They're trying to get the hotline set up by morning."

"Command Center, huh? You mean the War Memorial Building?" Luther asked, hearing a hint of snark in his own voice. And there wasn't any point in it. He'd already told Grant he wasn't happy about the woman having a responsibility that should have been his. But Grant didn't take the bait. He rarely did.

"Yes," was all his boss said. Grant leaned against the kitchen table. It was solid wood, built for leaning on, and Grant's own daddy had probably brought it in. It almost made Luther laugh sometimes, him and Grant working together, the son of a Sheriff and the son of a Beck, a family not known for their law-abiding ways.

"Alibi checked out on the last of our local boys on the sex registry," Luther said, scooping coffee. "He was at the VFW— drinking—from three p.m. until almost seven."

"Damn. I expected as much, but we gotta check off the boxes."

"No news on any other fronts?" Luther asked.

"Nothing good," Grant said. "I've notified everyone, put her in all the databases, there's an AMBER alert out. Everybody's stretched pretty thin, but I managed to pick up a few deputies on loan from Sheriff Tucker and Sheriff Webster. Just for the weekend. We can use them knocking door-to-door, searches, checkpoints, whatever. Bad roads between us and the interstate are slowing things down, but the Feds are on their way. A couple of guys from an advance team are helping Beth right now, and the rest of them'll be here first thing in the morning. Which brings me to your brother."

Luther waited, and his jaw clenched in anticipation before he could stop it. Forcing the muscles to release, he ran his tongue over his teeth, as if to get rid of a nasty taste. "Yeah?"

"I appreciate Leslie helping out with the searches this evening. To be honest, I was hoping they'd find her. That she'd just gone off somewhere and didn't make it back before dark hit."

Luther relaxed a little, hearing thoughts that echoed his own.

Grant continued. "It was worth a shot anyway. My only concern is, now we'll have everybody and his Federal agent brother in here. I'm grateful for the help, but all these alphabet soup guys are particular about how they do things. You think that's gonna be a problem with Leslie?"

Luther considered. He'd been surprised how gung-ho his brother was, quickly dividing up the search areas, organizing the teams and assigning them territories. The man hadn't shown a lick of enthusiasm for anything in a long time. It was a shame it took a missing child to bring it out, but that was better than the alternative. Now that he'd found a purpose, Les might very well bump against the higher-ups. But Luther couldn't bring himself to speak against his brother.

Grant said, "How about this? How about from here on out we let everybody know to coordinate the search stuff through you, instead of talking direct with Leslie?"

Luther nodded. Maybe Grant wasn't such a dumbass after all. "Sounds good. What else needs to happen?"

Grant looked lost, for just a moment, like a man trying to do the right thing but not sure what that is. He dropped his head, gave it a little shake, and cleared his throat. When he spoke, he lowered his voice, as if there were anyone else to hear them. "I've been putting it off, but I've got to go to Dorothy and Otto's again tonight. I figured I'd ask Otto to sign releases for us. Then Doc Hammond can bring the girl's medical records over tomorrow. I'll send someone to Plattsville to pick up her dental records tomorrow, too."

Luther swallowed hard. "You think it'll come to that?"

Grant started to shrug off the question, but met Luther's eyes instead. His voice sounded strained as he said, "It doesn't look good."

Luther felt a sickness in his stomach that made him wish he hadn't had that half a sandwich an hour ago. Somehow, the situation hadn't seemed that serious before. He'd assumed the girl would've shown up by now. But he, of all people, should've known better.

"My brother was there the night the guy took Danny Carpenter. Never thought we'd have to deal with something like that again," Luther admitted. The coffeepot stopped burbling, and he topped up Grant's proffered cup before filling his own and sipping at the bitter brew. "Your dad know what's going on?"

"I hope not."

Grant's father had been Sheriff during the Carpenter kidnapping. The man had hired Luther and been good to him over the years. Now he was in a care facility, and some days he didn't know what decade it was, much less what day.

"Stop by the Command Center on your way home, see what Beth needs, but other than that, I can't think of anything else you can do before first light. You want to meet me here in the morning? We can swing by the Nicholsons' together to check in, first thing," Grant suggested.

"What time?" Luther asked.

"Say six a.m.? No, six-thirty should do it."

Luther couldn't help cringing, just a little, as he checked his watch. It was nearing eleven p.m. now, and he'd be lucky to make it to bed before one. "You got it."

Grant looked at his own watch. "I better be getting out there with the releases, before it gets any later. You still got that inhaler?" he asked.

Luther pulled the device from his jacket pocket, already

sheathed in a labeled, plastic bag. "You know Dorothy's gonna freak out when she sees this," he said, handing the item to Grant.

"I was thinking maybe I'd show it to JJ first, see what she can tell me. With their kids being best friends, she's taken care of the girl a lot, and she's a nurse…" Grant trailed off, scratching the back of his neck self-consciously.

"Makes sense. JJ's got a cool head on her shoulders," Luther said. He smiled to himself as he thought of the scene Les had described earlier. *Especially when she's got a cold shotgun in her hands.* "That reminds me, my brother told me something. When they were wrapping up tonight, him and his buddies saw a strange car pull into JJ's."

Grant took a sip of coffee while he waited for Luther to continue. Luther thought the man was trying to look casual, but not doing a very good job of it. Especially since his cup was about empty.

Luther said, "It was Adam Rutledge."

Grant's tired eyes widened. "Adam Rutledge? Was Leslie sure?"

"Pretty sure." Luther grinned. "Although JJ was apparently doing her best to keep him out of sight while she chewed everybody out."

Grant didn't even smile at the image, just stared at the dregs in his cup. "Well, thanks for letting me know, Luther, but I can't imagine it means anything."

Suddenly Luther felt the heat building, the buzzing in his brain that forecast his temper, but he wasn't sure why. Because Grant had been dismissive? Or because it was Adam? Something was pushing Luther's buttons, enough that he should keep his mouth shut. But Luther had never been very good at that.

"Adam Rutledge was Danny Carpenter's best friend," Luther argued. "You think it's just a coincidence that the man shows up *within hours* of our first kidnapping since then?"

"Don't forget the girl, the one after Danny. Sarah Edmunds," Grant countered.

"That was in Plattsville."

"The town may have had their own police force, but the Beecham County Sheriff's Department helped out."

Luther's voice raised a notch. "Nobody ever proved a stranger snatched that girl."

Grant lurched to standing, with the table giving the tiniest scooch as it released his weight. "Technically, no one ever proved that of Danny, either."

"Maybe not, but Danny sure as hell wasn't a runaway!" Luther said. "He was taken."

"Yes, he was. And Adam was a kid at the time." Grant's voice remained calm as he asked, "Are you trying to say Adam had something to do with it?"

Luther held his breath to slow the words that would have tumbled from his mouth. He tried not to gasp audibly as he breathed in and responded. "I'm saying some weird shit happened around that kid. And now he's not a kid anymore."

Grant nodded. "Unfortunately, some people get more than their fair share of tragedy."

Luther remained outwardly still, but flinched inside at Grant's words, at the thought of young Adam crying for his mother while she bled out in a mass of twisted metal by the side of the road.

"Coincidence or not, Rachel Nicholson has nothing to do with Danny Carpenter," Grant said, rinsing his mug and setting it in the dish drainer alongside the sink. He reached out and squeezed Luther's arm briefly as he passed. "And she's not coming back unless we find her."

9

Curled up on the couch, JJ had her mother's afghan on her shoulders and Trooper's head on her lap while she watched a misty rain swirl in the light from the porch. It almost looked like snow. It would be soon enough.

Adam was long gone and wouldn't be back until morning, after a decent night's sleep. JJ had decided to leave Evie at her slumber party tonight, as had the other mothers. The girls wouldn't be getting any sleep, but then, no one had thought they would. Speaking with Melanie's mom (she wouldn't dare embarrass Evie by asking to speak with her personally) had helped ease JJ's mind. She'd said the girls were subdued, but not crying, so that was something. The female officer that stopped by to interview them about their classmate had tried to downplay any danger, to make it sound as if Rachel's absence was just a misunderstanding, but the girls weren't stupid.

JJ wasn't due to pick up Evie until early afternoon. Maybe she'd take Evie to her mother's. Evie would complain about staying with her grandmother in the next county, but the child would be conflicted enough about Rachel's disappearance without watching people coming and going trying to find her. JJ would call her mother tomorrow at a more reasonable hour to make sure she was free.

That resolved, JJ dozed off herself, just for a moment, when headlights shone up her driveway. She recognized the car, and she wasn't the only one. Trooper lifted his head, but he didn't bark. In fact, the dog's skull seemed to get heavier when he settled it back on her lap, challenging JJ to remove it. Which, of course, she did.

"Sorry, sweetie," she said, lifting his head and rising from the couch. She leaned over and whispered, "But if you promise not to tell Evie, I'll let you sleep on the bed with me tonight."

JJ scuffed to the door in old wool slippers that had been missing a right toe since Trooper's puppyhood. Heavy, hurried boots made their way up the front steps while she unlocked the deadbolt.

The stupid man hadn't worn his hat.

"Get in out of the rain," she said, as she opened the door. "Coffee?"

Trooper's tail thumped against the wooden arm of the couch.

"Hey buddy," Grant said, running a hand through his own wet, auburn hair until it stood on end. "Coffee would be great, if you don't mind."

JJ hit the switch on the coffeemaker she'd preloaded earlier, a habit she'd fallen into with him over the past few months. "Sit down. Can I get you something to eat?"

"No, thanks," he said, perching on the edge of the armchair and rubbing his hands along the top of his legs. It was a kind of tic JJ had noticed before, when he sat down. "I can't stay long."

JJ made herself a cup of chamomile tea. When the coffee was done, she brought a steaming mug (black) to Grant, who gratefully accepted it with both hands. Trooper had vacated his spot on the couch to rest his head on Grant's damp knee. Grant looked as though he could use all the warmth he could get. His brows were so light they were nearly invisible, making his green eyes stand out even more starkly against his pale face. Even his freckles seemed transparent.

"Well?" JJ asked. She lost a slipper as she tucked her feet beneath her and left it on the floor.

Grant stared down at his coffee, silent. Trooper nudged his knee gently, and for an instant, JJ thought Grant would cry.

"Oh, my God," she said softly. "How bad is it?"

Grant exhaled a heavy breath, then set his coffee on an end table and pulled something from his coat pocket. "We found this at the edge of the road, right before your driveway."

JJ took it from him and turned it in her hand, wishing it could speak. It was Rachel's asthma inhaler, in a small plastic bag. JJ choked back the sob that rose in her throat, and her voice sounded almost normal when she said, "This is an emergency inhaler, the one she'd use in case of an attack. Rachel never goes anywhere without one. She also uses a different one every day as a preventive."

"How long before she starts to feel the effects of not having either of them?" Grant asked.

"I don't know. It's outside my expertise—you'd really need to talk to her doctor. But I do know that this fall was tough for her, and she's had to use her emergency inhaler more than they'd like." JJ took a deep breath, trying to maintain in nurse mode without slipping into mother mode. "I also know that stress is a big trigger for her attacks. And when they start, she panics, which just makes it worse."

Grant leaned back, gripping the armchair with one hand while rubbing the other across his face until his forehead was pink. "I've done everything I know to do so far."

"What about help from outside?" JJ asked.

"Anyone and everyone." Grant's hand shook as he reached for his coffee. "JJ, I've never done anything like this before."

"If, God forbid, it were Evie, I can't imagine anyone else I'd rather have looking for her." She leaned forward and gripped his knee. "I'm sorry your father can't help you."

"I'm sorry yours can't either," he said darkly, only half joking. He'd seen the damage JJ's father could do to the deserving. "This might sound awful," Grant continued, "but I just hope my dad has a bad week, the kind where he won't understand what's going on, or wonder why I'm not there on Sunday."

JJ squeezed her mug of tea hard. "You don't think you'll find her by Sunday?"

Grant smiled. His chin was a little too narrow and stuck out a little too far for him to be classically handsome, but he was a good man. JJ thought maybe she loved him just for that hopeful, lying smile.

"Of course, we'll find her," he said. "But Sunday, I plan on sleeping in."

Grant gave Trooper one last pat before standing and chugging the rest of his coffee. He handed JJ his mug. "I have to go talk with Dorothy and Otto now. Thanks for the coffee."

JJ set his mug back on the end table and walked him to the door. They stood, feeling the cold radiate from the storm door glass, and watched the rain get heavier, pooling on the bottom step and in the bare part of the yard beyond.

"They say we might get snow tomorrow night," Grant said.

"Let's hope not," was all she said, but JJ couldn't help but wonder where Rachel was, if the child was out in this cold and wet without a decent coat... or worse. *Please God, let her be safe.*

"Good night, JJ," Grant said and stepped outside, pulling his coat close and bowing his head against the rain.

It was almost a physical ache, watching him leave. *Am I just going to let him go like this, every night for the rest of my life?* He'd almost made it to his car before JJ ran down the steps after him, still wearing only one slipper, following before she even knew what she intended.

Grant turned to her in surprise, hand on the cruiser door. "JJ, you're going to—"

She grabbed his face between her hands, pulled it down, and kissed him hard. Rain ran down his forehead, dripped off the end of his nose. She tasted it on her lips, along with coffee and chamomile and some indefinable something that must be Grant.

Finally, she let go of his face and would have backed away, but his arms wrapped around her waist and held her fast until they both had to come up for air. Albeit wet air.

"Well," Grant said, a little loudly so he'd be heard over the rain, "that's new."

JJ smiled and wiped rain from her eyes. "It's overdue, is what it is. Be safe."

10

———

Adam hadn't called Iris when he'd left Pennsylvania several hours earlier because he hadn't known he was coming, not exactly. And he hadn't known what to say. The good thing was, most of the things he was reticent to talk about, his grandmother was content to ignore as well.

He hadn't called Iris when he'd left JJ's either, and yet there she was.

The rain had let up, but it was still cold. Iris stood on the front step, waiting, pulling a chunky sweater tightly around her chest and shoulders. She looked good, younger than she had any right to, as many people as she'd raised and buried in her life. Her white-blonde hair fell to her shoulders with a hint of wave, much more bohemian than she'd ever allow any of her clients to be. If she still cut hair. Adam was ashamed to realize he didn't even know, not for sure. He slung his duffel over his shoulder.

"I thought I might be seeing you. So you heard about the girl?" Iris asked.

Her words echoed JJ's so closely, Adam had to suppress a little chill and spend some effort on his most charming grin. "Did you ever stop to think I might just have come back to see you?"

"Not for a minute, you pretty boy," she said, still smiling. She put her arm around his free shoulder when he reached the front door, but withdrew it almost as quickly. "Ugh, you're wet. Come on in before you catch your death of cold. Did you eat yet?"

"Yeah, I had something." Cheese popcorn, and maybe a bowl of cereal about twelve hours ago.

"Uh-huh," she said, heading toward the kitchen. "I'll make you a decent meal while you go get changed."

Adam ran upstairs and took a quick, hot shower. It didn't wake him up, but it gave him a nice, if temporary, fuzzy feeling that all was right with the world. It also helped that Iris had kept a room for him, just as she'd always done, ever since his parents died.

He tucked his duffel in the open closet to keep from tripping over it in the small room. Iris had removed the closet doors when he'd first moved in, traumatized and terrified that someone—or something—was hiding there. His grandmother was lucky she wasn't a hunchback, all the nights he'd startled awake to find her dozing in a child's hard, wooden chair next to his bed.

He sat in that same wooden chair and looked around. The room had belonged to Iris's son Bo years before Adam's arrival, though he'd never found any sign of his dead uncle in it. The bedroom walls were mostly bare, but a shelf on one side held a baseball and mitt; the skateboard Adam had desperately wanted but rarely ridden because there was no paved surface close enough; a pair of swim goggles (turned out the water at Poplar Creek was brown all the way down to its muddy bottom, not just at the surface); a crate of paperback books and *National Geographic* magazines; and a few other remnants from his childhood. The truth is, he and Danny and JJ hadn't needed much in the way of stuff to entertain themselves. They were feral, imaginative kids. On summer days, they'd disappear in the morning and return in the evening just before dark, with a couple of clandestine kitchen runs in between.

Of course, all that changed when Danny was taken. People got funny around Adam after that—superstitious, Iris said. JJ said stupid. Adam and Danny had been best friends, Adam was there when Danny was taken (along with a dozen or so other Cub Scouts), and Adam had already had such bad luck in his short life. It didn't help that Adam had difficulty dealing with his friend's disappearance, including a return of his vivid nightmares. Adam finished out the school year in Cold Springs—barely—but then Iris sent him to live with an aunt in Pennsylvania. That didn't quite work out, and it was on to a cousin's somewhere else in the state, and then on to another home from there. By the time Adam graduated high school, he'd lived with at least half a dozen friends and family members.

In the first years of his Exile—that was JJ's word for it—Iris still allowed Adam to spend his summers in Cold Springs with her. Wherever he found himself living during the school year, he counted the days until he could return to this very room. Adam must have been about fifteen when—through a combination of familial dysfunction and teenaged rebellion—the summer visits stopped. He hadn't spent more than a night or two at a time in Cold Springs since, and then never leaving Iris's house. But his room was always waiting, often for years at a time, with fresh sheets and enough clean clothes in the right sizes to get by. He pulled a pair of sweats and a T-shirt from the dresser and breathed deeply. No matter how long he'd been gone, the clothes Iris had waiting always smelled better than anything he'd washed himself at the laundromat. Or lately, in the bathroom sink.

An enticing aroma pulled Adam from his reverie and down the stairs to the kitchen. Iris checked something in the microwave, put it back, and punched a few buttons before returning to monitor a skillet. Adam bent over and rested his head on her shoulder.

"Thank you, Iris."

"Try not to drool on my shoulder, kiddo," she said, leaning her head into his.

He straightened, embarrassed to realize that was a real possibility, and stared at the mouth-watering, flour-dipped meat in the skillet. "Is that tenderloin?" he asked.

"Your favorite," she said. "After all, you coming to visit is a special occasion."

Was there a hint of judgment in her voice, or was he being overly sensitive? Adam spent a lot of time asking himself that question around his grandmother, and he didn't think that was an accident. Hers was a subtle manipulation.

"I thought deer season didn't start until next month," he said.

The microwave dinged. Iris turned off the stove before pushing Adam toward the kitchen table. "What are you, the game warden now? Go sit down and get out from underfoot. What do you want to drink—milk?"

Adam shuddered. He'd stopped drinking milk when he was ten, but Iris never stopped offering. She had it in her head that it was good for him, and when Iris got something in her head, it was there to stay. Adam pirouetted around her, getting a glass of water as she made him a plate: deer tenderloin, baked potato and a green salad. She narrowed her eyes and shook her head when he was a little too generous with the Ranch dressing.

"What?" he asked, indignant but grinning. "I'm a growing boy."

"You better hope not. Once you've passed thirty, the only growing you do is out." Iris settled down across from him with a mug of something hot and herbal. "Not that you couldn't stand a few more pounds right now. Have you been eating?"

Adam chewed and moaned around the tender meat. "Yeah, but not like this," he said, dropping a forkful of potato on its way to his mouth.

"Then don't eat like a starving person," she said. "Show some manners. You been over to see JJ?"

Adam looked at Iris, trying to figure out the subtext in her question, but the woman had several decades of practice on him. And he was tired. He nodded, then took a sip of water. "Stopped there first. Why didn't you tell me about her dad?"

Iris raised an eyebrow. *So you could do what?* That's what her eyes were saying, but fortunately her heart was much more kind. She shrugged. "Hard to see a man like that, so physically strong all his life, laid so low. Shrinking away to nothing so fast. If I ever get cancer, you're gonna have to get me a pistol or pull the trigger on that rifle of your grandfather's I've got in the back room. I am not spending my last days the way Max Tulley did..." She trailed off, drifting into some other place—uncertain future or unshakeable past, Adam couldn't tell—before changing the subject. "I imagine it's pretty crazy over by JJ's now, what with the Nicholson girl. You see anybody else?"

Adam finished his plate with a sigh. "You mean, did anybody see me? You're as bad as JJ." One reason Adam visited so rarely was that Iris apparently expected the town to arrive on her doorstep carrying torches and demand his surrender. He wasn't sure what crime he had to answer for, but Iris had lived here her whole life, so Adam figured she wasn't entirely wrong.

Iris continued to stare, waiting for an answer. If it weren't for the malleability of her morals, or more accurately, a total disregard for any laws she happened to disagree with, his grandmother would have made a fine cop.

"There was a group of guys at JJ's, just come back from looking for the girl. I don't think anyone recognized me. I didn't recognize them." Adam stood and rinsed his dish in the sink. He tried to speak nonchalantly over the sound of the tap. "Except maybe Leslie Beck."

"Leslie Beck?"

Adam turned to see his grandmother resting her face in her hands. He placed his hands on her shoulders and gave them a little squeeze. "It'll be okay."

She sighed and rose to see to the greasy skillet. "Fine, it'll be okay. But you need to stay clear of Leslie Beck. You know his brother's a sheriff deputy now?"

"Yeah, JJ mentioned that. I always thought Luther was all right," Adam said.

Iris made a sound suspiciously like a snort. "Honey, there ain't a

Beck been made that's 'all right.' Don't you go underestimating a single one of them. The meanness that was in their grandfather made my own husband seem a saint. And that he surely was not."

Adam's grandfather had died before Adam was born—shot himself deer hunting, too drunk to stand without leaning on his loaded rifle—but Adam had heard enough stories over the years that he was not sorry he'd never met the man. He waited until Iris set the skillet in the sink to soak before giving her a big hug from behind. This time, he noticed the prominent bones of her arms and shoulders, the thin veneer of flesh over her ribs that the cardigan had hidden.

"I think the pot was calling the kettle black," he said. "You been eating lately?"

"Of course I have. I'm not an idiot," Iris said, squeezing him back. "I have to take old Mrs. Gunderson to a doctor's appointment in Plattsville tomorrow morning, so you're on your own for breakfast."

Iris turned to face him. It didn't matter how long he'd been gone, she never asked him where he'd come from, what he'd left behind, or how long he was staying. It was almost as if he were a wild animal she was afraid of spooking. That's why her next question surprised him.

"Adam, why are you here?"

He tried to look straight ahead, over the top of Iris's head at the kitchen cabinets, while he got his thoughts in order. When that didn't work, he gazed at the ceiling, but the words he needed weren't there either.

"Sweetie?" Iris asked gently.

He took a deep breath, and the thought that had haunted him for the past eight hours tumbled out. "Do you think there could be a connection between this girl and Danny?"

Iris reached up to touch his face. "No matter what you do, you can't bring Danny back. You do know that, don't you?"

"Yes, I know," Adam said.

And he did, except for the part of him that was still a child back in Dead Hollow, looking down at the ground where there used to be a sleeping bag, and out at the dark woods where there was nothing. Not anymore.

"I'm going to bed now. Thank you, Iris. Love you."

"I love you, darling. Sleep well."

It wasn't until he flopped into bed, rolled onto his side, and pulled the blanket over his head that Adam realized his grandmother hadn't answered his question. Exhaustion weighed on his eyelids like an extra moon's gravity. Tomorrow. He'd press her on it tomorrow...

11

———

Rachel woke up. It wasn't the first time, she knew, yet she couldn't remember the previous times, or where she was. Now, she was cold and alone in a dark so black she couldn't see her finger touch her nose. In fact, she missed and touched the side of her face. Her chest ached, like Fat Justin had been sitting on it all night. (Not that she ever called him that. In addition to being huge, he was mean, and he was in the eighth grade, so she was afraid of him.) Had she eaten anything? Rachel wasn't sure. She felt like she had—like she had eaten a lot—but she was also hungry. She reached around in the dark and found a wrapper next to her. Holding it to her nose, she smelled oatmeal and sugar, and suddenly realized that yes, she was hungry. Very hungry. She licked the inside of the wrapper, but there was nothing left. She needed more food.

She rolled over onto her hands and knees. The surface beneath her was squishy, like a bed or a couch, and it was covered with something flannel. There were blankets tangled around her feet, too. Whatever she was on, she could feel the edge. She scooted over to it and started to jump down.

But maybe there was something else down there, something that wasn't a floor at all. Maybe there was just a space that went on forever. That's what it felt like in the dark.

Now she was just being silly. She could probably reach the floor if she *got flat on her belly again. Slowly, slowly, Rachel stretched her hand down... and touched bare wood. Grit stuck to her fingers as she traced the seam between the boards. The clench in her stomach relaxed a little as she wiped her fingers on the seat of her pants. Just a regular dirty floor.*

Rachel leaned forward and swung her legs down, thinking to stand, but instead she fell on her face. It scared her more than it hurt. She touched her nose (it was easier to find when it was throbbing), but there didn't seem to be any blood. She turned sideways, and that's when it registered that one of her legs was still on the bed.

She hadn't been clumsy.

She was tied to the bed.

No, no, no, no... She started to whimper, a relentless, rhythmic sound like the two branches that rubbed together outside her kitchen window when the wind blew.

But her whimpering wasn't the only sound in the room.

Rachel tried to hold her breath—to hide, to hear the other sound—but she couldn't. Her breath was a rattling wheeze, not under her control anymore. The pressure in her chest grew. Because she wasn't alone.

A light came on, bright as a sun, and kept getting brighter through her closed lids. When the blaze leveled out, she blinked and shaded her tearing eyes with her hands, slowly pulling them away until she could make out a shape.

A man shape.

A familiar man.

She heard herself saying, in a voice that was not quite her own, "Please, daddy, please don't hurt me."

12

———

P *lease...*

Adam jerked awake with a gasp, heart pounding.

It's happening again.

He didn't bother changing his clothes, just threw on his sneakers and his jacket, grabbed his car keys and ran out the door. His hands shook as he put the key in the ignition. The starter whined, but the engine didn't catch.

"Come on!" he screamed, slamming his hand against the wheel.

This time, the universe listened.

Adam swung the hatchback around, narrowly missing Iris's sedan, and raced down the driveway. The sky was the silver-gray of an antique mirror, with the objects in the yard clear enough to see but casting no shadows. The dim light faded as he reached the road, with the trees edging out most of the shoulder and a steep mountain bank rising on one side. The road seemed little more than a series of connected curves, and miles slipped by as he concentrated on making the curves as fast as he could without taking out a guardrail. The car's momentum carried Adam's body with it—left, right, left, right—and Adam tried not to hang on the steering wheel as his butt slid on the worn seat. His heart hammered and his foot tapped the brake when he saw a reflection ahead—a sign for a hunting lodge. Not his turn yet. He sped up again, hoping the deer were tucked in somewhere asleep already, urging his hatchback to go faster on a brief straight stretch.

Why hadn't he seen it? It was so obvious.

Was it that obvious with Danny? No, it couldn't have been. The Sheriff would have checked anyone and everyone close to him. And Danny would have been found. Possibly still alive.

It was that time of early morning when headlights didn't do anything useful, and his eyes made it even worse. No matter where he focused his gaze, his vision seemed to slide away, eyes unable to hold their position. If he had more time, he'd pull over and throw up. More time, and room to pull over. Adam avoided looking at the dented guardrail when he reached the curve at Dead Hollow, afraid the steering wheel would follow his eyes and he'd find himself reliving another nightmare.

He recognized the turn-off ahead, but at the last moment, Adam realized he hadn't slowed down enough. There was no one behind him—he should continue safely past the lane and reverse. Except he couldn't—the anxiety screaming in his brain wouldn't let him. Instead, Adam geared down and pressed the brake harder, steering against wheels that wanted to lock. The hatchback almost made the corner, until he hit the autumn leaves blanketing the edge of the road on the driver's side. It might as well have been ice.

"Frick!"

Adam's stomach pitched like a carnival ride as the wheels lost all traction, producing a sensation of leaving the ground. He jerked the steering wheel in the opposite direction, but it was too late. The front end lurched into the ditch, and he felt more than heard the grating sound as the driver's side continued slowly forward, dragging farther over the side.

He waited for screaming, for the impact of trees, but there wasn't any. Just silence.

Except for the humming in his ears. And maybe something

mechanical. Adam shut off the car and rested his head against the steering wheel, just for a moment.

He got up before the shaking could start.

Adam popped his door open and stepped out carefully. There wasn't much ground to step on; he had to swing his leg out and twist toward the back of the car to avoid the ditch. Adam clutched the side of the vehicle as he carefully closed the driver's door behind him, and kept clinging—palms flat against the car's body like a prayer—as he worked his way around to the rear of the car. Most of the vehicle was still on the road, but no way was Adam's four-cylinder, front-wheel drive engine backing the rest of it out.

Hopefully no one would hit the car and knock it the rest of the way into the ditch. Adam put a hand on the rear taillight, muttering an apology, and a shudder ran through his body. He had to move.

A few steps from the car brought Adam to what he thought was the center of the road, but with no flashlight and no brightly painted lines, he had to guess. He turned uphill, took a few more steps, and then his legs buckled, the dirt road biting into his knees and his hands as he fell. Kneeling, head to his knees and fists clenched, he tried to ride out the shaking that finally overcame his body. Eventually the spasms eased, and he tucked his hands behind his head, as if to protect himself.

What the hell am I doing here?

He stared at the dark road ahead, sheltered from the dawn by the shape of the mountain and the thick forest that covered it. A light mist in the air tingled against his face and made the trees looming overhead feel absolutely primordial.

Adam struggled to his feet. Alone.

I'm doing what I wish I could have done twenty years ago.

At least he'd worn his sneakers. He took a deep breath and began running up the steep incline. Soon he found his stride, breath hissing, arms and legs pumping, aware that with every movement forward, he was following in Rachel's footsteps. And every step was a step closer to reaching her.

13

———

JJ hadn't slept well.

She put on a jacket and stepped into her hiking boots. Then she took her coffee and Trooper, whose snoring, stretched-out bulk was one of the reasons she hadn't slept well, out to the front porch. Where she could see what was coming. She had a buzzing in her veins, like a lion watching over its pride and anticipating trouble.

JJ wandered down the driveway, still carrying her coffee, Trooper at her side. With most of the leaves off the trees, there was a spot partway down the drive where JJ could see into the Nicholson yard, all the way up to their front steps. From here, everything looked normal. Both cars were still in their driveway, as if this were just another day.

JJ wondered how early the next search would go out. Should she join in, or was her time better spent... doing what? JJ wished she knew. She wished *so much* that she knew how to bring that little girl home. Ask anyone, and they'd say JJ was one of the more rational, grounded people you'd find around these parts. And yet she found herself thinking things that didn't make rational sense.

Things like, *Adam is the key*. Now, what the hell was that supposed to mean? The key to what?

Some movement next door caught JJ's eye. Probably Otto.

No—there was a man next door, but it wasn't Otto.

JJ startled, spilling hot coffee on her hand, the coldness of her skin magnifying the burn. Was that Adam? Stepped straight from her thoughts to the Nicholsons' driveway. *What the hell is he doing here?* She walked toward the edge of the small wood that buffered the properties for a better look.

Adam staggered up the Nicholson drive in fits and starts, like a kid who's been beaten in a race but doesn't want to walk at the end, no matter how worn out he is. He knocked on the door and bent over, gasping for breath while he waited for someone to answer.

I've got a bad feeling about this.

"Stay, Trooper. Guard the house."

JJ set her mug on the ground and picked her way deliberately through the gray forest, careful of the hidden branches and pitfalls in the ankle-to-shin-deep blanket of dead leaves. It was hard to keep an eye on Adam while navigating the tricky footing, but JJ watched as he backed up, almost to the metal railing, to allow the screen door to swing open. He hesitated on the slab porch as Dorothy exited the house. Then Adam bolted, off the porch, into the yard and around back of the house.

Shit.

JJ took off running, pumping her arms, high-stepping in her loosely laced boots and hoping for the best. All she could hear was the pounding of her feet and her heart, and a roaring in her ears. Twenty yards, fifteen... and then the low brush got thick on the Nicholsons' side of the woods. JJ slowed and stuck her arms straight out in front of her to parry the blows. A stray branch slipped by and stung her face like a switch, right below her eye, but she kept running.

The roaring in JJ's ears grew even louder as she finally burst through the brush into the Nicholson yard. She ran around the corner of the house, toward the structures in the back. There was a chicken coop opposite an empty pigpen with a small covered area, and a barn beyond.

And there was Adam, trotting toward the barn.

JJ ran past Dorothy, who looked lost on her own property. On past squawking chickens, flapping next to their enclosure entry, the door levered shut with a baseball bat on the outside.

Otto emerged from the barn, looking almost as lost as Dorothy.

Adam stopped, a few yards away from the missing girl's father, short of breath. He raised a hand and pointed at Otto.

"Where is she?" Adam yelled. "What have you done to her?"

Otto tensed, bending his knees slightly, and then his arms. But he didn't speak. Neither did JJ. She just stood panting, with no idea what to say.

"She begged you not to hurt her. What the hell did you do?" Adam demanded.

Adam screamed, a primal sound from deep in his belly, and ran forward, launching himself at Otto. The two men landed on the ground together, flailing, but within moments Otto was on top of Adam, pounding his fists into the smaller man's body. At least Adam had the sense to cover his own face. Dorothy shrieked next to JJ.

"Goddammit, Dorothy! Why don't you do something useful?" JJ said, grabbing the woman's arm. "Like keep your husband from killing Adam!"

Dorothy kept shrieking, so JJ joined her, yelling, "Stop, Otto! Leave him alone! Otto!"

She didn't know it, but JJ's loud protests galvanized Trooper into action. The canine raced through the woods to meet her as JJ jumped on Otto's back, arms over his shoulders and legs wrapped around his torso. She could have been an insect for all the impact she made on the man. JJ slid her arms down Otto's as far as his biceps, but he easily flexed his arms free of hers. With nothing to hold onto but legs still locked around him, JJ fell backwards, jamming her wrist on the ground. She dug the knuckles of her other hand into Otto's kidney, and he flung an elbow haphazardly, narrowly missing her nose.

Sonuvabitch! JJ pushed off someone's leg (Otto's? Adam's?) and clenched her abs to get upright again. She quickly reached around Otto's neck with one arm, then wrapped the other arm around and tucked her hand behind Otto's head.

"Otto, if you don't let Adam go I will choke you out, just like my daddy taught me," she said in the man's ear. "I swear to God I will."

He dipped his chin toward his chest, forcing it between her arm and his throat to block her chokehold. JJ twisted and climbed, trying to get a better angle on Otto, but he was mid-swing, and her weight took them over. Otto fell sideways, off Adam and onto the damp ground, landing hard on JJ's arm and shoulder. Otto and JJ grunted, and JJ gasped for air.

"Get off him!" Dorothy yelled, baseball bat clutched awkwardly in her hands.

JJ had no idea what Dorothy intended to do. Smack her in the head? Beat on Adam some more? He wasn't even moving.

Dorothy glanced over her shoulder toward the house, as though she'd heard something, and then turned left toward the brush. Her eyes grew wide. Leg pinned beneath Otto, JJ raised herself on one elbow in time to see Trooper appear from the woods. Panting slightly, the dog circled around behind the JJ-Otto-Adam pile and lowered his head at Otto. His tail was held high. He and Otto locked eyes, and a low rumble radiated from the dog's chest.

"Easy, Trooper," JJ said. "Sit."

The dog shifted his hips, back and forth, back and forth, before slowly dropping his rear to the ground. His head and shoulders still leaned forward, and his body quivered.

"Dorothy," Otto said, eyes never leaving the dog, "Put the bat down. I want you to go in the house—"

JJ thought that seemed sensible.

"—And bring me the rifle from the bedroom."

"The fuck you will!" JJ told the back of Otto's head, but she didn't move, not wanting to trigger the dog and uncertain if she could control him, as angry as she was. "Trooper, stay."

"This is my property," Otto said, squeezing the words through his back teeth. "Dorothy, get the gun."

JJ glanced toward Dorothy as she dropped the bat, and noticed movement beyond the woman. Two uniformed men approached from the house at a good clip—Grant and Luther Beck. Relieved, JJ began untangling herself from Otto. She freed her legs and stood on shaking knees as Adam began to stir.

"Why'd you tie up your daughter?" Adam mumbled, and rolled onto his side.

Otto flinched, then froze, still on his knees. Mouth slightly open, his eyes stared ahead at the dark, wet ground that had left a smear on his cheek and marked his clothes. Finally, he blinked and turned, shoulders tensed, slowly toward Adam.

He's going to kill Adam.

Voices echoed through the air—Grant and Luther, now nearly upon them—but she was so scared and angry, JJ couldn't make out their words. Otto knee-walked awkwardly to Adam and grabbed the front of his jacket with both hands, lifting Adam from the ground.

"No!" JJ screamed, kicking at Otto.

She'd aimed for his ribs, but connected a glancing blow closer to his hips. Her unlaced boot tumbled awkwardly from her foot on the follow-through and landed a few yards away.

Otto ignored both the strike and Adam clawing at the hands in his shirt, so JJ pulled the boot from her other foot. Drawing back her arm, she swung at Otto's head—

And Luther grabbed her from behind, lifting her feet from the ground. The boot brushed Otto's shoulder and fell from her hands.

"Calm down, JJ!"

Her socked feet kicked in all directions, but the deputy maintained his firm hold. JJ shrieked with frustration, and suddenly

Trooper was moving, closing the short distance between him and the two humans in a slow stalk.

Luther dropped JJ to the ground and kept one hand around her torso while extending the other toward the dog. "Easy, now. Just take it easy." He pulled JJ closer and spoke in her ear. "JJ, now'd be a good time to call off Cujo."

She took a shallow breath—Luther was still holding her too tightly—and tried to make her voice sound calm. "Trooper, sit. *Sit.*"

The second time was the charm, and as the dog complied she felt Luther's heavy exhale of relief next to her ear. He released his grip and, hands on her thighs, JJ took a moment to catch her breath.

Dorothy had stopped screaming. Adam remained on the ground, knees lifted but not quite sitting. Grant stood next to him, acting as a buffer while Otto paced in a half-circle around Adam, taking care not to trip over the baseball bat on the ground.

"Otto," Grant asked, voice even, "where do you want me to be: hanging around your house, breaking up fights, or out there looking for your daughter?"

Otto stopped in front of Grant and glared down at the Sheriff.

"Okay, good. Me, too," Grant said, as if Otto had spoken.

"He started it!" Dorothy protested, pointing down at Adam.

Grant glanced over his shoulder at the woman, nodding. "Dorothy, I was wondering if you'd be so kind as to go inside and rustle up some coffee."

Dorothy looked at her husband uncertainly.

"It's all right," Otto said, barely out of breath. "Go on, and we'll be in directly."

Dorothy headed back to the house and the men waited, silent, until she was out of earshot.

"Y'all want to tell me what's going on here?" Grant asked, facing Otto.

Luther gave JJ a little nudge with his shoulder, and she nearly elbowed him in the gut for his trouble. But she didn't speak, and neither did anyone else.

Grant sighed and took a step back from Otto, creating enough space to keep an eye on the man while staring down everyone else. "Fine. We'll just have Adam wait in the car while we sort this out."

Adam sat, hunched forward, hugging his upright knees with one arm. He held his other shaking hand alongside his skull without touching it, or his swollen cheek. His mouth looked a little worse for wear on the same side.

"Sheriff," he said, his voice strained with pain, "I might need a little help with that."

Otto lunged suddenly, grabbing the baseball bat from the ground, and charged at Adam. Grant quickly moved in front of Otto, colliding with Otto's massive chest. The impact knocked both men back a step. Grant squared his stance, and Otto pointed the bat past him at Adam. "If you ever set foot on my property again, I'll kill you."

"Otto, this is a tough time for you, but you still can't be making threats like that in front of the law. You know that," Grant said.

Otto inched closer to Grant, so close he could have counted the whiskers the Sheriff had missed shaving that morning. "That sonuvabitch accused me of kidnapping my own daughter. So let me tell you, Sheriff—it's a promise, not a threat."

Grant held his ground, and JJ held her breath, staring at Otto's battered knuckles, pale from squeezing the bat. Her breath caught when Otto's grip shifted, and at the same moment, she felt Luther moving behind her.

Crack!

JJ flinched at the sound as the baseball bat hit a fence post. After flinging the bat away, Otto stepped around Grant and followed his wife to the house.

Grant closed his eyes, then took a deep breath and let it out, before turning his attention to Luther. "Go with him. I'd hate like hell for Otto to come back out here with a gun and kill us all."

Luther removed his hand from his holster.

"No shit," he said, and followed.

14

JJ looked at Trooper and said "Okay," to release him. The dog loped over to stand just behind her, where he'd remain until she told him otherwise.

"Are you hurt, JJ?" Grant asked. His voice held concern, with an edge of angry frustration.

JJ also noticed that Grant didn't seem all that surprised to see Adam. *Damn.* She should've said something to him last night before somebody else beat her to it. "I'm fine," she said.

Adam tried to stand, only to pitch over sideways in slow motion. "I'm still *not* fine," he said.

JJ was torn between helping him and kicking him, but either way she had to gather her boots first. She jammed them on her feet while Grant gazed down at Adam, shaking his head. The corner of Grant's mouth crept up slightly in an expression that seemed a hybrid of a grimace and a grin. A *grim*. JJ felt one cross her face as well.

"Otto really did a number on you, didn't he?" Grant said, as he and JJ each took an elbow.

Adam winced when one of their hands grazed his side. "Well,

yeah," he wheezed, "but he'll be thinking of me when his hands are too sore to hold the TV remote tomorrow."

Grant met JJ's eyes over Adam's fluffy, sleep-spiked hair.

"Anything new?" she asked.

Grant shook his head, and they pulled Adam the rest of the way to his feet. The three of them stood, with Adam the point of an uncertain triangle.

"You gonna fall down again if we let go?" Grant asked. He and JJ gently released Adam without stepping away.

"Maybe," Adam admitted, and slowly swayed, like a toddler who's just released his grip on his favorite stand-up chair.

Grant and JJ both put their hands back on Adam's elbows, enough to keep him steady and break his fall, come that eventuality. Their progress across the property was slow. When they finally turned the corner of the house, JJ saw a Beecham County Sheriff's Department SUV parked behind Otto's truck and Dorothy's car. Luther was waiting for Grant on the front step, leaning on his elbows on the metal railing, and made no move to help get Adam in the SUV. Fortunately, once Trooper settled next to the back bumper out of their way, it wasn't as hard as JJ feared it would be. At least not for her. Adam, biting off a painful moan as he climbed into the back seat, might have begged to differ. Grant made sure Adam's legs were fully inside before closing the door.

"JJ, I'd like you to wait with him," Grant said. "If you don't mind."

She looked at Adam in the back of the vehicle and the metal grill that separated him from the front, at Luther walking purposefully to join them, and finally back at Grant. "Am I under arrest?"

"No," Grant said.

Luther's sudden proximity set JJ's teeth on edge. "Is Adam under arrest?" she asked.

"No," Grant said, while Luther simultaneously asserted, "Yes."

She looked at them both. "Well, which is it?"

"Adam is not under arrest," Grant said.

Luther gritted his teeth and stared down at the ground, hands on his hips. "Yet," he muttered.

JJ got in Luther's face. "What the hell is your problem?"

The deputy straightened and shouted back at her, "What the fuck is yours?"

Trooper left his post at the bumper and trotted to JJ's heel. His growl was throat only, barely audible. Luther took a step back and his hand strayed toward his holster.

"Luther, if you harm a hair on my dog's head, I will cut your—"

"Hey! Both of you calm down," Grant interrupted. "Nobody's gonna hurt anybody, including the dog. Or did you forget why we're here?"

Grant left JJ and Luther standing awkwardly next to the SUV. JJ sighed and rubbed her eyes, exhausted already even though it was barely daylight. She walked around the back of the vehicle, Trooper at her heel.

"Trooper, go home," she said, hand on the back passenger door.

Luther, turning the front corner of the SUV, jumped when the dog loped by on his way to the woods. The deputy didn't reach for his weapon, but JJ still gave him her best stink eye.

"Goddammit!" Luther said. "I swear, I was just coming around to open the door for you. I wasn't going to touch your damn dog."

JJ stepped back and made a grand motion à la Vanna White for Luther to go ahead, but he shook his head at her, pissed.

"Fine," she said, turning away.

She leaned against the car window, catching sight of her own reflection. It embarrassed JJ, her expression of almost teenage petulance. She looked past her own face at Adam inside, eyes closed and arms held close to his body, obviously in pain.

Because of Rachel. Because he wanted to help her.

JJ was so ashamed, words burst from her lips before she could stop them. "I can't always protect my daughter, any more than they could protect Rachel. But Trooper will. That dog will kill for her, and he will fight for her with his last breath."

It was the closest Luther would get to an apology. She climbed in the back of the SUV and wrapped her arms around herself, but it didn't help. The shivering set in. Too much adrenaline, and too damn cold. JJ watched Luther join Grant on the front porch, even though looking through the metal partition made her feel like a criminal. The men were too far away to read subtleties in their expressions, but Luther looked as cold as she did, while Grant looked too tired to feel the temperature.

"I don't know what the hell you thought you were doing back there, but you better have some kinda story ready," JJ said. "Unless you *want* to be arrested."

Adam didn't reply.

JJ turned, ready to tear him a new one for being so reckless. But his eyes were closed, and he looked so vulnerable. She didn't have the heart.

15

Grant's nose was pink below his uniform hat, and there was a hint of fog when he breathed. But he still stood patiently out front, waiting for his deputy. It reminded Luther of Grant's father. He was the first man who'd shown any patience with Luther, and it was thoughts of the old Sheriff that prompted Luther to apologize. Even though Luther had been provoked.

"I'm sorry, Grant," he said. "I let my temper get the best of me. It won't happen again."

"Really?" Grant asked, deadpan, green eyes boring into Luther.

"Well, not today anyway." Luther tried to keep a straight face, but the corner of his mouth betrayed him.

Grant matched his half-smile. "I guess that'll have to do," he said, and reached for the door.

"Wait," Luther said, stomping his feet before he could stop himself. "Damn, it's cold. Listen, before we go in there... I stepped out because they were arguing and Otto asked for some privacy."

"What did you hear?"

"More than Otto intended. I pretended I'd camped out in the bathroom until they wandered in the living room and found me.

The upshot is Dorothy wants to press charges against Adam, but Otto's dead set against it."

"He say why?" Grant asked.

"Something about not muddying the waters while you're looking for Rachel."

Grant tilted his head. "That sounds surprisingly reasonable for someone who just pummeled a man."

Luther nodded. "Yes, it does. Which is probably why he said it. But it's bullshit."

Grant didn't disagree. "Any idea what his real reason is?"

"Not a one," Luther admitted.

Grant sighed. "Well, let's see what he has to say." He knocked, but didn't wait for a response before removing his hat and entering.

Luther followed suit. Stepping into the dry heat of the house made the skin on his face pucker. They found Dorothy with her back to the kitchen sink, arms crossed. Otto leaned against the perpendicular counter, in much the same pose. A bruise was coming up on his cheek where Adam—or maybe JJ—had gotten lucky.

"Luther probably told you," Grant said, "we don't have any news since we spoke last night."

"Yes," Otto said, "but he thought I might be of some help down at the Command Center today."

Grant nodded. "But first we need to resolve this issue with Adam Rutledge and JJ Tulley."

"JJ—" Dorothy began, but Otto interrupted her.

"There is no issue, Sheriff."

"You sure about that, Otto? Because I don't want to be getting another call to intervene in this *non*-issue."

"Yes, sir, I'm sure. I'd like to focus on finding Rachel."

Luther watched Dorothy while Otto acted as if she weren't in the room. The woman didn't look happy, but she didn't contradict her husband, either. Grant said a little more to the parents, but nothing that amounted to anything, and within a minute or two

Luther found himself back outside on the front step, freezing his ass off again.

"So what do you think?" Luther asked, blowing into cupped hands.

"I'd say you're right to be suspicious about Otto's sudden change of heart."

Luther glanced at the heavy door behind them and lowered his voice. "You really think Otto could've taken her?"

Grant stared out at the Sheriff's vehicle, where only JJ's head was visible in the back. "I think it's time we had a serious talk with Adam Rutledge."

"You want to take him in, maybe hold him for a while?"

Grant shook his head, then brushed off the hat in his hand. "I'm afraid we don't have that kind of time. And neither does Rachel Nicholson."

16

───────

dam sipped air, expanding his aching ribs as little as possible, as Luther hit every bump exiting the Nicholson driveway.

"Where are you taking us?" JJ asked.

"Home, if that's okay," Grant replied.

Luther's eyes kept searching for Adam in the rearview mirror. Or maybe it just seemed that way to Adam. JJ was right; he needed to have his story straight, but he didn't. He couldn't.

What if he was wrong?

He had to be missing something.

JJ's dog was waiting for them and sniffed Adam's leg as he struggled—with no offers of help—to get down out of the SUV. Once satisfied, the dog left him and fell back into line behind JJ, but Adam couldn't help but feel some sense of uneasy déjà vu around the creature. He watched as JJ picked up a mug from the edge of her driveway before going inside.

Adam paused, appreciating the solidity of the SUV next to him, until Luther motioned him ahead. Grant was already waiting on the porch. Adam held his breath against exclamations of weakness in front of either man (*God help me—steps!*).

"JJ, you mind getting your first aid kit?" Grant asked.

Grant was a tough man to make out. He had never been anything but kind to Adam growing up, even at the worst of times, and kindness doesn't always come easily to boys and young men. But that was decades ago, and now he was the Sheriff.

Adam waited until JJ left the room to ask, "Are you going to arrest me?"

"We need to talk," was Grant's careful response.

The three men sat at the dining table. Adam cringed as the sweatpants he'd worn to bed, now mud-streaked, touched down on JJ's clean chair. When JJ returned, he was still struggling to find a position on the unyielding wooden seat that was more forgiving to his body.

"You know, those ribs could be broken," JJ observed, sitting next to Adam. "You should probably get X-rays."

"He probably shouldn't have taken on a man with a fifty-pound weight advantage," Luther said.

JJ glared, but Adam said, "Forty-two, tops. And I'm sure most of it was water weight." Adam watched as Luther choked back a laugh.

Luther's good humor faded quickly, though, when JJ insisted, "Adam needs to see a doctor."

"He's got you," Luther snapped. "You're a nurse."

"JJ," Grant's calm voice cut in, "we need to speak with Adam *now*. When we're done, you can take him to the ER in Plattsville if you feel like it's necessary."

Adam touched JJ's arm, which happened to be the limit of how far he could reach without groaning. "He's right, JJ."

"Fine. At least let me get started before you bring out the rubber hoses," she said, opening a first aid kit big enough for an Everest expedition. "You want me to cut that T-shirt off, or help you pull it off?"

"Let's take it off," Adam said. "Cut it off, and I'll have Iris to deal with."

Adam stood and JJ tugged on his jacket sleeves, sliding it off in one painful move. For the T-shirt, Adam successfully raised his right arm most of the way, but getting the left one even to half-mast made him groan, so JJ peeled the shirt off for him, more roughly than he would have liked. His hand went to the chain he always wore around his neck. The key that had belonged to his mother still hung there. Reassured, he settled in the wooden chair, cold spindles hard against his back.

Luther leaned in for a better look and winced. "Ouch—Mike Tyson's gonna need some ice." Then his gaze traveled up to Adam's face, to the eye that was getting harder to see out of. "A lot of ice."

"I've got cold packs in the freezer," JJ said.

Adam watched, surprised, as Luther rose to get them.

He was still watching Luther rearrange frozen food when Grant said, "So, you want to tell me what all that was about next door?"

Goosebumps prickled on Adam's arms and chest, and he felt self-conscious being shirtless. What had seemed like such a reasonable idea moments ago suddenly wasn't. There was no other word for it: this was an interrogation. "Do I need a lawyer?"

Grant leaned across the table. "Goddammit, Adam! This isn't Charleston or Morgantown or even Scranton."

Adam's ribs twinged as his breath caught. *How the hell does Grant know where I used to live?*

"I've got a missing girl, and I don't have time for this crap. You can talk to the Feds over at the Command Center, and I'm sure they'll be happy to read you your rights and do it by the book. Or you can talk to me and we'll be done in five minutes. Why were you two beating the hell out of each other?"

"I didn't mean to," Adam admitted. In fact, he knew he hadn't done much of the beating at all, just the being beaten.

As if on cue, JJ's hands moved to Adam's torso.

"JJ!" Grant said brusquely. "Not now."

"What? It's my house," she protested, but she removed her hands and sat back in her chair.

Grant turned his attention back to Adam, waiting for an explanation. Adam grimaced as he shifted in his chair, now even more self-conscious and anxious. "You searched the Nicholson property? Top to bottom?"

"Of course," Grant said.

Adam turned his head away from JJ, relegating her to his peripheral vision. "And you looked at Otto Nicholson?"

"Adam! That's ridiculous," JJ protested.

Grant ignored her and nodded. "Otto and Dorothy. We always look at the parents."

JJ's look of shocked outrage swung first to Grant, then to Luther opening drawers in the kitchen. Adam pressed forward while he felt the moment's respite. "Are you sure Otto has nothing to do with his daughter's disappearance?"

"Are you kidding me?" JJ asked. "He didn't kidnap his own daughter—"

Grant held up a hand to preempt her rant. "Do you have some kind of evidence to suggest otherwise?" he asked.

"Not exactly," Adam said. "Not evidence."

"Then what?" Grant asked.

"Yes, what?" JJ demanded. "What gives you the right to come back here and accuse someone you don't even know—someone you'd never even met before last night—of being some kind of goddamned sicko? Answer me!"

Adam worked his jaw, back and forth. He couldn't look at JJ, couldn't think about how she'd react if he spoke. *Am I really going to do this?*

His guilt over Danny had been with him so long, it was a part of him. It was like his DNA. It would never be gone. But if he could do something to help this girl now, and didn't, he'd never be able to live with himself. What was the worst that could happen if he told them? They'd lock him up in prison? Well, actually, there was something worse. If he was wrong—if he was crazy—they might lock him up somewhere else.

"Can you promise me what I tell you will never leave this room?" Adam asked.

"No," Grant said. "I won't lie to you. I can't make that promise."

Adam's eyes drifted up, not really at anything in particular, just away from what was in front of him. His hand strayed back to the small metal talisman on his chest, praying for guidance. He could have sworn he felt a warm breath against his forehead.

He had to tell them.

"I *know* Otto Nicholson kidnapped his daughter."

"You *don't* know that," JJ said. "Otto is a good man."

"I do, because I saw it," Adam insisted.

"What do you mean, you saw it? You saw Otto Nicholson kidnap his own daughter?" Grant asked.

"No, but I saw *her*. I saw Rachel."

Adam flinched when JJ grabbed his arm.

"Then where is she?" she asked, voice frantic.

"He has her in a cabin."

"What do you mean?" Grant asked. "What cabin?"

Adam turned to JJ, and Grant and Luther didn't exist anymore. *Please let her understand.* "Do you remember, a few months after Danny was kidnapped, when I had the nightmare in the middle of class?"

JJ glanced down at where her hands were squeezing Adam's arm. She let go abruptly, fingers spreading away as if his arm were hot. "Yes, I do. That's pretty hard to forget."

"For me, too," Adam said. "That's why I remember the cabin. Rachel is in the same cabin I saw *her* in, in my old nightmare."

"What's he talking about, JJ?" Grant asked. "*Her* who?"

"I don't know—"

But suddenly, JJ did know. Adam saw it in her eyes. Because no doubt JJ had been thinking about that time, too, ever since Rachel disappeared. JJ leaned forward, and her hand gripped Adam's bruised arm again, painfully. "Your nightmare back then was about Sarah Edmunds?"

"Yes," Adam said, and felt the secrets that had bound him, that had kept him from breathing freely for twenty years, loosening their grip on his lungs. If he'd been standing, the release would have sent him to his knees.

"So when you say you saw Rachel," JJ said, "you mean you saw her the way you saw Sarah Edmunds. You dreamed about them both."

Adam let out a sigh of relief and felt tears rush to fill his eyes. She understood. *Now, please God, let her* believe *me.* "Yes, Janie. Rachel is in the same cabin I saw Sarah Edmunds in twenty years ago."

17

———

T *wenty years ago...*

ADAM WAS afraid to close his eyes.

He'd been afraid to sleep ever since the night Danny was taken. The evidence was there in the bathroom mirror every morning. Adam looked hollowed out, like a carved pumpkin left too long on the front porch. But the weather's too cold for pumpkins to rot come winter, so they just sink in on themselves. That's what he looked like.

Some of the other kids were afraid to sleep because they were afraid they'd be taken. Adam was afraid of that, too, but he was more afraid of what he might see.

Leslie Beck told him once that if you died in a dream, you died for real, too. Adam couldn't help thinking he was going to die in his sleep. And no one would ever know why.

But Adam was just so tired.

The classes after lunch were the worst. He put his head down on his desk. Adam had let one of his fingernails grow a little longer than the rest—not so much that Grandma Iris would notice, but just long enough that he could scratch himself. At first, jamming the nail into his palm had been enough to keep him awake. Not anymore.

Adam crossed his legs to bring his foot close. He slid his sock down and dug his long fingernail into the skin of his inner ankle. It was still sore from yesterday. He'd chosen that spot because no one would see it, unlike his arms or wrists. Adam was careful not to make it bleed too much, and he watched for infection. He'd learned that from Leslie. Leslie had been picking on someone, and JJ'd scratched him so hard that he still had the scar. Leslie had cried and said they might have to cut off his arm if it got infected, because people's fingernails were so dirty. Adam didn't believe everything Leslie said, but it would suck to lose a leg.

A shiver ran through Adam's body, and he suddenly realized his finger was wet with blood. He wiped it on the inside of his sock, but he couldn't get rid of the dark shadow under the nail. It made Adam feel gross, gross enough that he couldn't start on the other ankle. He'd just have to hope class was interesting.

Mr. Barnes's voice was soothing—something about the War of 1812. Adam imagined he could hear the ticking of the big clock on the wall, as seconds passed them by. He always thought the clock would stop keeping time when he watched it. The skinny, little hand paused, then lurched forward so hard he could see it shake with the effort of moving only that far and no further. Pause, *lurch*, pause, *lurch*... Tick, tick, tick...

∼

SARAH HAD BEEN SITTING on the concrete steps long enough to know her mom wasn't coming. She must have forgotten about the half day of school today. Sarah's mother was never the most attentive parent, but ever since she'd started dating someone from work, she'd been totally clueless. Dating is what her mother called it, but she didn't fool Sarah. Her mom was having sex with him. Bob Something. Sarah didn't want to think about it. But at least her mom never had sex at their house, and her mother and Bob should be at work, so Sarah didn't have to worry about interrupting anything this afternoon.

She could've asked one of the teachers to drive her home, but the last time Sarah had done that someone had called The County, though nothing had come of it. Walking home from school wasn't allowed anymore, not since a kid in Cold Springs disappeared. No one in her class was worried, though. Cold Springs may have a decent football team, but everyone knew they were dumb as rocks on the other side of the mountain. She'd heard Bob say the kid probably got lost, or accidentally locked himself in an old empty refrigerator. Sarah shuddered. That would be an awful way to go. She waited until the teachers were distracted by a kid throwing rocks at one of the buses, and slipped away down the street.

This was Sarah's favorite time of year to be outside. She hated hot weather and she hated to be wet, so the cool days before winter got socked in and they were buried in snow were the best. The air felt crisp and clean, and if there was one thing Sarah appreciated, living with her mother's mercurial attitudes toward housekeeping, it was clean, odorless air.

About half a mile from the school, Sarah reached the overpass, a short section of road raised like a bridge over a low spot in the surrounding forest. She stopped to look over the edge at the ground, twenty or thirty feet below. Sometimes a stream appeared in the spring, if there'd been heavy snow, but it was dry now, thick with leaves. She shivered as she felt and heard the rush of air as a car passed behind her on the road, and imagined what it would be like to fall that far.

The ground gradually leveled out again as it reached the grassy fields of the town park up ahead. Sometimes she saw deer on the slope, but not today. Instead, she saw a big, white van—the kind without any windows— pulling over to the shoulder a little ways past the overpass. Its hazard lights began blinking, and a man jumped out, leaving the engine running.

"Skipper? Skipper?" he called, disappearing for a moment as he hurried around the front of the van.

Sarah stopped.

The Platt Acres development lay beyond the town park, farther than

Sarah could see. In fact, there were no houses or businesses anywhere in sight. Sarah considered crossing to the other side of the road, to gain a little distance from the van, but she didn't want to draw attention to herself or look scared. Because she wasn't. Not really. She kept walking.

The man wasn't paying attention to Sarah. As she got closer, she heard him tell someone to stay in the van, saying it would be all right, that they'd find him. The man was about the age of the ones her mother dated. His clothes could use a washing and he needed a haircut, but lots of people around Plattsville worked dirty jobs and didn't have the energy left over to try and look their best.

He didn't look scary.

This close to the overpass, the ground dropped steeply away from the road. The man peered over the edge, into the woods beyond. Sarah sped up, hoping to get by him unnoticed, but he looked up as she approached.

"Excuse me—I'm looking for my dog. You haven't seen him, have you?"

Sarah tried to speak, but she couldn't, mesmerized by his eyes... Once, Grammy and Pappy had taken her to church (without her mom, who'd threatened to burst into flames), and the preacher talked about prophets in the wilderness. This man looked like that. His hair, brown and blonde and gray all at once, fell almost to his shoulders, and he had some color of pale eyes that were so intense and knowing... and sad.

Sarah finally managed to shake her head.

The man went on. "We were taking him to the park, and he jumped out the window—it was the damnedest thing." The man's face flushed and he looked down at the ground. "Sorry, miss. I guess I'll have to put up signs, but we don't have a photo of him, and I don't know nothing about dog breeds. He's one of them fluffy dogs—"

"What color?" Sarah asked, before she remembered she wasn't speaking to him.

The man's face squinched up on one side and his lips squeezed together while he looked up at the treetops, trying to decide. "Well, I don't rightly know how to describe it. Son, you still got that picture you drew?"

He walked back toward the van, and Sarah thought she heard someone inside, but she couldn't make out the words.

"In your book bag?" the man said. "A'right."

He opened one of the van's back doors and grabbed an olive green satchel, resting it on the bumper to rummage through it with his back to Sarah. "I know he ain't exactly Picasso, but maybe if you looked at this—"

Sarah walked over, hands tucked into her backpack straps. Her mom always yelled at her for that—said she looked like she was trying to pinch her own boobs—but Sarah couldn't help the nervous habit.

What did she have to be nervous about?

Maybe why it was taking so long to find his kid's picture. Sarah licked her lips, mouth dry. It was time to leave.

She stepped back, intending to run toward the park even if it made her look stupid, but the man swung around suddenly and clamped his hand over her mouth. Sarah couldn't get her own hands free from her backpack in time to stop him. The man's other arm encircled her, pinning her arms against her sides. Was there another shadow, someone else, in the back of the van?

The man put one knee on the bumper and raised up, lifting her inside. Sarah kicked her legs as hard as she could, screaming into his heavy hand, and fell hard onto the metal floor of the van. Her head—

ADAM FELL FROM HIS DESK, taking his chair over with him. The screaming sounds wouldn't stop, and it wasn't until Mr. Barnes grabbed him—"Adam, calm down!"—and he saw all the other kids staring at him, mouths open, that Adam realized *he* was the one screaming. But he still couldn't stop.

18

"So what'd they do with you?" Grant asked, face inscrutable.

Adam shrugged before remembering—with a little gasp —that the motion would be painful. "I don't know. Took me to the office, I guess. I was so freaked out, they said I kicked some of the teachers. Iris had to come get me."

Luther stood by the stove, forgotten cold packs on the counter next to him, but made no move to join them.

JJ asked, pointedly, "Can I look at his ribs now?"

Grant nodded.

Adam found it hard to meet JJ's eyes, unsure of what he would see there. But she was all business as she motioned for him to raise his arms and began moving her hands methodically over his torso.

"I know it hurts, but stop holding your breath," she said.

"Everyone in the school heard about it," Grant said, "but I guess nobody that wasn't in your classroom really knew what happened. Is that when Iris sent you away?"

Adam dropped his arms. "She didn't send me away."

Except she did.

Adam raised his arms again at JJ's prompting.

Sure, Iris had said he could come back, and had welcomed him in the summers for a while, but she'd also said he couldn't stay there. She'd made him leave his home. The closest thing he'd had to a home.

JJ tilted her head while considering a particularly tender area of Adam's ribs. She pressed harder, and Adam grunted.

"Sorry. I think you lucked out, though. Doesn't look like anything's broken, but you might want to get it checked out by somebody who knows more than me." She dug around in the first aid kit and made a frustrated sound. "I'll be back."

Adam watched JJ stride toward the back rooms, and felt Grant's eyes upon him. He felt raw, but it helped when Grant met his gaze across the table without looking away.

"You think I'm crazy," Adam said, somewhere between a statement and a question.

"Was there actually another person in the van?"

"I don't know," Adam admitted.

Grant pressed. "What's your instinct?"

"I don't know," Adam repeated.

"Don't suppose you got a license plate."

It was obvious by Grant's tone that they both knew the answer. Adam couldn't help a half grin. "No."

"Was that the first time you saw something like that?"

Adam swallowed, and he felt a tremble begin in his body. He looked down at his hands, but the vibration wasn't visible yet. He wondered if Grant could see the motion of his heart pounding in his chest, pulsing at his throat.

JJ set a bottle of pain meds on the table, and Adam jumped, triggering a pained grunt. JJ dropped a flannel shirt across his lap, too, but she made no move to help him put it on.

"Adam," Grant pressed, "was that the first time?"

Adam stared back down at his hands, unable to comprehend why they weren't shaking hard enough to knock the table over, because he was inside. "No, it wasn't. The first time was at Iris's, not long after Danny was taken. I woke up screaming on Iris's couch. And your father was there."

A wet thump sounded from the kitchen. All eyes swung to Luther, picking up a cold pack he'd knocked to the floor.

Grant turned back to Adam. "Did you tell him about your dream?"

Adam closed his eyes, but it didn't help. Nothing came back. "I'm sorry. All I remember is being afraid he'd arrest me."

"Adam, you were twelve years old," JJ said.

Adam shrugged, this time on just one side, but it still hurt like hell.

"What about Iris?" Grant asked. "Did you tell her?"

"Maybe," Adam said, unsure. "After your dad left, Iris told me to forget about whatever I'd seen. She said not to tell anyone, and if I didn't tell, the dreams would go away."

Grant raised his eyebrows, but not like he was surprised. More like he was stretching his forehead. "So, how does all this connect to Rachel Nicholson?"

JJ stood, grabbed the flannel shirt from Adam's lap, and held it in front of him. The first sleeve wasn't too bad, but getting into the second was so painful, he wished he'd stayed shirtless despite the cold. They left it unbuttoned and Adam sat, hands on his lap, until he had enough control over his breathing to speak.

"Thanks, JJ. Things got a little crazy for me at school after that. Iris kept me home for the rest of the week. When I went back, everybody was staring. I couldn't take it. Most days, Iris would drop me off in the morning and pick me up again by lunch. I'd hide in my room—quiet-like—all afternoon while she cut people's hair in the kitchen."

Adam pinched the shirt together at the bottom and held it between his long fingers. He felt the cold settling in. "I don't know how long things could have gone on like that—there's a limit to the leeway people are willing to give even an orphan kid—but it ended up not mattering. I had another dream about Sarah Edmunds one evening."

"And the girl was in a cabin in this one?" Grant asked.

Adam nodded.

"What cabin? Where was it? What did it look like?"

Adam shook his head. "I have to be honest, once these dreams are done, it's hard for me to remember them, especially after Iris told me not to. But when I saw the little girl this morning—"

"Rachel," JJ interrupted.

"Rachel," Adam repeated. "I dreamed about Rachel this morning. And when I woke up, I *knew* she was in the same cabin Sarah Edmunds had been in."

"Could you see her?" JJ asked, leaning forward. "Did she look all right?"

If this doesn't make them lock me up... Adam continued anyway. "I couldn't see her, but I know she was okay because I was seeing *through her eyes*. Like I was inside her."

Adam's shirt collar had slid sideways on his neck. He bent to adjust it and held his breath as his ribs twinged. That's when he remembered something else. "She was okay, but her chest hurt. It was tight, like maybe she'd been coughing a lot?"

JJ fell back against her chair, speechless. Grant asked, "What did you see?"

Adam closed his eyes. "All I have is impressions now. Blankets on a bed or a cot or something that her ankle was tied to. It was cold and it was dark—so dark— inside."

"Then how do you know it was the same cabin?" Grant asked.

Adam opened his eyes. "I just do."

"Wait a minute," JJ said. "If you thought she was in a cabin somewhere, why'd you go after Otto?"

"Someone turned on a light in the cabin. I didn't see who, but the last thing Rachel said before I woke up was, *Please, daddy, don't hurt me.*"

JJ's hand flew to her mouth.

"What kind of light?" Grant asked. "Electric?"

Of course—was the cabin off the grid? This was why you needed cops, trained professionals who could think straight. Adam closed his eyes again. "I don't think so. It got brighter slowly, so maybe a hurricane lamp."

"What about water? The smell of wood smoke? Anything else?" Grant pushed.

Adam considered. "I'm sorry. That's it. That's all I have."

Luther shifted in the kitchen. "Sheriff," he said, "how about I go get the truck warmed up?"

Grant nodded. He and Adam and JJ sat in silence at the table, until the sound of the SUV's engine stirred JJ to action.

"Can I send some coffee with you?" she asked, getting the pot going.

"No time," Grant said, rising. "We're done for now. Unless there's anything else Adam needs to tell me."

Adam wished it were easier to breathe. Then maybe he could think straight, too. "No. But Sheriff, no one else knows about this, the things I told you."

Heavy boots made their way up the front steps. Trooper barked at the door before Luther had a chance to knock, if he were going to. Adam's lips went numb, like the blood had drained from them, as he experienced another moment of déjà vu.

JJ glanced over at him and asked, "Are you okay? You've gone pale."

Adam took a breath, and the world seemed to settle on its axis again. "Trooper barked when Rachel was taken," he said.

"Of course he did," JJ said, sounding almost offended.

Grant stared out at his waiting deputy. "I gotta go. JJ, will you walk me out?"

19

———

JJ closed the front door behind her, joining Grant and Luther standing in the cold. "So what do you think?" she asked.

"He's crazy, that's what I think," Luther said. "Just like his dad. All this hocus pocus shit."

"Luther, that's not particularly helpful," Grant admonished.

"What? I know people didn't talk much about Virgil Rutledge, especially by the time you were growing up, but don't tell me you never heard any stories about him. He was crazy as a goddamned loon."

"Fuck you, Luther," JJ said.

"That's not particularly helpful, either, JJ," Grant said. "Did Adam tell you about his dreams back then?"

"No," she said. "I asked him, after the blow-up in class, but he didn't want to talk about it. Everybody was messed up after the way Danny was taken, but I knew there was something else going on. Something Adam wasn't telling me."

"Did you tell Adam about Rachel having asthma?" Grant asked.

Luther stared at JJ, arms crossed.

"No," she said, looking directly at the deputy. "It never came up."

Grant pursed his lips, thinking. He looked a little bit like Otto had beaten him up, too. "Would Trooper bark at Otto if he were passing by on the road?"

The gears were slow to turn—too slow by a long shot—but JJ eventually got there. "Driving, no. Walking, I doubt it. Unless he did something Trooper disagreed with. So you believe Adam?"

Luther snorted.

"Luther, if you want to wait in the vehicle, I'll be there in a minute," Grant said.

JJ almost stuck her tongue out at the deputy as he clomped down the steps. She may have, if Grant hadn't been watching her, and she hadn't been waiting for his answer.

"I think Adam believes it," Grant said, once Luther was gone. "And whether what Adam said he saw is... *real* or not, it's something to think about. We've got a chopper going up in half an hour. They'll be looking for places—including cabins—somebody could be holding Rachel. And I'll have somebody double-check with your other neighbor about hearing Trooper yesterday. But I'm not about to walk into a meeting with federal agents and say my psychic friend—whose best friend was kidnapped when he was a kid—says the girl's father took her."

Drumming his fingers on the steering wheel, Luther must have felt JJ glaring at him. He pointed at his watch through the windshield, and Grant held up a couple of fingers in acknowledgment.

The jerk could damn well wait thirty seconds more. JJ put her hand on her hip, feeling more solid, more grounded, now that she had some distance from Adam. "I'm not saying I believe him, either—I don't think Otto had anything to do with it—but no matter what Luther says, Adam's not crazy."

Grant just nodded in that way that said, *I hear you, but I'm not committing to anything.* "I'll let you know if I hear something. Keep Evie close."

JJ bit back an automatic, angry reply, because she knew Grant

—unlike her asshole ex-husband—wasn't challenging her ability to raise her daughter. Instead she said, "Good luck," and patted the puffy shoulder of his winter coat as he left.

Luther turned around in her driveway too fast for JJ's liking, and the Sheriff's vehicle rolled towards the road and out of sight. People said what happened to Danny—and the fact that his body was never found—had cracked something deep inside Grant's father, that he'd never been the same man after that. Grant was younger than his father had been then, and to be honest, softer. No, not softer—*kinder*. She hated to think what would happen to Grant if he didn't find Rachel.

It was finally starting to look like real daylight out. JJ stepped down into the yard and moved the bicycle Adam had nearly tripped over the night before. *That girl.* What would happen to Evie if her best friend was never found? Would she weather it all but end up married to an abusive asshole? Although JJ felt it wasn't a bad trade for an amazing daughter. Or would Evie end up stuck at this moment in time, in a perpetual limbo, unable to form meaningful connections with anyone, a ghost of the person she could have been?

Not if JJ could help it.

She trotted back inside the house.

"Everything okay?" Adam asked, still sitting at the table, still obviously in pain.

"Fine," JJ said, heading for the kitchen and pulling down plates. "You haven't eaten, have you?"

"No."

"You take cream and sugar with your coffee?"

"Yes, please."

She loaded a tray with coffee and muffins and carried it to the table. Adam immediately shoved half a banana muffin in his mouth, wincing a little at his torn lip. "Thanks, JJ."

"Don't get yourself too worked up," she said. "I'm a working mother, so they're store-bought."

JJ stared at the bran muffin on her plate, then switched it out for one of the blueberry ones. "You ever go see anybody about this stuff? A professional, I mean?" she asked, popping an unsatisfying bite of muffin in her mouth. Too much sweet, too little substance. She should've stuck with the bran.

"Are you asking if I've been to a hooker?" Adam deadpanned, but he couldn't hold off the grin for long. With that damn dimple, he probably hadn't paid for more than half a dozen drinks in his life, much less for sex.

"You don't shave sometime soon, a hooker's the only kind of woman who'll be interested," she said, pointing to some stray muffin caught in his stubble. "Not to mention that fancy shiner you're getting. Answer the question: have you been to a shrink?"

He wiped his chin, then looked at the napkin to see what he'd caught. "Huh. Thanks. I went once. The school referred me to somebody in Plattsville, right after Danny. I didn't have much to say. So you still don't believe me about Otto?"

JJ topped up her coffee, watching a slight post-adrenaline tremor in her hand as she poured. She might have to make another pot. "I know Otto. He and Dorothy and Rachel have lived next door for over five years. Plus, if you're right about Trooper, he wouldn't have barked at Otto. I'm pretty confident the man didn't harm his own daughter."

Adam didn't speak, but his eyebrows did the same funny curl toward his forehead—like upside-down commas—that they'd done as a child when he was considering Danny's latest scheme.

"Pretty soon, they'll have all manner of law enforcement on the ground and in the sky—thank God—and if anyone can find Rachel, they can." JJ sighed. "That's what my logical brain says. But when you showed up on my doorstep last night, I asked how you heard about the girl so fast, and you looked surprised. You didn't know, did you?"

"Not for sure," Adam admitted.

"So you had some kind of dream about her—and my barking dog—and you drove from where?"

"A little bitty town outside of Harrisburg."

JJ shook her head, trying not to look at her fingers while she did the traveling math. "Jesus, what'd you do—just jump in your car and go?"

"Pretty much," Adam said, picking at the final muffin on his plate.

He was too skinny. His face was drawn and there'd been no fat to mitigate the bruising on his muscled torso. One morning of muffins wasn't going to make that right, but still... JJ set the remaining pastries on Adam's plate.

"Finish them," she said. "I know I'm stepping outside the bounds of the Tulley family character here, but I have to think that you showing up here means something, even if I don't understand it. That you're here because you're meant to be here, and that together, we're meant to do what law enforcement can't. Or won't."

Like maybe not care if the bastard makes it to trial.

"So what do we do?"

JJ got up and retrieved the cold packs from the counter. She handed one to Adam, and set the other on the table with a clean dish towel. "Here, put this on your ribs. Over your shirt is fine. When you're done eating, wrap the other one and hold it on your cheek."

Adam's eyes strayed to an elastic bandage in the first aid kit, and he raised an eyebrow.

"Mummies don't have lips," JJ said, and Adam chuckled, even as the lines of pain in his face deepened.

Elastic bandages—and the little metal claw fasteners shaped like dog bones—had fascinated them as children. They'd once wrapped Danny's head in one, and he'd walked around JJ's house, arms outstretched, wide eyes staring and lips smacking. When JJ pointed out that mummies don't have lips, for some reason it had set them off, and they'd all laughed until they cried. That is, until Danny knocked over a lamp with his mummy arms. Seven years old at the time, they were all terrified of JJ's dad.

"Did your dad spank you for the lamp?"

JJ shook her head, still smiling, and a tear snuck out of the corner of her eye. She quickly wiped it and pointed at the bandage. "We don't wrap rib injuries anymore. It restricts the breathing, and may increase the likelihood of pneumonia." She opened the bottle of pain relievers and put a couple next to Adam's coffee. "Take these. If we're gonna figure this out, you gotta be as close to a hundred percent as possible. For that matter, so do I."

JJ's head had the dry ache of too little sleep, so she downed a couple with her coffee. Then she began pacing slowly around the living room with her mug. "If we go on the assumption that there is something to learn from your dreams, it seems to me there are two ways to look at it, like dreams in general. What you see could be literal, or it could be metaphorical."

Adam looked slightly comical with a faded, pink unicorn dish towel covering half his face. "Okay, if I get a vote, I'd say they feel literal."

"Or Option Number Three," JJ said, ignoring his vote, "somewhere in between. Could be another father figure."

"I'd imagine law enforcement's already looking at anyone who fits that bill. Do we know for sure that Otto is her biological father?"

JJ stopped suddenly, slopping a few drops of coffee from her cup. "What, it's not enough to slander her father, now you have to slander Rachel's mom, too?"

Adam held up the hand formerly securing his rib ice pack—albeit slowly and not very high—in penitent surrender.

"Fine," JJ said. "I'll interrogate Dorothy as soon as Otto leaves. Alone. What about you?"

"I should talk to Iris. Maybe she remembers something about my dreams I don't, or maybe she has a better understanding of them than I do." He adjusted the ice pack, then winced.

"You've gotten awfully wimpy in your old age," JJ said, grinning.

"It's not that. I just remembered I don't have a car. Well, not a usable car. I kinda drove mine into the ditch at the bottom of the road."

"Seriously?" JJ asked, visualizing the spot. "You think we can push it out?"

Adam plopped both ice packs on the table. "It's a small car, but I don't think I could push a tricycle out of a ditch right now."

JJ sat back in her chair, considering. "That's okay. I've got a couple of quick errands to take care of. I can drop you off on the way, and that'll give Otto time to leave."

"Okay, then," Adam said, rising from his chair in a series of furniture-gripping stages. "I guess we should be moving."

"Think you need a walker, old man?" JJ asked.

"Don't forget," he said, "I may seem old, but I'll always be seventy-two days younger than you."

JJ grabbed her coat and put her boots on, taking a moment to tie the laces more tightly this time. "That's only true if we die at the same time." Then she shook her car keys. "Ready?"

20

———

A dam knew Iris would be home. She had to be. He'd been waiting twenty years to have this conversation, and after doing—in JJ's words—a "thorough job" of driving his car into the ditch, he figured he was due some better luck.

Iris met him on her way out the door. "I was just going to pick up some bread at the market—what happened to you?"

"Long story," he said, moving awkwardly around her and through the door. "We need to talk."

"Okay." Iris followed him back into her house. "Have you seen a doctor?"

"JJ took a look at me. I'll be fine, just some bruises."

"Have you eaten anything?"

"Yes."

"I could make you some eggs—"

"Iris, please. It's about Rachel Nicholson, the girl that was kidnapped." Adam sat at the kitchen table but didn't remove his jacket. Putting it on had hurt too much to take it off until he knew he'd be inside long enough to bother.

"Is that why someone beat you? Because of the girl?" Iris asked, dropping her purse on the kitchen counter.

"No one—" Adam stopped, unable to outright lie to his grandmother about how he'd been injured. That gave him time to process the rest of what she'd said. "Why would someone beat me because of Rachel Nicholson?"

"You know why," Iris said, sitting across from him.

"No, I don't. If I did, I wouldn't ask."

Iris pushed her long hair back from her face. "When a child disappears, people get scared. And when they get scared, they get stupid. Is there any news about the girl?"

"No," Adam said, and stalled out for a moment. He could not imagine how to start this conversation, and perhaps worse, he could not imagine any good way for it to end.

"Sweetie," she said, reaching for his hand, "I know this has to be hard for you, after what happened to Danny."

"What did happen to Danny?" he asked.

Iris released his hand and grew still. "I don't know what you mean."

"There are gaps in my memory, pieces of things that you told me to forget—"

"Why would I do that?"

"—And I think it's time we remembered them," Adam said, his voice growing stronger along with his resolve.

He hardly recognized Iris's closed expression. This was not his grandmother; it was the woman the rest of the world had to contend with, the woman who'd buried her husband, then her youngest son, then put her eldest son and his wife to rest and raised their child, only to send him away when he wanted nothing more than to be with her. But, of course, her blood ran in Adam's veins, too.

"Tell me about my dreams," he said.

Adam saw a moment of confusion on Iris's face, and then... relief? *Good God, what else is she hiding from me?*

"I don't know what you mean," she said, calm stoicism back in place.

"I knew when Danny was abducted."

"Of course you did. You were there."

Adam struggled to articulate the inexplicable. "No, I knew about something else, something that happened to him later. But I can't remember." He stretched his arms toward Iris, ignoring the pain as he placed his palms on the table. "I also knew when Sarah Edmunds was abducted."

"So did half the state." The words were challenging, but her tone was that of an adult patronizing a child who says his plastic baseball bat is a pirate spyglass.

"And yesterday, I knew when Rachel Nicholson was abducted."

Iris's expression didn't change, but her face blanched as pale as her white hair. "Don't be ridiculous."

"I saw him take Rachel, just like I saw him take Sarah. That's why I came back."

"Saw whom?" she asked.

"I don't know," Adam admitted. "I was hoping you could tell me."

Iris sighed, and Adam watched the doting grandmother mask cover her face. It made the back of his neck tingle.

"Adam, sweetie, you always were a fanciful child."

"I know what I saw!"

Iris blinked at his raised voice, then narrowed her eyes. "No, you don't, and that's precisely the issue."

A tearing pain racked Adam's chest when he reached up to rub his face. He was already so tired, and standing up to Iris sapped his energy even more. It's probably why he did it so rarely. "You don't understand. What I saw about Sarah years ago, I think it can help us find Rachel now."

"How? The two things are totally unrelated," Iris said. Her confidence was unnerving.

"What did I tell you about Danny, when I had the nightmare?"

Iris got up from her chair, deliberately pushed it back under the table and moved to retrieve her purse from the counter.

"Tell me what you know!" Adam yelled, slamming a hand on the table.

Iris wheeled and placed her own hands on the table, facing Adam. "Oh, are we sharing things now? Then maybe you want to start with why you left Morgantown in such a hurry. Or any of the other places and things you ran away from. Would you rather share numbers? How about six. That's how many times you showed up on my doorstep over the past eighteen years. Forty-eight. That's the longest period—in hours—you ever stayed."

"Iris, please don't do this." Adam lurched to his feet.

"Or you could start by telling me who beat the crap out of you this morning. In my own town. If it's not about the girl, how did you manage—"

Adam's voice boomed over Iris's, "Please, just answer the goddamned question!"

They stared at each other in the silence that fell over the house. Until a powerful knock echoed through the front door.

Iris pushed off the table with her hands and said, "Who can that be," with no more emotional inflection than a phone service recording.

Adam hadn't heard a vehicle approach, but he suspected Iris had. He let his eyes slip shut and tried not to think about the words Iris had said in anger, to match up the events in his life with the times he'd run to her. He rubbed his hand against his face and felt the stubble crackle. JJ was right; he was starting to look and feel like a hobo. At least he'd have a chance to take a shower and shave if Iris made her excuses and slipped away.

"Luther!" came Iris's surprised voice from the door. "What brings you here this morning? I'd offer you coffee, but I'm afraid I'm on my way out."

Despite her assertion, Iris allowed the deputy to pass through the door. He stopped on the doormat, glancing down at his own boots.

Adam straightened too quickly, then listed to one side to ease the pain. He tried to disguise his grimace as a small smile as he walked over to join them. Not that he'd fool Luther.

"I'm afraid I don't have time for coffee anyway, Ms. Rutledge," Luther said.

"Is there any news on the girl?" Iris asked.

"No, ma'am, but we're doing our best. I was just checking in with some of the searches out this way. I stopped, since I was passing by, because I thought I might catch Adam," Luther said, hat literally in hand.

"What's up, Luther?" Adam acted nonchalant, but he wasn't sure he wanted to hear Luther's answer. Was Otto pressing charges? Was Luther here to arrest him? Either way, he'd prefer to not air the sordid details of the morning in front of Iris. Not just yet.

"I wanted to check with you about your car. What exactly happened to put you in the ditch out there by JJ's?" Luther's voice held a mixture of concern and mild interest, probably his default lawman mode of address. Adam couldn't read him, and he wasn't sure how to deal with this incarnation of the man who'd graduated high school about the time Adam started grade school, the much older brother of the boy who'd become the class bully.

Adam tilted his head in his best embarrassed, aw-shucks grin. "Nothing sinister, Luther. I can't even blame a deer. I just wasn't used to driving on the back roads and hit a patch of wet leaves on the turn."

Luther nodded in agreement. "Happens to the best of us. I'm heading in that direction, if you need a ride back out there. Obviously we're pretty swamped, but if all you need is a quick nudge to get her out, I think I could manage it."

"Thanks, Luther, but Iris and I—"

"That sounds like an excellent idea, Luther," Iris said. Her voice was tight, and Adam felt certain he'd get an earful from her about the accident. "I don't think I'd be much help pushing a car out of a ditch." She grabbed her purse and smiled at Luther as she brushed past him and out the door.

"We'll talk later," Adam called out to her.

Iris waved without looking back.

Luther shook his head. "Force of nature," he said.

"That's one way of putting it." Adam caught a glimpse of Luther outside of lawman mode when the man grinned back at him. "Let me just lock up."

Adam followed Luther out to the same vehicle Grant had used to take him to JJ's earlier that morning. It was easier to get in the front seat than it had been to get in the back a couple of hours ago, but only marginally so. And it'd probably be harder by tomorrow.

Luther laughed, and Adam heard just a hint of the bully his brother had been as he echoed Adam's own thoughts. "Boy, you're gonna be feeling it tomorrow."

Adam hitched his breath in a kind of stair step, double inhale, trying for maximum oxygen intake with minimum pain. "I don't suppose we could have a pact, that you'll drive better than I apparently do, and I'll pretend to wear the seat belt."

Luther's answering chuckle was softer. "Sorry. I'm afraid that'd be setting a bad precedent. We're not even really supposed to have passengers in the front seat."

"Having smelled your back seat, I appreciate the special dispensation," Adam said.

Luther raised an eyebrow in acknowledgment. "You gonna go picking fights, you could find an easier target than Otto Nicholson. Man's the size of a bear."

Adam turned to watch the trees pass by. In daylight, he couldn't seem to get over how darn many trees there were. Not many leaves left, though. Too bad. Iris had said an early cold snap, followed by a freak windstorm, were to blame. "I wasn't trying to pick a fight."

"Really?" Luther said, skeptical. "Don't get me wrong. Sheriff's Department's got too much else on our plate right now to give a shit about it, and I'm not trying to yank your chain, either. I'm just saying, Otto Nicholson could put a world of hurt on a man." Luther couldn't resist looking at Adam with a grin. "Especially a man like you. Where'd you learn to fight?"

Adam smiled, despite himself. There wasn't any advantage in annoying Luther, and he had a point. "Obviously, I didn't."

The two men laughed—Luther more than Adam—dissipating some of the tension in the stuffy vehicle. Adam still wore his jacket, and Luther had set the heat high enough to warm a lizard in the Arctic.

Adam kept waiting for Luther to say something about what he'd shared at JJ's—not whether Luther agreed that Otto was guilty of something, but whether he thought Adam was some kind of freak. As the miles rolled by in silence, Adam began to relax. Luther drove pretty conservatively, his law enforcement training prevailing over his Beck family heritage. Adam seemed to remember one of Luther's cousins coming to an early end in a souped-up Chevelle, drag racing on the straight stretch by the Howard Farm, with gruesome results. He wondered if Luther had been a deputy then, and if he'd been called to the scene. That might be enough to encourage a man to drive the speed limit.

And cue the arrival at the scene of my latest accident. Maybe I should give up automobiles entirely.

"I guess you never really had a chance to practice driving the roads around here," Luther said.

"Yeah, I was long gone by the time I was old enough to get my license," Adam agreed.

Luther pulled off to the side of the road a bit past Adam's hatchback before turning his hazards on. "Your car locked?"

"No, I never bother."

Luther opened the driver's door. Adam unlatched his seat belt and started to follow.

"No," Luther said. "You just stay put. I'll get you all sorted out."

If he hadn't been Leslie's brother, and a deputy, it probably wouldn't have sounded so ominous.

21

———

The woman at the post office had been chatty, so by the time JJ's driveway was in sight, she took a chance on Otto being gone and continued to the next one.

Dorothy's was the only car at the Nicholson home, and she met JJ at the door. The woman had every right to be upset—if Evie were gone, JJ would be a raving lunatic—but JJ wasn't in the mood for drama. It wasn't particularly helpful, and JJ was still harboring some resentment over the baseball bat this morning. She skipped the embrace and words of comfort that might have set Dorothy off.

"You eat anything today?" JJ asked.

Dorothy stared at JJ as if she were speaking a foreign language.

"I'll take that as a 'no.' Come on—don't be a zombie."

JJ took Dorothy firmly by the elbow, parked her at the kitchen table, and put a couple of slices of wheat bread in the toaster. There was a jar of apple butter on the counter. She held it up for Dorothy's approval.

"That's the first batch of the year," Dorothy said. "Will you have some with me?"

"You better believe it," JJ said, removing the canning lid with a little pop. Apples and cinnamon and cloves and sweetness assaulted her nose. "Mmm... smells good. Nice consistency, too." The dark brown spread was almost as thick as porridge on the spoon. JJ brought plates to the table and waited until Dorothy took her first bite before asking, "Otto out with the search?"

Dorothy nodded. "Believe it or not, I took Jacob to some kind of special practice this morning. Coach thought it'd be good to keep him busy, said he'd bring him home later."

"I think that was wise," JJ said.

"I feel like *I* should be doing something," Dorothy said. She set her toast on her plate, and her eyes began to tear.

JJ squeezed Dorothy's forearm. It felt no more substantial than a willow branch. "You're exactly where you need to be right now. And I'm sure that's what the Sheriff said, too. About this morning—"

"JJ, let's not talk about this morning," Dorothy said.

JJ didn't appreciate the woman showing a hint of backbone at the worst possible time. "Dorothy, I know you're under a lot of strain right now, but I don't want to take a chance on hard feelings festering. Adam—"

"Adam needs to keep his goddamned sick thoughts to himself."

And there's that pesky backbone again. "I'm not making excuses, but Adam got the wrong end of something and ran off half-cocked. And he got the shit beat out of him for his troubles, I might add."

"Well, of course he did. He's just lucky—" Dorothy snorted, "you were there to save him."

JJ looked at Dorothy from beneath her lashes, doing her best impression of demure. Then the women started to giggle.

"If you could've seen yourself, like a monkey on Otto's back," Dorothy said. She laughed, and tears started streaming down her cheeks. Then her face crumpled, and JJ watched in horror as the woman came undone.

"Dorothy!" JJ resisted the urge to slap her, moving alongside her chair and taking her face firmly in her hands instead. "Dorothy! You can't do this now. You have to hold it together."

Dorothy's lip still quivered dangerously, so JJ gave her head a squeeze, perhaps a little harder than was strictly necessary. "Are you done?"

She nodded, and JJ released her. "Good girl. Finish your toast."

The petite woman looked more child than mother, with her watery eyes and small pink nose, dutifully eating the toast she held in her diminutive hands. But JJ knew Dorothy wasn't a child. Far from it, and she hadn't been one for a long time.

"There's something I need to talk to you about," JJ said. "Something that might help us find Rachel."

Dorothy dabbed at the corner of her mouth with a paper napkin and said, "Go on."

JJ paused. Raised more by her father than by her mother, she'd acquired the man's distaste for anything that might be considered gossip. But she'd lived in Cold Springs her entire life, so she knew her father's reticence was in the minority. "We didn't know each other very well when you married Otto, or when Rachel was young," JJ began.

"That's true," Dorothy said uncertainly, obviously wondering where JJ was headed.

"Is there anyone else Rachel might think of as a father figure?"

Dorothy frowned, trying to make sense of the question. Then her face cleared. "You mean someone she might have gone to, someone she trusts."

I mean someone she'd call daddy and beg not to hurt her, but close enough. "Exactly."

Dorothy tugged on the ends of her hair, but just on the right side. Maybe that was where she kept her brain button. JJ closed her eyes, ashamed of her frustrated, exhausted thoughts.

"I told the Sheriff, I can't think of anyone, man or woman," Dorothy said. "My dad lives out of state, and we've checked— Rachel's not with my mother and her husband, either."

"I did notice," JJ said, vaguely indicating the framed photos on the entertainment center in the next room, "that all of your wedding photos are head shots."

"Ahh," Dorothy said, blushing. "Yes, I was already pregnant with Rachel when we got married. Is that what you wanted to know?"

"Not entirely," JJ said, wondering again why she'd agreed to interrogate the mother of a missing child. She slid the plates of toast out of range of stray elbows. "Okay, I'm going to ask you something, and I don't want you to get angry. I'm just trying to get the fullest picture of Rachel's life I can."

Dorothy clasped her hands, bracing herself. "Okay."

JJ's voice softened as she leaned across the table. "Is Otto Rachel's biological father?"

Dorothy's face flushed. "Of course he is! What the hell kind of question is that?"

JJ backed away from the woman yelling in her face. "I'm not judging."

Dorothy folded her arms across her chest. "Aren't you?"

"No, I swear." JJ shook her head so emphatically she felt her neck crack. She wiped her hair from the corner of her mouth where it had strayed. "Considering my track record, I have no right to judge anyone else on their mistakes. I was just wondering if there's anyone else who could... have an interest in Rachel."

A flush ran all the way from JJ's neck to her face. This was ridiculous. Of course Rachel was Otto's daughter. What had she been thinking? JJ put her head in her hands and tried to figure out her next step. She didn't have one.

But when JJ lifted her head, she saw that Dorothy was staring at her.

"How did you know?" Dorothy asked.

JJ was speechless.

Dorothy began fidgeting with the rings on her finger. "I'm ninety-nine percent sure Otto is Rachel's father. But there is a chance—a very slight chance—"

"Who?" JJ asked.

"I'm so ashamed."

"Who, Dorothy?" JJ wanted to shake the woman by the shoulders.

Dorothy sighed, still spinning the small, diamond engagement ring around her finger. "Otto and I had been dating for about a year, and I thought *this is it*, he's the one. But then along comes Becky Strawderman, flouncing around in her little cheerleader skirt. She was still in high school, for God's sake."

JJ rolled her eyes, but Dorothy was so caught up in telling her drama that she didn't notice.

"And me and Otto had a big fight about it, and we broke up. It only lasted a weekend—I found out Otto hadn't even touched her, that she was fooling around with this guy from Plattsville—but in the meantime..." Now it was Dorothy's turn to hide her head in her hands. "Promise me you'll never tell anyone else."

"I promise," JJ lied.

"Oh, God," Dorothy said, tenting her arms completely over her head. "I sort of hooked up with Leslie Beck."

"Leslie Beck? Luther's brother?" JJ couldn't have been more shocked if Dorothy had said it was their old shop teacher, a man twenty years their elder, rumored to be missing two toes on his left foot from a homebrewing accident.

"Well, he was a lot better looking back then," Dorothy said, defensively.

True, JJ thought, but he'd been just as much of an asshole. "What do you mean, *sort of?*"

Dorothy lifted her head from the table. "We were down at the tavern, and I'd been drinking a lot. He was flirting with me, and I was just so mad at Otto, I went out to Les's car. We started fooling around. Things got hot and heavy, and then Les said something about parking up on Daylor Hill."

Daylor Hill was the place sixteen-year-olds parked to finish the transaction. JJ wrinkled her face in distaste before she could stop herself.

"Exactly!" Dorothy said, pointing at JJ. "I couldn't do it. But Leslie wasn't in the mood to hear that. He had me pinned in the back, and I couldn't get out, but I didn't want to start screaming unless I absolutely had to."

"Because you didn't want everyone to know you were in the back of Leslie's car with him."

Dorothy nodded. "I tried kneeing him in the doo-dads, but I couldn't. He was so heavy. And my voice—I don't know. It just wouldn't work. I couldn't make it loud. I was afraid he was going to hurt me down there, so finally I just gave up and let him finish."

JJ became hyperaware of other sounds as Dorothy's voice faded away. Some kind of machinery droned in the distance—maybe a chainsaw—and the television was on low volume in the other room. JJ's eyes burned and she felt her bottom lip swell as she tried to match the other woman's stoicism. "I am so sorry, Dorothy."

"Don't be," she said. "It's not that big of a deal."

"Yes, it is."

Dorothy sighed. "You mean to tell me you never had a guy who wouldn't stop when you changed your mind?"

"Just my husband," JJ admitted.

Dorothy's mouth fell open. Her hand snatched JJ's and clasped it tightly, just for a moment. The two women took a couple of deep breaths together, dispelling the swirling emotions like sweeping leaves from a porch on a breezy day. It would do, for now.

"Have you had a paternity test?" JJ asked, and Dorothy released her hand.

"I know he's not Rachel's father."

"Does Leslie know?" JJ asked.

"I don't think so. We've never spoken about it, and Otto and I were married a few months later. I guess maybe Les could do the math."

"I'm not sure he can count to nine," JJ said, and Dorothy managed a wan smile. JJ stuffed the last bite of toast in her mouth as she took her plate to the sink.

"Your father found out, didn't he? About Marcus not treating you right?" Dorothy asked.

"Yes, he did."

Dorothy read the look of grim satisfaction on JJ's face and said, "Good." Picking at her toast, she added, "I thought Luther was going to kick Leslie's ass, too."

JJ dropped her plate in the sink more heavily than she'd intended, drawing a sharp look from Dorothy. "Luther knew?"

Dorothy nodded and paused to chew. "Les didn't any more than have his pants up when the door flew open. Leslie'd done half-tore my blouse off, and I was upset, so it was pretty obvious what had happened. Luther dragged Les out, threw him up against the car, and punched him. I guess Les got him calmed down after that, but they argued for a while, and then Luther gave me a ride home."

"Was Luther in uniform?"

"Yeah. I figured he was on patrol, because he drove me in the cruiser."

"Did he ask if you wanted to press charges?"

Dorothy's eyebrows wrinkled. "No," she said, as though the thought had never occurred to her before.

"I have to go," JJ said. "Will you be all right?"

Dorothy nodded, but her lips began to tremble, and she burst out crying. This time JJ let her, squishing onto Dorothy's chair with her and holding her until the tears subsided.

"Shh, sweetie. Rachel's going to be okay." That's what JJ whispered into Dorothy's hair. But the whole time, a single thought spun through her mind: if Luther was willing to risk his job by covering up his brother's rape, what would he do about kidnapping?

22

A dam couldn't see what Luther was doing in the back of the Sheriff's vehicle, what with the metal grill, the seats, and the height difference. He hated to leave the relative warmth of the SUV, but curiosity—or self-preservation—got the best of him. Adam grunted as he stepped down, lifting the outside handle to quietly close the door. He walked around to the back, startling Luther.

"You don't listen well, do you?" Luther snapped.

"Sorry," Adam said, hands in his pockets. "Thought you might need the keys. And since it's my car, I figured the least I can do is stand in the cold and do nothing, instead of sitting in the cold and doing nothing."

Luther lost the look of imminent growling, but Adam knew he was walking a fine line with the man and needed to stay on his good side. He stood clear as Luther pulled the tarp from a stack of cinder blocks.

"I'm taking notes," Adam said, tapping his head, "in case there really is no hope for my driving."

"Well, if you ain't figured it out yet," Luther grinned, and grunted as he hoisted a cinder block in each hand. "Said the hooker to the blind bishop."

Luther set the blocks on the ground next to the car. "If you're going to be here come winter—*real* winter—you might want to throw a few of these in the back of that little car of yours. Extra weight might help keep you on the road, and sometimes they'll even help you get back on the road when you've gone off. Some people use kitty litter instead, but I can't say I'm a fan."

Adam reached for a couple of blocks, but when he felt their weight, he decided one at a time would be enough to be getting on with.

Luther smiled and said, "You got nothing to prove to me, except that you're a dumbass if you try carrying a stack of cinder blocks when you can't even stand to wear a seat belt."

The deputy stepped down into the ditch next to Adam's car. "You're lucky. It's pretty shallow here, but the ditch gets deeper further up the lane. And it's been raining, but just enough to make it cold and wet, not enough to make the ground real soppy."

Luther placed one of the blocks in the ditch and wiggled it back and forth until he was satisfied it was secure. Adam stepped down for a better look. The hatchback's front tire was just a couple of inches above the block.

"No wonder you landed in the ditch. These tires are balder than my Great Uncle Whitney. Why don't you get your jack?"

Adam moved his blankets and other belongings aside to access the spare tire and jack beneath. Jack in hand, he returned to find Luther had added a cinder block parallel to the first one, and was placing another one on top of the matched set. Adam perched on the narrow sliver of road between his car and the ditch and wedged his crappy little jack beneath the car frame. He nearly dropped the handle on his toe trying to attach it to the rest of the mechanism.

Luther shook his head. "I hate those damn useless things. Might as well try and lift the car, Popeye-style. Go ahead and give me a few inches—I'll tell you when to stop."

Adam gritted his teeth, pumping the little handle slowly up and down, up and down. After about a dozen times, he suddenly discovered he'd been holding his breath, took a big gasping suck of air, and suffered the effects immediately. He leaned lightly against the car, the world lost in a swirl of grays. When the fog cleared from his mind, he realized Luther was watching him.

"Keep going, hoss," the deputy said, smiling. "I want you to know I'm only laughing because it's not me."

For some reason, that nearly made Adam laugh, too. Perhaps it was some kind of pain endorphins. He went back to pumping.

"Okay, that's good. Stop for a minute." Luther placed another cinder block on top, so he had two matched sets, and scooted the top pair toward the car until both sets lined up. "Perfect. Now let it down a little bit, until the tire settles right on top."

Adam did, then joined Luther in the ditch to take a closer look at his handiwork. "You sure this will work?" Adam asked.

"Are you asking me as a deputy, or as a man whose younger brother never met a ditch he didn't like?" Luther grinned. "If this was a bigger car, I wouldn't try it without stabilizing these cinder blocks, but this one doesn't weigh much more than a go-cart. And we're only supporting a small fraction of its weight."

Adam squatted next to Luther and reached out with his less painful arm to feel how much play there was in the stack.

"Goddamn, what's wrong with your thumb?" Luther asked. "Otto didn't do that, did he?"

Adam extended his right arm slowly, turning his hand so the deputy could get a better look. Instead of relaxing with the rest of his fingers, Adam's right thumb stuck out straight and at an awkward angle from his hand. The knuckle also seemed oddly square. Adam could bend it a little bit if he concentrated, but not much.

"No, it's been like that ever since I was a little kid. I always say I'm a lousy fighter because I can't make a proper fist," Adam admitted. "My handwriting's pretty awful, too. I'm one of the few natural righties you'll meet that was forced to go southpaw."

Luther focused on the stack of blocks again, adjusting their fit beneath the car's tire. "Okay, the blocks will probably settle a little, so lower the jack some more, but don't take it out yet."

The car shifted the tiniest bit as Adam slowly cranked the jack down, and he fought the urge to step backwards and land himself in the ditch. Once he was sure the car was stable, Adam returned to Luther's side. The deputy squatted, now examining the stack of blocks from a marginally safer side angle instead of directly in front of the car.

Adam wasn't sure what Luther was looking for, and his own gaze drifted to the sky. Mid-morning now, it was pretty out, even with the leafless trees casting bony shadows. Maybe they'd hit sixty degrees today. Fifty-five, anyway. A loud peep drew Adam's attention. A pair of cardinals—one drab female and one iridescent red male—tilted their heads to look down at the humans. In combination with their black masks and triangular beaks, the behavior appeared almost creepily intelligent.

"What'd you do, fall out of a tree?"

It took Adam a moment to figure out that Luther was still talking about his injured thumb. "Car accident," he said.

Luther's head jerked up toward Adam. Obviously he knew the history. Adam didn't like to talk about it, so it was always nice when he didn't have to add, *the one that killed my mom.*

Luther's eyes were still on Adam when a loud crack resounded through the air, heralding a chain reaction. The cinder block directly beneath the hatchback hung in place for a full second before splitting apart and triggering the next crack. Adam jumped up onto the road as the car's front wheel dropped. He grabbed Luther beneath the arms and yanked him backwards with a groan, just as the car's jack gave way in the soft earth. The hatchback lurched forward a couple of feet before the undercarriage came to rest.

"Sonuvabitch," Luther said, getting to his feet and leaning against the Sheriff's vehicle. "Never had a block fail like that before."

Adam's hands shook, and his knees were none too steady,

either. He could still feel the effort of lifting the large man tearing across his ribs. "Closest I ever want to come to auditioning for the Darwin Awards," he wheezed.

"No kidding," Luther agreed. "You okay?"

"I've been better," Adam admitted.

Luther snorted. "I should hope so. Thanks for that." He inclined his head toward the ditch. "I'm afraid you're going to have to get somebody to pull the car out. The department vehicle could probably do it with the tow hitch, but I've got to be getting up past the Nicholsons, and I don't have a decent tow line with me."

Adam nodded, hugging his bent arm to his ribs. "No problem, Luther. I appreciate the effort. Just drop me at JJ's and I'll figure it out later."

"That works." Luther put a hand gently on Adam's shoulder. "You look like you're about ready to keel over. Why don't you get back in the truck and I'll put that jack away for you."

Adam climbed painfully back in the SUV, not bothering with the seat belt. He doubted Luther would insist on it for less than half a mile on a back road. He thought maybe Luther was warming to him. That is, until he watched in the rearview mirror while the deputy spent far longer than necessary to put the jack away. About as long as it would take to rifle through someone's belongings in an unlocked car.

23

JJ had just gotten out of the shower when she heard Trooper bark—only once. She threw on a pair of jeans and a long-sleeved T-shirt and saw Adam hiking slowly up her driveway. She and Trooper walked down and met him partway.

"Luther dropped me. I thought the walk might do me good. You know, stretching stuff out," Adam panted. "I was wrong."

His color was not good, an unholy mixture of pallor and flush. "You're a dumbass," JJ said.

"Yeah, I'm getting that a lot today," Adam said, reaching down to give Trooper's ears a scratch.

"Was Luther going to see Dorothy? They haven't heard anything, have they?"

"No. He said he was headed up the road a little ways to rendezvous with some of the searchers. Speaking of which, I'm pretty sure he searched the back of my car." Adam told her about trying to get his car from the ditch and how solicitous Luther was at the end.

"Did you lock it when you left?" JJ asked.

Adam tilted his head in a gesture that, from a recently beaten man trying to walk uphill, was meant to pass for a shrug. "Doesn't matter. There's nothing incriminating in it. I haven't even smoked pot since I was fifteen."

JJ stopped. Luther might not find anything, but would he *place something* incriminating in Adam's car? She shook her head. Now she was just being paranoid. What kind of incriminating, and why?

Adam was waiting a few steps ahead, staring at her. "What?" he asked.

She told him what Dorothy had shared about Rachel's possible paternity.

Adam shook his head. "That sonuvabitch."

JJ was a little surprised; Iris had thoroughly instilled her aversion to cursing in Adam. "Which one?" she asked.

"Les! I mean, Luther should have reported it, but—"

"Damn right, Luther should have reported it! He should've arrested the asshole, brother or not." JJ knew it wasn't fair to take her frustration out on Adam, but she couldn't help it. She felt like anger was spilling out of her pores.

"Okay," Adam said, raising his hands as high as his waist. "You're right." They resumed their hike up the driveway, but this time Adam stopped, his voice incredulous. "Wait a minute—you think Leslie might be *daddy*?"

"What?" JJ snapped. "You're the one that's hung up on the daddy thing! I'm trying to make it make sense. I'm trying to help *you* not be crazy." JJ poked him in the chest with a finger, and Adam staggered back a step and nearly fell.

His gaze dropped to the ground, the blue irises barely visible beneath his heavy lashes. JJ recognized this expression from when they were kids. He'd been so damned sensitive, she'd always felt like she'd kicked a puppy when she yelled at him. She still did. Trooper moved over to sit next to Adam's heel. It felt like even the dog was giving her stink eye.

"I'm sorry," she said. "I just—I know it's been less than twenty-four hours, but I feel like we're running out of time, that *Rachel* is running out of time."

"I know," he mumbled. She watched him brace himself for the pain as he took a deep breath before meeting her eyes. "Don't worry—we'll find her."

She nodded. They would find her. They had to. Because Adam was the key.

As soon as she stepped inside, JJ checked the kitchen clock. How could it only be ten-thirty? She was glad more time hadn't passed, but she was also strangely overwhelmed by it.

"I've been thinking," Adam said, shuffling as far as the living room and dropping in the closest armchair.

JJ was so grateful for any glimmer of direction, she could have kissed him, but her face remained calm. "And?"

"After Danny died, we spent a lot of time in these woods."

"A helluva lot of time," JJ agreed.

Initially, the adults had watched them like hawks. But most people get complacent eventually, even after tragedy, and soon Adam and JJ were sneaking off to the woods looking for Danny. They weren't methodical by any means, but they were relentless and creative, getting rides to places that were too far to walk in an evening or a weekend day. The two spent their summers together searching, even after Iris sent Adam away, and summer days were long. Few spots in Beecham County escaped their scrutiny.

"I know it's been years," Adam said, "and a lot of things have changed, but maybe if we went down to the Command Center and took a look at what they have—the maps and aerial surveillance and what-not—we could see something they've missed. Do you think Grant would let us take a peek?"

JJ's brows raised. "I'm sure if we wander around with bottles of water, looking exhausted and doing our best imitation of volunteers, we can fly under the radar."

Adam smiled, and for just a moment, all was right with the world. Like when they were kids. They'd taken turns then, too, being positive.

But right now, JJ still thought Adam looked like shit.

"Tell you what," JJ said. "Why don't you take a quick shower while I make a few phone calls? Then we can head into town, be there within half an hour."

She grabbed a clean towel from the linen shelf in the hall and, rummaging in the cabinet beneath the sink, she even found the electric razor she'd given her ex-husband for Christmas one year. "Mint condition. I doubt if the asshole even turned it on."

Adam turned the device in his hand until he found the switch that made it buzz. "His loss," he said. "Thanks, JJ. You don't know how much I *need* a shower right now."

"Yes, I do," she said, wrinkling her nose. Adam wrinkled his nose right back at her, and JJ smiled. "I'll be in the living room. Yell if you need anything else."

JJ sat on the couch and gazed out at the sun beating down on the little patch of side yard, at browning grass and mountain laurel shrubs that stayed green, while she gathered her thoughts. The only thing JJ wanted more than to have her daughter Evie next to her was for her child to be safe. The best way to ensure that was to make the call JJ had been dreading—to her mother, who lived more than an hour from Cold Springs.

The two women had never been close, and JJ had chosen to stay with her father when her parents divorced. This marked the genesis of her mother's oft-repeated lament, *What kind of girl doesn't want to be with her mother?* Still, problematic as their own relationship had been, the woman was devoted to her granddaughter. She agreed to pick up Evie from her sleepover and keep her for a few days. "I'll make sure she has a good time, but don't worry—I won't let her out of my sight," she'd said, without once implying that JJ would have neglected her own child.

JJ then followed up with Melanie's mother, letting her know about the change in plans. Wary of the kill-the-messenger syndrome, Melanie's mom had insisted on bringing Evie to the phone. Evie loved her grandmother, but she was not happy that she wasn't going home. A combination of threats and cajoling by JJ ultimately brought the two stubborn females to a truce, but it was a hard-fought battle.

Evie could skip school for a few days with no ill effects, but JJ didn't have that luxury. She wasn't scheduled to work until Monday, but she was on-call for Sunday. It tended to be a slow day at the hospital, but she called and switched with another nurse to make certain she'd be free tomorrow, come what may.

JJ set aside the heavy, landline phone that had resided in her house almost as long as she had with an equally heavy sigh. It'd been years since Marcus left, and she didn't know what the appropriate length of time was for an adult male shower. She didn't want to rush Adam, but she'd thought he would have been done by now.

The shower was still on, that much she could hear from outside the bathroom door. She gave a timid *tap-tap-tap*. "Adam, do you need anything? Adam?"

Perhaps he couldn't hear her.

JJ cracked the door an inch or two and directed her voice through the gap. "Adam, it's me. Time's ticking, buddy. Do you need anything?"

No answer.

"Adam?"

JJ slowly opened the door the rest of the way. The bathroom mirror was fogged over, but the air was clear. After such a long shower, she'd have expected steam to roll out of the bathroom. "Adam, are you okay?"

Evie had picked their shower curtain—a bunch of ducks holding umbrellas on a white background. There was no silhouette, and no hint of movement, behind the plastic.

"Adam, you better not be *fucking* with me," she said, emphasizing the word to get her voice to stop shaking. "I'm opening the curtain now."

Adam was lying facedown in the bottom of the tub, head tilted to one side. Water streamed in channels past his gaping mouth.

24

Shower spray soaked JJ as she jerked the curtain back the rest of the way. No wonder there was no steam—the water was freezing. She cut off the shower and the faucets, then squatted and leaned over the edge of the tub to grab Adam beneath his armpits. His wet skin was slippery, and he was heavier than she'd imagined. She tried to lift him and slid on the edge of the tub, falling forward onto his naked back and bumping her head against the tile.

Don't panic, Janie Girl. Her dad's voice. The only person other than Adam who ever called her by her middle name. She took a deep breath, then tucked a hand towel around Adam's head and neck and started to roll him over. His skin squeaked against the tub and stuck a few times, but soon she had him lying on his back.

"Adam? Talk to me." She leaned down, cheek above his blue lips, counting off the seconds.

Jesus.

He wasn't breathing.

JJ threw Adam's towel over his midsection, less for his modesty than to protect her knees. Then she hopped in, trying as best she could to avoid turning an ankle or falling on Adam again. Thank

God her father had opted for the full-sized tub. Nestling her knees in the narrow gaps alongside his waist, she sat astride Adam and began compressions.

Rhythm, counts, nothing else... And... And... Keep the rhythm... And... And... Break for breaths...

"JJ?" a voice called from the front of the house.

"In... here," she said, keeping her rhythm, trusting that because Trooper hadn't barked, whoever knew her name wasn't here to kill her. *Breathe...*

There was movement in the hall outside the bathroom.

"Oh, my God."

It was Grant's voice. And Trooper's whine.

And... And... And...

"Do you want me to take over?" Grant asked.

And... And... "Not... yet."

JJ bent forward, cheek to Adam's face. Counting. Praying. Staring at the small key that hung down next to Adam's armpit, just free of the hair that curled there. She felt the slightest tickle against her face. *Yes, there.* And again. She hadn't imagined it.

JJ let her cheek touch Adam's forehead in thanks, just for a moment, then whispered, "Good job," in his ear.

A tear dropped off the end of her nose and landed on Adam's chest. "He's breathing," she said, turning to Grant. "Can you drive us?"

"Yes."

It was even harder climbing over Adam to get out of the tub than it had been climbing in. Grant caught JJ's elbow and steadied her during the final lurch.

"Help me get him out of the tub," she said.

Grant blinked, then disappeared.

What the hell?

He returned with folded fabric in his hands. "He's naked," Grant said, flinging a sheet from the hall linen shelf over Adam. "If I were naked, I'd want a sheet."

Men.

25

———

*I*n, out. In, out. Not enough in. There was never enough air coming in.

A man's voice said, "She's still alive."

In, in, in...

"Are you sure?"

That was a man's voice, too, but she couldn't tell if it was the same voice speaking, or a different one.

Pause. "Yeah, she's breathing. Look."

In, in, in... She wished she could figure out how many voices there were, how many people. She didn't know why, but it seemed important.

It sounded like the same voice, but that didn't make sense.

Her eyes felt heavy as stones. She couldn't see anything—it was so dark. But there was something, or someone, else... Are you still there? Are you still with me?

She wished the voice—or voices—would go away. But not the Other One, the one she couldn't hear. She wanted him to stay. She needed him to stay.

I'm so tired, I just want to let go.

The voice asked, "What if she stops breathing again?"

Someone laughed and answered, "Well, then, I guess she'll die."

26

So much darkness.

Adam woke suddenly in a strange bed with something over his face. He gasped—*pain*—and reached up to rip the thing off so he could breathe.

"Don't do that." A girl's face hovered into view a few inches from his own. "It's supposed to be there."

Adam dropped his hand and relaxed. He trusted her. The eyes —he knew those eyes. "JJ?" he asked, voice hoarse and muffled by the mask. "Where's Danny?"

The girl blinked. "Mom!" she yelled, still inches from his face. "He's awake!"

Adam put a heavy hand, trailing tubes, to his chest. His throat felt raw, and it hurt to breathe. He closed his eyes.

"You're not going to die again, are you?" the girl asked. "There was water all over the place when Grandma took me home to get my heavy coat."

Adam opened his eyes and turned his head a fraction. He saw an IV stand with a dripping bag. Lots of stainless steel and fancy medical equipment. He rotated his head the other way, slowly, slowly, and saw an empty bed. He was in a hospital.

A woman rushed into the room. She had long, dark hair, pulled back from a face haggard with worry. The divot between her upper lip and nose was well defined, with two distinct lines... *just like JJ*. Adam closed his eyes, dizzy as the world came rushing back.

JJ's voice was angry and whispery, with a hospital hush. "Evie, what are you doing in here? You know children aren't allowed."

Adam opened his eyes to find the girl (*Evie, not JJ*) still staring at him. She spoke in a calm, matter-of-fact tone, and rolled her eyes without bothering to turn her head toward her mother. "I was checking on him while you argued with Grandma. Remember, she's my ride."

JJ exhaled the long-suffering sigh of the mother of a precocious child. Evie smiled at Adam, said, "Bye—feel better," and strode past her mother as if the child owned the hospital.

JJ followed her daughter out of the room.

Adam's hand returned to his chest, careful of the IV. The pain wasn't piercing, but it was fairly intense, and pervasive. There was no escaping it. He was still drifting around its edges, trying to find its boundaries, when JJ returned.

The acoustics of the room seemed designed to absorb sound: the medical beeps, JJ's shoes crossing the floor, and even the chair scraping to the side of his bed. JJ sat in it, tucking her hands beneath her legs as she'd sometimes done when they were kids. Her dark hair swung forward as she bowed her head. Evie's hair was lighter, more brown with a hint of red, but Adam thought JJ's hair had been closer to her daughter's color when they were kids.

JJ lifted her head and removed the mask from his face. "They said your oxygen stats are better now, back where they belong. How are you feeling?"

Adam stretched his face a bit, feeling the absence of the mask's pressure. "Chest hurts. What happened?"

"I was hoping you could tell me."

He considered, tried to orient himself in his mind, and was swamped by vertigo. The nausea was overwhelming. "JJ—"

She grabbed a small trashcan and got it beneath him just in

time as Adam swung over the side, vomiting, somehow missing the IV line. The pain was so intense, he almost cried. He would've, if there'd been a second round of heaving.

"Sorry," he said, slowly sinking back onto the bed.

"Don't be stupid," JJ said, setting the trashcan down and reaching for a tissue from the nightstand. She wiped Adam's mouth and said, "I'll get the resident."

"No," Adam said. "I feel better. Really." He did feel better—not his chest, but the nausea was gone and his vertigo had subsided.

"Nausea is not something to mess around with. You could've hit your head when you fell."

"I didn't," Adam said, certain. "When did I fall?" About this, he was uncertain.

JJ rolled her eyes.

"I see the eye-rolling is a hereditary trait." That won him a wan smile from JJ. "When I woke up, I thought she was you."

Bigger smile. "Don't tell Evie that."

He wouldn't. He hoped Evie hadn't heard him ask for Danny.

Mouth softened and eyes relaxed, JJ's face held a combination of pride and vulnerability and... something else. Adam could've spent hours trying to figure out what, but there was a dissonant murmur in his mind, a sense of urgency he couldn't explain. So he asked the question sure to wipe all relaxation from her face.

"Why am I here?"

"Something happened while you were taking a shower. We—Grant drove us here—we aren't sure what. All of your test results are normal. They can't find anything wrong." Her voice was so even, so artificially calm, he knew she wasn't telling him the whole story.

"What do you mean, *something happened?*" Adam asked.

JJ looked away, but she answered. "I found you unconscious. You'd stopped breathing."

Adam stared up at the acoustic tile ceiling and tried not to panic. People—especially relatively healthy, thirty-something young men—didn't just stop breathing for no reason. The cause may be a mystery to the doctors, but he thought he knew how to find it. Adam closed his eyes. This time, he was ready for the nausea, the sense of falling, as he remembered.

He'd been so tired, almost asleep standing up. He'd put his hands against the tile beneath the showerhead, and they slowly slid down... That's when the voice started.

I can't breathe... I can't get away if I can't breathe... Chest constricting, throat...

Adam had tried to turn off the shower and get JJ. His fingers slid off the taps with a blast of cold that almost brought him around... then his hands were on the edge of the tub... he threw his head back, trying to breathe...

Help me, if you're there...

But it was no use. His knees hit the floor—

"Adam!" JJ's voice cut through his mind.

He opened his eyes, and she was out of her chair, leaning over him. She looked scared, and JJ never looked scared. Except when they took turns being brave.

"I have to get out of here," he said. "Now. How do I get this out of my arm?"

"You're in no condition to leave."

"Yes, I am," Adam said, lying through his teeth. At least they weren't chattering. "You said yourself, they couldn't find anything wrong with me."

"They won't allow you to leave yet."

The corner of Adam's mouth curled in a shadow of his impish grin. "They can't stop me."

JJ got in his face, her voice low and fierce, eyes filled with tears. "I had to do chest compressions on you. You selfish asshole! Do you understand, you practically died in my bathtub?"

He was filled with guilt as he had a flash of what that must have been like for her—had she found her father, too?—but he pushed it away and clenched his jaw until he was solid enough to go on. "I'm sorry, JJ. But you have to understand, it wasn't me."

"What do you mean, it wasn't you?"

"Well, it wasn't *just* me. It was her—Rachel—who stopped breathing in your tub. And we have to find her. Now."

27

The Sheriff was not looking one hundred percent when he walked into the Command Center. In fact, Luther wasn't sure he had the math skills to describe the man's harried appearance.

"Where'd you run off to?" Luther asked.

Grant waved a hand through the air, as if he couldn't muster the coherent thought to answer.

Fine. Be that way. Luther had more important things on his mind. He led Grant the long way around the warren of rooms where most of the agents and volunteers were gathered, until he found a secluded corner. "I checked with Otto's boss," Luther said. "He didn't go in to work yesterday at all. Had the whole day off."

"Shit."

Luther raised an eyebrow in surprise.

"Sorry," Grant said, as if he wasn't used to hearing worse out of Luther's mouth eight hours a day, five days a week. "There's a lot coming at me today. You tell anybody else yet?"

"No."

"Good. I'll talk to the agent in charge, see how he wants to handle it, but my inclination is to keep everyone else in the dark as long as possible. We've got too many civilians in here with nothing better to do but talk."

"Got it," Luther said.

"Is Otto here now?"

"Yep. Wandering around, looking lost."

Grant ran a hand through his hair, then looked at his hand, as if he'd just realized he wasn't wearing his hat. "I know the feeling. You want to meet me at the interrogation room upstairs—the bigger one—in say, fifteen minutes?"

"Will do."

They decided to keep it locals only, to use people Otto trusted to get him to commit to his answers first. Federal agents would monitor the interview from the next room and be available for any follow-up.

Grant asked Luther to join him for the interview. They sat next to each other, with Otto across from them, on matching metal, folding chairs that read WAR MEML BLDG in stenciled black letters across the back. Grant nodded at the recording setup next to the wall (which also allowed the real-time monitoring), and explained to Otto that they were going to tape the interview, that they were taping all of their interviews.

Luther had brought coffee for each of them and sipped at his mug. He found it hard to look at the man across the table. Either Otto had done something to his own daughter, in which case Luther would like to rip his lungs out his throat, or he was just a scared dad, in which case Luther felt like a total shit for suspecting the man of such a horrible thing.

Grant made the identifications for the recording and then began, calm and at ease. "Otto, I want to start by letting you know that you're not under arrest. You're free to leave at any time. But we do need to ask you some more questions. And in light of the fact that you weren't truthful with us before, I feel like I need to advise you of your Miranda rights." He read aloud from a small, well-worn card. "You have the right to remain silent. Anything you say can and will be used against you in a court of law. You have the right to an attorney. If you cannot afford an attorney, one will be provided for you. Do you understand the rights I have just read to you?"

"Yes," Otto said.

"With these rights in mind, do you wish to speak to me?" Grant asked.

"Of course I do, Sheriff. I want you to find my daughter."

"Then why did you lie to us, Otto? We know you didn't go to work at all Friday. Where were you?"

Otto glared at the recording system and pushed his hair back where it brushed the tops of his shoulders. "Does this have to be taped?"

"Yes, Otto. If you want us to find your daughter—and be able to successfully prosecute whoever took her—it does have to be recorded. Where were you yesterday?"

Otto generally struck Luther as a pretty cool customer. Even when he'd beaten the crap out of Adam Rutledge this morning, he'd done it with an icy anger, whereas Luther's own temper was all heat. But now, Otto was looking rattled. Luther had never seen that before, and he'd once witnessed Dorothy throwing a lit firecracker at the man's head. Otto clasped his enormous hands on the table in front of him and watched them closely, as if he was afraid they'd get away from each other.

"I took off work because I had to meet someone," Otto said.

"All day?" Grant's voice was interested, but not sarcastic. Luther didn't know how the man did it.

"I drove to Harrisburg to meet them," Otto said.

"That's an awful long way. Why Harrisburg?"

Otto rubbed his clenched hands back and forth on the table. "Because it's right on the interstate—easy to get to—and it was about halfway between us."

"Who were you meeting, Otto?" Grant asked.

He didn't answer, and Grant leaned forward, tilting his head so Otto had to look at him. It seemed to Luther that, in that position, Otto could raise either or both fists like a hammer right into the side of Grant's head and lay him out.

Some day, Grant's gonna trust the wrong person.

"Otto, are you having an affair?"

Luther braced himself to pick the Sheriff up off the floor, but it didn't happen.

"No, I am not having an affair."

"Otto," Grant said, pressing until the man met his eyes, "I believe you, but you need to tell us what you were up to, so we can figure out if it had something to do with Rachel's kidnapping. Maybe you set something in motion you don't even know about."

Otto unclenched his hands and wiped them on his pants. "It's not like that," he said.

"Then what is it like?" Grant asked.

When Otto dropped his eyes again, Grant yelled, "Hey!" with all the authority of a drill sergeant. "Stop jerking me around so I can do my job and find your daughter. In one piece."

Instead of getting angry, Otto's eyes glistened. "God help us." He took a deep breath. "I went to meet my mother-in-law."

Luther was supposed to sit silently, but he was so shocked, he blurted out, "Dorothy's mom?"

"No, not Dorothy's mom. My first wife's mom. I was married to someone before I met Dorothy. In New York."

"I thought you were from Kentucky," Luther said.

"No, somebody said that once, and I just never bothered to correct him."

"You're not a bigamist, are you?" Luther asked. Grant gave him a pointed look, and he sat back against his chair and vowed to keep his mouth shut.

"No, we're not married anymore. She—" Otto coughed, and then cleared his throat. "We married right out of high school. And one day—we'd only been married about eighteen months—she just disappeared. Her mom and I reported it right away, but they never found her. You didn't need a passport to go to Canada back then, so some people thought that's where she went. But her mom never heard from her. Neither did I. Nobody did."

"Were you a suspect?" Grant asked.

Otto sighed. "I'm sure I was, like I am right now. Which is why I didn't want to say anything. But I was never a serious suspect."

"So why were you meeting her mother?"

"Because she asked me to. She does that from time to time. Not because she's heard anything. I guess just because she wants to talk to someone else who understands." Otto wiped an eye with his thumb before continuing. "When I left Friday morning, I thought I understood what she felt. But now..."

He couldn't finish.

"We'll need her name and her contact information," Grant said. "Does she know you've remarried?"

"Yes. There were some legal things that had to be settled before I could remarry, and she helped me with that." Otto became agitated, reaching for Grant's hand. "You can't tell Dorothy! Please, Sheriff. She doesn't know anything about Marie. And she doesn't deal with that kind of stuff well."

Luther wasn't sure what else would fall into the category of "that kind of stuff" when it included "I have a missing wife who is presumed dead," but he knew what the man meant. Dorothy looked delicate and vulnerable, but she also had a touch of crazy. Maybe more than a touch.

"I'll do my best," Grant said, "but Otto, you know it's gonna come out. It's just a matter of time. You're better off telling her yourself. Does anyone else know?"

"No. When I finally gave up hope, I moved as far away as my gas money would take me, and I left everything behind. I never told anyone."

Grant slid a notebook and pen across the table to Otto. "All right. Contact information. Also anywhere you stopped for gas or food or anything else and how you paid. If you've got receipts, that'd be helpful, too." He shook his head and headed for the door, motioning for Luther to follow. "I just wish you'd told us this from the beginning."

Out in the hall, Luther waited for a volunteer to pass by, then asked, "Well, what do you think?"

Grant shrugged. "We'll see what the Feds have on the first wife, their relationship. Probably used cash to visit the mother-in-law, so I hope he kept his receipts. Even if the trip checks out, we still gotta do the math. Doesn't mean he didn't take Rachel somewhere when he got back. It'll be hard to rule him out."

Luther shook his head. "I know we gotta be objective, but it's hard to imagine the man harming his own daughter."

"You know the statistics. Kids are most commonly taken by family members." Grant glanced down the hallway and lowered his voice. "And the man's wife disappears, he starts a new life, and his child disappears. What are the odds?"

Luther couldn't argue with that. Either Otto was guilty of something, or he was just about the unluckiest sonuvabitch he'd ever met.

28

"I always thought Danny was the troublemaker," JJ said.

"I guess I figured it was time I did my share," Adam said.

She and Adam were getting a lot of stares, and she was sure she'd be getting an earful from her colleagues her next shift. *So, I hear you brought in a naked guy and then walked him out AMA. Yeah, good times.*

Fortunately, she didn't know the woman behind the wheel, not well. Even Against Medical Advice, after all the signatures and we're-not-responsible-when-you-die speeches, the hospital still pushed you out in a wheelchair. Providing transport to the door was not a bad idea, at least for Adam today. He'd moved slower than molasses back in his room, putting on a long-sleeved T-shirt and scrub bottoms she'd filched for him from a friend. Fake sheepskin slippers from the gift shop were the best she could do for footwear.

"Reminds me of the last time I saw you naked," JJ said in a low voice as the exit doors slid open.

Adam put a hand over his face before she helped him out of the wheelchair and over to a bench in the pick-up area.

"Well, you didn't just think I'd let the naked thing go," JJ said.

"I guess not. You do know that was a very cold shower."

"I do, and I know we'll be lucky if you don't get pneumonia." JJ sat next to him on the concrete bench and removed his chain from her pocket, where she'd put it for safekeeping.

"Here," she said, hooking it around his neck.

"Thank you," Adam whispered, and tucked the key safely beneath his borrowed shirt.

"You wore that the last time I saw you naked, too. That's when you were afraid you had leeches on your pee-pee."

Adam's mouth dropped open in horror. "Oh my God."

JJ nodded with an evil grin. "Uh-huh. Forgot about that one, didn't you? That glorified puddle out in the woods—"

"It was hot! And Danny said it was a swimming hole."

"Ha!" JJ laughed. "Told you he was the troublemaker. The only thing swimming in that patch of muddy water was leeches, waiting for dumb little boys."

"You didn't get in the water."

JJ raised an eyebrow. "Of course not. I wasn't a dumb little boy." She paused, looking out at the warm sky, at the mountains beyond the parking lot. The rolling slopes were mostly grayish-brown with bare trees, but there were occasional patches of red and orange color. "Even at the tender age of—what, seven or eight? —I'd figured out there was a little something different about being a girl, that maybe I didn't need to be sharing."

She laughed again. "Not that you two cared! Danny came splashing out, screaming, with a tiny leech on his arm, and you right on his heels. Next thing I know, you're both taking off your clothes, flinging them this way and that."

Adam covered his face while JJ giggled and flailed her arms.

"Two little boys, dancing around with your hands over your little boy parts, shrieking. It was a sight to behold." JJ sighed and wiped a tear from her eye before she lost control entirely. "Sorry. I needed that."

Adam dropped his hands from his face, and she saw they'd been covering a smile. "You didn't laugh then."

"Didn't I?" she asked, trying to pretend like she didn't remember.

Apparently Adam had never gotten a chance to shave, what with the almost dying in the shower, and his face was still shadowed with scruff and a growing bruise. And other things, even darker things, around the eyes. But there was still so much of the boy she'd known there. Danny may have gotten them into trouble, but Adam's grin had gotten them out of just as much. Just a touch of the imp, topped off with his you-know-you-can't-stay-mad-at-me magic.

"You told us to put our underwear on," Adam said, "and you checked the backs of our legs for leeches. But you didn't laugh then. You waited until the next day, when we could all laugh together."

"Well, I couldn't have you walking back to my house naked. Dad really would've tanned your asses, then." JJ tried to savor the moment, watching a pair of cardinals foraging in a patch of grass, until squawking blue jays swooped in and ran them off. Assholes. She didn't have many moments like this, when things were set in motion, and she couldn't do a damn thing except wait. She didn't think she'd have many more for a while, either.

"So you believe me? About Rachel?" Adam asked.

"Believe is a strong word," JJ said. "It sounds too much like religion to me. Let's just say, when a little girl's life is at stake, I can't see the harm in helping you follow through."

As soon as the jays were done, the cardinals swooped back in, and JJ relaxed again. So much so, a thought popped into her head, unbidden.

Yes, I believe him.

JJ barely had time to be surprised by it before a car entered the parking lot and headed in their direction. She stood with a sigh. "There's our ride."

Adam squinted. "Dorothy Nicholson?"

JJ turned to offer him an arm—which he refused—and watched Adam rise painfully to his feet. What the hell was she thinking?

He had no business being anywhere except in a bed. And yet, she also knew he was going right where he belonged.

"Iris didn't answer her phone. And when I called Dorothy to ask if she'd check on Trooper, she offered to pick us up," JJ said. Technically, Dorothy had said she needed to get away from the house for a little while, then offered to pick *JJ* up. "It's okay. Dorothy hits like a girl. I can take her, easy."

Adam laughed unexpectedly, only to groan. "You sure you didn't break any of my ribs?"

"That's what they tell me."

A brown, four-door boat of a car came to a stop next to them. Dorothy leaned across the passenger seat, trying to make sense of the *two* people standing there.

"Just get in the back seat and let me do the talking," JJ said.

It took Adam a couple of tries to get the back door open. JJ wanted to help him, but sensed that would only make things worse. Instead, she casually climbed in the front, as if she were just hitching a ride to the store. "Thanks, Dorothy."

Dorothy gripped the steering wheel tightly. "You didn't mention I'd be picking up your friend back there."

Adam slumped lower in the back and kept his mouth shut.

"You're headed to the Command Center, aren't you?" JJ asked.

"Yes."

"Good. So are we," JJ said, and left it at that.

It wasn't far back into Cold Springs proper, and JJ hoped they'd make it the rest of the way in uncomfortable silence. But Dorothy had come up with a sideways approach. "What's Grant think about that?" she asked. "About him coming in?"

JJ stared at Dorothy until the woman behind the wheel met her eyes, albeit briefly. "He thinks we should do anything and everything we can to get your daughter back."

Dorothy's eyes sought out Adam in her rearview mirror. "You look like shit."

JJ leaned to watch Adam in her own side mirror. He didn't speak.

"Looks like maybe Otto wasn't the only one that put a hurting on you," Dorothy said. "That's a gift, pissing people off that fast."

JJ almost smiled. Dorothy had a point. Except, of course, she didn't; it only looked that way. *Poor Adam.*

Dorothy twisted her hands forward and back on the wheel, as if she were throttling a motorcycle. "Why'd you think Otto did something to my daughter?"

Just keep your mouth shut, JJ thought. Nothing Adam could say would make it any better.

They were nearly at the first stop sign on the edge of town when Dorothy suddenly slammed on the brakes. The car lurched—even at a sedate thirty-five miles per hour, it was jarring—and Adam grunted in the back as the seat belt pulled tight across his chest. An SUV behind them laid on its horn, and Dorothy flipped the driver the bird. A man in a T-shirt and dirty work pants came rolling out.

"What the f—" He broke off when he recognized Dorothy in the driver's seat as he walked up alongside the closed window. "Dorothy, you all right?" he asked, voice muffled through the glass.

She'd undone her seat belt and turned in her seat to face Adam. She yelled through the glass without moving, "Fine, Carl. Just go around."

JJ raised a hand in acknowledgment, and the man shrugged before returning to his car and slowly pulling around them.

Once his car had passed, Dorothy demanded, "Tell me why you did what you did. Tell me why, or I swear I'll blow your goddamned heart out."

The woman was holding a revolver in her hand, pointing it at Adam.

"Jesus, Dorothy—put the gun down!" JJ should have known not to underestimate her; as a mother, she might have done the same thing in the circumstances.

Dorothy held the gun in her right hand and rested it on the back of the seat, so her body acted as a buffer between JJ and the firearm. Adam looked at Dorothy. His eyes held a mixture of kindness and resignation that made JJ want to scream at the stupid woman—again—that if she wanted them to find her daughter, to put the gun down and drive the goddamned car already.

"I had a dream about your daughter early this morning," Adam said.

Dorothy's lip started to tremble, and her left, bracing hand drifted away from the gun. "Was she okay?"

"Yes."

But Adam was lying, and they all knew it. A flash of desperate anger crossed Dorothy's face, and she gripped the gun in both hands again, tightly.

"She was scared," Adam admitted. "But she was okay."

Tears streamed down Dorothy's face. "Was Otto in the dream?"

"I don't know," Adam said. "I thought so at first, but now I'm not sure. And obviously if he came straight home from work yesterday…"

JJ remained still while Dorothy stared at Adam. At this range, was there any chance she'd miss?

Dorothy swiveled in her seat so abruptly that JJ flinched, afraid the gun would discharge. Then the woman shoved the revolver somewhere on her side of the car, brushed the tears from her face, and put the car in drive.

They rode the rest of the way in silence.

29

L uther knew trouble was coming when he saw Dorothy's old sedan swing into the lot in front of the Command Center, parking across two spaces and nearly taking out a federal agent's car in the process.

Dorothy always did have a penchant for drama.

He took a quick glance around—he was alone on the front steps, which was his intent in coming out here in the first place, to get away from all the crazy for a minute. The only time anybody used this entrance was if they'd rented the front room or wanted to have a smoke.

It was JJ—not Dorothy—that came rolling out of the car. She ran at Luther, dark hair streaming behind her. Considering she'd told him to fuck off this morning, he wondered what kind words she'd have for him this time.

"Luther," JJ panted when she reached the steps, "Dorothy's got a gun."

"So?" Luther asked, taking some satisfaction from noticing she was short of breath. "I hear you were aiming one at my brother last night. What's your point?"

JJ shook her head in frustration, and turned to watch Dorothy throwing on a jean jacket as she exited the car a couple of rows over. "My point is she's not exactly in her right mind now, and she's got a gun *with her*."

Luther noticed Dorothy's jacket was hanging a little lower on the right side. She wasn't carrying a purse, so it was probably just her wallet. It's possible JJ was overreacting, but Luther figured it couldn't hurt to pat Dorothy down before allowing her inside the building. He walked to meet her.

"Dorothy," he called out, "we've got some security procedures here you need to know about."

The woman could have been deaf and mute for all the response Luther got from her. That is, until her husband exited the building behind him.

"Otto Nicholson!" Dorothy screamed.

Luther wheeled around to see the man's long legs descending the steps.

"Dorothy? I thought you were staying home—" Otto began.

Dorothy pulled a revolver from her jacket pocket and aimed it at her husband.

Well, shit.

"Whoah, whoah, whoah!" Luther said. He already stood roughly between the two, but now he slowly sidestepped to help block the woman's view of her husband. "Dorothy, put the gun down."

"Where were you after work yesterday, Otto?" Dorothy asked. "Where were you when our daughter was being *kidnapped?*"

Luther did his best to keep his voice calm and outstretched hands steady, despite the adrenaline already pumping through his veins. "Dorothy, you need to put the gun down."

"You were with her, weren't you?"

What the hell had happened since Luther talked to the couple this morning? Did Dorothy actually believe her husband had taken her daughter? She couldn't know yet that they'd interviewed Otto.

"Weren't you?" Dorothy shrieked. "With that whore!"

Ahh, a her of a different variety. Luther wasn't sure if his chances of living to claim his pension had just gone up or down.

"Dorothy!" he barked.

Dorothy's eyes focused on Luther, finally recognizing him as a human being instead of just an obstacle on the bullet's path to her husband.

Luther walked forward slowly and prayed he wasn't imagining her gun hand lowering. "You need to put the gun down, Dorothy. I know you don't want to hurt anybody, but there's a lot of cops in there—FBI agents, even—that don't know you. What do you think's gonna happen if they step outside that door?"

Dorothy wavered, and the gun lowered another inch.

"They're gonna see some crazy woman pointing a gun at a cop, and they're gonna shoot you. Hell, maybe shoot me, too. Now, how's that gonna help Rachel? Huh?"

Her arm dropped the rest of the way, and the gun was pointing at the ground when Luther reached her. He took her revolver in one hand, wrapped the other around Dorothy's shoulder and pulled her to him. She was so tiny, shaking and sobbing against his side.

"Come on," he said.

Grant—no doubt summoned by JJ while Luther was otherwise occupied—nodded an acknowledgment to Luther from the front steps. Luther took his time with Dorothy while the Sheriff led Otto back inside. At least any subsequent altercation between the two would be behind closed doors, and unarmed.

"It wasn't even loaded," Dorothy mumbled.

Luther held his tongue. *Stupid damn woman.*

30

———

Grant was cloistered in a room with Dorothy and Otto and a young man in uniform that JJ didn't recognize. The door to said room had a narrow window in the center, but JJ couldn't very well press her face to it with Luther standing next to her. Backs to the door, each kept stealing glances inside when they thought the other wasn't looking.

Finally, Luther gave up pretending. He removed his hat and peered through the window, rubbing an itchy spot of his beard all the while. "I didn't see that coming," he admitted.

"What—Dorothy pulling a gun?" JJ asked.

"Nah, that didn't surprise me much. Especially after your warning—" He tilted his head at JJ. "Much appreciated."

JJ gave him the curled lip she reserved for people she thought were being smartasses, when she didn't particularly care if they knew it.

He laughed. "Why don't you tell me what you really think of me, JJ?"

JJ blushed. She and Luther had never been friends, but she was having trouble processing what Dorothy had shared and what it meant about the character of the man—now twelve years older—

standing in front of her. Still, there was nothing to be gained by pissing him off. "Sorry, Luther. It's been a long twenty-four hours."

"Don't worry about it. But I was expressing genuine thanks. We've got enough craziness already without Dorothy going batshit. As I was saying, what really surprised me was the idea of Otto stepping out on her."

JJ finally gave up pretending, too. Standing a few inches away from the door, they could simultaneously see inside without banging heads or being too obvious to the occupants. "You know Otto very well?" JJ asked.

"Can't say as I do," Luther admitted. "But Dorothy... now that's someone worth coming home to."

JJ nearly said something ill-advised, but when she looked at Luther, he was grinning. "Just winding you up," he said.

His grin faded as they watched Dorothy jump up from her seat. Grant encouraged her to sit down again.

"But I was surprised," he continued. "'Course, maybe there's nothing to it. Maybe it's just Dorothy getting excited because she's got nothing else to do except wait for us to tell her we found her daughter in a ditch somewhere. Or worse." Luther's eyes bore down on the people in the room.

JJ asked, "You think Otto could've had something to do with it?"

"Directly, meaning do I think he could've done it? I doubt it. But indirectly... he may not have been with another woman yesterday, but if he is having an affair, that opens up a whole other line of inquiry. Maybe a jealous girlfriend took Rachel, thinking Otto'd leave his wife." He turned to face JJ, crossing his arms and leaning against the door again, as if he'd seen enough. "Hell, for that matter it could've been Dorothy herself. Kinda like—what's that called? Munchausen by proxy? She gets all the attention, all the sympathy."

"You don't really believe that, do you?" JJ asked.

Luther sighed. "No, I don't. But, as the Sheriff reminded me earlier, that's why it's good to have outsiders here, somebody who can look at everyone objectively, without being blinded by the fact of knowing everybody and their kin."

Luther took one last look inside and said, "You might not want to be here when Grant finishes. I have a feeling he's gonna be pretty pissed about you bringing Dorothy over here." Luther held up a hand when JJ started to protest. "I know she was driving, I'm just saying that's how he's gonna see it."

Luther sidestepped a group of men unzipping hunting coveralls, faces still pink from the outdoors, on his way down the hall.

He wouldn't be JJ's first choice for relationship advice, but Luther was probably right about the reception she'd get from Grant. Although not true, it did *appear* that JJ was responsible for Dorothy showing up, and the woman's craziness did seem to be triggered by her talk with JJ and Adam in the car. Then there was Adam. Grant had rushed back to the Command Center right after Adam was admitted, so he didn't know JJ had helped him get discharged AMA from the hospital. Grant would not be pleased.

But Luther had been right about something else, too. They were all fools if they thought they knew who was and wasn't capable of kidnapping.

She had to see Grant, to tell him that Leslie could be the missing child's father.

THE UNIFORMED OFFICER bumped JJ on his way out the door a few minutes later. Grant followed soon after.

"Hey," JJ said, putting a hand on Grant's arm. "How are you holding up?"

"Not now," Grant said, closing the door behind him and giving Dorothy and Otto some privacy. They were still sitting on opposite sides of the table, but at least they were sitting, and not yelling.

JJ moved to block the narrow corridor and lowered her voice.

"I know things are crazy right now, but there's something I need to tell you."

The building had access stairways at both ends, so rather than pushing past her, Grant turned and headed down the hallway in the opposite direction. "I'm sorry, JJ," he said over his shoulder, "but believe it or not, the world doesn't always run on your timetable."

"What's that supposed to mean?"

Grant's shoes echoed on the dark wood as he descended the stairs to the lower level. JJ stood for a moment and watched. She nearly let him go. And then she remembered: *this is not about me.* It wasn't about her feelings or Grant's feelings or the embryonic relationship she'd decided to nurture at the worst possible time for both of them. Except, of course, it was. Partially. Because life doesn't allow for nice separate boxes or discrete categories.

She pounded down the stairs after him.

Around the halfway point, the enclosed stairway emerged from the lower level's ceiling, opening up to the workspaces on one side and adding a safety railing. Grant waited at the bottom, along with the smells of coffee and pastries and the sound of muffled male conversations. "When were you—"

Grant paused, glanced down the corridor and peeked in the closest open rooms. He put his fingers lightly on JJ's arm and nudged her past the open stairway, closer to the kitchen and the main exit. Then Grant edged closer, until JJ felt the paneled wall against her back, and asked the question she knew he'd been holding in all day.

"When were you going to tell me that Adam Rutledge was back in town?"

"I don't know," she admitted.

Grant extended his arm to the wall and his coat stretched wide, shielding JJ from the view of the kitchen. "The man's been here less than twenty-four hours, and he's managed to drive into a ditch, get the hell beat out of him, and have a heart attack in your shower."

"It wasn't a heart attack," JJ said.

"Whatever. Did I mention he apparently arrived within hours of Rachel's kidnapping?"

She probably should have been angry, but JJ wasn't. Instead, she found herself smiling. "Is this about the kidnapping, or because you found me sitting on him naked?"

Grant's face drifted closer to JJ's. "He was naked; you were clothed."

"Whatever," JJ said.

The corner of Grant's mouth twitched. "At least I know where he is, so that's one less worry on my list."

"About that... Adam's in the back of Dorothy's car right now. He checked out of the hospital, AMA."

JJ was sorry to see the twitch that might have been a smile recede. Once it was gone, she figured she might as well keep going. "Listen, I know I have shitty timing, but there is something I need to tell you. About Rachel."

Grant stiffened next to her. "Go on."

"Leslie might be her father."

Grant's mouth dropped. He looked over his shoulder and down the hall again. "Leslie Beck?"

JJ nodded, not trusting herself to keep her voice down if she said more. But she couldn't keep the distaste from her face.

Grant's eyes narrowed. "Was it consensual?"

"No."

Grant tilted his face away. The hand resting on the wall clenched into a fist, and JJ could hear him breathing. "Did Luther know?"

Now it was JJ's turn to check the corridor. "Yes. It sounds like he gave his brother a Beck-style talking-to, but he didn't report it."

Grant closed his eyes briefly as he shook his head, then exhaled hard. "What about Otto?"

"Hard to say if he knows, but Dorothy didn't tell him."

"This keeps getting better," Grant said. "Luther helped me interview Otto."

"Are you going to tell the task force?"

"Tell them what?" Grant said. "That the guy in charge of our initial searches had a motive for kidnapping the girl he was supposed to be looking for? And by the way, his brother is the Number Two man in my department."

JJ felt the need to play Devil's Advocate. "Les has a possible connection to Dorothy, but that's not the same as a motive. What's the statute of limitations on rape?"

"Sexual offenses, it depends on the circumstances, but for what you're talking about, there isn't one in this state. He could be prosecuted at any time."

That surprised JJ. "What about Luther?"

Grant shook his head. "Let's stop there."

"Why? He—"

"JJ, you did the right thing, telling me. Thank you. But I can't be talking to you about this stuff. The task force—not to mention our prosecuting attorney—will have my ass. As they should. Okay?"

"Okay." JJ let her head drop toward her chest.

"Hey," Grant said, pushing her hair back from her face. "Are *we* okay?"

She looked up at Grant, at the fear in his eyes that he couldn't —or maybe didn't bother to—hide. They had to find Rachel. Whole.

"Yes," she said, touching his hand.

Grant nodded, squeezed her shoulder, and moved off toward the kitchen.

JJ stood for a moment, resting her head against the wall and listening. No one had passed them while they were talking, but she could have sworn she heard—and felt—the clomping of boots going back up the stairs.

31

Adam waited in the car until Luther took Dorothy inside, and then he waited a little more. He'd lost any chance of going under the radar, as JJ had hoped to do, when Dorothy pulled the gun in the parking lot. Emotions were doubtless running high for the whole community, and Adam didn't exactly think he'd be welcomed with open arms once they figured out who he was. The last thing he needed was to set off someone else's crazy.

He'd been telling the truth when he told Dorothy he wasn't sure that Otto'd taken his little girl. But he also believed in what he'd seen. If nothing else, nearly dying had clearly done that for him.

He had to get a look at the maps inside.

Adam didn't have any outstanding warrants—he'd be willing to bet that wasn't the case for all the search volunteers—but that didn't make him any less wary of going into the belly of the law enforcement beast. He helped himself to an Orioles baseball cap he found on the back seat. His head ached as he pulled the cap down hard, but that was nothing compared to the agony of getting out of the car and upright. He unlatched the door and pushed it open with a leg to minimize the movement in his torso.

Adam leaned against the car, letting the warm sun soak into his cold bones while he recovered and got his bearings. Mostly brick with white wood trim around tall windows, flanked by flagpoles but bearing no fancy plaques or statues, the War Memorial Building hadn't changed since Adam's childhood. The last time he'd been inside was for someone's birthday party. He couldn't remember who or when, but they were young enough that they blew on noisemakers with a sense of fun rather than irony, and Matchbox cars were the party favors of choice.

Built on a slope, the building had multiple levels and multiple entrances, for which Dorothy should be grateful. Adam imagined most of the activity was on the other side, where there was additional parking. That entrance was closer to the main kitchen and the biggest bathroom.

The front entry wasn't raised more than half a dozen feet from the ground, but the designers had made the most of the distance with numerous shallow, broad steps. Adam kept slowly tap-tap-tapping his slippered feet on the concrete without feeling like he ever made any headway. He felt certain it was a fire hazard. To make matters worse, lifting his feet to ascend the steps took so much concentration, he kept forgetting to breathe.

Adam paused at the top, dizzy and breathless, just as the push bar handles rattled on the door. Adam dropped his head and looked away as a pair of men banged through the doors and lumbered outside. They ignored Adam, and he slipped inside after they'd passed.

He found himself in a transitional area, with a large, open assembly room to the right and a warren of smaller rooms to the left. Adam recognized the open room from the birthday party so many years ago, and stepped in that direction.

It was dim inside, all glare and shadows, with pools of light from the windows puddling on the dark, hardwood floor. A few long, folding tables broke up the open space, and the far wall was a mix of removable partition and solid, structural barrier. Beyond the partition lay a kitchenette, with a fridge and sink and plenty of counter space, but no actual cooking appliances, meant to supplement the workhorse, full kitchen downstairs.

Tables had been pushed up against the solid wall, and photographs were mounted on the wall itself. A couple of men—early forties, dressed in matching dark shirts and tan khakis with lots of pockets—stood in front of the tables.

Adam risked moving in for a closer look and found exactly what he was hoping for—aerial photos. It wasn't all of Beecham County, but they'd covered more than enough ground to keep Adam's eyes busy. Corresponding maps for the areas were spread out on the tables below—a mixture of National Forest, State Park, county road, state road, tax maps, topographical, and everything in between. Adam's eyes locked on a gray area he recognized. Even with the early loss of leaves elsewhere, it stood out. His fingers moved over the maps until he found the corresponding spot on one of them.

"They've got all this stuff computerized downstairs, but sometimes it's nice to be able to touch the paper," said the man next to him. He had dark hair and a blue polo shirt that identified him as FBI. "What is that?" he asked.

Adam focused on the photo, trying not to make eye contact without being obvious about it. "Dead Hollow," he said, holding his breath against the pain as he pointed at the corresponding map.

"And the trees are all dead? They didn't just lose their leaves?"

The inane question shocked Adam into staring at the man. A narrow scar over his lip caught Adam's eye. "They're dead, in that big patch in the middle. I don't know why. Some people say it's because something toxic was dumped there, but nobody really knows."

"Isn't that where the boy was kidnapped twenty years ago?"

Crap.

Adam had talked himself into a corner now. At this point, it'd be suspicious not to answer. Perhaps if he satisfied the man's—the *agent's*—curiosity, he'd go on his way and leave Adam to review the photos. Preferably before someone else recognized Adam.

"Danny Carpenter was taken from here, just north of the dead patch," he said, trying not to wince as he leaned across the table to point at the photos. "But locals call this whole big area Dead Hollow, from around that camp all the way out to the state road."

"You must have known him—the Carpenter kid. You look about the right age."

"Yessir," Adam said, perhaps his first *yessir* since he was fourteen. He tried to shove his hands in his pants pockets, only to realize he was wearing scrubs. *Nice. That's blending in.* "Yessir, it's a small town. Everybody knew him."

"Were you there—"

The man was interrupted when his khaki-clad companion appeared at his side and said, "Blake wants us."

The two men left without another word to Adam, as if he were no more than a piece of furniture.

Adam breathed a pained sigh of relief and got down to the serious business of finding a cabin he'd only seen in his mind.

ADAM UNFOCUSED HIS EYES, blurring the photos in front of him, to get a different perspective. He'd been staring at them long enough that the blurring part wasn't that hard. A man sidled up next to him, carrying a Styrofoam cup. He was tall and skinny, wearing a short-sleeved T-shirt over another long-sleeved one, and he smelled like dead leaves and sweat.

"You back from a search?" Adam asked.

"Yeah." The man's wrists stuck out from the bottom of his shirtsleeves as he reached forward to indicate on the maps. "Here and here."

"So y'all checked that cabin, over near the old Taylor homestead?"

"Damn Skippy, we checked it out. Les said all those old buildings are at the top of the list. Didn't find so much as a critter's nest, though. Doubt if anybody's set foot in there in years."

"Same for all the rest?" Adam asked.

"I heard there was one closer to the road some teenagers were using—found empty beer bottles and used rubbers—but that was it, so far as I know. Les checked out most of them himself."

Of course, they would have searched the cabins. Adam wasn't sure what he'd imagined he could contribute that no one else had thought of. "I don't suppose anybody took pictures of the cabins, on the inside, I mean."

The man shook his head. "Nope. In and out." He held up his cup. "Off for a refill if you want one."

"No, thanks."

The man walked away, but Adam heard his voice again before he reached the stairs. "Hey, Les, I think you got another volunteer in there."

Well, crap. If Adam pulled his hat down any farther, he wouldn't be able to see, but maybe if he just moved slowly down the table, looking the other direction...

"What the hell kind of pansy-ass pants are you wearing?" Leslie asked.

Or maybe not.

Adam stopped and turned to face the man.

"Well," Les said, "if it ain't Adam Rutledge. Those must be the kind of pants you get when you're screwing a nurse."

Adam knew Leslie could probably wipe the floor with him on a good day, much less one when he couldn't bend to tie his shoes. He also figured the back offices and the bottom floor of the building were crawling with law enforcement, and he knew from experience that his inability to reside at a single address for more than three months made a lot of those types suspicious. Finally, Leslie was a caveman, so it wasn't worth starting anything.

But the caveman made it so very hard.

"Believe it or not, I fell in the shower. Hate to think what the hospital'll charge me for these when I get my bill. And they're so thin, I can feel the wind blow right through 'em."

"Huh," Leslie said. "You ought to be more careful."

"I know. How's it going with the searches? Anything?"

"Nope, not a goddamned thing."

Adam leaned lightly against the table behind him, trying to look more casual than he was capable of feeling. "You've gotta know this area as well as anybody. You think somebody's really got her somewhere out there?" Adam asked.

"Well," Leslie said, pulling a piece of hard candy from his pocket, "what's the alternative?"

Adam shrugged, then tried to make his pain look like a thinking pose. Experience had taught him to never let someone like Les know how bad he was hurting. "So what *wouldn't* show up on these maps or these photos?"

Leslie popped the candy in his mouth before resting his head on his chin and gazing at the maps. "Well, obviously there's a lot of unofficial structures—hunting cabins, tree stands, whatever—that wouldn't show up on the tax maps, or probably any other ones for that matter. Now, I believe they just took photos of areas that were interesting, places they might want to search, but I heard they've got people going over satellite coverage of everything. With the leaves mostly gone, you'd probably get a decent view in."

He pointed at a green patch on a photo while rolling the candy with his tongue. "I don't know shit about the tech, but I'd imagine it'd be hard to see a structure where there's dense conifers overhead. And if it's something small..." he shrugged his shoulders. "We're looking at hundreds of square miles. That's a damn lot of ground to cover."

Adam felt like they were missing something. He leaned on the table, closed his eyes, and took a deep breath. Slowly it got darker, darker than his shuttered eyelids alone could account for, and the table dropped away beneath him—

A big hand squeezed Adam's arm. "Hey!"

Adam opened his eyes again, fighting a familiar wave of nausea.

"Y'alright there, Rutledge?" Leslie asked. "Don't go passing out on me."

"She's still out there," Adam said, confident. The question was whether she would make it through the night.

Leslie looked at him uncertainly, almost as if he were frightened of him. Then he inched even closer and squeezed Adam's arm harder. "I don't know what the hell you think you're playing at. You might have the sheriff and his little whore fooled—"

"Les!" A voice yelled from across the assembly room.

The break gave Adam just enough time to connect Leslie's verbal dots. He straightened, finding himself eye to eye with the man (surprising, since Adam had never been within four inches of his height as a kid), and twisted his arm free of Leslie's hand. "If you ever—"

"Leslie!" Luther cut in. "This is no time for shitting around. We got a tip on the girl."

———

32

Adam remained chest to chest with Luther's brother. He might not be able to fight worth a damn, but Luther had to hand it to the man: Adam had heart.

Two ass-whoopings in a day would be a bit much for me. He wondered if he was going to have to break them up.

"What do you mean, you got a tip?" Adam asked, eyes shifting to Luther but holding his ground.

Luther hesitated, but knew—whether anything came of the tip or not—word would be around Cold Springs by dinner anyway. "Someone saw a van they didn't recognize yesterday. It's gone now, but we're sending some people to check out the scene. Adam, could you excuse us?"

Adam gave Leslie a dirty look, then said, "Sure, Luther," and went on his merry, hobbling way. The man looked even worse than he had a few hours ago.

"Says he fell in the shower," Leslie volunteered, following Luther's eyes.

"Is that right?" Luther scanned the empty room out of habit before nudging his brother down the line of tables toward the exterior wall with its tall windows. They were all closed, and

Luther leaned his head against one for a moment, watching a young woman dressed like it was summer enter the convenience store down the street. "I don't know why you've always got to make such an ass of yourself."

"What?" Leslie protested. "You're the one that told me to keep an eye on Rutledge."

"Not by picking a fight with him, I didn't."

Luther reckoned that his brother protested entirely too much. Nothing was ever his fault, and everything came as a surprise. He had the righteous indignation of a preacher in the pulpit, sermonizing to an empty church on Super Bowl Sunday.

At the moment, Les was shaking all over—just a little, like a shimmy on a bad quality video—and Luther wondered if it was purely from adrenaline. The man's hair was standing up straight and his body odor was for sure something interesting. "Put your hat back on. You look like a doofus. Worse than Adam in his silly blue pants."

Leslie slapped his hat back on his head like a petulant child.

"This tip they got was over by state park land," Luther said, surveying the empty room.

"Oh, yeah. Where at?"

"Almost to the top of the mountain, the pull-out near that old cabin DNR keeps talking about tearing down. Did y'all search there?"

"Of course we did," Leslie said, glancing at the maps next to them. As if he needed to. And as if any of them showed the area they were talking about.

"Les, look at me." Luther wanted so badly to grab his brother by the face, but figured that's when someone would walk in to check on them. "You searched the cabin, or you just half-ass cruised around it?"

"We didn't get on our hands and knees and search it top to bottom, but we went in," he said. Then, less defiantly, he admitted, "I opened the door and went in enough to see there wasn't anybody there. Nobody else went in."

Luther put one hand on the edge of a table, wrapped his fingers around and squeezed until he could swear he felt the metal bend. He didn't speak until he'd stopped imagining it was his brother's throat.

"You think they're gonna find anything when they search it?"

"How the hell should I know?" Leslie asked.

Luther squeezed the table one more time, with feeling. Leslie noticed, and the younger brother instinctively crossed his arms in front of his soft stomach.

"I'm asking," Luther said, in his most patient voice, "if they're gonna find anything of yours when they search it."

"No... hell, no! There's nothing to find. I told you, I'm not into that anymore. I'm done."

"Okay," Luther said. He didn't really believe his brother, but it was hard enough for Luther to keep his own nose relatively clean. He couldn't work miracles on Leslie, too.

He turned to leave, but Les caught his arm. "Wait," Leslie said. "There's something I need to tell you, too."

Luther felt a pang when Les quickly backed up, out of range. He told himself it was because of their dad—the twitchiness—but he knew that wasn't entirely true.

"What, Les?"

Les looked around, but more as if he were working up his nerve than anything else. A couple of men passed by on the far end to exit the building, but the brothers were still alone in the assembly room. Les scratched his neck, and then finally, with no other way to put it off, said, "They know I had sex with Dorothy."

"What? When?"

"What do you mean, when? The time at the tavern when you beat the crap out of me, that's when. The slut must've told somebody."

Les made a choking cough, and something flew from his mouth. His head barely made a sound when it slammed against the heavy windowpane. It took Luther longer than it should have to realize he'd put it there.

"You mean the woman you had to rape to have sex with you? That slut?" Luther asked, hands around his brother's throat.

"I didn't rape her, but if I did, you covered it up," Leslie croaked.

Luther released Les's throat, and looked at his own shaking hand. What the hell was going on? How had it come to this? It was as if the whole damn town had gone crazy. He flexed his hand to get the tightness out. "It was a long time ago."

"Eleven years and nine months, to be exact," Les said, rubbing his throat.

Now it was Luther's turn to stare, uncomprehending.

Finally, Les said, "I just heard JJ tell the Sheriff I might be Rachel's long-lost daddy."

A rapist daddy kidnapping his natural child: now that was a scenario law enforcement could sink their teeth into. Luther sighed.

"Uh-huh. Just let that one sink in for a minute," Les said. He bent down and picked up a piece of sticky, wet candy from the floor, using a dark green wrapper he pulled from his pocket. "JJ also told him you knew about it."

Sonuvabitch... Luther thought back to what he'd said to JJ in the corridor, about Dorothy and Otto, about being objective when it came to people in the community they thought they knew. He almost had to laugh at how well JJ had taken his words to heart. It'd be a lot funnier if he weren't a short step away from losing his job, and his brother two steps away from prison.

He'd figure something out.

"All right," Luther said, and pretended not to notice that Leslie flinched as he patted his arm. "Thanks for letting me know."

"You still want me to keep an eye on Rutledge?" Les asked.

"Sure, from time to time. If you can keep that temper under control," Luther said, and waited for his brother to say something stupid.

He didn't. There were limits even to Leslie's stupidity.

33

———

Adam found JJ sitting outside, waiting for him on the front steps.

"You see all the fancy shit downstairs?" she asked, standing.

"I successfully avoided a trip downstairs with all the officers," he said. "Impressive?"

"Yes, I'd have to say it was. A lot of equipment I didn't understand, a lot of people wanting to do something... I just hope it helps. Come on. Dorothy's waiting. She said she'll drop us on her way home."

"Will her gun hand be on the wheel?" Adam asked as they walked to the car.

JJ grinned. "Yeah, that was one of Grant's conditions. He confiscated her gun, and he's gonna pick up the rest of their guns later. For safekeeping, until this is over."

Adam whistled through his teeth, more than anything just to prove to himself he could muster that much air. "You think he'll catch any flak from the Feds about her waving a gun at Luther?"

JJ cringed as she opened the door. "Let's just hope they don't find out."

"Hey!" a deep voice called from nearby. Adam scanned the parking lot across the top of the car and saw a large, pale, bearded man approaching.

"Shit," JJ said, under her breath. "Otto, we don't want any trouble. We're just catching a ride home with your wife."

"You," Otto said, pointing at Adam. "You need to come with me."

"Otto," JJ warned as the man came closer. "Back off."

"It's okay, JJ," Dorothy said, leaning from behind the wheel. "He doesn't want any trouble, either. He just wants Adam."

And how is that not trouble for me? Adam wondered. But he put on his best, disarming smile, ignoring the pain in his face as his cheek moved to accommodate his wishes.

Dorothy reached out her car window and took Otto's hand in hers, kissing the backs of his fingers.

"It'll be alright," Otto said. Then he rested his arms on the roof of the car and addressed Adam. "There's someone you need to see."

Otto's size, longish hair, and arresting eyes put Adam in mind of a Viking. It wasn't the most merciful image.

"Please," Otto said.

Suddenly, Adam didn't see a Viking anymore. He saw a desperate father, asking for help.

Unless he'd actually had something to do with his daughter's disappearance.

Unless he was *daddy*.

But there was only one way to find out.

"Okay," Adam said.

JJ slammed her car door. "The hell you will!"

"I think I need to do this, JJ. And we all want the same thing— Rachel at home, safe and sound."

JJ's eyes met Adam's. Her eyes—good God, how he'd missed them! When they were kids, Adam felt like he hadn't finished anything until JJ's deep brown eyes had seen it. A tear snuck out of the corner of one now. Adam wanted to wipe it away, but JJ brushed it off so quickly herself that he almost thought he'd imagined it.

She turned to glare at Otto. "If you hurt him again, I'll cut your balls off and feed them to my dog." She opened the door, telling Dorothy, "I mean it."

JJ grabbed Adam's hand and clung to it, almost pulling him on top of her as she sat in the passenger's seat.

"You're not gonna mash my hand in the car door, are you? Because my hand is one of the few parts of my body that doesn't hurt at the moment," he lied. It was actually the hand he'd had an IV in, and he was trying not to wince.

"Of course it doesn't—you didn't get a decent punch in." She squeezed Adam's hand one last time and told him, "Be safe."

"Always." He fell in behind Otto, shuffling his feet through the parking lot so he didn't lose his slippers on the gravel, telling himself all the while that he wasn't the proverbial condemned man following the executioner.

Climbing in the truck was like ascending the Command Center steps again, if all the steps were condensed into one painful, yanking lurch. By the time Adam was up (and relatively upright), Otto had already walked around, gotten in the driver's side, and belted up.

"I'm not having an affair," Otto said, pulling out onto the main highway. They were headed the opposite direction from the Nicholson home.

"Okay," Adam said.

"I did once. Just one time, a few years ago. It was cheating, but I don't even know if that counts as an affair."

Adam wasn't sure what sort of response was expected, so he stuck with, "Okay."

"I'd have to be an idiot to hit you while I'm driving and risk killing us both," Otto said.

"True."

"In other words, relax," he said.

"Okay," Adam said, because he had nothing else to say.

Within minutes they passed the bar that marked the limits of Cold Springs. The houses on the edge of town still looked like "town" houses, with mailboxes at the ends of driveways and lawns browning but mowed, punctuated by little jockeys (some black, some white) and birdbaths, and anchored by an old oak or elm. The ground began rising in another mile or two, manicured yards giving way to unruly woods and the occasional rusted tractor.

How much light was left in the day? Adam looked at the clock on the dash, but it was flashing twelve.

"Is my daughter still alive?" Otto asked, when the first ridge came into sight.

"I think so," Adam said.

"But you don't know for sure?"

"No, I don't."

"Dorothy told me what you said, about why you came over this morning," Otto said. "She didn't know what to think of it."

"That makes two of us," Adam admitted. He wondered if Dorothy had mentioned she was holding a gun on him at the time. Considering the events of the day, Otto might have assumed as much.

"You know about Rachel's asthma, don't you?" Otto asked.

"Yes, I do." *Now*.

"You've got that same look." Otto took a hand from the wheel to point beneath his eyes before gearing the truck down. "The same look she has when she gets a bad one. Like a stain beneath your eyes."

Death warmed over. That's what Iris would say, when she saw him.

"I had an uncle—nobody talked about it, but we always knew he saw things."

"Is that where we're going? To see him?" Adam asked.

"No. This was back in New York, and he killed himself. Blew his brains out."

Adam cringed, but didn't have the energy to maintain his horror, and leaned his head against the window.

"Sorry," Otto said. "You asked. But I think the man we're going to see can help. I heard about him when I first moved here—years ago—and went to see him about someone else. He couldn't find her, but with you... I think he can help us find Rachel."

"What do you mean, *with me?*" Adam asked.

"That's why you're here, isn't it? Why you came back? He lives over toward Pine Gap. You got about twenty minutes—time for a quick nap, if you want it."

And he did. Adam wasn't sure he'd ever been so tired before. The window was hard and cold, but the mountain curves had always felt like a lullaby, rocking him to sleep, ever since he was a baby. Iris said that's how they'd gotten him to sleep when colic and every other baby ailment in creation had made him cranky. Swaying gently, side to side...

Except once. One time there was a crunch, and the car lost the asphalt, flying into the air and tree limbs, and suddenly—

Adam jerked upright, heart pounding, throat dry. He looked down and saw he had adult hands, wonky thumb and all. That feeling—falling into a flashback to the accident—hadn't snuck up on him in a long time.

He was alone in the idling pickup. He raised his weary eyes at the sound of metal clinking across metal. Otto stood in front of the truck, unlooping a chain from a gate and swinging it open.

"We're almost there," Otto said, climbing back in the driver's seat. He didn't bother closing the gate.

They crept slowly over an old cattle guard, then passed open fields on either side. There was a barn in the distance, just before the forest picked up again. Adam rubbed the side of his face where it was cold and clammy. The air outside pressing against the window was much cooler than it had been in town. The sky was thick with clouds, and he felt disoriented, still unsure where the sun was or how much longer it would provide warmth.

"There's an extra jacket in the back," Otto said.

It got even colder when the truck rolled under the canopy, leaving the ghosts of prancing colts and cud-chewing cows behind. Adam rubbed the tops of his legs to warm them. What he really needed was another pair of pants.

"You got a cellphone?" Adam asked.

"Naw. No point out here, 'til they put a bunch more towers up. Dorothy knows where we're going. She'll call his neighbor if she hears anything."

After another mile or two, they came to a winding driveway, with trees crowded so close to its edges that their destination remained cloaked in mystery. Otto drove slowly past a patch of trees with dented trunks and bark scraped away at truck height.

"How the heck do you manage that driving uphill?" Adam asked.

Otto said, "Easier than you'd think. There's a matching track on the downhill side, too. I didn't make either one."

Adam was just starting to shiver when the shape of the cabin came in sight through the trees. He racked his brain, trying to remember if he'd seen the structure on the maps or photos. They were all starting to run together. Everything was starting to run together.

"You okay?" Otto asked.

"Yeah," Adam said. "But I won't say no to that jacket."

"Harlan'll have a fire going."

Adam looked at the sky above the cabin and saw that Otto was right. Smoke never looked so good. The chimney was stone, and as they made the last bend he got a good look at the cabin it was attached to: simple, one story, with logs stained dark and bright white chinking. Split wood lay stacked all along the outside wall under the porch's overhang, and also in the driveway under tarps, ends exposed where the tarps had ridden up. The woodpile was the height of the truck and about three feet wide, making a wall of potential warmth.

Otto pulled up alongside an old red truck parked in front of the cabin. He cut the engine, and the vehicle gave a few extra sput-ters, as if he'd bought bad gas. They sat for a minute or two, listening to the engine tick in the cool air, giving the man inside the cabin time to come out to greet them.

Adam gave another shivering shudder. "So, that jacket?"

Otto reached easily over the back of the seat, a move that Adam looked forward to performing again someday, though probably not for quite a while. Otto handed Adam a camouflage jacket with green cuffs. Resisting the urge to smell it, Adam threw the jacket over his upper body. He couldn't put it on properly in the cramped truck cab, and possibly not without assistance.

"How long do we—"

Adam's question was answered when a gray-haired man in a dark flannel shirt and jeans stepped out the front door.

"What are you waiting for, an engraved invitation? Get your asses in here." He banged back in through the door so quickly Adam never even got a decent look at him.

"Harlan, huh?" Adam asked.

Otto left the keys in the ignition when he got out. "Yeah, Harlan Miller."

Otto's passenger door was old and temperamental, and Adam had to push it harder than he would have liked to ensure it didn't swing back and mash his legs. He slid off the seat and down to the ground. Only a tight grip on the doorframe kept him upright. The jacket crept off his shoulders and fell to his feet.

Adam stood, unsteady, looking at the garment and wondering if he should join it on the cold, damp earth.

Otto appeared next to him and picked up the jacket, giving it a little shake. "You won't need that inside. I'll take my hat back, too." He plucked the Orioles cap from Adam's head and tossed it and the jacket in the truck.

Adam looked toward the cabin. Harlan Miller had left the door open except for a screen, so cold air would be rushing in. Harlan Miller... "You mean, Crazy Harlan?" Adam asked.

"Some people call him that."

Adam knew he'd heard stories, but for the life of him he couldn't remember any at the moment. "He doesn't move like an old man."

"No, but you do. Come on," Otto said, eyes urgent and fingers bruising Adam's arm. "Now."

34

—————

Otto waved Adam ahead, and Adam did his best to walk normally up the steps and through the screen door.

"You can leave that open," Harlan said, from the kitchen. "Afraid we might've let it get a little too hot in here, with the fire."

The cabin layout was open as you entered, with the kitchen to the right and a seating area with a fireplace to the left. A hall presumably led to the bedrooms and bathroom in the back. The interior walls were the same as the exterior—the logs were visible—and undecorated except for a large quilt. It hung between two windows on the wall across from the fireplace. The floor was real wood, with the occasional bit of persnickety millwork sticking up at the seams, and a large, round, braided wool rug lay in front of the fireplace. Adam desperately wanted to lie on the concentric circles of earthy color.

"Put your filthy shoes by the door and come sit down," Harlan said.

Adam should have guessed—the place was immaculate. He toed his slippers off, leaving his feet naked, and crossed to the kitchen table. Otto remained standing at the entry while Adam took the nearest chair.

Harlan set a steaming enamel mug in front of Adam. "You look like you could use some coffee."

"Thank you, sir," Adam said, letting the mug warm his hands and steam warm his face.

"It's traditional to drink that, not just inhale it," Harlan said, sitting across from him and smiling. He was a handsome man, with silver hair and trimmed mustache, but striking dark eyebrows, and a tanned face that made the silver shine. He must be in his sixties —well into his sixties, and perhaps beyond—but he had a vitality that transcended his age.

The screen door made a scraping sound, and Adam felt a surge of cool air. Forgetting that twisting was not his friend, he turned to see Otto leaving.

"No promises," Harlan said.

Otto bowed his head at Harlan and backed out the door.

Adam didn't know whether to follow. He placed his hands on the table and braced himself to stand.

"It's okay, son," Harlan said. "There's nothing more he can do here, and you're staying with me. When was the last time you had anything to eat?"

Adam wasn't sure. Had he eaten today? He'd had muffins at JJ's. *Was that today?* But then he threw up in the hospital, so the muffins probably didn't count.

Otto's truck rumbled outside. Adam listened as it reversed and made its way down the drive.

"Man drives like a paranoid," Harlan said. "Just because I had an incident or two. I tried to tell him I was drunk at the time, but I don't think that helped."

Harlan got up and went to the gas stove. Adam had noticed the pair of big tanks outside, nearly as high as the roof. The man slipped a plain, white apron over his head and turned on the burner under a cast iron pot. "Just take a minute to warm up," he said, stirring. He retrieved a heavy bowl from an open shelf. "We'll get some food in you, and then you can tell me how you came to be dressed like a homeless man."

Adam looked down at his scrubs and his bare feet. He wasn't sure his shirt wasn't on backwards, too.

Harlan brought a plate of biscuits to the table with some butter. Adam looked at the smooth tops and round brown edges, and he could imagine the flaky layers inside, butter melting over the side...

"You wait for the soup, or I cut your fingers off," Harlan said, setting his knife next to the plate. He was smiling—sort of—but Adam still wasn't sure if the man was serious.

Now that Adam's salivary glands had woken up, the aroma of the soup was intoxicating: light tomato-based broth, with the starchy smell of potatoes and other veggies, and the primal tease of chunks of meat. He hadn't realized he'd closed his eyes until the clunk of the bowl on the table in front of him made them shoot open.

"Thank you, sir," he said, grabbing a spoonful and pausing only long enough to blow the heat away. "Mmm..."

"Best soup you'll ever eat, but I can't take all the credit," Harlan said.

Adam reached for a biscuit and slathered it with butter, trying to pace himself so he didn't burn his mouth on the broth. "Reminds me of my grandmother's soup."

"Then you're in for a treat."

Harlan smiled a Cheshire cat grin as a woman ambled from the back of the cabin, face shielded by a pale blue towel as she rubbed the crown of her head.

"Harlan, I thought I heard a truck. I hope it wasn't Jim again." She reached the wet ends of her long, white hair, glanced up, and dropped the towel on the floor. "What the hell are you doing here?"

Adam's mouth nearly hit the floor along with the towel. "Iris?"

"Iris, language," Harlan said, eyes twinkling.

Adam dropped his biscuit on the plate, confused thoughts tumbling through his head.

"Son, eat your soup," Harlan said. "Having food in your belly'll help you think of nasty things to say later."

Iris ignored him. "How did you get here?"

"Otto kidnapped me," Adam said, which he felt was only mildly hyperbolic. "So when you didn't have time to talk to me, what did you do? Go to the market, make a wrong turn at the bread aisle, and fall into somebody's bed?"

Iris stalked toward the table. "How dare you—"

Harlan stood and stepped in front of her. "Iris, before you go getting all pissed, just take a minute, process what he said, and look at the kid."

"He's a couple of decades past being a kid," she said.

"Yes, he is," Harlan agreed, and motioned her to the chair on his other side. "And you, *kid*, don't you disrespect your grandmother again or I'll show you what a real beating is. Now eat your goddamned soup."

So Adam did, while Harlan watched and Iris stared at the table.

It felt strange, and not just because Adam was being watched. All the years he'd lived with Iris, it had only ever been the two of them at the table. Occasionally Danny and JJ ate with him, but then Iris never sat. She'd just hovered, grabbing bites at the counter while she fed them and did seven other things. He missed that, that feeling that someone was ready to swoop in as needed. Iris had done that for him. It may not have been forever, but the decade he'd spent with her was the safest he'd felt in his life.

Adam used the last bit of biscuit to clean the bottom of his bowl, wiped his face, and stared at the same spot on the table his grandmother was staring at. "Iris," he said, "I'm sorry."

Her stare didn't falter.

"Don't worry. She'll be so pissed at me in a minute, she'll forget all about you," Harlan said, fixing his gaze on Iris. "Otto Nicholson called me last night. Well, he called Jim last night, looking for me. Asked if I knew anything about his daughter, Rachel."

Now Harlan had Iris's attention.

"I told him no, I was sorry, but that wasn't the way it worked. Then this afternoon, when Jim came by, it was to tell me Otto was calling again. That's why I had to go by Jim's. Otto told me Adam came after him this morning because of some dream he'd had about Rachel." Harlan glanced at Adam. "Neglected to mention he'd beaten the crap out of you. Anyway, when Dorothy told Otto what you'd said, she didn't make the connection, but Otto's got a history with these kinds of things. He put two-and-two together pretty well when he saw you and found out you'd been in the hospital."

"What do you mean, hospital?" Iris asked.

Adam lifted his hand and slid the plastic admission cuff from beneath his sleeve.

"I mean, it's too late," Harlan said. He reached across the table and took Iris's hands gently in his. "I'm sorry, darling, but he's got a link to the girl."

She sucked in air and tucked her lips back in her mouth so far they disappeared, not peeking out again until she exhaled. Her voice was calm, words measured as if she'd chosen each one after careful deliberation, although in the end all she did was repeat what Harlan had said. "What do you mean, he has a link to the girl?"

"I mean, he can save her."

"No," she said, trying to pull her hands away. The scattered wrinkles in her face deepened with the effort, but somehow she looked younger. Like a frightened adolescent. "That's not his job."

"Iris," Harlan said, holding her hands firmly. "Maybe it is."

"No! It's not!" she yelled, slamming their hands into the table so hard a salt shaker tipped over, then yanking hers free. She knocked her chair over when she stood, screaming, "You promised me!"

"I'm sorry," Harlan said. And he looked it. "There's nothing I can do. And I don't think he has a choice."

Iris was having none of it. She retreated until her spine pushed against the window, her small form backlit by the weak sunlight. "You promised me," she whispered.

Adam said her name—"Iris?"—but she wouldn't look at him, just edged her way to the door.

"No," Harlan said, when Adam would have followed her outside. "She needs time."

Adam heard her car start. It must have been parked on the other side of the woodpile.

"She'll be back," Harlan said. "She hasn't broken yet. It'll just take a little time for her to snap back. Let's just hope it's not too much time."

Harlan took a sip from his own mug, savoring it in a way that made Adam think it contained more than just coffee. The older man stared out the windows, at a view of nothing but tree trunks and the mottled shadows of their unseen canopies.

"Only a few hours of daylight left," he observed. "Now that you're starting to look human again, I think it's time you told me about these dreams of yours."

35

After Dorothy dropped her off, JJ headed back toward Cold Springs in her own car. She was reminded, as she passed it yet again, that something needed to be done about Adam's car in the ditch. Maybe she'd drop by the garage on the edge of town, see if they still did towing. She imagined there was a flat call-out fee, but a guy who worked there owed her a favor, so maybe he'd give Adam a deal.

JJ took the back roads, not exactly sure where she was going and in no particular hurry. About a mile outside of town, the pullout where the big power line came through looked like a parking lot, and she stopped to investigate.

A search team had gathered, under the direction of the most recently hired Sheriff's Deputy. The woman's uniform stood out among the sea of jeans and sweats, despite the fact that she wasn't more than a hair over five feet tall. The deputy was in her early thirties, trim, but with a wide face that made her look heavier. Her blunt haircut didn't help.

"Beth, is it? I'm JJ Tulley," she said, sticking out her hand. "I live next door to the Nicholsons, and I was wondering if you could use an extra set of eyes."

JJ hadn't asked if the deputy *needed* an extra set of eyes, because she obviously didn't. There were a couple of dozen people present already, for a small search area that was unlikely to hold anything of value—not Rachel, nor a clue to her whereabouts. But what the community *needed* was to be doing something, and Beth realized that as well as anyone.

"Beth Marshall," the deputy said. "Thanks for coming out. If you head over to that end, the gentleman in the yellow shirt will tell you what to do. We'll be moving out in just a few minutes."

JJ checked in and moved to her designated spot. The road people had parked alongside wrapped around the hill, much like a line on a topographic map, well below its summit. The view downslope was mesmerizing. Laid bare in a corridor a hundred or so feet wide, with forests of trees crowding on either side, the hills seemed stacked end on end, all the way to the state line.

The deputy was true to her word, and soon they traversed the ground in some kind of pattern JJ couldn't be bothered to figure out. It was enough that she knew to stay between the same two people, all the time. The team would work their way down the relatively steep hill and up to the crest of the next one before turning around.

The searchers kept their eyes to the ground, occasionally bunching closer together when conditions—sometimes rocky, sometimes heavy brush—dictated. It was quiet work, the only sounds an occasional car passing on the road above, the echoing scream of a hawk hunting nearby, a bunch of dogs barking farther away. The sun was surprisingly intense, and JJ wished she'd thought to wear a hat.

JJ found herself thinking about Rachel, about the girl's personality. She'd been glad when Rachel and Evie became good friends. Aside from the convenient proximity, the girls provided each other balance. JJ sometimes wondered if her daughter knew what fear was at all. Rachel, on the other hand, was a sweet girl, but a little on the timid side.

What kind of person could have kidnapped Rachel? Who

would she have gone with? It was a stupid question, really. Rachel would never have willingly gone anywhere with anyone other than her parents, or JJ. Of course, it didn't matter if she was willing or not when she was physically outmatched by anyone—male or female—over five feet tall and a hundred pounds.

A man stumbled farther down the line of searchers, and the person next to him paused to help him up. They were good people, doing a useless task but so desperately wanting to do something to help. They'd be in church tomorrow morning, praying for a miracle, bringing casseroles to the Nicholsons if this dragged on, or if —God forbid—the worst came to pass. And yet...

And yet, these were the same people that threatened their own children when no one was around to hear them, that beat them and their wives and their elderly parents and even their dogs when no one was around to stop them.

A sudden breeze came up and gave JJ a chill. At least, that's what she told herself. That it was the breeze rather than the stark acknowledgment that any of these people could have taken Rachel. That any one of them could have the child tucked away, waiting for his—or her—return.

～

JJ GRATEFULLY TOOK the bottle of water Deputy Marshall offered. "Thanks."

"Thank you for... you know," the uniformed woman said, looking around uncomfortably.

"No problem." JJ had convinced one of the local elderly dears to coordinate new arrivals (i.e., tell them to go home) rather than hiking down to search with the younger folk, undoubtedly breaking an ankle. She leaned against the hood of her car, snapping the bottle cap and taking a swig. "It'll be easier when people know you," JJ said. *And it'll be harder, too.* "Let me ask you something. If somebody files for a restraining order, is that public record?"

"Has somebody been bothering you, Ms. Tulley?" the deputy asked, cracking the seal on her own bottle.

"Call me JJ," she said automatically. She found that she couldn't be bothered to muster a convincing lie. "I just wondered about the procedure."

"Have you spoken with Sheriff Mason about this?"

The woman's tone of voice suggested she already knew JJ and Grant were *friends*—whatever that word meant. It seemed to be in flux. "No," JJ said. "It's nothing. Forget I asked."

"The hearings aren't necessarily public, but the paperwork would be. And you know how fast things get around in a town this size."

Yes, JJ did.

Both women watched a car pull over, squeezing in as one of the volunteers left. JJ recognized the white blonde hair behind the wheel.

"Excuse me, Deputy," JJ said.

"Beth. And if you'll forgive me for butting in, when someone of your temperament—what I've heard of it—" she said, with a hint of self-consciousness, "When someone like that has gotten to the point of wondering about procedure, then I'd say whether it's public or not should be the least of her concerns."

"That may be," JJ admitted, thinking of the gun in her glovebox. Unlike Dorothy's, hers was loaded.

JJ found Iris standing next to her car, almost in the road, gazing down the power line to the mountains beyond. Her hair was damp, and she looked upset, unfocused in a way the woman rarely was.

"Iris?"

She startled. "Oh, JJ. I saw the crowd and just wondered... nothing?"

"Not yet. Are you all right? You seem distracted." A sudden image of Adam in his slippers, being driven away in Otto's truck, flashed into JJ's head. "Adam's okay, isn't he?"

Iris shook her head with frustration. "That boy."

"Iris," JJ said firmly, "he's not a boy anymore."

"That's what I said."

To whom? What had JJ missed while she was searching for Rachel? "Iris, what's going on? Where is Adam?"

Iris's eyes settled on the horizon again where a turkey buzzard rode the air currents, cruising above the next ridge as though it had all the time in the world. Maybe it did, but JJ didn't. Having made everyone sweaty, the sun seemed now determined to beat feet behind the mountain and give them all a chill. And bring darkness. Again.

"You think that little girl's still alive?" Iris asked.

"I do," JJ said, "Partly because I want to, but mostly because Adam does. Where is he?"

"So you know about all this, too?" Iris looked around, self-conscious, but no one was paying them any mind. "These *dreams* of Adam's?"

"I know that if something bad happens to Rachel, and he thinks he could have helped her but didn't—whether that's true or not—he'll be devastated." *And so will Grant.* "Especially after Danny."

Iris pushed her hair back, shoving it behind her ear on one side, and gave JJ a sad smile. "You thought I didn't have a clue, didn't you? When you kids were tramping all over creation trying to find the boy. I knew, but I didn't say anything. I was so scared that something might happen to you—you'd fall or get lost or someone would run you over on the highway—but I was even more scared of what it would do to you, both of you, if you had to stay put. So was your father."

"Dad knew, too?"

Iris nodded, then sighed and stepped around JJ to get in her car. "Adam's at Harlan Miller's. If you don't know the way, you can follow me. I'm headed there now."

36

———

Nice, warm day, down here close to town. He ran a hand through his hair, distributing the sweat from around his temples, before firmly settling his cap back on his head.

It had been a long time, but he'd recognized her instantly. Something in the set of her shoulders, that fierce independence that, even as a little girl, had said she didn't need anyone. That she would personally protect Adam and Danny and whoever else she chose.

Silly JJ. That hadn't been true then, and it wasn't true now.

He'd faked a stumble, used it as an excuse to head back to his car early. And then he sat there and watched her. Her and Iris. Poor Iris was looking her age today.

The women spoke for a while, and JJ walked back toward her Bronco.

The man started his car and swept out onto the road, turning his head away as he passed JJ and Iris. He'd already made a phone call to the police, but he still had things to take care of. Besides, he was pretty sure he knew where the women were headed. And he'd see them there soon enough.

37

Adam gave Harlan a quick overview of each of the three dreams about Rachel—her kidnapping, the scene with the man she'd called daddy, and when Adam had nearly died in the shower. The final one clearly unnerved the older man. Harlan didn't bother hiding the bourbon he added to his own mug, roughly one-to-one with the French Roast, when he topped up their coffee.

"Tell me more about the scene with the man, *daddy*. What did he look like?" Harlan asked, closing his eyes.

"I told you I didn't see him."

"*You* didn't see him, or *she* didn't see him?"

Adam stammered, "I didn't see him."

Harlan said, "Are you sure? There is a difference, you know."

Adam sipped his coffee, followed the bitter taste over his tongue, felt an ache in his ribs as he swallowed before the liquid ran down his throat. This was *him*, *Adam*, drinking strong, now tepid coffee. But when he'd dreamed of Rachel... he'd felt hunger as she licked an empty wrapper. *He'd* felt it. "If there's a difference, I don't know how to see it," he said, frustrated.

"Okay, let's move on to something else. You were in Pennsylvania when you dreamed about Rachel being taken. Correct?"

"Yes, sir," Adam said.

"And obviously you were at Iris's this morning," Harlan said, worrying a toothpick between his teeth and watching the light outside the cabin as if it were a clock. "You ever have these dreams about anybody who wasn't somewhere in Beecham County?"

Adam thought about it. He'd had some vague feelings of... what? Dissonance. Something just not being right. But he'd never had anything vivid, anything he remembered details of after the fact, that didn't have to do with Beecham County. "I don't think so."

Harlan raised a dark eyebrow and pointed his toothpick at Adam. "Now that's interesting. That's very interesting." He began leaning his wooden chair on its back legs. "And when's the first time you had one?"

Adam thought back to his earlier conversation with Grant. "The first one I know of was at Iris's, and Sheriff Mason was there. But I don't remember it."

Harlan sighed. "Well, unfortunately Old Sheriff Mason won't be much help at this point. But maybe when Iris gets back."

"So you think she'll be back."

"I know she will," Harlan said, and barreled ahead. "You said you see through Rachel's eyes. Does she know you're there?"

The idea shocked Adam—even repulsed him. It somehow felt like a violation if Rachel knew he was there, which made no sense. It's not like Adam asked to be there. Of course, *she* didn't ask to have *him* there, either.

"Hey!" Harlan said. "Don't go down that road."

Adam narrowed his eyes at Harlan.

"No, I'm not psychic. I don't think. Hell, I don't even know what that means. But I wouldn't have to be, because I've been where you are. I've asked myself the same kind of questions. And eventually, I learned not to. So just answer my question. Does she know you're there?"

How could Adam tell what Rachel knew?

Adam received sensory input in his dreams, but he was somehow getting it secondhand and specific details eluded him. It was a little like trying to remember how a food tastes based solely on what you read or what someone told you about the flavor. *What someone told you...* Words made the connection between two individuals, acting as a bridge for shared experience. Adam remembered what Rachel *had said*, even when the sensory details of his visions were fuzzy. So maybe he could remember other *words*.

Adam let his mind go blank and sink down. Further... further... back to when he collapsed in the shower. There was nothing there.

But before the hospital, there was a moment. Adam recalled lying in the tub. JJ was there with him, knees pressing against the outside of his hips. He felt her face above his, and heard voices, hers and... *it must be Grant*. But theirs weren't the only voices. Rachel, in her darkness, could also hear someone speaking. Possibly more than one person, although the raspy tone was so similar, it could have been a single voice.

Adam tried, but he couldn't capture any of the words. Except... except he could hear Rachel's words, never spoken out loud... *Are you still with me?*

Adam's eyes flew open.

Harlan stared at him, lips pursed, waiting.

"I think she knows now," Adam said. "I think Rachel asked if I was still there, after JJ found me and brought me back around."

"You mean after you'd stopped breathing, and after JJ did CPR on you?"

Adam nodded.

Harlan pointed at the cup in front of him. It no longer contained tepid coffee. It radiated warmth, filled with some kind of smelly tea. "Drink that," Harlan said.

Adam obeyed. The liquid was pungent, but not unpleasant. He couldn't identify the flavors, but they seemed familiar. Adam paused for breath, then drank the rest in one long draught. "What was in that?"

"You don't want to know. I brewed it while you were in la-la-land."

"Meaning?" Adam asked.

"Meaning you sat there without speaking for a good fifteen minutes. When your mouth started turning blue, I thought a hot beverage might be in order."

Adam touched his lips. Now that Harlan mentioned it, they did have a hollow, tingly feeling that made him want to rub the life back in them. His arms felt icy beneath his shirt. The tea was helping, but Harlan was right. Adam probably didn't want to know what was in it.

"Does this happen to you?"

"Not usually," Harlan said. "It's different for everybody, what they see and how. What it does to them. And to be honest, I don't see that much anymore. Thank the Lord."

But Adam noticed Harlan was now drinking the same pungent tea, not the corrected coffee he'd been drinking earlier. That had to mean something. "What is it like for you? And why did Otto bring me here?"

"Let's just say I have a certain reputation among some people."

"So you've got something woo-woo going on?" Adam asked.

One of Harlan's dark eyebrows rose like a blind. "Woo-woo? Do I look like a goddamned train?"

Adam wasn't certain if Harlan was mad, but there was an edge to the man's voice. "No, sir. I just meant—"

Harlan waved a hand. "I know what you meant. I guess I just don't get much of a chance to practice my social skills out here. But it's my own choice."

Adam followed Harlan's eyes to the half-empty bottle of bourbon. He wondered how many more the old man had stashed away.

"Couple of cases," Harlan said, and grinned.

Adam glared at him, but couldn't maintain it, and found himself grinning, too. "Not psychic, huh?"

"Actually, I'm not," Harlan said. "Not like a *Twilight Zone* episode, with voices in my head. Sometimes I get flashes of insight, like intuition. And I get them more with some people than others. You seem to be one of those 'some people' I get them from a lot."

"Have you always been like that?"

Harlan nodded, leaning back on his chair legs again. "Long as I can remember. But the real strong stuff—the visions, like your dreams—for me, those come with touch. Skin to skin contact."

Adam thought back. From the moment he'd entered the door, Harlan hadn't touched him. "All the time?"

"I wouldn't say *all* the time." Harlan got a distant look in his eyes, and added, "But I would say *any* time. I never know when."

Adam had avoided contact himself—physically certainly, but emotionally even more so—in his adult life. The thought was still staggering. Casual contact would be bad enough, but what about any kind of physical intimacy?

Harlan brought his attention back to Adam. "Exactly," he said.

Adam wrapped his arms around himself and noticed his pain seemed to have receded, just a bit. Harlan bumped his chair back down to the floor, got up, and closed the front door against the chill. Shadows fell around the table as he did.

"Does Iris know?" Adam asked.

Harlan gave a rueful chuckle. "Even Iris doesn't know what Iris knows, from one day to the next. But she's interesting. I've never met anyone who can shield herself—from things going out or coming in—the way she does. I think it came from being married to Lawrence Rutledge." He strode toward the fireplace, where the briskly burning fire clearly did not need tending.

"What do you mean?" Adam called out to the man's back.

Harlan poked at the fire, moving the screen back into place afterwards to help protect his rug. Finally, he said, "Son, it's complicated. And I'm afraid that's not my story to tell."

Adam got up and shoved his chair under the table. Then he set his plate and bowl in the sink, perhaps a little too forcefully.

"Easy," Harlan admonished. "Those were made by a man in Pine Gap who was one of the best ceramic artists I've ever seen—

rest his soul. He was crazy as a bedbug, though. I always wondered if it was something he put in his paints."

"Well, if it was, you're eating it," Adam snapped, staring out the window over the sink at the nearly naked trees beyond.

"Fair point," Harlan said.

Adam watched a brown leaf fall from an oak's high branches, doing a lazy, end-over-end, cradle-jerking spiral toward the ground until it hit a gust that sent it sideways. He tried not to be angry, and he was mostly successful. He didn't really have a right to be angry with Harlan, or even with Iris. There were undoubtedly things she'd never told him. But Adam had stopped asking, and then he'd stopped coming back. He'd made it easy for her. Not that anything had ever been easy for any of them.

Harlan sighed and leaned against the sink, crossing his arms and getting the hem of his shirt wet on its edges. "I'm sorry, son. I will tell you this. I never liked Lawrence Rutledge, for a lot of reasons. Didn't help that I loved your grandmother from the moment I set eyes on her, and she was already his wife."

Harlan looked toward the road. "And there she is," he said, stepping around Adam to set a kettle of water on the stove to boil.

Hearing the car a couple of seconds later, Adam thought the man must have the ears of a bat. They walked to the front porch together. The shaded back roads were dim enough that Iris's headlights were lit up, and Adam caught a flash of another set behind her. It was JJ.

"Told you she'd be back," Harlan said. He watched as Iris got out of her car, pulling something from the back. "Mmm-mmm. It's been damn near thirty years, and that woman's still got the finest ass in Beecham County."

Adam cringed. "I did not need to hear that."

Harlan smiled unapologetically, eyes locked on Adam's grandmother as if she were the only thing worth gazing upon in the whole wide world. Adam found it touching, despite the edge of creepiness. He didn't want to spoil the moment. And yet, he had to ask.

"Harlan, do you really think we can find the girl?"

"No," Harlan said, honestly.

He was so certain that Adam nearly vomited his belly full of soup and tea. *Then why am I here? What's the point?*

"I don't think we can find her," Harlan continued. "And I think it might damn well kill both of us, one way or another. But I think we have to try."

38

Luther drove past the other parked cars, squeezing his way as close to the old park cabin as he could. He blocked someone else in—Virginia tags, so it was probably one of the task force guys. *Tough shit.* Luther wouldn't be here long. The tape barrier crossed the lane just ahead of his vehicle, and again farther on, marking off a twenty-foot span of road. He wondered if there was anybody on the other side, wanting to get out. If so, he doubted they'd stop for a couple of orange cones and some flimsy tape.

The deputy nodded at a couple of State Police guys that looked vaguely familiar. Some of the other men milling around wore FBI khakis and jackets. He hesitated. Things were getting complicated, and for once he did not envy Grant's position. Luther could avoid making an ass of himself most of the time, but knew he didn't have the temperament for interagency politics. Today was a good day to be a simple investigator.

Luther turned in a slow circle, taking in the gravel road, the leaf-strewn parking area with room for a couple of vehicles, the patchy grass and pine needles between the parking area and the cabin, and the people tramping around. The scene was a clusterfuck. Either they'd processed it lickety-split and decided there was nothing there, or they'd decided whatever was there had already been trampled. Too many cooks by the fire.

So what had the man (Luther decided to play the odds) been thinking? Why had he come here?

Luther stared at the woods in front of him, until the various shades and textures of gray trunks merged, taking over the space between them. He currently stood about eight miles from the girl's house. Unless the kidnapper was either really stupid or didn't care about getting caught, this couldn't have been his final destination. It had been searched less than eighteen hours after the abduction, albeit apparently half-assed, thanks to Luther's brother. Maybe the man was taking Rachel (*"the girl"—stick with "the girl"*) to meet someone. That scenario would make sense if it were a custody dispute, but for once that wasn't an issue.

Goddamn, Luther hoped they didn't really think his brother was the poor child's dad. Things would get awfully complicated, awfully fast.

Luther brought his attention back to the taped road. So the kidnapper had brought her here for a quick stop. He could have been meeting someone, even if it wasn't about custody. Luther tried to pull his mind back from the dark places where people sold children, reminding himself that there was no sign of a meeting. Of course, with the state of the scene, there probably wouldn't be.

Please, God, don't let forensics find any blood.

Maybe the man just needed to pause for his peace of mind, take a moment to ensure the girl was secure, that he hadn't messed up anything before continuing to his final destination.

"Deputy Beck!"

Luther felt as if he'd jumped out of his skin, but anyone around him wouldn't have seen a flinch. Grant had just exited the cabin and was headed in his direction. Luther waited for the Sheriff to catch up, and together, elbow to elbow, they walked back toward the road and the Beecham County vehicle Luther had driven in.

"Anything?" Luther asked.

Grant glanced over his shoulder, back at the cabin. "There were a few things from Rachel's backpack—a piece of candy, her school ID, a set of keys on some kind of puffy keyring. Maybe he thought the keys had some kind of kid tracker or something."

"Did they?"

"No, just sparkles and ribbons. Looks like he wiped her stuff clean before he left it. We're checking the cabin for hair and fiber, but as of now, there's no indication that she was ever inside. He could have left her in the vehicle, taken her bag inside to search it."

There was a stilted awkwardness to their conversation. Luther wasn't sure if it was just the circumstances—standing at a crime scene that gave them nothing, aware of the clock running against the child—or if Grant was trying to decide how best to fire his senior deputy for being complicit in a major crime.

"Who called the tip in?" Luther asked.

"Someone who didn't want to get involved, probably hunting where he's not supposed to be. He said he saw a dark-colored van yesterday evening when he drove by, and that's all he said."

"Any reason for me to go in there?" Luther wasn't sure if he wanted to or not, but he was leaning toward not.

"Not unless you want to be under foot," Grant said. He rubbed his nose on either side, then out to his bruised-looking eyes.

"They get a decent tire cast?"

Grant shrugged. "We'll see. They got a couple, but who knows whose it is or whether there's enough detail to give us anything. Don't suppose you know how close your brother's teams have been driving in, how much of it they're doing on foot?"

Luther shook his head.

"Well, that's something we'd better brief them on. Just in case," Grant said.

Grant had left the county cruiser at the Command Center and ridden to the cabin with the federal agent in charge, so he said he'd catch a ride back with Luther. They found that another vehicle had blocked them in (*yeah, yeah, that's what I get*), so Grant sent someone to track down the owner and the keys.

The two men leaned against the county SUV, contemplating the cabin while they waited. It was a simple wooden structure, weathered to a dark, moldy color, with a ten-foot overhang in front. There was no porch to speak of, but a picnic bench that had seen better days sat under the shelter. The overhang sagged on one side thanks to a cattywonkus post, and looked in danger of burying the bench, given the excuse of the slightest breeze. The main roof didn't look a whole helluva lot better.

Luther definitely didn't need to go in. "Tell me," he said, "did Les and his boys miss anything? Anything they should have seen?"

"No, I don't think so," Grant said. "It's not like the stuff was out on a table, or sitting in the middle of a circle in the dirt or something crazy. But it might be good to include that in the brief tonight, too. Things to watch out for."

Luther nodded, then hesitated. Les was in enough trouble already, but he had to know. Had Les searched the cabin himself because he was incompetent, or because he was covering something up? This was the kind of place his brother used to take advantage of. "There wasn't anything else in the cabin? Any sign of other illegal activity..."

His voice trailed off, and Grant looked at him, hard enough that Luther knew he wasn't fooling the man. The Sheriff might be softhearted, but he wasn't soft in the head.

"Leslie hasn't run into any more problems with DNR, has he?" Grant asked, voice low.

Luther stared at his boss. He didn't know how Grant had heard about Leslie's first "problem" with harvesting ginseng illegally, since nothing had been filed. Except it was Beecham County. Eventually everybody knew everything here, and the man was the Sheriff.

"No, sir," Luther said, intending the formal response to be the end of it.

"Good," Grant said, absently rubbing a finger along one of his brows. "Nobody would have cared so long as it stayed local. But I guess anytime there's easy money to be made, somebody'll show up to make it."

Luther snorted. "Easy, my ass. Tramping out there in the woods. I'll take sitting in my nice, warm car with a radar gun any day."

"Yeah," Grant admitted, "me, too."

Actually, it did seem like easy money to Luther, but—he'd never admit this to the Sheriff—it offended his sensibilities, digging up what grew wild and shipping it off to some rich bastards in China or wherever who couldn't get their peckers up. As far as Luther was concerned, they could all stick the ginseng trade up their asses, which is where he'd like to kick Les for ever getting involved with it. That in itself was a bit of a mystery, since Leslie was not the most motivated person Luther'd ever met. He must've needed the money. The big question—the one that kept Luther up nights because his mother wasn't there to ask it—was why.

39

G rant was quiet on the drive—too quiet. The silence gave Luther's mind plenty of space to spin out scenarios around his future and Les's, and none of them were good. He drove directly around back of the Command Center, where Grant had left the department cruiser, and parked. The deputy cut the engine. Grant removed his seat belt but seemed in no hurry to move.

Luther sighed. He could keep pretending, but he knew it would only get worse. It was time. "So, you know about Les and Dorothy?"

"Yes." Grant scooted his seat back a notch and raised his knee against the door, like a teenager getting comfortable.

"She's not Leslie's kid. All you have to do is look at her and look at Otto to know that he *is* her daddy."

"Luther—"

"Look, I'm not condoning what Les did," Luther said. He couldn't look at Grant, and kept his eyes on the steering wheel, where one hand picked at a flaw in the grip.

"I didn't think you would. But then, I didn't think you'd cover it up, either."

"I didn't cover it up!" Luther shouted, too loudly for the enclosed space. "And I didn't lie. I just didn't tell anybody."

Grant inclined his head, regarding Luther with cold eyes. "Luther, you're an officer of the law. You've sworn to protect people that can't protect themselves. You don't get to not tell anybody."

Luther held his tongue against the explanations and justifications that threatened to burst from him, because it didn't matter. Grant was right. It didn't matter what he had done; it mattered what he hadn't.

"But what's the point *now?* Who does it help for Les—"

"Dammit, Luther! I'm not wasting time sitting in the parking lot—while Rachel Nicholson endures God knows what—because of your brother. I'm sitting here because of you."

Luther dragged his eyes to his boss. "What do you mean?"

"A girl's life is at stake, and unlike you, I don't have the luxury of keeping this to myself. That means shit is about to get even more complicated." Grant's face was flushed, somehow making the decade's difference in their ages more apparent. "When I got this job—hell, even before I was elected—one of the first things my father told me was that I could trust you, that above all others, I could *always* trust you."

Luther dropped his eyes, feeling a lump of shame and pride in his throat—all mixed together—that made him sick.

"What I need to know, before I go in that building and all hell breaks loose, before I put my reputation *and Rachel's life* on the line, is whether he was right." Grant grabbed Luther's arm. "Look at me. Can I trust you?"

Luther opened his eyes wider against the pressure he felt building in them, and pressed a single word through his constricted throat. "Yes."

The pinching around Grant's mouth eased, and he relaxed his grip on Luther's arm. "Okay," he said, and reached for the handle of the door.

"Okay?" Luther blinked. "That's it?"

"Triage," Grant said. "Right now, we do what it takes to get Rachel back. We'll figure out the details on everything else later. Let's go."

Inside, they passed the kitchen and continued to a large room with computers on one end and tables and whiteboards on the other. Most of the half dozen or so people were some sort of law enforcement. Leslie was an exception. He stood calling out place names and making checkmarks on a big whiteboard while Deputy Beth entered the data on a computer next to him.

Grant had been on his cellphone since they left the vehicle, but seemed unable to make a connection. "Has anybody seen Adam Rutledge or JJ Tulley?" he asked of the room at large. A generally soft-spoken man, Grant had one of those voices that was clear as a bell on the rare occasion he raised it.

"Ms. Tulley volunteered on one of our searches, maybe an hour ago," Beth said. "Mr. Rutledge wasn't with her."

Leslie used the edge of his shirt cuff to erase a smear of dry erase marker on the board before turning to add, "Otto gave Rutledge a ride."

"Otto Nicholson?" Grant asked, surprised, but no more so than Luther was himself. The two men hadn't exactly been bosom buddies a few hours ago.

"Said something about taking him out to Crazy Harlan Miller's. I don't know why," Les said, before turning his attention to the deputy next to him. "Beth, I'll be upstairs in the map room if you can't read the rest of my chicken scratch."

Grant had suggested they keep the morning altercation under wraps as best they could, and Luther hadn't told his brother about it. Now he half wished he had.

"You want me to head out there and pick Adam up?" Luther asked.

"No, that's okay. I'll take a quick drive out. You check in with the task force and make sure they're not having any problems getting the evidence from the scenes transported to—" Grant stopped when a man stepped into the room and waved him over. "Speak of the devil," he muttered.

Luther watched the two men retreat to a corner. He would've recognized the federal agent even if the man hadn't been wearing tan commando-wannabe pants that stuck out like a sore thumb in Cold Springs. Luther thought of the agent as Scarface—even though the scar on the man's lip was barely noticeable and the name made him sound like some kind of badass—because nothing else about him stood out at all. It was hard to trust a man like that; such invisibility could not be natural.

Their voices weren't raised, but Scarface and Grant were obviously arguing. Grant shook his head vigorously and stepped close to Scarface. The two men were of similar height, and if Grant had been wearing his hat, it would've connected with the other man's forehead. Scarface didn't respond, but scanned the space. His eyes stopped at Luther, although his expression didn't change. He said something else to Grant, and the two men left the room.

This does not bode well. Luther bowed his head and thought about what Grant had said, and about all the things he hadn't done. That led him to think about Rachel Nicholson, something he hadn't done enough. He'd been afraid to, afraid to make it any harder than it already was, especially should the worst come to pass.

The last time he recalled seeing Rachel was about a year ago during a class field trip to the jail. She was a beautiful little girl, pale as a ghost with big blue eyes. She'd been afraid to touch anything, as if every surface could bite. Luther had offered her a peppermint from the dish on his desk, but she'd politely declined because her mother didn't allow candy.

Luther smiled. Rachel had been trying to stay close to JJ Tulley's little girl, but that firecracker'd had none of Rachel's qualms. She'd stuck her arms through the bars, examined the cell door, done everything she could to figure out how she'd escape from it. Luther had almost offered to lock the Tulley girl in for a while, but he figured that wouldn't go over too well with anyone but her. Maybe JJ would okay it when the girl turned a teenager.

The candy...

Luther strode to a table at the back of the room covered with plastic bags, banker's boxes and other evidence-related detritus, but no actual physical evidence.

"Hey, Beth," he called out.

She looked up from her keyboard warily as Luther crossed the room. "Yes?"

"Where's the physical evidence from the scene? The cabin scene, I mean. Not the abduction point."

She glanced toward the table he'd just left. "If it's not there, it's either still at the scene or en route."

"En route to where?"

"Depends on the evidence. From the scene to here, or if it's been logged already, from here to the state lab, or the federal lab, or the department, or—"

"What about photographs of the evidence?"

"That depends on who took them and whether the camera's back yet. You can see everything that's been downloaded over there." She pointed to another computer terminal.

"Thanks." Luther scooted his chair close and squinted at the monitor. The downloaded folders of pictures were labeled by date and time. Luther clicked through a few before he found the first shots of the cabin interior. The entire cabin had been documented from multiple angles, but Luther focused on a small bookshelf that sat beneath one of the windows. It was covered with so much dirt, it almost looked as if it had sprung from the earth rather than the hands of man. The top shelf held an empty votive holder and a small, cracked plate that had served time as an ashtray.

The bottom shelf was what interested Luther. It held a stack of rotting hardcover books, their spines illegible, and pieces of Rachel's life. There was the puffy, ribboned key ring that looked like a cross between a pool floaty and the handle of a little girl's first bike. Luther rotated the photo for a better view. There was the school ID, on its nylon strap in its plastic holder. And there was the piece of candy, the candy that probably hadn't come from Rachel. He zoomed in and sent a copy to the printer.

"Luther," Grant said, entering the room. The man's pinched face suggested he was not bringing good news.

"Sheriff," Luther said, "there's something here you need to see."

Grant shook his head and pointed Luther toward the exit. Luther didn't argue, but he picked up the page from the printer, folding it in his pocket, and left the photo file open on the monitor.

Their feet crunched on the gravel as the two men walked around the corner of the building. Grant looked over his shoulder before settling against the brick wall. The man looked exhausted.

"How bad is it?" Luther asked.

"It could be worse. Your brother will no longer be involved with the searches, or anything else associated with the kidnapping investigation."

"He's not being prosecuted?"

"We'll see," Grant said. "I told the task force that he had a relationship with Dorothy. I did not go into details of the circumstances."

"You mean you didn't tell them about the rape?"

Grant opened his mouth to speak, but the words didn't come out. He sighed and tried again. "That's within our jurisdiction—not theirs—and I need to talk with Dorothy about it, *after we find Rachel*. It should be Dorothy's decision then, about who knows what happened and where we go from here."

"But they'll argue the rape is relevant to Les's motive." Luther knew he wasn't telling the man anything he didn't know, but it had to be said.

"I made a judgment call," Grant said, voice final.

Luther hoped it wasn't one that would come back to bite the Sheriff in the ass. "And what about me?"

"From here on out, you won't have direct or supervisory responsibility for anything in the case."

"What does that mean?" Luther asked.

"It means, keep your head down. For now, head back to the department and check in with... I don't even remember who's answering the phones. See if we left any fires burning that need to be put out."

Luther nodded. "Fine. But before you kick me off the case, I noticed something." He told Grant about his experience with Rachel and the candy at the scene.

"That's good," Grant said. "I'll check with Dorothy about Rachel's habits, see if we can confirm the theory that it came from the kidnapper. If it is something unusual—"

A khaki-clad young man rounded the corner, and Grant straightened abruptly and raised a hand in acknowledgment. "Be right in."

The man turned on his heel, heading back inside at something more than a walk but less than a run.

"That's right, don't wanna keep Scarface waiting," Luther said.

Grant looked confused.

"Agent Banana Republic," Luther said by way of clarification. "Captain Khaki."

After a beat, comprehension dawned, and Grant put a hand up to his eyes, almost hiding a ghost of a smile. "That's Special Agent D'Antonio. Luther, we've worked together for—how long now?—and I'm still occasionally taken aback by your way with words."

"Promise not to fire me before then, and I'll make you a book with all my reports in it for Christmas."

40

————

Luther took care of a couple of things first, but he had every intention of returning to the Sheriff's Department as Grant had suggested. But when he climbed into his vehicle, a piece of folded paper jabbed him in the crease of his hip. Luther tugged it from his pocket.

It was the printed photograph from the cabin scene. He hadn't had a chance to look at it yet, so he held it toward the car windshield for better light. There were no words visible on the candy wrapper, or at least none he could see. Luther pulled a magnifying glass from the glovebox. The photo's resolution wasn't great, thanks to the zoom, but he could make out some small symbols around the margins, possibly some kind of foreign writing. A white pinwheel shape dominated the small, dark green wrapper.

Luther's breath caught in his throat. *It can't be.*

He launched himself from the SUV and ran across the parking lot, back into the Command Center. Someone greeted him in the kitchen, but Luther ignored her, rushing to the stairs. He was breathing hard by the time he clomped his way to the top in his heavy boots, around the corner and into the map room.

Three men wearing hunting fatigues crowded around the

maps on the wall in back, but Luther wasn't interested in the maps. He grabbed the trashcan from the corner, carried it to an unoccupied table, and dumped its contents on top. A few sheets of crumpled paper drew his eye with their brightness, while mostly empty coffee cups dribbled dark, viscous liquid—some coffee, some tobacco spit—on the table's surface. There were empty chip bags, some paper towels, cellophane-looking candy wrappers... and there it was. A dark green wrapper, pinched around the sticky piece of hard candy Les had nearly choked on. Luther rotated his hand and saw the pinwheel shape on the bottom of the wrapper.

Luther put a hand on the table to steady himself. *Jesus, Les, what have you gotten yourself into this time?* There had to be an explanation.

"Hey!" he yelled at the group of men in the corner. "Has anybody seen Les Beck?"

A short, round man in a NASCAR hat said, "Yeah. He went storming out of here a while ago, looking pissed."

Grant must have sent him packing already because of Dorothy. "He say where he was going?" Luther asked.

"No. You gonna leave that shit on the table?" Luther didn't speak, but he didn't have to. The man raised placating hands. "Hey, just asking."

Luther's heart hammered as he ran back down the stairs, bypassing all the law enforcement personnel and heading straight to the kitchen, to the woman who'd greeted him earlier. "You seen Grant?" he asked.

She shook her head. "He took off, maybe fifteen minutes ago."

Shit. Luther pulled his cellphone out as he walked through the parking lot. Grant's phone went straight to voicemail, and Luther didn't leave a message. He was probably on his way to Harlan Miller's to see Adam. There wasn't any cell reception out that way, but Luther might be able to raise the Sheriff on his radio. The question was, did he want to?

Leslie's phone went straight to voicemail as well. Luther slammed his hand on the hood of the vehicle and listened to the metallic thump echo through the parking lot while the numbness spread across his palm.

His brother hadn't been good for much lately, probably not since he'd hurt his back at work last year. But something about the kidnapping had galvanized Les, pulled him from the hole where he'd been sulking.

There had to be an explanation.

Luther had promised the Sheriff. But he'd also made promises to his mother, years before. He couldn't turn in his brother until he'd heard what he had to say.

41

JJ parked her car directly behind Iris's. Even this close to the cabin, the driveway had enough incline that JJ was careful to set the emergency brake and leave the car in gear.

"You ever met Harlan Miller?" Iris asked. She had a paper bag in her hand as she walked casually toward the front steps, definitely not a stranger.

"Maybe, when I was a kid," JJ said, sweeping her head around to take in the mixed forest that stopped just shy of the cabin. There were some clear patches in back, probably where they put in the well and septic. "Heard the stories from my mom. She said he was a crazy, old drunk. Dad seemed to think there was more to it than that, but he wouldn't give particulars."

A tall, striking man who looked a bit like an aging, punk rock lumberjack stepped out onto the front porch.

"They were both right," Iris said. "As is often the case." The sound of Iris's boots, slowly climbing the front steps while he waited, was somehow reassuring. She stepped into the man's arms and was lost in his flannel-limbed embrace long enough to make JJ uncomfortable.

The man's chin rested on Iris's head. He said, "You must be JJ. Adam is waiting inside."

It was warm in the little cabin—almost too warm. Adam sat at the kitchen table, and he gave JJ a small smile when she entered.

"Hey," he said. "Boots by the door."

JJ saluted and coaxed her footwear off without bothering to sit or untie the laces, mostly just to see if she could. The answer was, barely, as she put a steadying hand against the wall. Iris and Harlan followed JJ in, and Iris slipped her own short boots off with half the effort and twice the grace.

Iris crossed the room, seized Adam's head with her free hand, and kissed the top of his hair, lingering. If she spoke, JJ couldn't hear the words. Then she set the sack on the table and turned toward Harlan. "Think we could get some fresh coffee?"

Harlan went to the stove, moving a kettle from its burner just as it began to whistle. "Already on it."

JJ hovered, unsure where she belonged. When Iris sat directly across from Adam, JJ went to the kitchen instead. "Can I help you with something?" she asked Harlan.

He looked over his shoulder at JJ, then at Iris and her grandson staring each other down at the table. "Chicken," he said, grinning. "You'll find a tray on that shelf. Load it up with some small plates and mugs, maybe even some napkins if you're feeling fancy."

JJ did as he suggested and carried the tray in, and Harlan followed shortly after with the percolator. Once they settled, Iris asked, "What do you want to know?"

"Adam says the first dream he recalls was at your house, and Old Sheriff Mason was there," Harlan began. "What can you tell us about it?"

Iris blew out her breath. "Not much. I remember it—obviously. Adam was very upset, but he didn't say much that seemed coherent at the time. We just figured it was a nightmare."

"Is that why you sent me away? Because of the dreams?" Adam asked. His chin was tucked, making his eyes appear even more intense, peering from beneath his dark brows.

To Iris's credit, she didn't fidget, and, with the exception of a quick glance at Harlan, she didn't look away from her grandson. "People around here were scared, even more so after the girl went missing. Every time you did something like that... I could feel something in them change. Not everyone, but enough that I was afraid what would happen if you stayed."

"So why didn't you go with me?" Adam asked.

Iris worked her jaw back and forth, and JJ could feel her own eyes tearing up as the older woman clamped down to maintain control.

"We're here to find Rachel," JJ burst out, unsure whether she did it to save Iris's feelings or her own. After all, where was her own daughter right now? *With someone else.*

Adam hesitated, then turned his scrutiny on Harlan. "You think I have some kind of link with Rachel. Why can't I just use that? Reach out to her somehow?"

"Because this morning she almost killed you," Iris said.

JJ had to agree, but then she had been the one waiting, waiting, waiting for that magic breath to brush her face, without ever feeling it. She shivered.

"She's just a child," Adam said.

"That's true," Harlan cut in, "but just because you're on the verge of your first gray hairs doesn't mean we're ready to trade you in yet. Besides, as of now, this isn't exactly a two-way radio you've got going on here. Even if you can initiate the connection, what do you propose to do with it? Maybe there's something in what you've already seen—"

"Grant tried that already," Adam said.

"The Sheriff knows about this?" Harlan asked, looking perturbed for the first time.

Adam nodded. "I don't think he sees me as a suspect, but he might think I'm crazy."

"He hasn't tried to commit you yet," JJ said.

Adam smiled an acknowledgment. "Small miracles. He's probably too busy."

"So what did you tell the Sheriff?" Harlan asked.

"That I saw Rachel get kidnapped, but I didn't see who did it. And that I saw when Sarah Edmunds was taken." Adam paused.

"And you remembered the details of that? From twenty years ago?"

"Yes, I did," Adam said.

"Why do you think that is?" Harlan asked.

JJ felt as though the distance between Adam and Iris suddenly shrank to nothing, and that she and Harlan had fallen away, that neither Iris nor Adam knew they were there.

"Because you told me you dreamed about Sarah Edmunds," Iris said. "That's why you remembered it."

She and Adam had both gone pale, but Iris's face seemed to disappear against her long, white hair—ethereal—while his features stood out all the more, a dark-haired corpse, freshly slain.

"I didn't think it was real—" she began.

"You didn't think it was real?" Adam yelled, his features contorted in disbelief. "How does a kid make something like that up? Twice? With Sarah, and with Danny?"

"People don't just *see things*..." Iris said.

JJ glanced at Harlan, but he kept his eyes on his coffee.

"Losing your parents when you were so young—and then Danny—it was enough to traumatize anyone. I told you, we just thought you were having nightmares."

"What if someone had listened to me?"

"I did listen!" Iris slammed a fist on the table. "I listened to every word you ever said in that house, any time of day or night." She let out a deep breath and finally admitted, "I just didn't want to believe you."

Adam stared down at his hands, rubbing one knuckle over and over like a genie's lamp. Iris watched him, and waited. JJ recognized that kind of waiting, when you're hoping your child will figure out something on her own (*Dad's not coming back, is he?*), but you're ready to tell her if you have to. Because it's too important to go unspoken.

"The night I had the dream when the Sheriff was there, that's when Danny was killed, wasn't it? Is that what I said then?"

A tear spilled from Iris's eye. "Yes."

Adam nodded, seemingly to himself. He gave a little shiver, then rubbed his legs, still covered in thin hospital scrubs. "Harlan, you have any clothes I could borrow?"

Harlan looked him over, top to bottom. "I think I've got something that'll do. You might need a belt, though. We'll see."

Harlan was a big man. JJ could hear him padding around barefoot, down the hallway, into the bedroom in the back.

"So, Danny's dead," Adam said.

"That's what you said," Iris confirmed.

"What exactly did I say?" Adam asked.

"I don't know." Iris paused and leaned her head on her hands, elbows on the table. "The only thing I remember clearly is you screaming, 'Danny, no!'"

Harlan lumbered back to the table. "Left your clothes folded in the bathroom."

"Thanks," Adam said.

He stood to change, then sat back down abruptly and stared across the table at JJ.

What had Iris said that was significant? *Danny, no...*

JJ's eyes widened. What if Iris had misheard her distressed grandson twenty years ago? Adam's brows drew together, and his head dipped, almost as if he were giving JJ a nudge. He needed JJ to ask the question he couldn't. She didn't know why—she had a feeling she was still a step behind him—but it didn't matter.

"Iris," JJ said, "could Adam have said, *Daddy,* no?"

42

Adam watched Iris lift her gray head, confused. "It's possible that's what he said, but it doesn't make sense."

Harlan stiffened next to Iris, then volunteered, somewhere between a question and a statement, "That's what Adam heard Rachel say. *Daddy*, don't hurt me."

"But we pretty much decided Rachel wasn't referring to Otto," JJ said. "And Leslie's our age, so even if Rachel meant Les, obviously he didn't father Danny. What ever happened to Danny's dad?"

"You might remember, Danny's parents didn't have the best marriage, even before he disappeared," Iris said. "Mrs. Carpenter left her husband to live with her family, and Danny's father moved away not long after that. I think he ended up in Maryland, but I wouldn't swear to it."

"Did he leave before or after Sarah Edmunds was kidnapped?" JJ asked.

Adam didn't hear Iris's reply. He was recalling the camping trip twenty years ago, when everything changed. He almost hadn't gone. After all, it was the Cub Scouts, so JJ couldn't go. But Danny convinced him they'd have fun, even without her. Adam had told Iris about it, and said he didn't need a tent, but a sleeping bag would be good. Iris never said, but he always knew money was tight for them, and he saw the worried look cross her face. It was gone as quickly as it had come—that's the way Iris was—but Adam had gotten good at reading her. He never blinked when he told her something important, so he wouldn't miss her split second of response.

No problem, Iris had said, and he'd known she'd check the secondhand shop in Plattsville. So long as the sleeping bag wasn't pink, he'd be happy with whatever she got.

And then, a couple of days before the trip, she'd come home with a surprise... a Batman sleeping bag that appeared suspiciously new. Adam had been so thrilled, he hadn't questioned it. And yet, on some level a part of him had. But not out loud.

"Iris," he began, his ribs twinging as he forced out his voice. Everyone waited quietly for him to continue. "Where did the sleeping bag come from?"

Her brows wrinkled, puzzled. And then they cleared and Iris went pale with shock—her face, her lips, all the way down to the gums flashing from her open mouth.

"Oh, dear God," she said.

Yes.

"Adam?" JJ asked. "What's going on?"

Adam looked at Harlan, whose face grew ashen beneath its tan. The man had either intuited or deliberated his way to the same place.

So Adam told his story.

∼

"And that's *why they call it* Dead Hollow."

The groans of a dozen or so disappointed boys rumbled through the cool, night air.

"Dude, that wasn't even scary. You gotta have a hook if you want it to be scary," Leslie said, demonstrating with a curled finger.

The boys had gathered in a ring around the campfire, most with their hands around tucked knees. The camaraderie, the crackling hot barrier, and the presence of adults combined to make Shawn, the smallest boy in the fifth grade, unusually brave.

"I don't know, Leslie," he said. "You looked pretty scared to me. Adam, you want to check his pants?"

Adam, sitting next to Leslie, grinned but didn't take the bait. The idea of "haunts in the holler" wouldn't keep him awake tonight, but sleeping a few feet away from an angry Leslie would. He glanced to his right and saw Les already planning his revenge against the younger boy. If he were Shawn, he'd stick close to the troop leaders until the moment his mom picked him up tomorrow.

"All right, guys. Time to turn in," Chad Henderson's dad said, watching Les.

Adam was glad Mr. Henderson was one of the leaders for this trip. Obviously he knew which direction trouble would be coming from.

"Last chance on tents," Mr. H continued. "Danny-Adam-Leslie-Frank-Joey—any takers?"

The boys all declined. They tried to pretend like they hadn't brought tents because they were tough, but everyone knew it was because they couldn't afford them. No one really cared—most of the boys that had equipment had gotten it hand-me-down or secondhand. Still, the tentless boys had their pride, and since it was a clear night, Mr. H had said they could go without.

"Don't be waking me up when you get cold and wet," Jeremy's dad said. He tried to make it sound like a joke, but everyone knew it wasn't. Jeremy's dad was a dork, and no one could figure out why he went on the trips.

"Okay, then. Tarps and rope are over here if you get desperate in the middle of the night. Where's my Campfire Team Three?" Mr. Henderson asked. "Let's put this puppy out and get some shut-eye."

Danny and Adam walked over to the patch they'd claimed at the edge of the clearing. "Did you see the look Leslie gave Shawn?" Danny whispered.

"See it—I could feel it sitting next to him," Adam said.

Their friend Frank was struggling to get in his sleeping bag. The Scout leaders were still sifting through the ashes with Group Three, so Danny took a chance and swatted the back of Frank's head as he passed. Frank grunted and toppled over on his side, and all three boys snickered.

"What do you want to bet Les accidentally kicks Shawn in the nuts tomorrow on the hike back?" Danny asked. He kept his voice low, even though Leslie was on the other side of Frank and would need superpowers to hear him.

"I don't want to bet anything," Adam said. He'd enjoyed the trip so far, but he was secretly tired. He wasn't about to admit to it, though, or Danny would say he was a wimp. If Danny had his way, they'd be awake all night.

"How about that fancy new sleeping bag? You want to bet that?" Danny asked.

"No!" Adam said, too loud. His voice carried across the now nearly dark campsite.

"Boys, do I need to separate you?" Jeremy's dad called out.

"No, sir," Adam said, and Mr. Dork turned off the last lantern. Adam made a face at him, and at Danny, in the dark.

They'd put their sleeping bags on tarps on the ground, and the plastic crackled as Adam snuggled in. The smell of fabric softener overwhelmed the odor from the extinguished campfire and the ever-present hint of pine. It made him think of Iris. If she was a camp leader, they'd have had hot chocolate. And not from a packet, either. Adam smiled and drifted off to sleep.

Adam awoke with the moon up and the clearing almost bright. He couldn't say what had roused him. He lifted his head and looked around at the other sleeping bags and the three tents, all approximately the same color in the moonlight. He smiled and looked down at his legs. There was still no mistaking the shape of the Batman symbol against its yellow beacon in the dark. Except from this angle—upside down—it looked strangely like a baby's open mouth with a few teeth.

There was a sound coming from the other side of the campsite. He scooted to a sitting position and squinted, then opened his eyes as wide as he could. He saw a shape, a person standing at the edge of the trees.

"Adam..."

It didn't seem as if the voice had come from the person-shape, but it must have. There was no one else awake.

Adam knew he should be scared, but he wasn't. He crawled out of his sleeping bag, cringing at the sound of the tarp crackling beneath him, and slowly crossed the campsite. Frank made some kind of sinus-cacking sound in his sleep as Adam stepped past him, and there were actual snores coming from the big tent.

The figure moved a few feet into the woods now, but still waited for him, beckoning with a pale hand.

With her hand.

Adam reached up to touch the chain at his neck.

He knew it was crazy, but he could swear that was his mother waiting for him. Adam sped up, trying to catch her, and nearly tripped over one of the tent lines.

"Wait!" he whispered.

But she kept gliding into the woods, keeping the same distance no matter how fast he moved. And he did move fast—faster than he should have been able to—under the leafy canopy. The trees blocked most of the moonlight, but he ran anyway, dodging branches and tree trunks before he'd even seen them. Down one slope and up the next rise, where the bottom, damp layer of leaf litter slid beneath his feet until he was scrambling with his hands.

Adam was panting now, and he stopped to catch his breath. Where is she? Was that her, up ahead, where the light seemed just a little bit brighter?

"Mom?"

He listened to his voice echo.

But there was no answer.

And it was dark.

Adam had no idea where he was, or where camp was. And now, he was scared. He sat down, back against a scratchy tree trunk, and started to cry. Not because he was scared. Because he'd just wanted to see his mom, one more time. His only memory of what she looked like was imprinted from the photo that sat next to his bed.

"Adam..."

He jumped up from the ground, but this time when he heard the voice, he didn't see anyone or anything nearby.

Until the flashes.

They flickered through the trees in the distance, far below him, and then he saw solid lights. He thought he heard shouting. It must be camp. They must have figured out he was missing and gotten worried.

Adam let out a sigh of relief and wiped his eyes. He didn't want anyone to know he'd been crying. It's not like he could tell them why. In fact, he'd need a story to explain his absence. One of the kids in his class said his dad sleepwalked out into their yard once. Adam wasn't sure anyone had really believed him, though, so no sleepwalking. He'd just say he'd gone to use the bathroom and gotten lost. If they asked for more, he could always say he'd seen a fox and followed it. That was almost believable.

It seemed to take forever to make his way back, but it probably wasn't more than ten minutes. The lights from camp were a guide, a target, but they didn't help him see where he was going. If anything, they made it harder to see. So he walked slowly, keeping his eyes toward the ground to help preserve his night vision, and hopefully keep his eyes intact if he ran into a branch.

It occurred to Adam that he'd be in big trouble for wandering off and waking everyone up. He was surprised he hadn't run into any searchers yet. When he'd almost reached the circle cast by the camp lanterns, he called out, "I'm here!"

Lights flashed in his face, blinding him. A man came rushing at him before he had a chance to speak—Jeremy's dad—and grabbed him, physically picking Adam up as if he were a little kid and carrying him into the center of camp. The boys were all sitting on the ground, huddled together in a pile against the cold.

"It's Adam!" Jeremy's dad yelled, before setting him down and running his hands over his arms. "Are you okay? Did he hurt you?"

Adam tried to pull away, but Jeremy's dad wouldn't let him. "Let go! I just had to pee—"

"Adam, hold still." Jeremy's dad looked over his shoulder as Adam squirmed. "Is Jim still gone?"

"Yeah. We never should have let him go out there alone," said the other

leader. He was the new kid's dad, and Adam couldn't remember either of their names. The new kid's dad grabbed Adam's free arm and demanded, "Where is he?"

"Who?" Adam asked.

"Where's Danny?"

43

A hush fell over the room.

Everyone in Cold Springs had assumed Danny's kidnapping was a crime of opportunity. After all, it was no secret that the Scouts were having their annual trip, with flyers and reminders scattered all over town. Danny just happened to be lying farthest from the center of the camp... *after Adam left to chase a ghost*. Adam had always felt guilty because his friend was taken from the spot he should have been occupying. But it was worse than that.

He gently asked, "Who gave you the sleeping bag, Iris? It was my father, wasn't it?"

Iris's shoulders convulsed once, then she took a deep breath and lifted her eyes to meet his. "Yes."

Adam's voice remained calm and even. "He gave it to you for me, so he could tell which one I was in the dark, with that black symbol against the bright yellow. Dad kidnapped Danny."

It couldn't have been easy, but Iris matched his calm. "Yes, I suppose he did."

Adam nodded. "I'm going to change clothes now," he said, and left the table.

Harlan had left garments stacked on the edge of the bathroom sink, including a pair of boxers on top. Adam told himself Harlan had intuited rather than observed he was going commando in the scrubs. *Back in Beecham County less than twenty-four hours, and I'm already reduced to wearing another man's underwear.*

Placing his hands on the vanity, Adam let his weight drop forward, slowly intensifying the pain in his ribs and chest. He welcomed the sensation; it helped cut through a vague numbness that spread through his body and mind.

Getting the scrubs off was relatively easy, but pulling new bottoms on required Adam to sit on the toilet. At least the jeans were a little big, or he'd have had to call for assistance. He got them up as far as his knees and paused, resting a moment.

Adam's mind wandered back to Danny, the kind of child he'd been, the kind of children they'd all been. No one in Beecham County had much in the way of material things, but none of the three of them had a complete, functional family, either. They avoided Danny's house because his parents were always yelling. JJ's mom and brother had left when she was eight, so it was just her and her dad. And Adam had lost both parents—he'd thought—and only had Iris.

JJ had said earlier that Danny was a troublemaker, but Danny was more a prankster, though he could sometimes be a bit of a sneak as well. And Danny had coveted his sleeping bag.

Adam braced an arm against the sink to help him rise. *Jesus*, the pain in his abs. He was glad no one could hear the whimper that escaped him. Zipped up, he gingerly pushed his arms through the sleeves of a lined flannel shirt, emerging from the bathroom in time to hear JJ finish his own train of thought aloud.

"So when Adam left camp that night," she said, "Danny got in Adam's sleeping bag. Either thinking he'd scare Adam when he returned, or that he'd pretend to be asleep and make Adam spend the night in his empty sleeping bag instead."

Iris's head rested in her hands, and Adam wasn't sure if she was listening. Harlan responded, "Sounds reasonable. Danny burrows down out of sight, pulls the bag over his head. Virgil comes to get Adam, grabs the bag with the boy in it, none the wiser until... who knows when."

Danny's muffled cries had roused the camp, albeit not quickly enough. Would they have been recognizable to anyone? Had Danny screamed words, or just terrified sounds? He'd never thought to ask. Adam stood, gripping the back of his chair for support. "He knew he had the wrong boy when he killed him."

Iris's head jerked up. "We don't know Virgil killed Danny."

"Yes, Iris," Adam said, "yes, we do. *I* do. Remember, I saw it happen." He winced as he sat back down in his chair. "I thought dad was dead."

"So did I," Iris said.

It was too much for Adam.

"Not when he brought you a fricking sleeping bag, you didn't!" Adam spit on the table as he shouted.

"Adam," Harlan warned, but Iris touched the older man's arm.

"That was the first time I'd seen him since your mother died," she said. "You have to understand, your father always had... issues."

"You mean he was crazy," Adam said. "Don't look so surprised. You never talked about him—it seemed like nobody ever talked about him—but I guess somebody did, because I always knew."

Iris twisted her hands on the table. "I hate that word—*crazy*. For some reason, when we say it, it sounds like a value judgment, like it's the person's fault. But your father couldn't help it. He was a diagnosed schizophrenic."

Adam's eyes widened.

Iris nodded. "See. Don't be so sure you know everything, either. Charlotte was the best thing that ever happened to him, but even your mother couldn't fix what was wrong. And then when she died, that broke Virgil, and he disappeared. Once I thought I saw him watching us when we visited your mother's grave, but I convinced myself I was mistaken."

"So he just abandoned me," Adam said.

Iris ripped her hands apart and laid them flat on the table.

"What do you not understand about, *the man was broken?*" She pushed Harlan away as he reached for her. "But as broken as he was, as confused as he was, I can't believe that my son would ever willingly hurt a child."

"What about Adam?" JJ asked, pointedly. "You said you thought he was having nightmares, but whatever they were, in them he was begging his father not to hurt him."

Iris rose in her seat and leaned over the table at JJ. "Virgil *never* harmed Adam. Never."

Harlan stretched a long, restraining arm toward JJ as she stood. "Hey! Everybody just take it easy. Ladies, sit."

The two women stared at one another, nostrils flared. Harlan's muttered words about *women* and *pissing contests* rolled over Adam as he tried to recall... he had very few memories of his father, and certainly none of being abused by him. And yet something hovered on the edge of his memory that filled him with uneasiness, like an inexplicable shadow in his peripheral vision.

Movement around the table—Iris and JJ returning to their seats—helped Adam focus again on Harlan's words.

"Thank you," Harlan said, eyes on Iris. "You know, JJ's on to something. Even if Adam had no reason to be afraid of Virgil, that's not true for the children Virgil kidnapped. Adam would have felt their fear. So what if Adam was speaking *through* Danny and Sarah, not just hearing them? He recognized his father, and spoke through the other children, using their voices."

"Daddy, don't hurt me," Adam whispered.

"And Rachel," JJ said. "Danny and Sarah *and* Rachel said that. So Virgil took Rachel."

Had his father taken the girl? And if so, why? Adam struggled to find some coherent rationale that could explain such a chain of events. He wasn't alone.

"Oh, this is ridiculous," Iris said, and stormed out of the room.

"We need to tell Grant," JJ said.

Adam's eyes shot at her.

"Adam, he already knows about your dreams, so it won't sound that crazy."

"Even if we're right," Adam said, "how does knowing that Virgil may be involved help Grant find Rachel? If everyone thought the man was dead, how will that give Grant any leads?"

"I don't know," JJ admitted, "but it might."

"JJ's right," Harlan said. "It'll probably be easiest to head down to Jim's, see if we can raise the Sheriff on his phone. But first, I need a minute with Iris."

Soon, Adam heard the bedroom door close behind Harlan. Without planning to, Adam and JJ simultaneously scooted their chairs back and rested their foreheads on the table, like they had when they were kids. It was the three of them back then, peering at made-up worlds that teemed with sharks or alligators below, while they rested their feet on the safety of the chair crossbars.

"All that time we looked for him…" Adam said.

"I know." JJ took his hand in hers.

Adam squeezed an acknowledgment, then got up from the table and crossed to the front door, gazing out at the deepening darkness. He grabbed a jacket from a hook, stepped into his slippers and said, "I'm gonna get a little air," before closing the door behind him.

44

———

He'd just gotten into position, nestling down in the bed of pine needles, when Adam stepped out onto the front porch. Adam wore proper pants now, but he still had slippers on his feet and walked like a cripple.

It almost didn't seem fair.

He watched as Adam picked his way to the parked cars and looked up at the sky. He wondered if Adam knew his constellations. Did the Scout leaders teach kids that? Not that it mattered now. It was too early to see anything but the brightest planet, and cloud shapes were building on the horizon. Still, there might be decent visibility later. Who could say?

Maybe he should take Adam now.

It wasn't the way he'd planned it—not that he was a slave to planning—but Adam was *right there*. It was almost too perfect.

Except Adam was only a piece. The most important piece, but he still needed the other pieces to line up. He watched a shadow move across the cabin door and stand in front of it. It would be JJ, of course. Because wherever young Adam had been, JJ had been there, too. And everything was coming full circle. Well, almost.

He lay motionless in the dark as Adam shuffled slowly down

the driveway, head down, closer and closer. He imagined he could smell Adam—not the stink of body odor, but the distinctive aroma humans begin to emanate after sufficient exposure to the cold. Yes, he had a plan, but it was *so tantalizing*, after all these years of dreaming and making do with substitutes, to have Adam *so close*.

He wondered if Adam was a restless sleeper, prone to getting up in the middle of the night and wandering outside. That would be even better. And it wasn't that cold; he could wait, for hours if need be.

Normally a decisive man, he realized he was enjoying his moment of indecisiveness, even wallowing in it. *Enough*. It might be better to take Adam later, when everyone else was asleep, but he was here *right now*. And how long would it be before anyone started looking for him? He smiled. If it was a fraction as long as it had taken them to look for Rachel, he'd have plenty of time. Plenty of time...

Wait—what was Adam doing? It appeared the man was trying to lie down on the ground, as if he'd given up entirely. *Yes*. The universe had spoken. It was time to take Adam. *Now*.

45

———

Adam wanted to stand in the dark, disconnected from everything and everyone, until he couldn't stand anymore. That wouldn't take long, as unsteady as his legs felt. Perhaps he should lie down instead, although he may never get up again.

He slowly lowered himself to one knee. The driveway was cold, and tiny rocks pressed through his jeans. Adam painfully brought his upright knee to join the other one on the ground, and, legs tight, sat on his heels.

Adam wanted so desperately to not think, to not *be*. But then where would that leave Rachel? *Where is she—*

There was a rustle in the trees, and something moved off to Adam's left. It stopped, but as he stared into the trees—*what is that shadow?*—he heard another sound. A car engine. Headlights approached in the distance, disappearing briefly, only to orient toward him when they reappeared. The car had turned below, onto Harlan's driveway.

Adam grimaced as he stood. Staring at the headlights had dampened his night vision, and he couldn't tell where he'd seen... whatever he'd seen a moment ago. It didn't matter. The vehicle came rocketing up the driveway, lights bouncing. Remembering the scars on the trees, Adam tramped quickly into the woods out of its way, leaving a slipper behind.

The vehicle was a car, not a pickup. It passed so quickly in the dark, Adam couldn't see much more. Brake lights shone like dim, red beacons through the trees as the car stopped in front of the cabin. Adam meant to follow, but first he had to find his slipper.

It was so dark beneath the canopy that Adam had to concentrate to make out the tree trunks at eye level in front of him, much less anything on the forest floor. *Crap.* He rotated slowly in a circle, his cold, naked foot on its tiptoes, looking for anything unusual. Finally, he glimpsed a lighter spot next to a mass of mountain laurel. Adam bent painfully and ran his hands around until he felt the soft shoe, matted with twigs.

Adam shook the slipper off and—

He heard something behind him. Again. A rustle. Long gone were the days when he could identify any shape or sound in the woods, but something was there. Adam jammed the slipper on his foot and stepped back out on the driveway in time to see the vehicle's headlights switching off at the house.

Adam trotted uphill, ribs and chest complaining. He paused halfway, sipping air into his aching lungs and tried to listen over the sound of his own wheezing. Whatever was in the woods, it was still there, moving parallel to Adam, rustling just inside the trees.

I'm being stalked.

Adam quick-stepped up the drive toward the vehicle. It was a Sheriff's Department cruiser, and Grant was just mounting the steps.

"Sheriff!" he called out.

Grant turned, hand on his holster, and slowly made his way down the steps. His other hand reached for a flashlight, and Adam was suddenly blinded, so much so that he didn't see Harlan open the front door and step out onto the porch.

"Adam?" Grant asked. "What are you doing?"

Adam was too winded to speak. When he got close enough, he simply pointed toward the woods behind him.

Grant unholstered his weapon, adjusting his grip on the flashlight to handle both objects at once. He waited until Adam passed behind him to ask, "What's going on?"

"Something out there," Adam panted. "Something big."

"Like a deer?" Grant asked, lowering his weapon.

"No. It was following me."

"Could be a bear," Harlan's voice called from the top of the steps. "Woods are thick with them lately."

"Mr. Miller, sir," Grant said. He removed his uniform hat as he climbed the front steps, then waved it toward Adam. "I was hoping I might find Mr. Rutledge here."

"Both of you, come on in out of the cold, before our friend decides he's hungry," Harlan said, ignoring the hand Grant held out, and added automatically, "Leave your shoes by the door."

Grant meticulously unlaced a pair of boots, while Adam shucked off his jacket and slippers and headed back to his prior seat. Concentrating on getting his breathing under control again, Adam noticed JJ staring at Grant, and Grant avoiding staring at JJ.

Finally, Grant stood, shoeless, glanced at JJ and said, "Can't say I'm surprised to see you here."

"Cup of coffee, Sheriff?" Iris asked.

"I'm afraid I can't stay," Grant said.

"Then you can drink it while you're standing," Iris said, back to her imperious self, and poured him a mug anyway.

"Thank you, ma'am." Grant took a sip before placing the beverage back on the table. "Please, don't let me disturb you. This won't take but a minute."

Grant pulled a digital camera from his coat pocket and started pushing buttons. "I was hoping you could take a look at something for me," he said, handing the camera to Adam. The back had a big view screen to preview photos. "Do these mean anything to you?"

Adam scrolled through dark shots of a rustic interior thick with dust and dirt and years of neglect. "How do I zoom?"

Grant demonstrated and Adam slowly went through the photos again, enlarging a bench here, a scrap of debris there. "Sorry," Adam said. "I don't recognize it."

"Would you?" Grant asked.

Although Adam hadn't seen the cabin from his dreams in person, he'd had enough recall tucked away somewhere to make the connection between Rachel and Sarah before.

"Yes, I think I'd know if it was the place I saw. And there's nothing."

Grant took the camera back and turned it off. "Okay," he said, tucking it into his coat pocket.

"Is that where the van was seen?" JJ asked.

"Yes," Grant said. No doubt half the county had already heard about the search, so he wasn't letting them in on any secrets.

"Sheriff, your trip wasn't entirely wasted," Harlan said. "I was about to call you with some information, someone you may want to add to your list of suspects."

Adam waited, anxious to see how they were going to play this. JJ's expression suggested she wondered the same, so Harlan and Iris must have decided without her.

"I've been speaking with Iris, and we believe her son Virgil Rutledge could be involved," Harlan said.

"Really? You and Iris, huh?" Grant asked. He pursed his lips, but didn't seem particularly surprised. A little angry, but not surprised. Grant let out a breath and stared down at his socked feet on the floor. Then he caught Adam's eye. "Did you see something else?" he asked.

"Sheriff—" Iris began, but Grant held up a hand, interrupting her.

"Adam?" Grant asked.

"Nothing new. But we've found some... commonalities, in the things I saw before. With Danny, and Sarah Edmunds, and Rachel. And it's possible Virgil Rutledge is still alive." Adam couldn't bring himself to call Virgil his father.

Once again, Grant didn't seem all that surprised. Maybe he hid it well, or maybe Grant knew things he wasn't telling them. "Okay," he said. "I'll see what I can find on Mr. Rutledge. Any thoughts on where he might take Rachel, if he has her?"

Adam had no idea. Presumably JJ didn't either. Iris tugged at her lip until Adam thought she'd pull it off. Finally, Harlan said, "I'm sorry, Sheriff. We were just getting to that part. But do you mind showing me where that cabin was?"

Harlan led Grant to a desk in the corner of the living room and raised the wooden top. "Maps are a hobby of mine," Harlan said, shuffling through the stacked, heavy paper within until he found the one he was looking for.

The two men bent over the desk, mumbling and pointing until they were in agreement. Adam stayed where he was, one hand straying to his chest to feel the imprint of his mother's key beneath his shirt.

The Sheriff finally headed back toward the door, JJ's eyes following. "Sir, do you have a phone out here?" Grant asked.

"Afraid not. No cell reception, and I never paid for them to string a landline in. But if we come up with anything, we'll call you from my neighbor's. And if you need to reach us—" Harlan wandered back over to his desk and scribbled on a sheet of paper. "Jim Henderson's only half a mile down the road, and willing to drive out if need be."

Grant put his hat back on as he headed out the door. Seemed silly, since he'd just have to take it off again when he got to the car. Adam rubbed the key some more, then realized JJ was watching him. With Grant gone, Adam supposed she had to have something to look at.

"How are those ribs?" JJ asked.

Adam had a flash of her pushing the key aside to put her hands on his chest and beat the life back into him.

"Adam!" Harlan's voice cut through his morbid thoughts. "Where we at, son?"

He wished he knew, or rather, he knew too well. Where they

were at was sitting around, the final hours and minutes of the evening slipping away. And so was Rachel.

Harlan had said Adam had a link to Rachel, that Adam could save her. Adam didn't know if that was true or not, but it was time he tried.

"I'm sorry," he said. "My chest hurts, I'm exhausted, and I need to lie down for a while."

Everyone stood.

"Alone," Adam said, pointedly.

The guest room was simply furnished, like the rest of the house, with an emphasis on rich, natural wood. Rust-colored curtains picked up one of the shades from the bedside rug, and along with the warm light from a lamp on the nightstand, helped the room look inviting. The full size bed was made up already, with a heavy quilt to combat the evening chill. Harlan had left a pair of gray sweats on top for Adam to sleep in, but for now he didn't bother, just stretched out on top of the bed in jeans.

After his discussions with Harlan, Adam wasn't sure he needed to be fully asleep to connect with Rachel. Alone and relaxed was a good start. He lay still, and the bedroom's cool air caressed his cheeks and made them feel flushed. Adam tasted woodsmoke as he breathed just enough to satisfy his body's needs and no more, and realized his chest *did* hurt. He *was* exhausted. And sleep wasn't as far away as he'd thought...

SHE RUBBED *the rope against the sharp edge, where the leg met the furniture frame. Except the binding on her leg wasn't really a rope like her dad used, but rather twisted strands of fabric that stretched slightly when she pulled. She thought she'd almost worn through the next to last section and she had to hurry—she didn't know how long the man would be gone.*

Suddenly she was swamped by a wave of tummy-sick dizziness, so bad that her hand slipped and she cut her finger in the dark. It wasn't serious, but it hurt. She whimpered, just a little.

But before she could really start crying, she realized, someone else is here. *The man hadn't come back yet, but the Other One was with her somehow. And she felt a little less alone.*

So she went back to scraping the rope against the metal, until her hands suddenly jerked back as the strand snapped free. Just one more to go… And then what? Where would she go? She didn't even know—

~

ADAM ROLLED over and made it to the edge of the bed, just in time to vomit into a waiting trashcan.

He retched again before recovering enough to lift his head and see Harlan, holding the trashcan and scowling.

"You stupid, sneaky sonuvabitch," Harlan fumed. "Don't bother trying to bullshit a bullshitter. I know this didn't just happen. You didn't just fall into the girl's head by accident; you did it on purpose."

Adam couldn't have answered if he'd wanted to, retching once more before sinking onto the bed, ribs in agony.

"I won't tell Iris and JJ—in fact, I'll even help you—if you answer two questions for me," Harlan continued.

"Okay," Adam groaned.

"First, did you see anything that will help us with a location?"

Adam nearly threw up again when he shook his head. "Too dark," he said. "But she's alone, and she's trying to escape."

Harlan blew out his breath. "At least we know she's still alive."

"Second question," Adam prompted.

"Second question," Harlan said, but took a moment, as if he were gathering his thoughts. "What the hell did you do to your finger?"

Adam lifted his right hand. It was shaking, and he watched as blood trickled down his index finger toward his palm.

46

L uther shifted in the driver's seat and wondered if the department vehicle's suspension needed work. It was relatively new, but took a beating on the rural roads. More likely, he was the one that was worn out.

He'd spent most of the day looking for Les, checking everywhere his brother might have gone: Les's trailer, his friends, all the local bars and hangouts. Nothing. The only place he hadn't checked was their father's house, but Luther figured Pop was the last person Les would want to talk to right now. The man had a gift for cruelty, especially when it came to belittling his youngest son.

Luther had also checked the convenience stores and anywhere else he could think of, but no one local sold the green-wrapped candy. He knew it was time to tell Grant, but he still hadn't been able to reach him on his cellphone. And while he trusted the Sheriff's discretion, Luther feared someone might overhear them speaking on the radio. It wouldn't do to have Les picked up by some over-eager law enforcement officer, looking to make a name for himself.

He'd even dropped by the Command Center again, but only gotten more bad news for his trouble. People were already gossiping about why Les was gone, and someone—no doubt someone looking to settle a score—had mentioned that he'd once seen Les watching Rachel. Of course, Luther was getting his information second- or third-hand; no one would admit to either being the source or believing it.

Musing over where his brother might have gone, Luther had realized Les could be angry with Dorothy for two reasons. One, her confession to JJ had set a sequence of events in motion that led to Les's humiliation when he was removed from the search team, and might lead to his prosecution for rape. Two... well, the second possibility didn't bear thinking about. That Dorothy's confession had put Les under suspicion for a crime he had actually committed—that Les had kidnapped Rachel.

The deputy didn't believe that, but he did believe his brother was vindictive, and he knew they shared a nasty temper. That's why Luther had spent the past four hours parked on the road across from the Nicholson driveway. He'd eaten and drunk everything he could scrounge from the vehicle, as well as peeing twice in the woods, but he hadn't seen anyone coming or going from the Nicholson property. He hadn't seen anyone around JJ's either, so she must still be out and about with Adam.

Luther pulled up the Nicholson driveway far enough to turn around. It was time to make one last run at his brother's place. If he couldn't find Les, he'd track down Grant in person and tell him what he'd found. He concentrated on the road, on his headlights, the dark asphalt and the walls of exposed rock, the guardrails and their black void, the tunnels of trees with branches like witches' fingers. Before his quick drive-by this afternoon, he hadn't been to his brother's place in a long time. Four months? Maybe more. He'd thought Les might have moved, though it seemed unlikely considering his recent state of inertia.

It was hard to see at night, but the trailer should be coming up soon. Les's neighbors were pretty sloppy with their kids' toys, and occasionally their livestock, so Luther slowed even more. Last thing he needed was a tricycle—or a goat—wrapped around the SUV's axle.

There it was, and so was Les.

Luther's headlights reflected off the white siding of Les's trailer and the dead taillights of his pickup. The hypnotic blue flashing of a TV screen was visible through the sheer curtains covering one window. Luther pulled up next to his brother's truck, and the porch light came on before he'd unclipped his seat belt. There was no proper porch, just some stacked cinder blocks. Les stepped down on them, wobbling a bit, and came out to meet Luther, probably hoping to talk through the window and keep Luther from going inside. Well, sinners in hell hoped for swimming pools.

Luther stepped out of his vehicle. "Where the shit have you been?" he asked.

"Out," his brother said. "What do you care?"

"You haven't been answering your phone, either."

Les shrugged, and his shoulders stayed close to his ears in the cold. "Battery's dead."

Luther looked around his brother's yard, not that he could see much of it in the dark. Cleared in front, forest in back. But he felt like something was missing. Then it hit him. "Where's your dog?"

"I sold him to Malcolm a few months back," Les said. "I wasn't around enough to use him, and Malcolm was happy to take him off my hands. You want to come in? Have a beer?"

No, I want to stand out here all night freezing my nuts off, waiting for you to show me a little hospitality. Luther slammed his door and listened to it echo. Sounds always seemed to echo more in the mountains when it got colder. "Yeah, that'd be good."

Inside, the trailer was illuminated only by a kitchen light and the TV, tuned to a football game, but from what Luther could see it was relatively clean. He moved a magazine from the couch to the coffee table (*thank God it's not porn*) and took a seat. The dark upholstery's texture was like a rough, cheap, wool sweater, so he rested his hands on his legs.

"Replay of the 'Skins game," Les said from the kitchen. "I ain't seen the news, so don't tell me who won."

"You want to talk about what happened at the Command Center?" Luther asked.

"What happened was the Sheriff's a pussy. His Federales masters said jump, and he shit-canned me. There's not much else to say." Les joined Luther on the couch, setting a couple of bottles of beer on the coffee table.

"Can you blame him?" Luther asked, popping the top off his beer.

"Hell, yes, I can blame him. What the fuck, Luther—has he got you under his thumb now, too?"

Luther reached for the remote and clicked the TV off.

"I'm trying to watch the damn ball game," Leslie said, indignant.

"Yeah, I must be under the man's thumb, because I can't imagine why he wouldn't want you searching for a little girl when you'd raped her mother." Luther's voice was thick with sarcasm.

Les threw his hands up. "Oh, so we're back on that bullshit again."

Luther pointed his finger at his brother. "You and I both know it's not bullshit, and I told you if I ever hear about it happening again—"

"What?" Les challenged.

Luther clenched his teeth, grinding them so hard a pain shot into his jaw. "Don't push me."

Les reached for the remote on the coffee table, but Luther snatched it first and threw it across the room to the sound of cracking plastic. Les opened his mouth, but didn't say anything.

Luther still held a beer in his other hand. The bottle vibrated slightly as he set it on the table, and his hand bumped against the tacky ashtray Les dumped his pockets in every night. A gift from their father, it was shaped like a large, naked, blonde woman, shallow in the center except for two large breasts standing at attention. Les's key ring was looped over one breast. The rest of the dish was filled with dirty change, his wallet, and a few pieces of hard candy with a familiar pinwheel on the wrapper. Luther picked up the ashtray, gave it a shake, and held it toward his brother. "Where'd you get the candy?"

"I don't know," Les said. "What are you, Weight Watchers?"

"Did you buy them?" Luther asked.

Leslie leaned in for a better look. "I don't think so. I don't buy much candy, except maybe Jolly Ranchers, and a chocolate bar once in a while."

"Did someone give it to you?"

"Hell, I don't know. I guess they must've."

"Who?"

Les's voice dropped. "I don't know."

Luther tilted his head and stared at his brother. "I don't believe you."

"I said, I don't know. Now leave me alone."

Luther lifted the ashtray and brought it down hard on the table. He felt the shock of the impact and the splintering force of ceramic shattering, heard the keys and change ricochet off the table as he screamed, "Don't lie to me!"

Les flinched, his face blanched and his eyes opened wide. His pupils looked large in the dim room. "Luther, you're bleeding."

Luther kept his gaze on his brother, unblinking. He didn't want to ask, didn't want to cross that bridge, but it couldn't be helped. He had to know for sure. "Did you take Rachel?"

"Did I—" Les stammered, then stopped. His face twisted in disgust, and he jumped up from the couch, banging his shins on the coffee table and knocking over the beer that had so far miraculously remained upright. "No! Hell, no! How could you even think such a thing?"

Luther breathed a sigh of relief, a sigh that almost transformed into a sob. He believed him. Sweet Jesus, he believed him.

"Luther, what the hell is going on?"

The deputy spared a glance at his hand. *What do you know? I am bleeding.* Blood had trickled from his fingers as far as his wrist. He moved his arm over the table just ahead of the first red drops. They slowly mixed with the beer splatters, smeary pink tendrils appearing around the edges. It felt as though the angry heat had gone out of him, alongside the blood dripping on the table. "Somebody said they saw you watching Rachel."

"I never!" Les said, face flushing. "I'm not a perv."

"And that kind of candy was found at a crime scene, at the cabin you searched this morning. Did you pick them up there?"

"I—" Les stopped, mouth gaping like a fish. "I don't think so. I'm pretty sure I didn't. But maybe. If I didn't buy them, they came from somewhere, and hell, I pick up shit all the time."

Luther considered. It strained credulity to think that even his brother was dumb enough to pick up discarded pieces of candy from a filthy cabin while searching for a kidnapped child. But it was just within the realm of possibility. Maybe he wasn't lying about the candy, or the lie wasn't relevant, it was just one of those compulsive untruths.

"I'll just throw the candy away."

"Dammit, Les, it's not that simple. If you got it from the cabin, it could be evidence. It might even have the asshole's fingerprints." Luther scanned the mess on the table, trying to find the pieces. Maybe they'd landed on the floor. "Little brother, did it ever occur to you there's a limit to how much shit I can bail you out of?"

"Pop says—"

"Pop is a dumbass. The man hasn't done an honest day of work in his life, and maybe if he'd got off his lazy ass once in a while, Momma'd still be alive."

If Luther expected his brother to argue with him, he was wrong. Instead, Les said, "I still miss her."

"So do I. Every day," Luther admitted. Maybe she could've told him what to do, how to get his brother out of the downward spiral that seemed to have caught hold of him. "Now, what are we going to do to find Rachel and keep you out of prison?"

47

The cabin was quiet. Harlan puttered around, doing JJ wasn't sure what, while Iris heated more soup. JJ and Adam sat on opposite ends of the sofa, staring at the black windows covered with condensation, each apparently lost in thought. JJ felt a twinge of guilt over Trooper. She'd fed him before she left, and he'd be fine in his doghouse for the night, but JJ hated leaving him tied out. She wished she'd asked Harlan how far she had to go to find a cell signal... down the driveway? The next county? Maybe his neighbor had reception. She'd like to call Evie, hear her voice right now.

The four adults ate with little enthusiasm and even less conversation, then retired to sit near the fire with the bag of cookies Iris had brought. Harlan took one to his desk, where he pored over several sheets of topographical maps like a man on a mission. He wiped his hands on his pants before tracing the lines with his fingers.

"These cookies are too moist," Iris said.

Harlan looked over his shoulder, pushing a set of simple, black glasses higher on the bridge of his nose. "I didn't know there was such a thing."

JJ took a bite. Oatmeal raisin. Evie would have loved them, but then Evie liked raw cookie dough. She watched Adam eat one, but was pretty sure he didn't taste a bite, eyes fixed on the fire. He was, if possible, even more pale than he'd been before lying down. His face was bruised and he still needed to shave. Her eyes were drawn to a cookie crumb at the corner of his mouth. Once a mother...

Adam blinked, seeming to notice the room again. "My father kidnapped Danny because he wanted to kidnap me. So, if he did kidnap Rachel, why did he do it?"

"If he did kidnap her," Iris said, now willing at least to discuss the possibility, "it's probably not going to be for a reason we can understand. It will make perfect sense to his own internal logic, but during a psychotic episode he doesn't have... linear logic, for lack of a better term."

The cookie, over-moist as it was, stuck in JJ's throat. She cleared it, then noted, "The why only matters to the extent it tells us what he's going to do with her next."

"Most mentally ill people do not harm others," Iris said. "If they harm anyone, they harm themselves."

"He killed Danny," Adam said, and raised his hand when Iris would have protested. "And Sarah Edmunds. The only thing we might have working for us is his timeframe—at least with Danny, he kept him alive longer—but we don't know what the trigger for the abduction was this time. Not just why Rachel, but why now?"

"It's been about twenty years since Danny was abducted, but it's not exactly the anniversary. Maybe he's been gone all this time and just came back," JJ suggested.

Harlan stood from the desk, wiping his hands on his pants again, before picking up another cookie. "We'll never figure out the why. But we might figure out the where."

JJ went to the kitchen and got a pile of napkins to distribute to everyone, unable to watch the man dirty his pants more. It must be his cleaning blind spot.

"If they're considering him a serious suspect, I figure the law'll have access to all kinds of property records for the Rutledge family," Harlan said, wiping his hands gratefully. "But folks around here don't always care much about what a sheet of paper says. I'm trying to come up with places Virgil might go, that might have meant something to him or his family but wouldn't show up on a computer."

"I can help you with that," Iris said, wrapping the rest of her cookie in her napkin before throwing it in the trash.

Harlan gave her a dirty look for wasting perfectly good cookies, but his face softened as she brought him the rest of the bag. "That's what I was counting on, darling."

"So what should I be doing?" Adam asked.

"Get some rest," Harlan said, pointing at Adam as he continued. "I mean it. We don't know yet how your... unique skills will come into play. But they won't come into play at all if you're dead on your feet. Get some shut-eye while you can."

JJ went to do some cleanup in the kitchen. She was filling the sink with soapy water when Harlan appeared next to her.

"I don't want Adam left alone," Harlan said, too softly for Iris to hear over the sound of the running faucet. "His connection to the girl makes him too vulnerable."

Harlan had checked on Adam earlier, and JJ wondered if the man had a particular reason to be suspicious, something he hadn't shared with her and Iris. But she simply nodded, dried her hands on a dishtowel, and went to check on Adam.

She knocked at the guest room door and waited until Adam called out, "Come in."

"I thought I'd tuck you in," she said.

Adam grinned and crawled awkwardly into the bed. He didn't complain, but he was obviously in pain, and JJ winced for him.

"Missing Evie?" he asked, and patted the bed.

"How'd you ever guess?" JJ lay on top of the quilt next to him. The pillow beneath it was a little too squishy for her tastes. Her eyes were drawn to follow the lines formed by the tongue and groove ceiling above.

Adam disentangled his arm from the blankets and reached for JJ's hand. "What's her favorite ice cream?"

JJ laughed. "Chocolate peanut butter."

"You mean, Charlie Brown?" Adam asked. That's what the flavor had been called at the local High's convenience store when they were kids, and it had been Adam's favorite. "Smart kid."

"Very smart," JJ agreed. Her free hand found the little tufts of threads where a quilt piece had been tied together and worried the tiny knot. "Sometimes too smart for her own good."

"Can't imagine where she got that," Adam said, shifting his head on his pillow. "So tell me about this ex-husband of yours, the sperm donor for your amazing daughter."

JJ tried to pull her hand away, but Adam wouldn't let go. "You do know you're hurting my injured ribs," he said.

"You do know that if you could fight worth a shit, your ribs wouldn't be injured," JJ responded.

She was surprised when he skipped the easy comeback about her breaking his ribs in her shower, and instead squeezed her hand until she looked at him.

"Please, Janie. How bad is it with your ex?"

She'd missed Adam so much that it suddenly felt like a punch in the gut, only from the inside out. She didn't ever share a lot, but from time to time when they were kids, she had shared things with Adam, and only Adam. Or she'd found that simply by being around him, she didn't need to share anymore.

JJ felt her lips pressing together tightly—a reflex action—and forced them to relax. To let the words out. "I don't know," she admitted. "We've been divorced for a little over five years. Marcus goes through these phases, and every once in a while, he comes back. Thinks we belong together again. He might be entering one of those phases."

"Does he ever get violent?" Adam asked.

"Sometimes he tries. Last time was almost two years ago, when dad was still around. I don't know what's kept him away for so long."

"Probably took him that long to heal," Adam guessed.

JJ laughed unexpectedly, remembering the condition her father had left her ex in. "It probably did. But a few months back, he started showing up again without warning."

"Did you go to the Sheriff?"

"Yeah, Grant knows."

"Grant seems like a good man," Adam said.

JJ almost got defensive, like the dreaded tween Evie was about to become, and denied her feelings for Grant. But then she remembered she was an adult, and sidestepping was a more appropriate response for the emotion-sharing averse. "He is. Legally, there's just not much that can be done about it at this point."

"Well, then," Adam said, voice soft, "maybe this is something we can work on, too. While I'm here."

JJ didn't reply, just turned toward him on her side and closed her eyes, content to hear his breath next to her and pretend—just for a few minutes—that life was simple again and that everything would be okay.

48

———

Adam jerked awake and immediately regretted it. One hand was trapped beneath a quilt, and his instinctive struggle to free it triggered knife-stabbing pain in his side.

Harlan stood over him.

Adam shifted in the bed, trying to sit, only to find that his other hand—fingers still entwined with JJ's—had fallen asleep, as had JJ.

"Just stay put," Harlan said.

The man's voice was low, but combined with Adam's movements, it made JJ stir. She lifted her head, blinked sleep-blurred eyes and asked, "What's wrong?"

"Nothing," Harlan said. "I'm sorry I woke you. I just—well, I figured you'd be more comfortable with Iris for the night, and I'd bunk with Adam."

JJ pushed her hair back, still sleep-groggy, and said, "Oh, okay." She rolled off the bed and made it as far as the door before remembering to say, "Night, Adam."

"Good night, Janie."

Harlan followed JJ to the door and stood in the hallway,

watching until she made it to the other bedroom. "She's even cuter when she's sleepy," Harlan said, smiling and pulling the door shut behind him.

"I dare you to tell her that," Adam said.

Harlan settled in a wooden chair next to the bed. Portions of its frame were roughly spindle-shaped, but looked as though they'd been carved by hand. It was the kind of thing that would sell for a fortune to a weekend visitor from Washington, D.C.

"Are you sleeping in that chair?" Adam asked, now upright.

Harlan chuckled. "No, not if I can help it. It's time to get this undertaking under way."

Earlier, Harlan had told Adam he had a plan, but it would take a little time to get ready, and Adam needed some time to recover.

"Okay. So tell me about this bold plan of yours," Adam said.

"Calling it a plan is a might bit grandiose. More like, an experiment." Harlan winked.

Adam had worked in more than his fair share of bars over the years, and it was the first time he'd ever seen a grown man successfully pull off a wink. That, and the idea of Harlan being humble, made Adam snicker briefly, despite the pain.

Harlan's smile was just as brief. He reached down to unroll his sleeves in the cool room. "We've been doing a lot of dancing around because Virgil is your dad and Iris's son. But the plain truth is we don't know what he'll do, and we don't know when. I've come up with about a half a dozen possible places for where, but I've got no reason to think any one is any more likely than any other. But that's where I think you can help me. Where we can help each other."

Harlan tugged on his cuffs, and Adam wanted to yell at him to just fix his stupid shirt already. That is, until he realized Harlan wasn't being OCD; he was stalling.

"How?" Adam asked.

The sharp contrast between Harlan's dark brows and silver hair seemed to make his expression alternate between wry amusement and utmost seriousness. Now it had swung to the latter. "What you do—your visions or dreams or what-have-you—it's dangerous. You do understand that, don't you?"

"Yes," Adam said.

Harlan motioned for him to elaborate, so Adam said, "I have very little control. I don't know how to come back, and I'm never sure I will. I imagine myself, stuck inside some horror that I can never leave. Screaming to get out, but no one can hear me." Except there was something even worse. Adam cringed inside as he added, "Or one person can hear me, and I'll drive that person insane."

Harlan nodded, but wasn't entirely satisfied. "And you could die."

"And I could die," Adam agreed. It may have been the most irrevocable of the risks, but to him it was in many ways also the simplest, and perhaps even the least disturbing.

"Okay," Harlan said, slapping his palms against his thighs. "So long as we're on the same page. Here's what I'm thinking." Harlan leaned forward, elbows on his knees. "What if we could connect you with Rachel again, right now, and see what she sees?"

Adam reached to the chain resting on his chest for reassurance. He pushed the key against his bruised sternum, using the pain to clear his mind. "And you're here to bring me back?"

"Right here next to you," Harlan said. "Your lifeline, if you will."

Adam was half afraid of being more harm to Rachel than help, but if Harlan were able to intervene, should things go wrong... "Obviously I'm willing to try, but what if I don't see any more than I did the previous times? Or what if I still don't understand what I'm seeing?"

"Oh, don't worry—I've been thinking about that, too." Harlan's eyes twinkled. "What if you had an extra pair of eyes?"

Harlan handed Adam a mug of hot tea.

"This smells like..." Adam couldn't go on because he wasn't

really sure how to finish the sentence. The odor was so primevally wrong, he couldn't even pick out different notes.

"I know, it smells like ass. Hey, I'm drinking it, too," Harlan said, holding up a steaming mug that said *Eastern State Plumbing*.

Adam's mug featured a cartoon character so faded that he couldn't tell if the species was a bear or primate. "You think twice about your friend's ceramic paints reacting with whatever's in here?"

Harlan took a sip and winced. "No, I just didn't want to risk breaking my good cups when the ass tea kicks in."

Gee, that's reassuring. Adam sipped and made a face. It tasted as good as it smelled, sort of sulfury and musky, with a hint of bile. Harlan had warned him not to chug it, or he would have, faster than a fifteen-year-old with his dad's Jim Beam.

"How are you going to sleep in that chair?" Adam asked.

"I'm not," Harlan said. "That's the point. Remember, I don't have to sleep to see things. All I have to do is watch you sleep, and take your hand when the time is right."

It sounded so simple, so rational. And yet, Adam had misgivings. "Have you ever done this before?"

"Nope," Harlan said, his voice entirely too chipper under the circumstances. "It might not even work."

"And what if it does? What'll it do to Rachel, having you piggyback on me piggybacking on her?" Adam asked between sips.

"I don't know, son," Harlan said through heat-flushed lips. "But I don't think anything we can do to her from here is half as bad as what Virgil—or whomever—has in store if we don't try it."

The man had a point. But so did Adam, at least one more. "Then why not tell Iris and JJ? What if something happens to you? Do you have, I don't know, any kind of medical conditions?"

Harlan barked a laugh. "I'm an official senior citizen in one of the poorest states in the country. What do you think? Iris would have a shit fit if we told her. And we don't need that on top of everything else to deal with." Harlan leaned over and set his empty mug on the nightstand. "Look, if you have a better idea, I'm all ears. But you and I both know that little girl will be lucky to make it through the night."

When he put it that way... "Okay," Adam said. He slowly drained the rest of his tea, then choked on some kind of nasty sediment at the bottom, coughing hard until his eyes watered.

"Easy there. We don't want the nurse next door to make a house call."

Adam wiped the tears from his eyes before rubbing his hand across his mouth to remove whatever had adhered to the corner. Then he lowered himself to the bed, painfully scooting. Pillow, then body. Pillow, then body. Harlan reached to help him, but Adam waved him away.

"I've got it," he grunted.

Adam closed his eyes, but opened them again almost immediately. He couldn't get past the sensation of being watched. "I don't know if I can get to sleep. This feels pretty weird."

"Don't worry," Harlan said. "The tea will help you relax."

Adam's tongue was starting to thicken, making words more difficult. "Then how will you be able to stay awake to watch me?"

"Because I've used this stuff before. It won't affect me as much."

"Who taught you—"

"Adam, shut up. You can't fall asleep if you don't stop talking." Harlan pulled the quilt up to Adam's shoulders and patted it gently. Adam rolled his eyes at him before letting gravity take his lids. He started slowly counting, to give his mind something to focus on. Before he made it to twenty, a warm, fuzzy feeling—just shy of a tingle—spread from his ears all the way down to his toes. The pulsing in his bruised cheek disappeared, and the aching in his ribs eased. A smile crept across his face before he knew it was happening.

"See, I told you," Harlan said, but it sounded as though his voice was slowly moving farther away. "Just pretend like I'm a kindly old grandfather, watching over you as you sleep."

"Never met my grandfather," Adam mumbled, his lips heavy and unresponsive.

"If I haven't mentioned it already, that's something to be glad about," Harlan replied.

If Harlan said anything else, Adam couldn't hear it. He lost himself in the most restful sleep he thought he'd ever had. Except if he knew he was sleeping, was he really sleeping? He didn't care. It felt so safe. Wherever he was, he never wanted to leave.

But then, he found himself falling...

49

———

*S*tumbling in the dark, Rachel tried to catch herself and banged her elbow on a nearby tree. She held in the whimper of pain while she fought a funny feeling in her stomach. She was so scared, her whole body vibrated and her breath wheezed at the edges. But she knew that feeling, that sense that the ground was not quite where she expected it...

Are you there? Did you come back?

The Other One probably couldn't answer, but she could tell he was there. And she felt a little less alone. She shook out the pain in her elbow, and then—

"Girl!" It was the man's voice, yelling for her from the ridge above. He knew she was gone.

Oh God, Oh God, Oh God...

Easy, Rachel, *she told herself. Or maybe it was the Other One who told her that.* Don't panic.

The trees overhead were mostly leafless and the moon was bright, high-lighting a path—a game path, not a human one—that meandered down the slope. It wasn't too steep; she could make it.

But so could he. And that's the way he'd expect her to go. Maybe she should go a different way through the trees, without a path. Except it would be noisier.

"*Girl! Where are you?*" *The voice was coming closer.*

She had to move. Fast.

Forget the path.

She scrambled straight down the slope instead, bending her knees and keeping her arms low to keep from falling. But sliding was even faster—tree surfing, she and Evie called it before her asthma got so bad that she wasn't allowed to play in the woods. Rachel took a few steps and jumped forward, landing slightly sideways and planting her legs a foot or so apart. Then she slid, faster and faster down the hill on the thick bed of leaves, only picking her feet up when she had to, tree trunks flying past.

But it was too fast!

Rachel pitched forward onto her knees and elbows and rolled, avoiding hitting a tree, but losing the momentum she'd built up. The hill was leveling out, and she couldn't get a good slide going again. It didn't help that her knees were shaking so badly. She ran the rest of the way down the slope like a slalom, eyes straining and arms flailing as she dodged trees. Suddenly there was a bit of bank—not much, only a couple of feet drop—but she couldn't stop in time and landed in a heap on level ground.

"Unh!" She'd hit hard, hard enough to knock the wind from her with a big thump. She could still feel the force, the pressure of the slamming exhale, but nothing else happened. She couldn't inhale. Rachel lifted her face from the damp leaves. There was something wrong, and her chest and throat muscles wouldn't work. They were just stuck. Her blood rushed in her ears like a waterfall while her brain screamed for air. She rolled over onto her back, and finally her diaphragm released, sucking in a ragged gasp of air.

But one wasn't enough, and it wasn't deep enough, so she sucked in again, and again, the taste of the leaves on the air scratching her throat raw.

Calm down.

That was the Other One. And she wanted to—oh, how she wanted to! —but it didn't work that way. She held her breath for a moment, tried to control it, but she couldn't. She struggled to sit up—sometimes that helped. But not this time. It was too late. The more she gasped, the tighter her throat and chest became. Her vision grew darker, and she fell over on her side.

Stop it, Rachel!

A new voice ran through her body like an electric current. Her eyes flew open, but even with her cloudy vision she could tell there was no one there. Not physically.

Good girl! Now look around.

She felt as though someone else were animating her limbs. Her vision cleared, and she saw she was on a leaf-buried trail—probably an old logging road, recognizable but no longer wide enough for a four-wheel-drive truck. The bank she'd fallen from was formed when the road was cut from the mountain. She looked back in the direction she'd come from— uphill—and her sliding path was clearly visible on the scarred hillside. The downward slope continued below the trail she kneeled upon. It was hard to tell in the moonlight, but the ground seemed to rise again in the distance.

"Girl! Where do you think you're going?" the man yelled, the man who was really here and not the one in her head.

Instantly, the panic kicked in, and she felt the tightness in her chest, a tightness that had never really gone away, just been masked by the electric voice. She was too scared to scream, too scared to cry.

Hide.

That was the electric voice in her head, but it wasn't as strong or as loud as it was before. Still, it was enough to make her move. There was a big patch of mountain laurel below her, just off the edge of the path. She crawled toward it and circled until she found an easy way in. It wasn't perfect cover—the branches were sparse and its glossy, evergreen leaves were smaller than she'd like— but it was better than lying in the middle of the road.

A rustle sounded from the ridge above, a light shushing sound as the man's feet passed through the leaves. She lifted her eyes and peered through the branches to see a dark shape descending the hill. He hadn't bothered using his flashlight. A shiver rocked her small body, but she was glad she wasn't wearing her pale yellow, puffy jacket, the one Evie said made her look like a marshmallow Peep. He'd have seen it for sure, practically glowing in the dark.

Maybe he already saw her.

He kept coming down the hill.

She held her breath, trying to keep a cough in, and her shoulders rocked with it. She hoped she wasn't making the branches move, or if she did, he'd think it was just a breeze.

"These woods are full of bears," the man said, close enough now not to have to yell.

She'd take a bear she'd never seen over the man in front of her anytime.

"You and I both know that's not the only reason you're not safe. It's time to come out," the man said, his voice even softer.

He was so near—about the distance they made the little kids run to first base in P.E. class—that she could see the strings hanging down from his hooded sweatshirt, swaying as he moved. He had the hood pulled up, and his pale face was a blur in the shadows. She was half surprised that she couldn't see his eyes glowing. Rachel knew his pale eyes were like angel eyes, only if angels were bad.

"I can't protect you if you don't come out."

She held her breath—what little she had—as he stepped down off the bank and onto the trail. He turned in a slow circle and looked up through the trees toward the moon. For a second, she was afraid he'd howl and turn into a wolf. Instead, his head turned back toward the ground again, and he clenched his fists.

"Don't make me find you, girl!" he roared.

She flinched.

That was enough.

The man lunged toward the shrubbery, and she tunneled on her hands and knees, head down and eyes closed to protect them from the branches. They poked her—in her exposed neck and the palms of her hands—and tugged at her hair.

She was surprised when she felt herself finally burst through the undergrowth into exposed space. She opened her eyes and—

His rough hand clamped across her mouth, cutting off her scream. Almost as quickly, her connection to the electric voice—and all of the relief he'd given her—was severed. It was as if her chest had turned to stone, heavy and immobile.

But the Other One was still there.

Breathe, Rachel... Breathe...

50

—————

JJ was sure she'd heard something. She didn't want to wake Iris, lying on the other side of the bed. But she also couldn't sleep without seeing what had disturbed her. Fortunately, Evie had given her a lot of practice at clandestine sliding out of beds.

From the hallway, JJ could see a glow of diffused moonlight streaming in through the windows in the front rooms. There was an odd sense of expectancy in the living room, as if the space were waiting for something to happen. Harlan had let the fire burn out, and it was cool, if not downright cold. JJ crossed the room and negotiated a couple of deadbolts and a chain before breaching the front door. At least she didn't have to worry about an alarm. She wondered why Harlan didn't have a dog. Iris had never let Adam have one, so maybe it was in deference to her. If they had that kind of relationship.

JJ pulled the front door shut, jiggling the doorknob first to make sure it wouldn't lock behind her. She should've grabbed a jacket—better yet, she should've grabbed *shoes*—but she wouldn't be outside long. A railing ran the length of the front porch, and she leaned on the cold wood, trying to make out any sound, any movement in the dark.

Someone out there is watching me.

It was a ridiculous thought, but one she couldn't shake. Her eyes scanned the driveway as far as she could see, down to the first bend. Was there something there? Adam's bear? JJ stood and walked to the steps. She wasn't stupid enough to walk outside barefoot in this weather, or check out something that might *be something* on her own. But sometimes a few more steps was all you needed to see what you were after.

She went as far as the bottom stair, feet sticking slightly to the cold, wooden surface. Was there a shape on the ground by the driveway curve? Before she realized what she was doing, JJ felt sandy, gravelly dirt beneath her feet. She'd just go as far as the hood of Iris's car.

Was that a pile of clothes?

Okay, maybe as far as the trunk.

There was a bit of movement, then suddenly—

"Adam!" Harlan's voice called out in the house, just loud enough to reach her.

JJ blinked, then looked toward the house.

"Adam!" Harlan's voice again, louder.

She looked back down the driveway.

There was nothing there. She must've imagined it.

JJ reached out to the cars for support as she jogged back toward the house, gravel poking the soles of her bare feet. She ran up the steps and inside, then swiped the stones from her feet on the doormat before slamming the door behind her.

She arrived at the guest bedroom just as Iris flung the door open and flipped on the light. Harlan was on his knees on the floor next to the bed, arm outstretched toward a motionless Adam.

"Are you praying?" Iris asked.

Adam sat up abruptly with a gasp, eyes wide and lips blue-tinged.

Harlan sighed and let his head rest on the bed. "Not anymore."

"Just what the hell were you playing at?" Iris demanded.

"Language," Harlan said, but his voice was so weak it was barely audible. JJ was monitoring his pulse—trying anyway, as his whole arm trembled in JJ's hands—while Iris banged around in the kitchen, supposedly making coffee. "You wouldn't mind using gloves, would you?" Harlan asked.

JJ glanced at the man to make sure he wasn't joking. He wasn't; he stared at JJ's fingers where they touched his skin.

"No, not at all," she said, and stood.

"Good," he said. "They're in the bathroom under the sink. Please check on Adam while you're there."

JJ paused in the hallway outside the bathroom door. She knocked hard on the door, using the pain in her knuckles to block out thoughts of the last time she'd checked on Adam in a bathroom. "Adam, I'm coming in," she said.

He was kneeling by the toilet, staring into the bowl.

"Are you okay?"

"I'm done throwing up," he said, flushing before leaning heavily against the wall to stand up.

He hadn't entirely answered her question, but if he was capable of standing under his own power, that was something. JJ squatted and opened the cabinet beneath the sink. Unlike her own precariously stacked storage spaces, it was well organized, with spare shampoo and shaving supplies, cotton balls and Q-Tips in their own small bins. She finally spotted a box of white cleaning gloves and snagged a pair.

"Anything I should know about Harlan's condition?" she asked.

"Nothing you don't already."

She stared at him, and Adam clarified, "Don't touch his bare skin."

JJ stood. "If I leave you here to get cleaned up, I'm not going to come back and find you on the floor, am I?"

Adam's cheeks were sunken, and his eyes looked as if he'd been punched (*oh yeah, he had been*), but they were clear. "No. I promise. I'll be out in a minute."

Back at the kitchen table, Harlan's lips had regained a little color, and his voice a little of its strength. "You don't really need to do that," he said, as she reached for his arm with a gloved hand.

She ignored him and felt the familiar thump beneath her hand. Pulses had personalities. This one, like Harlan, was strong and even, regular. It was a little fast, but even as she sat, counting, she could feel it slowing. When she'd gone a minute, she glanced up to find him staring at her and almost smiling.

"Now do you believe me?" he asked.

Before JJ could answer, Iris slammed a couple of plates of biscuits and thickly sliced cheese on the table next to them. Harlan raised a dark eyebrow, but didn't say a word about the precious ceramics he'd lectured JJ about while dishwashing. Iris returned with a tray of coffee just as Adam arrived and took a seat, hair still wet from washing his face.

"I assume none of us are going back to bed anytime soon," Iris said.

Harlan and Adam stared at each other, Adam hugging his arms around his body. "Was that him?" Adam asked.

"I don't know," Harlan said. "Drink some coffee."

"Drink some coffee! She's still out there, and *someone's* got her... *again*. What are we doing here?"

"We're getting warmed up and calmed down enough that we're actually worth something to somebody," Harlan said firmly, splitting a biscuit to make a cheese sandwich, "and then we're going to find her, and send in the cavalry."

Adam leaned forward onto the table. "Do you know where she is?"

"Not yet," Harlan said, biting off a piece of biscuit the same way he might pull on a pair of work pants. "I'm not even positive *when* she is—we don't know for sure that what we experienced has even happened yet. But I think I can figure out the where. Now leave me alone for a minute." He rose and went to sit in one of the chairs across from the cold fireplace, taking his biscuit with him. Once he'd finished shoving it in his mouth, he closed his eyes and bowed his head, letting his hands rest on top of his thighs.

JJ wasn't sure what he was doing, but she lowered her voice in deference to whatever it was. "Care to fill us in?"

Adam followed Harlan's culinary lead, but once he'd taken a bite, he tore into the rest like a starving man. He washed down the crumbs with a gulp of coffee before answering.

"Rachel escaped tonight," he said, "but the man who was holding her—and no, I didn't see him well enough to recognize him—found her. And there was nothing we could do but watch."

"We?" Iris asked.

"Harlan and I. He was able to see through me somehow, through my link with her."

Iris closed her eyes and shook her head, obviously pissed. JJ's mind raced. She *knew* Rachel was still alive. "We've got to tell Grant."

"Tell him what?" Adam asked, reaching for another biscuit. "That I had a vision she's being held somewhere in the woods? Gee, that narrows it down to the entire fricking state."

JJ didn't respond, but the sarcasm stung, and it wasn't like him. She could see Adam's hands shaking as he set the biscuit down.

"I'm sorry, JJ. I just..." He looked at her with eyes that were pleading for—what? Forgiveness? Understanding? She was sure he didn't know. "Rachel was so scared. And I couldn't do *anything. Again.*" A sudden sob jerked through his body.

JJ reached Adam before Iris did and held his head against her chest as he gulped air. His was a natural, physical reaction, one she'd seen a hundred times before in the emergency room. The body coped with the adrenaline dump that had gotten it through whatever trauma it had just encountered by shaking, crying, even fainting.

Except, of course, it wasn't just a physical reaction. It was who Adam was. These dreams or visions or whatever affected him physically. In fact, she was pretty sure they could be fatal. But JJ was even more afraid of what they were doing to his mind. Perhaps he'd gradually become unable to distinguish the reality he was personally experiencing from the reality of his dreams, and from his thoughts about what *might become* reality. Was that what had happened to Adam's father?

And then there was the emotional part—the guilt. Every time Adam experienced something as an observer, a voyeur who could do nothing to change what was happening, he added another layer of guilt to the structure he'd begun in his psyche with Danny so many years ago. How many more would it take before it came crashing down and took him with it?

He'd gone quiet, and the shaking had subsided, but she held him anyway. As she would have Evie. "Shh... we'll find her," she said, stroking his hair.

They had to.

Otherwise, she was afraid they'd lose Adam, too.

51

———

Adam pulled gently away from JJ. He felt like a shell, an empty meat and bone husk, yet when Harlan rose abruptly from his spot by the fireplace, touching the high back of his chair to steady himself, Adam was compelled to follow.

"What is it?" he asked.

Harlan went straight to his desk, with its pile of maps and his glasses. "Iris, can you help me with this?"

She didn't move.

Harlan turned, looking over the tops of the black frames and deepening the creases in his forehead. "Iris, you can be pissed at me later. If we're going to save this girl's life, I need your help, and I need it now."

Iris relented, and Adam and JJ crowded around both of them, anxious to see what Harlan had discovered.

"My recollection is that there were a couple of pieces of property your late husband was fond of, but may not have actually owned. Here—" Harlan's finger moved perpendicular to the contours, effectively ascending a hill, "near Orndorff Run is one of them. Not all that far from the park cabin where they found Rachel's stuff."

Iris squinted at the map. "Give me your glasses," she said, and held them in front of her. "Your eyes are even worse than mine. But I think you're right. What's the other one?"

"Just beyond that ridge," Harlan said, pointing out through the dark windows before shuffling to a second map. He squinted to find the spot. "Here."

Iris set the glasses on her nose and held the map down with both hands, as if it were going to fly away. She traced something with her finger, then put Harlan's glasses back on the desk and walked to the windows, wet with condensation. She made a fist and cleared a circle with the side of her hand, then leaned her head against the glass.

"My God. You're right." She closed her eyes. "I don't know who it ever did belong to, but it has a small cabin—single room, no running water. And there's a rock outcrop nearby—less than half a mile?—with a good bit of drop to it, almost like a cliff."

She opened her eyes again. "What am I saying? No *almost* about it. It is a cliff." She demonstrated with her hands. "It sticks out, like somebody jammed an upright book into the side of the mountain. The way the ground slopes, the front end must be more than thirty feet high. I don't know how broad it is. We didn't go around—there are boulders all over—and I couldn't see past it."

"Exactly," Harlan said, and turned to Adam. "I think the area where we saw Rachel was between the cabin and the little cliff."

"Harlan," Iris said, "that's just a few miles from here."

"I know," he said, rolling up the map. "Let's go."

"Wait," Iris said. "If Virgil has Rachel here, why was her stuff found in the opposite direction over by Orndorff Run?"

"I don't know," Harlan said. "Maybe he did it to throw us off his scent. But I'm sure Adam and I saw her here, near Pine Gap. So let's move."

"Where to?" JJ asked.

"First, we'll head to Jim's," Harlan said. "We can use his landline to call it in. Son, what size are your feet?"

"Ten," Adam said.

"Close enough," Harlan said. "Can't have you going outside in slippers again. There's an extra pair of ten-and-a-half hiking boots over by the door. Iris, would you grab him a couple of pairs of socks from my room so his boots aren't falling off?" Harlan listed a little, crossing the room as if it were a heaving boat deck.

"Are you okay?" JJ asked.

"Nothing a good night's sleep and half a bottle of bourbon wouldn't fix." Harlan lowered his voice once Iris was out of sight. "Listen, you two might end up out in the field—so to speak—before this is all over, so dress accordingly."

There was a bottleneck at the shoe bench by the entry. JJ was ready first because she was the only one physically capable of putting shoes on while standing on one leg. Adam envied her, wincing as he bent forward to pull a boot painfully onto his foot.

"You have a thermos?" JJ asked.

"You'll find a few on that middle shelf on the back wall," Iris said.

Iris had made enough coffee for a small army. Adam watched JJ fill two thermoses from the percolator while he finished lacing his boots. JJ kept one and handed the other to Iris.

Harlan scowled at JJ's dirty boots but didn't comment. He was the last one suited up and had difficulty locking the door, he said because he hadn't left a porch light on. Adam thought it more likely that Harlan was still feeling the effects of their little experiment. Adam certainly was.

Finally, Iris took the keys from Harlan and said, "Get in my car. I'm driving."

Harlan didn't argue.

Adam and JJ got in the back seat. It was cold enough to see fog from their breath in the car. Iris lingered at the front door, apparently unable to see keys and locks by moonlight any better than Harlan was. The man turned in the front seat.

"No matter what happens tonight, don't try to connect with the girl again," he told Adam. "Not without me there."

Adam hugged himself, cold even in his borrowed layers. "Okay," he said.

"Adam, I mean it. And JJ, don't you dare let him do it, either." Harlan twisted around until Adam thought he'd climb in the back seat with them. "Hopefully, sometime soon we'll have the leisure to figure out the ins and outs of what happened tonight, but for now, you have to trust me. It's too dangerous. I'm afraid I might have tweaked your link with the girl somehow, changed it into something even more unpredictable."

They all jumped when Iris's door flew open. "Are we ready?" she asked.

"Ready," Adam said. He'd heard what Harlan said, but Adam figured it was a little like airplane emergencies. Yes, the flight attendants tell you you're supposed to secure your own mask before securing your child's, but when push came to shove, he wondered how many people would do it that way. Their way made rational sense, but a child in danger often forces you to hurl rational sense out the window.

JJ gasped as Iris nearly hit her parked car in an effort to avoid the woodpile. Iris either didn't hear JJ or pretended not to, and they were on their way. It wasn't far down to Jim Henderson's place, but Adam felt himself getting more and more amped as seconds ticked away. He rested a hand on his jiggling knee to try to calm it, but that just made him unable to distinguish his knee's motion from that of his shaking hand. Adam felt strongly that, one way or another, it would be over tonight. They would either have Rachel, or she would be beyond their help. Maybe he would, too.

Even with a full moon, Adam couldn't see much beyond the outline of the trees until they reached Jim's driveway. The forest stopped at his property line, leaving the Henderson house visible less than a quarter of a mile from the road. White in the moonlight, the house was two stories with a narrow, peaked second floor and very little embellishment. A couple of pickups and a car were parked in front.

The woods picked up again behind the house and on the right next to Harlan's property, but in front and to the left it was all cleared, with the exception of the occasional solitary oak. Hills rolled down and away from the house, naked without the trees as dressing. An unpainted barn sat nearby, as well as another outbuilding of some sort off to the right between the house and the woods.

A dog started barking almost as soon as Iris turned up the driveway, and it was waiting for them by the house when Iris parked. Some kind of collie mix, it sniffed Iris's tires, let out one last bark, and then made its way to the front porch and lay down.

"What time is it?" Iris asked.

"Near three a.m.," Harlan said. "We'll sit here a minute, give everybody a chance to get their bearings before they decide whether to shoot us."

A couple of minutes later, the porch light came on and a man emerged from the front door in sweats and a jacket. He approached their car, and when he saw that Iris was driving he went around to Harlan's side.

"Evening, Jim," Harlan said through his open window.

"I'd say that's debatable," Jim said, leaning on the roof of the car. "Some people would call this part of the day morning."

"I'm awful sorry to bother you again, and at this crazy hour, but we need to use your phone to call the police. It's about the Nicholson girl."

"Well, hell, why didn't you say so?" Jim opened Harlan's door for him. "Hurry up and get in out of the cold."

Adam thought it must be even colder on the Henderson property, maybe because of the open field. They all hurried (so much as anyone can at three a.m.) to the porch, where the dog thumped its tail a couple of times but otherwise ignored them.

"Don't worry about your shoes. I'm not as anal as this one," Jim said, waving a thumb at Harlan. He'd only turned on a few lights in the house, presumably to keep from waking everybody else, but Adam could see that the man was about a decade younger than Harlan. He looked familiar...

Adam nearly gasped with recognition. A little stooped now, Jim Henderson wasn't as tall as he'd been in Adam's memory, and his hair was thinner. But there was no doubt he'd been one of the Cub Scout leaders twenty years ago, on the trip when Danny was kidnapped.

"Jim, this is—"

"I know who it is. Good to see you grown up, Adam. And damned if you aren't the spitting image of your mom. Harlan, you know where the phone is. Don't let me hold you up."

Harlan headed into the living room, with the rest of them close on his heels. Jim indicated a love seat for Iris and JJ. He and Adam were left with a couple of wooden chairs with inadequate cushions, the sole shining lamp standing between them.

"What's going on?" Jim asked, directing his attention at Iris.

"We think we know where the girl's being held," Iris said.

"You mean, Harlan... *Harlan knows?*" Jim asked, obviously dancing around a way to articulate something he didn't fully understand. Adam almost corrected him—that they'd both seen her—but Iris jumped in first.

"Yes, Harlan knows," she said firmly, with a glance at Adam to keep his mouth shut.

"Whew," Jim exhaled. "I hope they can get there in time."

Not, *I hope he's right*, but I hope the law can act in time. Adam wondered how Harlan had gained the man's confidence with something they couldn't even name, and how long it had taken.

Harlan walked toward them, carrying a phone with a cord that had been stretched long by the years, hand over the mouthpiece. "They patched me through somehow, but Grant's all the way over on the other side of Beecham County right now with most of the task force. Unfortunately—"

Harlan turned his attention back to the phone. "Yeah, I'm still here. Don't worry, I'll wait." Then he covered the mouthpiece again. "He said they can get a team to Orndorff Run pretty quick, but it'll be a while before anybody can get over here." Harlan dragged Jim's coffee table over to the lamp and pushed short stacks of mail order catalogs aside to spread out his map. "Jim, help me out here—what's the easiest access for whoever they send?"

Jim pulled his eyeglasses from his front shirt pocket and bent over the table. "Let me think a minute," he said, and paced slowly around the room.

Adam felt his eyes drawn to JJ. She stared at him steadily, confidently, as if to say, *This is it.* Adam gave a small nod in return, just enough for her to see.

"Okay," Jim said, bending over the map again. "They don't want to come in our road, Harlan. They can get closer in their vehicles if they stay on the state road until they get to here," he said, pointing with the frames of his glasses. "Dirt road—I don't even think there's a sign, but if they get to Pine Gap, they've gone too far."

Harlan kneeled next to Jim, resting the crook of the phone handset on his shoulder. "Then what?"

"It's not showing up on here, but if I recollect, it meets up with the old logging road right about in here. But you'd have to take four-wheelers or mules or whatever from there on in."

Harlan stood abruptly, grabbing at an aching knee as he did. "Yeah, still here. You catch any of that?"

He explained what Jim had told him, talking Grant through his maps on the other end. Then he paced and listened, while everyone else watched. It was quiet in the house, and they strained to make out words every time the tinny voice echoed in Harlan's ear.

"I understand, but goddamn, Sheriff—"

Harlan covered the phone and explained, "There's no way he can get a team in before daylight." He looked to Adam and JJ after he spoke, waiting, and when the two of them stood, Adam could swear Harlan almost smiled.

"Then you better tell them not to shoot me and JJ when they get there," Adam said, "because we're going in now."

52

J J knew they'd made the right decision. For the first time since he'd returned, there was a spark of hope in Adam's face, a sense that maybe things would come out all right after all. Not that *she* could imagine any scenario in which everything would come out all right, not if they were right about Virgil Rutledge being involved. But JJ would settle for taking Rachel home in one piece.

"Are you crazy?" Iris asked, a hoarse edge creeping into her throat. The poor woman must be tired of acting as the voice of reason for their little windmill-tilting group. "You're just going to run off into the dark, trying to find someplace you've never been to confront *we don't know who*, on the basis of a hunch."

"Yes," Adam said.

"I've got a four-wheeler you can use, if you don't mind doubling up," Jim said. "It can't be more than five miles from here to the cabin, and it's a pretty smooth ride once you get to the logging road."

Iris was up from her seat, glaring at Harlan as if it were all his fault. He turned away to fill in Grant on the phone while they hashed out the details.

"And what do you think you're going to do when you get there?" Iris asked.

"Get Rachel," JJ said. It occurred to her that she'd left her handgun in her car at Harlan's cabin. "Don't suppose you have some extra firepower we could borrow, too, just in case?"

Iris threw up her hands in disgust. "It just gets better and better."

JJ understood the woman's anxiety, but she didn't have time for it. More importantly, Rachel didn't have time for it. "What if it had been Adam instead of Danny? What would you have done to bring him back?"

"Anything. I wouldn't have hesitated to kill or torture or both," Iris said, matter of fact. And then she admitted, just as calmly, "But that's because he's mine."

Again, JJ understood. Iris's family had had it tougher than most, and she'd spent her considerable energy protecting what was left of it. But JJ didn't have those boundaries of protection, and she was pretty sure Adam didn't, either.

"JJ," Harlan said, holding out the phone, "Grant wants to talk to you."

Great. She'd been hoping she could dodge this conversation. JJ took a deep breath, and Harlan gave her a sympathetic look along with the handset.

"I'm here," she said.

"JJ, what the hell do you think you're doing?" Grant asked. His voice sounded angry, not to mention decades and miles away on the old phone, but it still gave her a little lift to hear it.

"I'm a nurse, and she knows me. Can you think of anyone better to respond?" she asked.

"Yes," he said. "A trained law enforcement officer. At least wait until I track down Luther. I can send him in if he's any closer than we are. Adam isn't exactly trained backup."

"Don't worry," she said, glancing over at Adam. "I'll take care of him."

Adam stuck his tongue out at her. He was getting giddy; they both were. They needed to move before their adrenaline peaked.

"What was that?" she asked, having missed a few words through distraction and static.

"JJ, as the Sheriff, I can't condone this."

"I understand. But right now, you're in no position to stop us, either."

"Damned, hard-headed woman," Grant muttered, and JJ heard his sigh of exasperation over the phone. "If you do find Rachel, for God's sake, don't make a move on your own. Stay out of sight and keep an eye on the situation until I can get trained officers up the mountain. The last thing you want to do is spook the kidnapper into an action we'll all regret."

"Got it," JJ said.

"Promise me you'll come back safe and sound," he said. "For Evie."

"Okay, I will," she said easily. JJ had no intention of being an idiot, but she couldn't think too much about her own daughter right now, or she'd never have the courage to help Rachel. Evie would be safe with her grandmother, no matter what happened.

Grant's voice grew louder and fuzzier, as if he'd moved the phone closer to his mouth. "No, that's not a promise. *Promise me*, JJ."

His voice was so intimate—not the voice of the Sheriff—that JJ flashed back to kissing him in the rain... was that just last night? She felt herself blush as she said, "I promise."

"Better," he said. "I wish I could be there."

"Me, too," she said, and tried not to think about everyone watching and listening, on both ends. "I guess you'll just have to make it up to me after."

"Okay," he said. "I will. I promise, too."

JJ handed the phone back to Harlan and tried to get her game face on again. It helped that Jim was waiting for her with a shotgun in his hands, a camouflage sling already snapped into the swivels. "Will this do?"

"Perfect," JJ said, and set it on the table. "Mama's little security blanket."

He handed her a box of twenty-five Federal shotshells. "I don't know where you want to stow these. It's not loaded."

JJ opened the box. It wasn't full, but she only needed a few. She shoved three in each jacket pocket for lack of something better. She looked at Adam, but he raised his hands in surrender.

"You know me. I'm more likely to shoot myself than do anything useful with any kind of gun."

"How about ATVs? You got any experience on them?" Jim asked.

"Afraid not," Adam said, with a rueful smile.

"That's okay," JJ said. "That was one of my ex-husband's loves. One that wasn't another woman, I mean. His was repossessed years ago, but I'm pretty sure it'll come back to me."

"Well, damn, Adam. No offense, but what good are you?" Jim asked.

"You taught me to build a fire twenty years ago," Adam said, and Jim's face softened at the memory. Adam went on, "And I'm a ninja with a blender."

Jim laughed. "I think the blender's more of a summer skill, but hopefully we'll get a chance to see it in action. Now let's get you all saddled up and on the road."

Iris had disappeared, and Harlan was still on the phone. They followed Jim outside to the building adjacent to the forest. It was still dark out, but he'd left the porch light on and the moon led them the rest of the way. The building, the same unpainted wood as the barn, had padlocked double doors that swung out. Once Jim released the padlock, Adam and JJ helped him pull one of the doors open. It swung free of the ground, but it was heavy. The building was wired with electricity, and when Jim flipped a switch, a couple of bare bulbs attached to the ceiling joists flashed on. A workbench off to the right had more lighting for detailed work, but they didn't need it. The ATV was right in front. JJ removed the cover while Jim went to get a gas can.

It was a no-frills, one-person machine with faded red paint and tires that had seen better days, but at least it was an automatic. Not that JJ couldn't drive a manual ATV, but she didn't relish the idea of doing it with Adam hanging on her back. Jim came over to top up the gas tank.

"What's the mileage on this thing?" she asked.

Jim looked at her and Adam, then toward the mountain, as if he had its terrain laid out in his head. "Don't worry. It's smooth trail most of the way, so even doubled up, you should have seventy-five, eighty miles in it."

Jim and JJ pushed the ATV out of the building into the open air. JJ jiggled the handlebars and took a closer look at the tires while Jim went back in and checked the ground for any fluid leaks.

"Looks good," Jim said. "You want to start it up?"

"In a bit," JJ said. Iris and Harlan were approaching, Iris with a backpack and Harlan with the shotgun slung over his shoulder. "Let's make sure we've got everything first."

Iris, a woman who didn't waste words when there were things to be done, had given up arguing. She unzipped the pack and pulled out a couple of dark, knit caps.

"Toboggans," she said, handing one to JJ and one to Adam.

"My cousins made fun of me for calling them that," Adam said, yanking his down over his hair.

"What else are you supposed to call them?" JJ asked, gathering her hair at the base of her neck with a band from her wrist, then sliding the cap down over her ears.

"Hats." Adam shrugged, and grinned. "Some people got no love of the language."

"Adam!" Harlan said, taking Adam's cap-covered head in his hands, careful not to touch his skin. "Focus, son. I know you're exhausted and you're punchy, but you got to focus if everybody's gonna come out of this alive. Okay?"

Iris turned her face away, but Adam just looked earnest and said, "Yessir."

Harlan nodded. "Good man. Just remember what I said. Don't

be stupid." He gave JJ the shotgun, and she slipped the sling over her head, adjusting it until it felt stable on her back.

Iris edged back in and handed the backpack to Adam. "I also packed a bunch of granola bars and some water in there, a small blanket, and a thermos of coffee. Jim, could we have a minute?" Iris asked. Her nose had gone pink in the cold, and a breeze had picked up, wrapping strands of white hair around and into her face. But her eyes were clear, and she otherwise seemed to be holding up.

Once Jim was out of earshot, Iris took Adam's hand and said, "Remember—if it's actually him—that man is *your* father, and he's *my* son. Somewhere, deep down, he is *still* both of those things. That is something that cannot be undone." Then Iris lifted his toboggan and kissed his forehead.

Turning to JJ, she said, "Both of you remember," and kissed JJ's forehead as well. Her lips were surprisingly warm, and JJ could still feel their imprint after Iris pulled the cap back down in the front and tucked her bangs back up beneath it.

JJ nodded. Iris handed each of them a small headlamp, and once JJ had secured hers over her knit hat, she climbed on the ATV. *Just like riding a bike.* Turn the key in the middle, flip the switch, hit the power button...

The engine caught easily, jumping around a little at first but settling into a steady idle within a few seconds. Jim smiled and gave her a thumbs-up. She waved to Adam to climb on. Even with his long legs, it was quite a stretch for him to get over with JJ already astride.

"Grab on," she said.

Adam wrapped his arms gingerly around her. Once they got underway, the ride was going to kill his ribs. "That is unloaded, right?" he asked, shifting the shotgun away from his face. "I feel like you're gonna blow my brains out."

"Not as long as you keep your hands where they belong," she said, and heard his pained laugh as she shifted into low and pointed them into the forest.

53

L uther and his brother had talked at length about the Rachel situation, but didn't solve anything. Les didn't have so much as a Band-Aid in his medicine cabinet, so while they talked he'd cleaned and bandaged Luther's finger with the first aid kit from the Sheriff Department's vehicle. It wasn't a serious cut, but it bled through the gauze almost as fast as Les could wrap it and ultimately stuck out like a chubby snowman's digit. Then Luther awkwardly gathered the stray bits of pinwheel candy using a handkerchief so Les could mop the bloody beer slop from his coffee table. Luther placed the candy in a sealed, plastic sandwich bag. He doubted they had any evidentiary value, but he wasn't taking any chances.

"I'm taking this out to the car."

Luther was locking the candy in the vehicle's glovebox when a noise from the cup holder startled him. Decent reception was so rare that it always surprised Luther when his cellphone rang. Caller ID showed it was the Sheriff. Stretching across the seat from outside the vehicle, and unable to bend his mummy finger, Luther nearly dropped the phone before he could answer it.

"What's up, Sheriff?" Luther said. "Did the task force get

something?"

"Not exactly. Are you anywhere near Pine Gap?"

"I'm in the neighborhood, over at Leslie's. Why?"

"You might want to sit down for this," Grant suggested.

"Give me a minute." Luther circled around the vehicle and climbed in the driver's seat. It was damn cold again, and he started the engine to get the heater going. "All right, go ahead."

"I went out to talk to Harlan Miller this evening. He thinks Virgil Rutledge is still alive."

"Virgil Rutledge?" *Jesus Christ.* Thoughts tumbled over each other in Luther's mind. That was a name he'd hoped he'd never hear again. "What makes him think—"

"It doesn't matter," Grant interrupted. "He also thinks Virgil Rutledge took Rachel, and he has an idea where the man might have taken her."

Luther struggled to make sense of what Grant was saying, of everything he'd seen and heard over the past twenty-four hours. "Wait a minute. It's not Harlan saying this, is it? It's Adam Rutledge."

"It's both of them," Grant admitted.

"Then they're both fucking crazy."

"Luther," Grant said, "do you really believe that? And if you do, do you believe it enough to bet Rachel's life on it?"

Luther sighed. Harlan Miller wasn't much more than a name to him, but Adam... if he hadn't known about the man's "dreams," Luther would think Adam was one of the more sane people he'd met of late. More importantly, if Grant was putting enough stock in the idea to want to check it out, there might well be something to it.

"I don't know what I believe. But I trust you. What do you need?"

There was a pause on the other end, and for a moment Luther thought he'd lost the call. Then Grant said, "Harlan thinks Virgil has Rachel in a cabin out by Pine Gap, not too far from Harlan's house. You familiar with the area?"

Luther went deer hunting once in a while, but very damn rarely, and—outside of work—that was just about the only reason he'd go tramping in the woods. But his brother was a true backwoods boy, even before his recent forays into lucrative botany.

"I'm not, but I know somebody who is," Luther said. "How do you feel about Les being involved in this?"

"All things considered, including him being on our list of potential suspects..." Grant blew out his breath on the other end. "I trust you, Luther, and you shouldn't go alone. I'll leave it to you."

Luther shut off the vehicle and jogged toward the trailer. "You're not gonna sign us up for some kind of workshop now, are you? Walking on coals and falling in each other's arms and shit?"

"I'll have to check next year's budget first."

"You do that. Hold on a minute." Luther put his hand over the phone to speak with his brother. "The Sheriff's got a line on the girl. You can be a self-absorbed dick like Pop, or you can do the right thing and help me find her. What's it going to be?"

Leslie reached for the phone, and Luther smacked him affectionately on the back of the head. "Hey Sheriff, this is Les... uh-hunh... uh-hunh... Oh, yeah, I know where that is... Now?" Les went silent and looked up at the ceiling, his thinking pose. "Yeah, he's probably right. Okay." Leslie gave the phone back to his brother.

"Luther here."

"I warned them not to, but JJ and Adam Rutledge are heading up there now from the other side—Jim Henderson's property—so try not to shoot them," Grant said. "Your brother says he can find the trail to the cabin. We'll send someone as soon as we can, but let's be honest—the locals are the only ones nimble enough with our timeframe, and you're the only person I trust that's anywhere close. You okay with this?"

"Yes, sir," Luther said automatically.

"No, Luther, I appreciate it, but this isn't a 'yes, sir' kind of situation. We need eyes on the ground. But if Virgil Rutledge—or someone else—has that girl up there, he could be dangerous. He could be mentally unstable. And you're already a persona non grata with our friend D'Antonio. So if something goes wrong—"

"I get it," Luther interrupted. "But the answer's the same."

"You're going to need an ATV."

"We'll pick one up on the way. I've got the county vehicle, and I'll check in before we go off road."

"You do that," Grant said. "Good luck."

Luther shut off the phone, and found Les watching him and apparently listening in. "There's only one place I can think of to get an ATV on short notice," Les said.

"Yeah, me too," Luther said. "But it can't be helped. Let's go."

PEOPLE SAID RUDY BECK, aka Pop, was a mean sonuvabitch from the time he could speak a full sentence, and getting old hadn't done anything to mellow him. If anything, he was worse. He had a kind of fatalism that comes with the approaching certainty of death, after decades of getting away with shit you shouldn't have. The people he associated with were no better, either hard-edged bastards or sycophants. On balance, Luther found the former to be more predictable, thus often less dangerous.

"Who all you think's gonna be at Pop's?" Luther asked.

"I don't know," Les said. "The usual Saturday night crew, I guess. Whoever was too fucked up to go home."

"He got people dealing out of the house?"

"No! Pop might be dumb, but he ain't stupid."

Luther thought that might be a distinction without a differ-ence, but he took Les's point. After all, Pop had been shady all his life and had never done any hard prison time. He'd had a short stint in jail here and there. But avoiding prison, that was still quite an accomplishment.

Luther pulled up into a yard full of scattered vehicles, some abandoned, and scattered bodies, some of which seemed the same. A couple of feet stuck out the window of the car he parked alongside, an old Falcon that had to've died long ago. It looked like the only conscious people were gathered around a burn barrel, spewing flames from God knows what fuel. Their father was among them.

"The devil never sleeps," Luther muttered.

"Listen, Luther—" Leslie began.

"Don't worry," Luther said. "Just let me do the talking."

All open, bleary eyes swung toward them as the two brothers got out of the Sheriff's vehicle.

"Hey, Pop!" Leslie said, but the man ignored him.

Rudy Beck stood in work pants—an irony that was not lost on Luther—and a formerly white, short-sleeved undershirt. That was yet another reason Luther thought of his father as the devil—he'd never seen the man cold. The spare tire on his front provided insulation, but he'd only had that for the past fifteen years or so.

"Well, well, well. If it isn't my long-lost eldest. You here to arrest me, *son?*" he asked, and held out his bare wrists. His voice was full of phlegm, cheap booze, and cigarettes.

Luther did a quick situation assessment. Of the half dozen other conscious people, the skinny woman a few feet to Pop's right was the only one that worried him. She was scratching and had twitchy jitters, coming down off some kind of amphetamines. The rest of them—all men—looked as if their brains had fallen asleep but forgotten to tell their bodies. That probably wasn't far from the truth.

"Jail's too good for you, Pop," Luther said, in his best good old boy voice. "I'd rather watch you rot from the inside out. All that nastiness has gotta catch up with you sometime."

"You ought to know, boy," Pop said. "I might have my doubts about that one, but there was never any question you were my natural-born son. Despite your choice of profession."

Luther smiled, a mirror of the scary smile Pop turned on him. Pop had always cultivated his smile, that and his hair. Habitually clean-shaven, he wore his hair slicked back like a mini pompadour. Brylcreem was one of the indelible scents of Luther's childhood.

The deputy put his hands in his coat pockets, casual as could be, while keeping his eyes on Pop, the skinny chick, and a twitchy guy in a ragged, stained sweatshirt who'd suddenly appeared out of the dark on Pop's other side. "As much as I'd like to stand around and freeze my nuts off trading insults, I'm here on business. And I don't mean drug business. I'm here to help you do your civic duty."

The old man's eyes narrowed, and he stopped smiling. "Really. How's that?"

"Don't worry," Luther said. "It won't cost you a dime. Just the use of one of your vehicles."

"Like hell," Pop said.

Against his better judgment, Luther decided to tell his father the truth. "You heard about Otto Nicholson's little girl?"

"A' course."

"We've got a possible location on her. Les can help me find it, but we need a vehicle that'll get us there. Now." Luther wondered if he'd miscalculated, and wavered between threatening his father or making up some kind of bullshit regulation to save the old man face. Then Pop surprised him.

"Follow me," he said.

Luther waved for Les to go ahead of him. The house was another fifty yards or so away—Luther hadn't set foot in it since his momma died—but Pop veered right instead, toward a couple of spotlit, prefab buildings that might fall apart in a year or two, though the pieces and parts would last forever.

The deputy kept his hand near his holster. Walking toward the buildings entailed a night vision-confounding stroll through alternating patches of darkness and blinding, glaring light. On closer examination, Luther found the structures would last longer than he'd thought. He stopped in front of the smaller one—maybe eighteen by twenty feet. It was made of steel and had a combination padlock.

"Don't get any ideas about anything else you see in here, and don't get any ideas about what's in the other one," his father said, popping off the lock. He grunted as he slid the door up on its tracks until it disappeared, then flipped a light switch just inside the entry.

Luther blinked against the bright fluorescent light. "I don't think a riding mower is gonna get us there," he said. There were two of the big buggers in the front, and Luther started to step around them for a better look at what else was there.

"Hey!" Pop said. "I didn't give you permission to enter. You can just stay right goddamn there until I tell you to move."

Luther kept his mouth shut and stayed put. He didn't have the leisure to piss the man off any more than he already had. But he did let his eyes roam, making mental notes, in hopes of returning someday and confiscating every last thing of worth in the man's possession, all of the weed whackers and other lawn maintenance and—why the hell was an armchair squeezed in there?

"Yep, I got what you need," Pop called from the back. "Go on around the outside to the other door."

Luther pulled out his flashlight. He didn't trust anybody here any farther than he could throw them, and he wasn't about to wade through the weeds in the dark.

"Come on, Les."

As the brothers neared the corner, they could see light spilling from the open door on the end and hear Pop banging around, moving things inside. Les jogged ahead of Luther, like a kid that never tires of being smacked.

"Oh, Luther, but this is a thing of beauty!" he called out. "It looks like something the Terminator would drive."

Leslie stood before a brand new, utility terrain vehicle. The beast was metallic black, with bench style, side-by-side seats, a bad-ass-looking molded laminate hood, and a roll bar that could withstand a T-Rex. Luther guessed it retailed for close to fifteen grand, with bells and whistles.

Pop came out grinning. "I think that'll get you where you're going, come hell or high water."

Luther had to agree. "I daresay it will."

54

———

Luther and Les had rigged up a light trailer to the Sheriff's vehicle—another Pop loaner—and were on the road with the UTV in about fifteen minutes. Les had been quiet since they left Pop's place. Luther's mind was going over logistics and watching for the turn off the state road when Les finally asked, out of the blue, "You think that's why he gave me a girl's name?"

It took Luther a moment to figure out what Les was referring to, although it probably shouldn't have. Jibes about Les's paternity were among Pop's favorite mind-fucks.

"I told you before," Luther said, "don't let him get under your skin. Leslie isn't a girl's name—"

"Yes, it is," Les interrupted. "Bob Radnor named his girl Leslie."

"Bob Radnor's a dumbass. And Leslie O'Neal made it to the Pro Bowl six times as a defensive end. While playing for the Chargers, no less," Luther said, slowing the vehicle. "Is this my turn?"

"Yeah."

Luther put the SUV into low gear before making the turn. It was a steeper drop off the road than he'd expected, and the trailer jounced over the edge. Luther hadn't driven a truck with a trailer in a long time. Splitting his attention between the narrow road in front of him and the expanse of metal behind him—lit only by his taillights—and hearing the sounds of the trailer's heavy metal pursuit, he was reminded why he had avoided the experience.

The road leveled out a bit, and Luther let out the breath he'd been holding. "Look, Les, we got to have our heads in the game now. And there are lots of ways I could pretty this up, but I'm just gonna say it straight out. What are the chances our momma would have had an affair?"

He heard sputtering noises from Leslie, but no words. "Exactly. You realize, he says that to insult her as much as he does to insult you. And if, by some miracle, she'd been lucky enough to find someone else to love her while she was still married to the bastard, what do you think Pop would've done to her?"

"He would have killed both of them."

"For starters," Luther said.

"I guess I didn't think about it that way," Leslie said.

Luther did. He'd prayed when he was growing up—before Les was born—that his mother would find someone else. But even in his fantasies, he knew they'd have to run far enough away that Rudy Beck wouldn't find them. When Luther got older, he'd spoken with his mother about leaving. She wouldn't hear of it. She was a very religious woman, and if God had joined her with a bad man, then it was her cross to bear. Until she died.

It was getting harder to concentrate on the road. Maybe because the adrenaline was wearing off, Luther hadn't been to bed yet, and it was... whatever the hell time it was. He couldn't make out the numbers on the digital clock on the dash, much less his watch, but it wasn't anywhere near light yet. He was suddenly damned tired.

"Les?"

"Yeah."

"Are you okay to operate that thing?" Luther asked, gesturing toward the trailer.

"What do you mean?"

"I mean, you had a rough day, it's Saturday night, and you seemed about half shot in the ass when I showed up."

"I'm fine."

"So how much farther?" Luther asked.

"I don't know. Maybe a couple more miles. You'll get to what looks like a real sharp turn, but it's actually where the logging road loops in."

Sure enough, just under three bone-rattling miles later, Luther saw something ahead he could not begin to navigate with the trailer. But Les was right—he didn't have to, because it was the logging trail. All the fallen leaves had made it impossible to distinguish from his road.

"When's the last time you were out here?" Luther asked.

"It's been a good long while. Probably... April? Yeah, April sounds right. I was out hunting for morels."

Luther didn't bother pulling off to the side of the road, just parked. He wasn't sure where the side of the road was, and the only traffic this time of night was likely to be the four-legged variety. Luther handed his brother a headlamp and the two men went to work unstrapping the UTV from the trailer.

"I didn't know you hunted morels," Luther said. "That'd be worth going out in the woods for. How do you fix them?"

"Same way Mom used to. Soak them in vinegar water for a bit, then fry them up in butter with a little flour. I'll let you know come spring, if you want to go out."

Luther grunted as he pulled out the sticky ramp to get the UTV to the ground. "Yeah, that'd be good."

Once they got the machine down, Luther left Les to move it up the trail a little and out of the way. Meanwhile, Luther worked to leave room for backup to get in, if it came to that. He fought to get the trailer to the side of the road, pulling back and forth and swearing every time he oversteered in reverse and the trailer bucked. Then he pulled out his cellphone to call the Sheriff.

No service.

The enormity of what Luther was about to do hit him. For the past hour since he'd spoken with Grant, Luther had managed to stay in denial about why he was here, to lose himself in the rush of successfully getting from one step to the next to the next. But now, it hit him. He was here to save a little girl's life. And he might already be too late. Or he might be in time, but still fail.

Or I might freeze my ass off, sitting here whining about it.

Luther used the car's radio to call in and gave Grant his location. Law enforcement didn't speak in radio codes so much as they used to in Luther's rookie days, but he still found the clicks and static reassuring. "Any word from Adam and JJ?" he asked.

"Negative," Grant said. "I don't know how they'd get word to us, anyway."

Luther agreed. "I got no cell service now, and the reception's not gonna get any better."

"Copy that. You wearing your radio?"

"Yeah, but this kind of terrain, it won't take long to get out of range of the vehicle, and I got no way to boost the signal." The car's radio went silent long enough that Luther finally asked, "Sheriff, you still there?"

"The cabin's about two miles from your ten-twenty," Grant responded. "I'll tell you what I told JJ—surveillance only. If the child's there, hold tight until we can get a full team in for a recovery. You got that?"

"Copy, Sheriff. Eyes only."

"If you meet up with JJ and Adam, send them back down with your assessment. And watch your back."

"Will do." Luther sat, listening to the bubble of relative silence in the car. The drone of the UTV's engine at the edge of the trail could be a big lawnmower on the last day of summer. If you'd never heard a lawnmower before. Assuming Virgil Rutledge was behind it all, Luther wondered if he'd recognize the man. He wondered if the man would recognize him.

The deputy traded out his broad-brimmed campaign hat for a black toboggan that covered his ears and wouldn't bang into every damn thing in creation if he had to start sneaking around. Then he stepped out into the cold and checked his equipment, reminding himself how everything on his duty belt interacted with his coat when it was zipped. He made a few adjustments, then locked the vehicle, stowed his flashlight and fired up a headlamp instead to keep his hands free.

Time to roll.

55

The rhythmic sound and vibrations of the ATV traveling through Adam's body; the constant pain of his stretching ribs as he hung on to JJ, punctuated by the sharper pain of unpredictable jounces; and finally, the passivity of Adam's position on the back—all of these combined to make him not entirely present, caught in a dissociative haze.

The ATV's headlights illuminated the path directly in front of them, but with his head turned sideways, Adam saw little more than an impression of the dark woods passing by. The way had gotten easier, and less painful, when they'd finally reached the logging road. An occasional hidden rock still gave them a wake-up call, but JJ no longer had to dodge among the trees and game paths, ducking down as low as the handlebars with Adam following her lead. JJ was also able to pick up the pace, and the engine tone changed as she accelerated and continued climbing the mountain.

Adam knew Harlan was right; something had fundamentally changed when Harlan tapped into Adam's link with Rachel, something that made connecting with her even more dangerous. Harlan had tried to hide it, but Adam was certain the man's exhaustion after the vision with Rachel wasn't "normal." Adam believed that he'd acted as a conduit between Rachel and Harlan, that Rachel had drawn upon both men to carry on her escape attempt when she otherwise would have collapsed. That may have even been Harlan's intent, to help the girl. However, Adam didn't think Harlan had meant to leave the line between them open. In fact, he wasn't sure Harlan knew how to close it.

Adam's memory of falling unconscious in the shower was muddled, but it occurred to him that JJ may have saved Rachel's life as well as his. Perhaps, even then, Rachel was drawing upon Adam to help mitigate the effects of the severe asthma attack. But that time, it was as if she'd been sucking his energy through a straw. Tonight, Harlan had opened a fire hose.

Harlan was probably safe from the effects now, so long as he wasn't touching either of them. But there was a growing certainty in Adam's mind that if he let Rachel in again, she would kill him, without ever meaning to. And it was getting harder and harder not to slip away, to release his tenuous grip on the conscious world. And on JJ...

Adam felt himself falling, felt the nausea kicking in. JJ grabbed Adam's arm as it dropped from her waist, jerking the vehicle's handlebars so the ATV slid sideways in the leaf litter and Adam was thrown back into his seat. JJ cut the engine and set the brake, twisting sideways to avoid kicking Adam in the face or beating herself in the head with the shotgun while she dismounted. Then she chocked the wheel for good measure.

Adam sat, rocking a little as if the ATV still moved, still hearing and feeling the engine drone through his body.

"Hey!" JJ said, placing her cold hand against his cheek. "You in there somewhere?"

Adam nodded, struggling to engage his brain to form words. He finally managed a "Yeah."

"Good," JJ said, giving his cheek a gentle slap before cutting the ATV's headlights and switching her headlamp on, using the red light setting so it didn't blind him. "How about some of that coffee?"

Adam stared at JJ, uncomprehending, until she tugged at the strap on his shoulder. The backpack strap. The backpack that held the thermos, and thankfully a blanket that kept it from constantly bouncing against his back. Adam slid the pack from his shoulder, unzipped it and gave the thermos to JJ. She poured a little into the metal cup and handed it back to him.

"Drink," she said.

The metal felt cool and somehow wrong against his lips, but the coffee was still surprisingly hot, burning the tip of his tongue. He took a few careful sips and held it back to JJ.

"No, I don't need it," she said. "Finish it."

He did, and found that the bitter liquid helped his sluggishness, his sense of disconnection from the physical world. It also made him remember how cold he was. He switched on his own headlamp and screwed the cup back on the thermos.

"I think we should go on foot from here," JJ said.

"Noise?" Adam asked.

JJ nodded, her red beam bouncing like a strobe. "We're at least a half mile from the cabin, so hopefully if he heard the ATV, he won't think anything of it. You ready?"

Adam shuffled back into the pack, moving his ribs as little as possible, and they set off up the trail. The moon had set since he'd seen Rachel, and he figured they probably had another hour before there was even a hint of light in the sky. His toboggan helped keep the headlamp strap from giving him a headache, but the light still made him queasy. He was never quite sure when his foot would strike the ground. The red color wasn't very bright and had a limited range. Adam couldn't see much beyond the six-foot half-circle that moved with them. At least, he told himself, that meant it'd be harder for someone else to spot them as well.

They'd been hiking up the trail for about fifteen minutes, silent save the shush of their feet in the leaves, when something changed. There was a familiarity to the landscape, even though he couldn't distinguish the details.

Adam put a hand on JJ's arm, asking her to stop. "Would you put out your lamp for a second?"

She did, and Adam switched his over to bright white light, just for a few seconds.

"Adam!" JJ hissed.

He took in the rise to their right and the patch of mountain laurel below that seemed to go on forever, then switched back to red light. "Rachel was here," he said.

He and JJ walked to the uphill side of the trail. The dirt along the edge crumbled as they stepped up onto the bank. There were long tracks in the leaves above them where someone's feet had slid, sometimes digging down deep enough to expose bare, dark, moist earth.

Adam turned and hopped off the bank back down to the trail. He knew how the story ended, or at least this part of it. There was an indentation and broken branches where Rachel had burrowed into the evergreen shrubs. She'd had her eyes closed, so he wasn't sure where Rachel had finally emerged. He and JJ approached the track from the adult pursuer's point of view instead, walking around the vegetation where a large man would have walked to intercept a child.

"Oh, God," JJ whispered in front of him, hand reflecting the headlamp like a flash as it flew toward her mouth. "She *was* here."

Rachel hadn't left anything behind—no scrap of fabric or cherished toy or scratched initials—but JJ was right; there was no doubt the child had been here. There was a deeper indentation at the edge of the shrubs this time, where she'd emerged, and the leaf litter was disturbed in a large area around it. Almond-shaped mountain laurel leaves lay, bruised and torn, where Rachel had pulled them from the branches she'd desperately clung to.

Adam picked up one of the leathery leaves. It was damp, from the ground and its rough treatment. And the scent...

Adam got down on his knees and rested his face against the ground. The items in the pack shifted toward the ground with him, the thermos nearly cracking him in the head. His red light masked what color remained in the decomposing leaves, and their musky, organic scent of decomposition made him start, like a squirt from a lemon. He felt molecules of the odor sticking to his throat, making their way to his lungs. Adam got to his feet abruptly, before the sensations could take hold.

"Are leaves a trigger for Rachel's asthma?" he asked softly, stifling a cough.

"They could be."

He was sure he knew the answer, but Adam had to ask anyway. "Can she die from an asthma attack?"

This far away, JJ's pupils were indistinguishable in her dark eyes, and the red light highlighted the planes of her face, the hollows beneath her cheeks. Adam shivered—she looked like a vampire. He couldn't shake the image from his mind until she spoke.

"Fatal attacks are generally less common among children than among adults, but yes, it's possible," JJ said. "And it's more likely if she had a severe attack recently."

Adam remembered Rachel gasping, falling over to her side, before Harlan jumped in and altered the connection, before— together—they'd given her the strength to hide in the shrubs. Then when she'd burst through, and the man grabbed her, Harlan left and her chest turned to stone. Adam's had, too—like a vacuum with no release—until Harlan had pulled him free of her.

Adam scrambled back toward the trail. JJ chased after him. He slipped and fell to his knees, and his head cracked her cheek hard as he tried to stand.

"Ouch!" JJ hissed, and grabbed Adam's shoulder before wiping her watering eyes. "Wait! Slow down. We're supposed to find her and sit tight. We can't risk provoking Virgil, or whoever it is that has her."

Adam took a moment to straighten his headlamp—he'd knocked it askew, too—and find his voice. "JJ, you don't understand. We can't wait to see if he harms her or not. She's already dying."

56

─────

JJ looked in both directions, bringing up the map in her mind.

By the time they'd reached the trail, Adam had convinced JJ he was right. They'd hiked another hundred yards or so up the trail before a path diverged from either side. Both had obviously been used recently and regularly.

"That's the direction of the cabin," JJ said softly, pointing uphill to the right. Gesturing toward the left, she said, "That one goes down a little ways and then swings back around the side of the mountain to the rock thing Iris mentioned. I'm guessing he took her to the cabin."

Adam nodded, conciliatory, but JJ had a feeling he was about to pull something. His face was too... what? Calm? Superficially candid?

"That makes sense," Adam agreed, "but we can't afford to be wrong. We don't have time to be wrong."

I knew it, you sneaky... JJ's voice rose a bit as she said, "We're not splitting up."

"I wasn't suggesting that." Adam lowered his own voice, as if trying to lead by example. "I think I should try to make contact with her, reach out through whatever link there is between us."

"No," JJ said. As if she could stop him. As if she wanted to. She *did* want to—of course she did—but what if he was right? What if this was the only way to save Rachel? She knew Adam was watching all of her thoughts play out, just waiting for her to come to the same conclusion he had. He knew her well enough to realize that he couldn't win against her from a position of opposition. But if *she* convinced *herself*...

"Okay, fine," she said.

Adam had the gall to grin, and she nearly smacked him. He must have seen that, too, because the grin disappeared just as quickly. Adam sat on the damp ground—which seemed a wise precaution from what she'd seen of his forays into whatever-it-was so far—and she sat a few feet away.

"Don't be stupid," JJ said, "or Harlan will kick both our asses."

Adam shut off his headlamp and closed his eyes. JJ almost turned hers off as well, but removed it from her head and held it in her hand instead, pointed away from Adam. She wished she'd thought to get one of Rachel's inhalers from Dorothy or Grant or someone, sometime. But then, it's not like she'd seen either of them before running off on this harebrained rescue attempt. She wasn't omniscient.

Apparently, Adam wasn't either. JJ tried to be patient, but she didn't do patient well. At some point she wondered, *if I ran to the cabin and checked it out on my own while he sat here, would I have made it back yet?* Then she remembered that she was the one who'd said no splitting up, and Adam would have been vulnerable sitting on his own. Did he even know she was there? She shone her red light in his general direction, but avoided his eyes.

"Another minute or two," he whispered.

JJ watched as he pulled a bent leaf from his pocket and began running it through his fingers, a little like some teenaged boys did with quarters, from digit to digit to digit. Then he sighed and leaned sideways, somehow descending slowly instead of landing on his face.

"Adam?" She crept closer.

He didn't answer, and his body suddenly went rigid.

"Adam!" She bent over him, shoving her lamp back on her head. Was he holding his breath, or just not breathing? JJ flicked his face. No response.

"Don't you dare pull this shit again!"

JJ tried pinching the webbing between his finger and thumb, but that had never worked well for her. She wasn't about to do a sternal rub on someone who'd had CPR that morning, but she had to get him to snap out of it—fast—or he'd be getting CPR again. She unzipped Adam's jacket, so there was less fabric between her hands and his body.

"I can't believe I'm doing this," she muttered, then reached out and grabbed Adam's nipples through his shirt and twisted hard.

Adam's eyes flew open and he gasped, then covered his chest with his arms. She rolled him over to his side, where he gasped a few more times before settling down to a shallow panting.

"Are you all right?" she asked.

"Next time, buy me a drink first," he wheezed.

"I'm going to help you sit up now. Okay?" JJ said.

He nodded, and she gently looped her arms beneath his and pulled him upright, then zipped his coat for him. He winced, and the facial contortion was even more disturbing in the red light.

"What did you see?" she asked, kneeling next to him. Adam was still having difficulty breathing, so she slipped a hand over his wrist, checking to make sure his heart wasn't completely arrhythmic or about to explode. When he had enough presence of mind to push her hand away, she let him. His hands were shaking, but his pulse seemed normal enough under the circumstances.

"I didn't see anything," he said, then twisted to grab at her arms. Adam's eyes were too wide, and he still didn't seem entirely present with her, shifting his head from side to side as if he kept catching movement in his peripheral vision. "She's in bad shape. We've got to help her, Janie."

"Shh..." She turned his face toward her. His skin was so cold beneath her hands, and his lips were colorless enough to be indistinguishable from the rest of his face. JJ finally realized she must be blinding him and angled her light to aim a little higher, above his head. "We will, sweetie, but we have to find her first. You said you couldn't see anything. Is that because her eyes are closed?"

"Yes," he said, rubbing his face. "That's why I couldn't get through. She's unconscious, but I think at the end, she knew I was there. It's like, she *draws* from me. She doesn't mean to hurt me—"

"But that's what Harlan was warning you about."

"I think so." He shook his head and slapped his own cheeks hard, then shook his head again. He closed his eyes, and—without thinking—JJ punched him in the arm.

"Ouch! It's okay. I'm okay now, I'm just trying to remember." He closed his eyes again, but JJ restrained her fist. A few moments later, Adam said, "I think I could hear the wind—there was a breeze, tickling at the hair by her temples. And I could feel the ground beneath her. Cold. There was a rock under her right side, rounded but hard, like it was sunk into the ground."

That could only mean one thing. "She's not at the cabin," JJ said.

"No. She's by the rock outcrop." Adam got to one knee, wobbled, and said, "Help me up. And don't argue."

She wanted to argue—especially when she had to support most of his weight to get him upright—but what was the point? No matter how much of a mess he was, they were better off together and more vulnerable alone. Plus, if she did leave Adam behind, she didn't trust him not to reach out to Rachel again and lapse into a coma. Or worse.

"Fine." She blinked against the glare while she turned on his headlamp for him. "But if we get to something you can't physically do, you're staying put. I'm not carrying you, and I'm not waiting."

He managed a pale imitation of his usual grin. "I figured you'd just push me off the cliff."

JJ led the way, downslope for about seventy-five yards or so before the path began gradually veering right. Soon their course was roughly parallel to the logging road they'd left, and they were heading uphill again. Unlike the logging road, at times this path was narrow enough to reach out and touch the rough bark of tree trunks on either side. Adam bumped into JJ's heels once, with a whispered apology, but otherwise he kept up.

Eventually the trees began to thin, and the species shifted toward more conifers and fewer deciduous trees. The forest floor was strewn with pine needles, and the path became less claustrophobic, but with more rocks encroaching. JJ kicked the edge of a particularly large, low stone with her booted toe. More rocks clustered beyond it... she angled her head up and to the right, and there was the outcrop.

She and Adam stood alongside the broad base of a massive pinnacle of rock that rose higher than their headlamps could reach. Vertical crevices and horizontal plates showed as narrow, parallel shadows, sometimes intersecting. JJ reached out to touch the surface of the formation—hard but slightly knobbly. She spun her fingertip and felt individual grains in the stone grinding down her skin.

It was hard to get a sense of scale with her headlamp in the dark, but if anything, she'd guess Iris had underestimated how big it was. As JJ faced the outcrop, to her right she saw a field of boulders. They ranged in size from small benches to Volkswagens, resting on a slope steep enough to require scrambling on hands and knees, but not quite so steep as to be considered technically climbing. To her left, the ground continued dropping away from the formation. The forest ridge sloped down sharply behind them as well. JJ imagined there would be a fantastic vista come daylight. For now, she wouldn't say the sky was brightening exactly, but she could tell that it was there, that there was a feeling of spaciousness even in the dark.

"Wow," Adam whispered.

There was no sign of anyone, so Rachel must be on the other side of the pinnacle. JJ had no landmarks in the dark, and her lamp range was limited. Rather than backtracking on the path, hiking through the woods, and making her way back toward the pinnacle from the other side, it seemed simpler to climb up and over it, not to mention more likely to preserve the element of surprise.

Adam would never make it, at least not without injuring himself even worse. He'd come to stand next to her, their combined lamps forming a deeper pool of red.

"So you think she's over there," he said, anticipating her thoughts as always.

She nodded, and he reached out to squeeze her arm.

"Okay," he said. "Be safe."

"Always."

57

Adam should have stopped JJ. He should have said, *I don't think Rachel's over there*. But he didn't know for sure. And he was so tired. Placing one foot in front of the other without tripping took almost everything he had.

But those weren't the real reasons he hadn't stopped her.

There was something else.

There were *things* out there, things in the forest that he could *almost* see, but not quite—just glimpses as he walked past. Flashes. Shadows. They wanted Rachel. And it was his job to protect her.

Part of him knew that he should have told JJ about them. But another part of him, a *whispering* part of him, said the things were easier to see without her, so didn't that mean that JJ shouldn't be there? That he'd have a better chance of protecting Rachel without her? *Maybe,* it whispered, *he couldn't even trust JJ*.

Adam stopped.

Of course he could trust JJ. He shook his head. Red light reflected off his pale hand and blinded him. Adam pushed the headlamp against his forehead, pressing the case through his cap into his skull, until he was afraid he'd break the light. *Snap out of it.*

Adam looked around. His hand strayed to his chest, wanting to touch the key around his neck, but he couldn't feel it through his coat and it was too cold to take his coat off. Where the hell was he anyway?

He could make out a stunted pine a few yards away, grown not more than knee high, but nothing beyond it. Against his better judgment, Adam switched the light over to the brightest white setting for greater range. He was on a level ledge that, a few yards ahead, tapered off to a slope. Even the brightest light was swallowed up trying to penetrate the dark sky that hung in front of him. Mostly coniferous forest stretched out on one side, and likely on the slope below him. He must be directly in front of the rock pinnacle.

Adam slowly tilted his head back, looking for the remote but reassuring touchstone of stars, but couldn't find any. He tilted farther back—

"Jesus!" he gasped.

There was rock—not sky—directly overhead. Adam wasn't in front of the pinnacle; he was *beneath* it.

Adam's heart pounded as he was overcome by a fear of being crushed beneath thousands of tons of rock. He stumbled forward, trying to get free of the tomb, and fell hard to his knees. Hard enough to tear a bloody gash in his (*Harlan's*) jeans, and hard enough that the pain jolting from the edge of his kneecap to his hip helped push the panic away.

He lay beneath a few feet of overhang—not even a proper cave —an overhang that had probably been there for thousands of years. He wasn't sure why he had panicked. Perhaps because he had no memory of strolling beneath a chunk of mountain. Adam rolled over to a sitting position and manipulated his knee, wincing. Despite the tenderness, it seemed he hadn't done more than superficial damage. He took a deep, calming breath and gazed at the rock above his head. The white LED light illuminated a washed-out hint of color variations, stains where water and minerals must have seeped through over the millennia like a ceiling under a leaky roof.

But he wasn't supposed to have the white light on. Why was that again? *Focus.*

Adam's knee held his weight when he stood, so that was good. Just one of those things he needed to walk off. Calm or not, he wasn't about to pace under a cliff. He reached up and switched the lamp back to red, waiting a few seconds for his eyes to adjust before hiking out. He emerged from beneath the overhang and picked his way carefully over ground strewn with rocks. It was crazy to think he couldn't remember coming this way. But maybe he hadn't. Maybe he'd come a different way—

A jolt ran through Adam as a familiar, cold breeze brushed his cheek, singing softly while it cut its way up through a ravine, or wrapped around some unseen geological feature. He recognized that hollow song.

Rachel was here.

But where?

Adam strayed from the base of the formation and followed what felt like a path but didn't look it, heading back the way he'd presumably come in. Most of the scattered rocks were knee height or higher. Although it tugged at his aching ribs, he found it easier to sit on these boulders as if they were stools, swinging his legs around rather than stepping over or between them. It felt like a strange, painful, children's game.

Right about the time his forward motion became automatic, unthinking, Adam reached a section of smaller rocks—too small to comfortably sit on, and small enough that his boot wedged among them in the dark, stuck. He tugged his foot free and perched precariously on one hip on the offending stones, trying to secure his loosened boot with fumbling, unresponsive fingers. He blinked hard, unable to decide if the laces were properly tied. The shape of the loops looked foreign. Adam looked away, trying to give his brain an opportunity to reset.

And that's when he saw her. Lying in the dead space between the pinnacle and the forest. Unmoving.

Oh, God. Adam rushed to Rachel, knelt next to her and put his face above hers. He couldn't tell if she was breathing, but when her lips brushed his face they were cold, colder than his own skin. *Where are you, JJ?* He reached down, clasped Rachel's icy hands between his—they were so *tiny*—and rubbed them, gently but vigorously.

Rachel didn't react at all; the only time she moved was when he moved her. Adam put his fingers to her throat. Nothing, so he pushed a little harder, a little deeper beneath her jaw. And there, like a little moth... there was something, he was sure of it. He brushed her dark hair back from her face and pulled a stray twig free. "Rachel," he whispered. "Rachel, it's me, Adam. You know who I am. It's safe to come back. Please come back."

Something moved in Adam's peripheral vision—a shadow—and he whipped his head around. But there was nothing there. Just rocks, too squat to hide behind. *Great, now I'm losing my fricking mind again.*

"Rachel, please, don't make me come get you. I don't know if I can bring you back on my own. Please come back." And what if she didn't? Was it better to pick her up and carry her out, back to the logging trail? Could he even find his way without JJ? He'd have to—

Movement again. This time it was back toward the ledge. Just a flash and it was gone, but he had the impression of a girl, one bigger than Rachel. Adam's hand brushed against Rachel's while he continued watching (*there's nothing there—not really*), and he instinctively clasped it. Did he feel a tightening of her small fingers in response?

"Rachel?"

Adam bent double, assaulted by a wave of nausea as energy was suddenly yanked from him into the child. His heart fluttered in his chest, but Rachel's breath became tangible, animating the stray hairs around her face. Adam released her hand, and felt the drain ease to a trickle. He braced his legs, and without giving himself time to think about it, lifted the small girl in his arms.

"Argh!" Adam couldn't hold in the sound as her weight

shredded his ribs and aching sternum and brought tears to his eyes. He struggled to lift Rachel into a stable position, until her head finally came to rest against his shoulder.

Patches of bare ground appeared as he stumbled—he thought—in the direction of the logging trail, but it was difficult to see where he was going. Simply walking took so much concentration that it was a relief when he reached a recognizable path. Adam still caught his toe on the uneven ground, and Rachel's forehead brushed against his bare neck, instantly triggering the familiar tug of vertigo. He maneuvered sideways around the next rock, nudging Rachel's face back against his jacket, and the sensation passed.

As Adam grew weaker, he lost what little confidence he'd had in his perceptions. Shadows slithered and coiled in the periphery, just beyond the range of his headlamp. Were they natural products of an exhausted mind in low light conditions, or dark manifestations of beings with consciousness? He didn't know, so he pretended not to see them and kept walking, step after staggering step.

He'd protect Rachel as long as he could, but her only chance was for Adam to find a place to hide, a place she'd be safe until more help arrived. If she kept draining him at this rate, he'd be dead—or insane—before daybreak.

58

JJ focused on not breaking her neck in the dark, which was more difficult than she would have expected when mostly crawling on one's hands and knees. She paused for breath and a wardrobe adjustment, tugging at her pants as she stretched to mount the next boulder. The damn jeans didn't have as much give as she'd thought. Of course, the shotgun on her back didn't help, either. Glancing over her shoulder, she couldn't see a hint of Adam's headlamp anywhere. Maybe she was just out of range, but she didn't think so. She had a bad feeling, deep in her bones. She never should have left him.

Too late to turn back now. About halfway across the rocky ridge, JJ hit a bare spot—no boulders, just plain dirt—and wondered if she had glaciers or humans or something else entirely to thank for scraping it clear. It wasn't more than ten or fifteen yards, but her muscles were grateful to stand upright and walk again, and she felt like she made up some time crossing it.

She'd be glad to see the end of this night. JJ hadn't been working the garden or chopping wood lately, so her soft hands were sore and abraded, and one of her fingernails was broken and bloody. She was tired, and the headlamp—either its dim, red light or the tight strap around her skull—had given her a headache. At least the batteries had held up so far.

On and on, stretch and crawl and climb, until the next boulder patch. JJ told herself that she was almost there, almost finished. She sighed. The rock in front of her was so large, she couldn't see the end of it as she hoisted herself on top. She traversed it slowly, with her hands and knees feeling almost equally raw. This particular stone had more fissures than most, knobbly sections that caught at her fingers and prodded her palms and kneecaps. The next rock must be lower; she couldn't see it yet. As soon as her fingers cleared the front edge, she lay flat, swung her hips around, and stretched out her legs—

Toward nothing.

There *was* no next rock, only empty space.

JJ was falling. First her leading leg, then her hip. She dug her back leg into the ground hard, and one hand locked onto a small rock spur while the other clawed for finger holds, but her mass still dragged her down. Suddenly her butt and her remaining leg were suspended in open air. She gasped as gravity seized her and her falling weight wrenched her shoulders. The shotgun banged against her back.

Fortunately, the rock face was neither entirely vertical nor absolutely sheer. JJ managed to gain an initial foothold around knee height to her left, then twisted sideways, slowly inching her way back onto the top. Grunting, she pulled herself forward until her thighs, then her knees, finally touched solid ground.

JJ rolled over onto her side and lay shaking and panting with shock, adrenaline, and relief. *Damn, I tore another fingernail. No more nighttime rock climbing.* But she realized she hadn't actually seen the ground when she was falling. It might only be ten feet or so, just far enough to make her panic because she couldn't touch. JJ crept forward, body perpendicular to the rock edge so her head would be the sole portion of her body not on solid ground. Only then did she allow herself to look down.

Unlike where she'd begun, this side of the outcrop had no

gradual slope, only a cliff. The final rock hadn't been a separate boulder; it had been the pinnacle itself. JJ estimated it was a drop of about twenty-five feet before hitting the solid rock below where she lay. It was hard to say exactly; she wasn't certain her light quite reached the ground. Inching in reverse until her head was a safe foot or so from the precipice, she switched off her headlamp, rolled over on her back (and the shotgun—she shifted a little to her side to accommodate it) and gazed at the black sky.

Shit. She'd wasted all that energy and time—time Rachel didn't have—nearly crawling off a cliff, and for what? Not to mention, she'd left Adam alone. Stupid, arrogant... Why did she always think she was the only one who could—

A sound somewhere below cut off JJ's self-recriminations. She kept her light off, but rolled onto her belly, crawled back to the edge and peered over. There was a man below, wearing a headlamp.

It was not Adam.

How could she be sure? The figure's white LED light shone out of a tunnel-like hood that covered his head, not a toboggan. He was carrying something—a rock? Probably. JJ watched him pick up a similar object from the ground. Then he continued walking toward the steeper end of the rock pinnacle, the front of the formation. JJ had assumed there wasn't an easy access around the front. Of course, she'd also assumed the formation would be the same on both sides—symmetrical—and that climbing over the back edge would be most efficient. Obviously, she didn't know shit about geology.

If the figure—Virgil Rutledge, or whoever the hell it was— knew a path around the front, he could approach Adam unaware. Alternatively, JJ had been right all along: there wasn't a front passage, and the man was keeping Rachel on this side, but closer to the leading boundary of the pinnacle. Either way, she'd have to follow him to find out.

Considering she'd nearly walked off a cliff with her headlamp *on*, there was no way JJ was following him with it turned off. With the limited range of the red light and as high as she was above him, she wasn't that worried about being seen if she didn't stray too close to the edge. Still, it was nerve-racking.

So long as JJ stuck to the pinnacle rock itself and stayed clear of the loose boulders, the ground was a solid slab and relatively easy to traverse. But she still had to approach the precipice occasionally—with her light off—to check the man's progress. As she advanced toward the front of the pinnacle, the wind grew stronger, not enough to buffet her off her feet but certainly enough to add to her uneasiness. On the bright side—since Adam wasn't here, it was her job to come up with a bright side—the lonely, whistling howl of the wind would cover any stumbles she might make.

JJ had a sense that the front cliff face was imminent before her headlamp told her it was there. Maybe the sky was beginning to lighten. She crept—squatting more than walking—slowly to the edge and knelt down for a closer look. The man must have picked up another rock along the way. His own lamp reflected off two tucked into the crook of his left arm and one in his right hand. He'd stopped and seemed to be searching the woods at the periphery with his light, as though he'd heard something. Then his gaze turned to the rock formation next to him, and the light swung in JJ's direction. She didn't dare move except to close her eyes.

JJ held her breath. By the time she decided it was safe to open her eyes, he was gone.

Dammit! She opened her eyes wide, straining to see anything, and finally—there it was. A flash from his headlamp, coming out from somewhere beneath her.

There was a passage around the front after all.

The quickest way around—back to Adam—was to stick to the pinnacle rim, to continue skirting the precipice and avoid her previous bouldering adventure. She could have moved much faster if she'd had a walking stick. JJ thought of the shotgun on her back, and almost as quickly thought of her father looking down from heaven, giving her stink eye for even thinking such a thing in jest. Well, now that she'd gotten her dad's attention, hopefully he'd stick around for a while and keep an eye on her and Adam. They could use all the help they could get.

She never saw the rock-carrying man again and eventually stopped checking for him. That helped her make decent time around the front sweep of the rock formation, but soon after she turned back toward the mountain—what she thought of as "really solid ground"—JJ hit a snag. A cleft sliced through the pinnacle, leaving a gaping fissure that was too broad and deep to cross without wings. Bypassing it sent her, and her aching hands and knees, back into the central boulder field. Except, of course, it wasn't just in the center on this side. The boulders stretched from the pinnacle all the way to the forest.

Stretch and crawl and climb, on and on, again... Finally, JJ stood in a familiar area on the broad slope where she'd originally begun. It seemed forever ago, and JJ wanted to lie down and cry with the futility, but she kept moving. She told herself that, regardless of the temptation, there wasn't a decent spot to lie down. Still, JJ was aware that she was entering a state of exhaustion where she was getting stupid. She'd begun to lose touch with why she was out here at all.

Perhaps that's why the voice sounded so surreal, echoing suddenly in the dark, when a man yelled, "You can't have the girl!"

The voice wasn't Adam's.

59

———

Adam nearly dropped Rachel when a man appeared seemingly out of nowhere. Bright light shot from the man's brow, and a hood shrouded his head and obscured his features.

"Who are you?" Adam asked. His arms quivered with exhaustion. He'd told himself he could put Rachel down when he reached the path through the trees, the path the man was now blocking. He wasn't going to make it.

"Damn you, I said leave her in peace!" The man raised a weapon—something long—over his shoulder.

Adam didn't wait to see what it was. He wheeled with the girl, back the way he'd come, and heard the resounding clang of metal on rock behind him a second later. There was nowhere to go. Adam couldn't leave the path while carrying Rachel, and ahead, even the path itself was rocky enough to slow him down. He'd never get away with her.

Still, Adam hurtled over and around obstacles faster than he would have thought possible, Rachel bouncing in his arms. If he could make it to the overhang, maybe there was a place to hide her. Just up ahead—

Something struck the heel of Adam's boot from behind and sent him flying. He twisted his body as he fell, elbow hitting the ground and hip landing on a stone. Pain shot down Adam's leg and up into his back, but he avoided crushing Rachel.

A groan echoed through the air and Adam thought it was his own, until he looked up and saw a shovel swinging at him. Its arc seemed slow, slow enough that Adam was able to roll the rest of the way over, Rachel still tucked in his arms, before the metal edge struck the rock behind him. Then Adam looked back and realized the shovel wasn't slow; time was.

He watched tiny grains erupt from the sandstone, arcing out through the white beam of the man's lamp. The shovel hung there, time ticking away, as if the tool were too heavy to bother swinging again. But Adam knew it wasn't. He struggled to move in slow motion, pushing Rachel up against the edge of a boulder, shielding her body with his. Resting his chin on top of her head, he tucked his knees toward his torso and arched his back. Then he breathed deep, chest and ribs screaming, and held the air in his lungs, bracing for the next impact.

Adam flinched as a shotgun blast assaulted his ears and reverberated across the mountain. He didn't think he'd been shot, but he didn't dare move.

"Drop the shovel!" a woman yelled. It was JJ's voice, but Adam still stayed put.

"I didn't mean to—" The strange man's voice was hoarse, and JJ cut him off before he could finish.

"Where is she?" JJ screamed, closer this time.

Adam finally risked a look over his shoulder. The man had taken half a step back, away from Adam, and balanced the shovel on its metal end, his fingertips steadying the tip of the handle. JJ closed the distance between them, stopping about fifteen feet away. Her headlamp was also bright white now. A soft mist hung in the air, and the individual droplets reflected in the light.

"JJ, she's right here," Adam said, his voice even raspier than the other man's had been. Adam untucked and leaned back on his haunches so she could see. Then he turned and smiled at her. "And she's alive."

It never occurred to Adam that he'd just moved back into range.

"Liar!" the man screamed. He pulled the shovel toward his shoulder and swung at Adam's head.

60

____

Something shifted in Adam as the shovel sped toward him, as if the safety mechanism that kept his capacity for violence in check had irrevocably snapped. The white light on the man's head was mesmerizing, but Adam tore his eyes away and focused on the weapon's arc. He ducked his head, hunching, and the rounded back of the shovel blade hit his thin backpack, glancing off the metal thermos within.

Adam was already rising, launching, as the shovel continued its arc and finally came to a jarring stop, striking the same scarred rock it had struck before. Adam followed it, grabbed the wooden handle and yanked it to the side to clear the rock and block the man who was holding it. Then Adam let his momentum—and his anger—carry him forward, shoving the man to the ground beneath him.

He roared and bore down on the man's chest with his knees, pushing the wooden pole toward his throat. At the same time, some portion of his mind was observing and logging details: the white beam of a headlamp on the ground, where it had been knocked from the man's head; the rough texture of the shovel's handle, the individual splinters of wood of that made it whole; JJ's shape approaching from the side, the shotgun still held in her arms. But most vivid was the man beneath Adam: the lines on his hands like shadows as he pressed up against Adam's weight, his bearded face and shaggy hair, and the deep creases that bracketed eyes so pale Adam could distinguish the pupils in his red headlamp.

The eyes of a prophet.

The whispered words must have come from inside Adam's head, but seemed to come from the mountain itself. Adam thrust the handle until it ground against the man's collarbone, and inched it toward his soft throat.

"Adam, that's enough!" JJ yelled. "Just step back."

Instead, Adam pushed harder, and the wooden handle began to dent the man's throat—not much, no more than someone checking for a pulse in the wrong place. The more Adam filled with anger, the more calm the man beneath him seemed to become. The man barely struggled, but he shifted his grip, and his hands brushed against Adam's—

A wave of images washed over Adam, so many that he couldn't breathe, drowning beneath them all. Some he'd seen before, but they were gone as instantly as he recognized them. Others made no sense, frightening nightmarish visions of terrors that could not exist in this world, thankfully gone just as quickly. But the final image lodged in Adam's brain, an infant—no, a toddler—screaming in the woods, autumn woods like these. Dead woods. And the child was alone.

Adam gasped, and found himself sitting on the ground, not sure how he'd gotten there. He felt an odd sensation of time tunneling down to the present moment. He could see the man's booted feet in front of him and heard JJ say, "If you don't put the shovel down this time, I'll blow your motherfucking brains out."

There was motion, and the sound of metal on rock reverberating through the handle. Adam breathed deep, listened to the air rush into his mouth and hiss down his throat.

JJ asked, "Adam, you okay?"

His lips were numb, and he couldn't seem to find words.

JJ's light never wavered from the man on the ground, and her voice was almost steady as she said, "Adam, if you can, please get up and help me so I can help Rachel."

Rachel. Adam's head swung toward the figure on the ground, tucked in so well he couldn't see anything. He felt every joint, every muscle protest as he rose and went to JJ.

"Unclip my strap," she said.

Strap... What strap? The one on the shotgun, with the swivel clips. Adam's fingers were slow and clumsy, but JJ held the weapon steady until he handed her the strap.

"Get on your stomach," JJ demanded, "hands behind your back."

The man complied. When he was facedown on the ground, JJ traded Adam her shotgun for the strap he held. Adam wasn't sure he had the dexterity to pull the gun's trigger, but he certainly couldn't have bound the man's hands as JJ did, either.

Once she'd secured Adam's attacker, JJ went to Rachel. Adam was aware of her examining the child out of the corner of his eye, but he couldn't stop staring at the man on the ground.

"Who are you?" Adam asked the man's back.

The man lifted his head and turned the other cheek to the ground, so he was facing Adam. "I don't know; who are you?"

"Rachel's breathing, but barely," JJ said.

Adam forced his attention away from his father. Because that's who the man was. Virgil Rutledge may not have recognized his son, but on some deep molecular level, Adam recognized him.

"What needs to happen?" Adam asked, kneeling next to JJ and setting the shotgun on the ground.

"I'm afraid her brain's not getting enough oxygen, and there's nothing I can do for her. We need to get her out of here—to the hospital—as fast as possible."

Adam nodded. "You take her on the ATV, and I'll stay with him."

"I'm not leaving you again—"

He held up a hand, both interrupting JJ and blocking her blinding lamp as her head swung toward him. "You need to take her, and you and me riding double on that ATV was already one too many. I'll be fine. You'll send someone for us. Can you carry her as far as the ATV?"

JJ gazed down at Rachel and smoothed the child's hair back from her forehead. "Of course, I can. But I'll need to secure her somehow."

Adam slid out of his backpack, then winced as he shucked off Harlan's coat and held it up in front of JJ for size. It'd be huge on her, big enough for two. "Here. Put this on and zip it up over both of you. Should be enough to help her stay put if she's sitting in front."

"No! I'm not taking your coat. Are you crazy? You'll freeze to death."

Adam put the coat in her hand anyway, and JJ stared at it, lips pursed. She'd be weighing their options, trying to either convince herself he was right or come up with the argument to convince him he was wrong.

"I'm telling you, the girl's dead. And she shouldn't be alone. If you'd let me finish—" Virgil's voice was deep and resigned and rose from the ground behind them like a specter.

JJ turned and stalked toward her prisoner, pointing her finger. "Shut up! Just shut the fuck up!"

"I was trying to protect her. From *him*," Virgil hissed, jerking his head to look over his shoulder for someone who wasn't there, who had never been there. "*He's* the one who did it. He's the one who always does it. And I can't stop him. You have to help me stop him."

"You crazy sonuvabitch..."

JJ continued yelling at Virgil, but her voice fell away as Adam knelt next to Rachel. JJ was right; his father was crazy. But Virgil wasn't entirely wrong. Rachel would never make it down the mountain alive. He reached down and grasped her tiny wrists, then gently pulled her toward him until they sat side by side, backs against cold stone. Rachel's head slumped against his chest. Adam raised his knees because it felt warmer and more secure. He pulled his mother's key free of his shirt and touched it to his lips one last time. Then he took Rachel's bare hands in his, and let himself fall.

61

JJ screamed at the man on the ground. Her foot itched with the desire to feel his face beneath it. The sole of her boot seemed to rise off the ground of its own accord, and the man's eyes widened. But not in fear.

She turned, and saw Rachel was sitting up, next to Adam. Propped up, more accurately. But wait—had the girl's eyelids just fluttered?

JJ rushed to her. "Rachel? Rachel, can you hear me?" she asked, running her hands over the girl's face.

Rachel's lips were still pale, but were they less blue? *God, what I wouldn't give for some real light.* JJ held the girl's wrist. Her pulse was definitely stronger—it had been so faint before. Adam's pack... JJ scrambled for the thermos, now dented on one side from the shovel strike. She shook it, then peeked inside—*good*, stainless steel through and through, not a glass lining. Steam rose as she poured a little coffee in the metal cup. It was warm, but not hot. Still, the warmth and the caffeine might help dilate Rachel's bronchial tubes and help her breathe.

"Rachel, sweetie, it's Evie's mom. Can you drink this for me?" she asked, holding the cup to Rachel's lips. The girl didn't respond.

JJ dropped her gaze (*so close*) trying not to cry, and saw Adam's hand squeeze Rachel's.

"Try now," he whispered.

JJ lifted the cup again, and this time, miraculously, Rachel sipped. Well, sipped might be overstating it, but she at least facilitated pouring and dribbling. JJ quickly refilled, but she was too enthusiastic with the second cup. Rachel choked and began to cough. It was a painful sound—too much raw, hacking exhale and not enough inhaling. JJ told herself (true or not) that the coughing wasn't necessarily a bad thing; it was a sign of things loosening. She told herself the same thing when the girl began to wheeze, eyes still closed. JJ stretched one arm across Rachel's chest and used the other to rub circles on her back.

"Redneck seat belt," Adam said, voice faint.

It took JJ a moment to make the connection (that's what they'd called the arm across the chest move when they were kids). She smiled at Adam—

"Oh, God," she whispered.

Adam looked even worse than he had in the hospital—eyes glassy and sunken, cheeks hollow and ashen face lined with pain. JJ glanced down and saw his hands clasping Rachel's.

"That's enough," she said. She settled Rachel more firmly against Adam's shoulder and gently pulled his pale fingers free. She met no more resistance than she would expect from a sleeping child. "Adam, you've done enough," she repeated.

JJ dragged the backpack over and set it on her lap. She pulled Iris's promised blanket from the bottom and draped it over Adam's legs. As she did, a bag of granola bars and a small coil of rope fell free. *Good job, Iris.* JJ hadn't had a lot of confidence in the gun strap as a long-term restraint. She peeled back the wrapper on one of the bars and handed it to Adam, along with one of the water bottles.

"Eat this. And drink some water," she said, then went to work tying up the man on the ground. If she'd had more rope, she'd have been tempted to use a four-point restraint, another of the skills her father had thought was important to impart to his daughter. She'd just have to make do.

The man didn't speak or attempt eye contact while she tied his hands behind his back. The rope was tight enough, but not as tight as she would have liked, and just a few inches of it hung down like a double tail when she was done. Only then did JJ remove the gun strap binding. She looked at the sky and did the math. The sun would cross the horizon in an hour or two, but it wouldn't warm up for hours after that, and she had no idea how fast Grant could get a team up here.

Adam's eyes were closed, but he'd done as she said—there was an empty wrapper on the ground next to him, and at least a little water missing from the bottle. He'd leaned ever so slightly into Rachel, and it looked as though they had dozed off together on a couch while watching a boring movie. *Except Rachel's wearing the same clothes she left home in three days ago, I can hear her labored breathing, and Adam looks like complete shit.*

JJ took a deep breath through her mouth and felt the cold air burn her chest. The temperature was mid-forties, maybe? It wasn't freezing, but it didn't have to be anywhere near that for hypothermia to set in, especially the condition Adam was in. And the damned mist wasn't helping.

JJ bent over the man on the ground, close to his head but not too close, in case he tried some crazy head butt maneuver. She spoke in a low voice. "Your name is Virgil, isn't it?"

"I have been called that," he said.

JJ rolled her eyes and resisted the urge to kick the man in the teeth. "Do you know who that is?" she asked.

She jerked back as he lifted his head to face her and the harsh light from her lamp.

"He's the first son of man, resurrected," he said, simply.

JJ took a step back in her mind, so she could gaze at him from a distance and tell herself, *He's even got the crazy eyes to go with the crazy talk.* But the whole time, part of her was shivering inside. She pulled the lamp from her head, holding it so it reflected off the ground and they could see each other's faces.

"He is *your* son," she said. "And I'm Max Tulley's daughter. Do you remember Max Tulley?"

The man actually grinned, and this time JJ couldn't suppress a shudder. Despite the body odor, the grime worn into his skin, the heavy beard woven with multiple shades of brown and white and gray and small curls at the margins of his chin—despite all that, it was like looking at Adam when the man grinned.

"Maxwell Tulley is a righteous man," he said.

Present tense. He thought her dad was still alive, and for those who didn't know JJ, the old man was a whole lot scarier than she was. "I don't care if you are too batshit to recognize your own son. If you do anything to hurt him—" she pointed at Adam, "—Max and I'll have your guts for garters. And that's not a metaphor."

"But he can't be killed," Virgil said, still smiling.

Waste of fucking breath. But JJ still felt funny turning her back to him.

She didn't need the extra weight, so she'd leave the shotgun behind. Adam wouldn't use the gun, but Virgil might figure something out. She wouldn't trust the crazy bastard not to use his toes, so JJ gathered all the shells and dropped them in the pocket of Adam's coat before she put it on, tugging at the extra inches of sleeves until her hands popped out the end. Then she tucked her arms under Rachel, gently sliding her away from Adam. He jerked awake, eyes wide, as soon as the child left his side.

"It's okay. It's just me," JJ said. Rachel's eyes were still closed, but JJ managed to get the last few sips of now-cool coffee in her. Then JJ picked up her own jacket and tossed it on Adam's lap. "Here."

Adam held it up awkwardly, as if only portions of his arms were under his control. "I don't think my hands would fit through the cuffs."

Not to mention the arms probably only reached his elbows. JJ pulled the blanket from Adam's lap and helped him lean forward as she draped it around his shoulders. "Put my coat over your legs," she said, dropping it on his lap. Well, one leg anyway. "I'll get back here with the cavalry as soon as I can. Try to stay awake."

He nodded, but his lids were drifting shut already. JJ kneeled down and got in his face. "Hey! You better fucking be here when I get back. Don't go tramping all over creation, seeing the sights."

Adam touched her face with the heel of his hand, but his fingers didn't seem to be responding. "I'll be here."

JJ nodded, then picked up Rachel, grunting as she stood with the girl's weight. *I will not cry.* She hitched Rachel up until her head rested across JJ's shoulder, then headed toward the forest trail. JJ didn't even spare a look for the crazy asshole on the ground as she passed.

The only time JJ paused was to shift Rachel's weight to her other side. By the time she reached the woods, JJ couldn't distinguish Rachel's wheezing from her own. She wished she'd worn a watch, so she'd know how long it had been since she left Adam. So she could try to calculate how much longer he had. The faster she marched, the harder it was to think about anything except her next step, so she picked up the pace even more.

Finally, her headlamp caught a flash of red, a hint of reflected taillight ahead. JJ set Rachel on the ground for a moment while she got her bearings and unchocked the ATV's wheels. Then she unzipped Adam's coat and carried Rachel to the ATV, propping the child awkwardly on the seat while she struggled to wrap the small limbs around her torso and zip up the coat. JJ nearly lost an eye to the vehicle's handlebars while climbing on the seat, and Rachel's feet came free from the garment at the bottom. Still, it seemed a workable, if cumbersome, solution.

Adam, you're a fucking genius, she thought, starting up the ATV. She put it in low gear to slow their descent and began rolling down the mountain. *And I'm still not going to cry.*

62

———

He moved over and sat next to Adam, listening for his breath as Adam slipped in and out of consciousness.

Maybe the first son of man could die, and maybe he couldn't. But if he was going to die, this wasn't the way it should happen, with him gradually slipping away into the darkness.

He sighed.

The first son should be awake for death, and know it was coming.

He nudged Adam with his shoulder. "Come on. Let's go."

63

Luther had decided, about a mile back, that he hadn't slept enough to deal with all the damn noise from Pop's machine. He hadn't slept at all, come to think of it. He could imagine the vehicle being fun on a summer day when you were tanked up and didn't know any better, but not in the cold and the dark when you were on Sheriff's business. This was like some kind of torture, the constant vibration when your brain knew damn well it should be in bed.

That's why Luther almost didn't believe his eyes when he saw a flash of light above them. He tapped Leslie's arm, but his brother had seen it, too.

The light disappeared behind a loop in the trail.

Wait, there it was again; it must be JJ and Adam. Les slowed down, and soon there was nothing but a straight stretch of fifty yards or so between them and the other vehicle. *It better be JJ and Adam.* Luther reached for his holster and nearly dropped his gun. He'd forgotten about the damned mummy finger, where Les had bandaged his cuts. It would be his trigger finger. At least it seemed unlikely that whoever was approaching could maneuver their ATV and fire at the same time.

Les and the other ATV stopped a few yards short of each other. It was a lot smaller than theirs, and held only one passenger. The ground felt funny when Luther stepped down, or more accurately, Luther's legs felt funny, like they didn't quite want to hold him. They felt even funnier when a bulky JJ rolled off the ATV, nearly falling, and an extra head popped out of her over-large coat.

Luther gripped the vehicle's roll bar as his knees buckled.

Good God. The girl was actually alive.

~

Luther wasn't sure he'd make it up the mountain in one piece. There was a reason these damn little machines were so popular with young kids. His thighs cramped from angling his knees in to keep his seat.

He'd sent Leslie with JJ and the girl—both half-frozen, and Rachel still unconscious—down the mountain in the side-by-side and taken JJ's little ATV back up the mountain. JJ had held it together, but just barely, and probably wouldn't have if it hadn't been for the girl. Luther had never seen JJ so close to losing control, even when her daddy was dying. She'd begged Luther, *just do what you can for Adam*. Well, maybe the Lord had two miracles in him today. Luther had to wonder, if he was in any kind of shape at all, what Adam must be thinking now, sitting across from his crazy as a bedbug, recluse-turned-kidnapper dad.

He slowed. He didn't have far to go—they'd met JJ near the cabin trail—but the little ATV's headlights were nothing compared to the after-market upgrades on Pop's side-by-side, and he was afraid he'd miss the path to the pinnacle. He needn't have worried; the ground was torn up where JJ had left the ATV before, so Luther had no trouble seeing where to park. He headed down the slope into the woods.

The ATV lights might've been a letdown, but they were high noon in the middle of August compared to Luther's headlamp. His steel-toed boots did a better job of helping him find the path, until

Luther tripped over a rock and almost brained himself on the nearest tree. *I'm too damned old for this shit.*

He kept walking, and walking, and soon he couldn't hear past the sound of his own panting. It became more and more difficult to rein in the flights of fancy his exhausted mind took (*if I make it to Canada, I can hitch a ride with a Mountie*) almost as if it were chattering to keep the dark things at bay. Finally, the path opened up and Luther could see the barest hint of light in the sky ahead.

Luther emerged into the treeless patch and saw movement out of the corner of his eye, in amongst some boulders to the right that were on higher ground than he was now. Or at least, he thought he did. He didn't turn his head—he was better off relying on his peripheral vision than the damn lamp. Of course, he was trying so hard not to look that he ignored what was right in front of him. A rock slammed into Luther's shin and bent him over.

"Sonuvabitch!" he said, as the pain shot up through his leg and gave him shivers. Luther used the opportunity, writhing and cursing, to take a good look around, all sides.

Nothing.

He must have imagined it. That happened sometimes in the dark, when the peripheral vision got an incomplete picture and filled in the gaps, trying to make the world make sense.

Luther stumbled on a little farther, then stopped. It was a tough job, making the world make sense. Take, for instance, the fact that there was a shotgun lying on the ground in front of him, all by its lonesome. The back of Luther's neck prickled as he bent down to inspect it.

It was unloaded. And Adam and his crazy-ass father were nowhere to be seen.

64

———

JJ sat next to Rachel's bed. She felt mildly guilty holding the girl's hand, because JJ's own hands were still cold, and because JJ suspected she was doing it more for her own benefit than for Rachel's. The child looked lost in a sea of white sheets, and the IVs and oxygen mask made her look even more fragile, made JJ fear she could damage the tiny hand. But there was no doubt Rachel was alive, and that was nothing short of amazing. That was worth celebrating.

JJ heard a light knock at the door before Grant entered. "There's another chair—" she said.

"No, I can't stay. I just wanted to see how she's doing." He stood next to JJ, and together they watched the girl intently, as if something might change at any moment. Grant already knew, from her intake, that Rachel hadn't been sexually assaulted. She also hadn't yet regained consciousness, so JJ stuck with the physical.

"We'll see how she responds to the asthma treatments, but breathing on her own is a good sign. Assuming everything goes well, they'll be able to transfer her to the children's ward tomorrow. They're also treating her for dehydration, and she has some superficial cuts, but she doesn't appear to have any serious injuries."

"Good," Grant said. "Otto and Dorothy are on their way."

"Any word on Adam?" JJ asked, eyes locked on Rachel because she was afraid to look at Grant. She stiffened when she felt his hand on her shoulder.

"No, not yet. Leslie's guiding a small recovery team up there—" he glanced at his watch, "any minute now, with the full investigative team to follow. I promise, I'll let you know as soon as I hear anything. Either way. But he'll be okay."

JJ reached up and squeezed Grant's hand, so the three of them were linked in silence. There was a quiet in hospitals, in private rooms in the wee hours, if there weren't any codes, that JJ always found reassuring. She thought it must be like the peace some people found in empty churches, a kind of reminder of why we were here, and a sense of timelessness.

Except there was no true place of timelessness in this world. She felt Grant look at his watch again.

"Go," she said. "We'll be fine." JJ put his hand to her lips and kissed it softly, then held it against her face. His hand was warm and solid and safe, like Trooper's neck, without all the fur. Although she could feel a few little hairs, curling on the backs of Grant's fingers. Finally, reluctantly, JJ released his hand.

Grant opened his mouth to speak, but Rachel stirred—just the slightest bit—drawing their attention. The girl's breathing changed, lost its soft rhythm to become more deliberate, and JJ thought she heard a murmur through her mask. She stood up and put her face next to Rachel's.

"What is it, sweetie?" she asked.

There was a brief exhalation of sounds, and then Rachel grew quiet again, and her breathing returned to normal.

"Well?" Grant asked.

JJ's brain struggled to put the soft sounds together into words that made sense. "I think she said, 'Don't hurt him.' And maybe something about a panther."

Grant looked down at the girl and touched the thin blanket at the foot of the bed, as if to transmit whatever reassurance he could without disturbing her. "Haven't had a credible cougar sighting here in close to a hundred years. She must be dreaming," he said. "Who knows when we'll be able to get a statement from her."

Maybe Rachel was dreaming. But JJ thought—preferred to believe—the girl had somehow caught a glimpse of Adam, somehow tapped into their connection. And no matter what Rachel had been trying to say, at least that meant Adam was still alive.

65

"Adam?" Luther called out.

There was no answer.

He followed his own voice's echo, forward toward the open sky and a pinnacle of rock that rose out of the mountain to his right. He tried to take its measure, but it was still too dark. It was impressive, though, or at least it would be to a Sunday picnicker. To him, it just felt like a helluva lot of ground for getting picked off by a sniper.

Luther turned off his lamp for a moment and sat on a rock, to see what he could without its glare and to feel less like a target. He stretched his eyelids open wide, blinked a few times and waited. Luther heard a little something up the ridge, no doubt a combination of his paranoia and actual deer or raccoons doing their nighttime rounds. He couldn't see anything more without the light, not even the outline of the pinnacle. Except *there*, out in front. He could swear he saw a glow, flickering. Like the reflection of a campfire.

Hunh. There was no way in hell Luther would make it more than three steps in the dark without breaking his neck, but turning his light on was like hanging out a neon sign.

Luther's teeth surprised him by starting to chatter. He could make them stop, but it took some conscious effort. *Damn.* That's what he got for sitting on a damp, cold rock. He took stock and revised his assessment to wet, not damp; he was probably soaked through to his underwear by now. Continuing to sit on a wet, cold rock until daybreak was not a viable option. He switched his light back on and set out for the leading edge of the pinnacle. The footing was less than ideal, which was another way of saying Luther couldn't make it more than three steps without swearing. JJ had said she and Adam carried Rachel this way. Luther shook his head, triggering a moment's dizziness from the light. JJ might be a pain in the ass from time to time, but she was tough. With Adam, on the other hand, Luther suspected a sheer act of will kept one foot moving in front of the other until he dropped. That was a good way to end up doing so much you'd never recover. Luther hoped it hadn't finally caught up with him.

The wind picked up as the ground grew more exposed, a soft, mournful whistle that did nothing to alleviate the tingling target Luther's mind had conjured on his back, nor did it dissipate the eddies in the shadows. The atmospheric resonance might help cover his approach, but frankly, Luther would rather be heard.

Luther switched off his light when he was close enough to distinguish the front margin of the rock formation, and hugged the rock wall. The formation jutted out for a few yards, creating an overhang about eight feet from the ground, and Luther suspected a bit of a cave as well. There was no doubt in Luther's mind now that he was seeing a fire, and also that he would be blinded by it as he rounded the corner.

He drew his weapon awkwardly from his holster, getting hung up by his unbending, mummy trigger finger. *Dammit!* Why hadn't he taken the bandage off earlier when he'd had the chance? Luther holstered his gun and gave a tug on the finger's wrap. Les must have used half a roll of tape, because it sure as hell wasn't moving from his finger. He'd just have to make do.

Shooting left-handed, he knew he'd probably blow his own foot off. Instead, Luther stuck with his right hand and adjusted his grip after he drew, settling his middle finger over the trigger, gun pointed at the ground. A sardonic smile crept across Luther's face. If he made it through the night, it wouldn't be on his own deputy merits, that was for sure.

A little more than arm's length from the corner, Luther raised his gun, keeping it close to his body. *Here we go. Deep breath, slice the pie.* He shuffled sideways, eyes taking in the images rapid-fire, in a broad arc. Clear rock wall... blazing fire... prone body (Adam?)... man sitting against the back wall—

"Show me your hands," Luther said.

The man raised his arms—his hands were free—but stayed seated.

"Keep them up, and stay where you are," Luther said, and the ragged-looking man complied. Luther slowly made his way to the far side and cleared the outside corner. The rest of the space was empty.

The suspect didn't move, even when Luther approached him. The man wore layers—long johns peeked from his jeans, as well as multiple shirts and a hooded sweatshirt under a waterproof jacket —and he was sitting, so it was hard to get a good sense of his size. He'd no doubt layered clothes for warmth, but Luther appreciated that it also helped keep the man's body odor manageable. The man's hair reached almost to his shoulders and was a mix of browns and grays, but it was in dire need of washing, so it was hard to say what lay beneath the grime. His full beard had more gray than the hair on his head, and tended to curl around his chin.

"Hold your hands straight out," Luther said. Luther noticed a little blood and chafing on the man's wrists, but they were strong with wiry muscle. His arms didn't budge from horizontal while Luther cuffed him. Luther checked the man for weapons, but didn't find any, and his pockets were empty. "How'd you get the fire?" he asked.

"My son learned to make a fire in the Cub Scouts," the man said.

Did he, now? If that was the case, it looked as if Adam had managed it just in time. He was lying on his side near the fire, wrapped in a thin blanket that shifted with his breath.

So Adam was breathing. He was alive, too.

Luther sank to his knees next to Adam, feeling a little sob hitch in his throat. Goddamn, he was wrung out. He jumped when he heard the voice behind him.

"I told Maxwell's daughter, the first son can't die."

Tiny hairs stood up on Luther's neck. He cast a glance over his shoulder. Yep, that was Virgil Rutledge all right. He might look like a homeless guy now, but he still had those damn spooky eyes. Luther had known people who were crazy before, but this… there was something in Virgil now that set off alarms in the old lizard brain.

Luther pulled his gaze away, back to Adam. JJ's instructions had been to concentrate on his head and his core, not the extremities. And keep him dry. He started at the top. The toboggan on Adam's head was damp, so he pulled it off.

"Don't hurt him," Adam mumbled through pale lips.

"Adam, it's me, Luther," he said, holding Adam's head still with one hand. "You're gonna be okay now."

Luther's breath caught when Adam opened his eyes. His pupils had dilated to swallow all but a rim of blue.

"Luther," Adam said, and his arm fumbled in the blanket trying to get free. He finally gave up and said, "You're safe," before drifting away again.

It struck Luther as a helluva strange pronouncement, but then, Adam's brain was obviously up against the wall and trying to do its best. Luther pulled the blanket free, and found that Adam's shirt was damp. It was probably five degrees warmer in their protected mini-cave, but Luther's own hands were still freezing. His disobedient fingers tore off one of the flannel shirt's endless buttons. Adam was back to being a dead weight, so peeling the shirt off him without cracking his head open was no easy task. His cotton undershirt seemed dry, but Luther could feel the cold from Adam's body through the thin fabric. Luther saw a lump beneath and pulled out an antique-looking key, hanging from a chain. It was cold, too. Luther's fingers were too clumsy, so he rubbed the key between his palms until it warmed, then tucked it inside Adam's shirt and patted it against his chest.

Adam's jeans were dry except for some dampness below the knees, so Luther decided to leave them on. He pulled his own deputy's coat off, thankful that he had a couple more layers beneath it. Adam roused just enough to be a pain as Luther dressed him. The younger man tried to help, but didn't have reliable control over his limbs.

"Am I on the payroll now?" Adam asked.

Luther was surprised to hear him say something so coherent. Adam's pupils were still pretty blown, and his gaze rested vaguely on the stone ceiling, giving an unnerving impression of blindness. "You got it. But don't go shopping for those new tires for your car yet," Luther said, grunting as he finally got one of Adam's arms through. "The salary's about enough to keep you in Pop-Tarts."

"I like Pop-Tarts," Adam said, his voice strained. And then he started shaking. Luther thought it was probably from the pain, sitting up with nothing to lean against, all angry core muscles and pissed-off ribs. Or maybe it was hypothermia.

"'A' course you do, dumbass," Luther said. "Everybody likes Pop-Tarts. Now lay down before you pass out. I can get the rest."

Adam closed his eyes, the fight gone out of him. Luther was considerably thicker around the middle than Adam, so it wasn't hard to slide the other coat sleeve up over Adam's right arm. Adam's hand stopped short of the cuff, and Luther reached inside to pull it through, for just a moment having a flash of what it would have been like to have children, or maybe of what it had been like to be one. Adam's thumb got caught, and Luther struggled to tuck it down without hurting him, eventually stretching the cuff to pull his hand free.

Luther was transfixed by the thumb, that damn wonky thumb

that was a souvenir of Charlotte Rutledge's death. And he wasn't the only one.

"Did you do that?" Virgil asked, rolling forward on his knees. "Did you break his thumb?"

Luther flushed. "Sir, you need to sit your ass down, and stay down."

Virgil kneed forward, but overbalanced, falling on his face. "I have to see."

The deputy gently set Adam's hand on the ground before addressing the Virgil situation. Luther had a pair of plastic cuffs to secure Virgil's ankles if need be, but he was reluctant to use them. Honestly, he was reluctant to even touch Virgil again, as if the man's psychosis might be contagious.

"Either settle down, or I'm going to make your life considerably more uncomfortable for the next couple of hours," Luther said, standing over the man.

"Show me his hand!" Virgil roared.

Luther's temper rose up to meet Virgil's crazy. Luther grabbed the man by his jacket front and dragged him across the ground toward the back rock wall. Dust clouded around them, choking Luther into a coughing fit. That break gave the little voice that Sheriff Mason (the elder) had trained into Luther time to reassert itself. It was the voice of reason and avoiding lawsuits, and it was all that kept Luther from throwing Virgil against the stone wall.

Meanwhile, Virgil changed tactics and tried to speak reasonably. "Deputy, I need to see, because if there is an injury, then the first son has not been resurrected. Or he is not truly the first son of man."

Luther looked at Adam wearing his coat, lying by the fire, unconscious again. *Sheer force of will.* "I thank God above that I never had a child, Virgil Rutledge, because I cannot imagine anything worse in the world than not recognizing my own son."

Luther wrapped the blanket around Adam from beneath, trying to insulate his body from the ground. Luther's own toboggan felt dry, so he put that on Adam as well. Then he chose the rock wall spot closest to the fire to sit against and pulled Adam between his knees, nestling Adam's back against his own chest as if he were a child. He used his free arm to sweep the small coat JJ had left behind across Adam's legs.

"Why'd you search my car?" Adam's hollow voice made Luther jump, as if a corpse had spoken.

"What's that?" Luther asked.

"The back of my car, in the ditch," Adam said, words spent.

Luther thought back, tried to remember why he had done it. "I wanted to know if you were sticking around," he said, honestly. "Are you?"

But Adam had faded away again.

I'm supposed to keep an eye on you.

And a helluva job he'd done of it.

Cold seeped from the stone through Luther's layers and chilled his spine, but it would warm up soon enough. Luther gazed out at the shadows flickering in the dark—*spooky shit*—but he could just make out spiky silhouettes of the treetops from the slope below, jutting into the sky.

Daylight would come. And he'd be watching for it.

66

———

Adam could feel his pulse's labor all through his body. Each beat was like a drum reverberating under water. The air was warm and wet, like a rainforest entering his lungs. But he was so cold.

Any movement was a monumental effort. Every time he pried his eyelids apart, their weight brought them back down. Adam kept trying until finally, he glimpsed a familiar face leaning in.

"I told you not to check out AMA," JJ said.

He tried to smile, but the mask made it harder, and he slipped away again.

Adam had impressions of Iris sitting next to him, of JJ, and occasionally a nurse that wasn't JJ, but he didn't really feel *present* until the following day. That was the first time Grant came to see him.

"How are you feeling?" Grant asked.

"I'm not really sure," Adam admitted, raising the head of his bed a few more inches. He was still having difficulty connecting his mind and his body, corralling thoughts and recognizing sensations.

Except pain. That sensation he knew very well. "Alive. How is Rachel?"

"She's doing well," Grant said. "She's over in the pediatric wing now, and they might release her tomorrow."

"Good," Adam said. His mind had already drifted away again, come untethered and forgotten anyone else was in the room, when he heard a quick knock at the door. Luther stepped in, carrying a small brown sack.

Adam smiled. "I hear I should be thanking you."

Luther grinned, and Adam felt something release in his chest. "Damn right you should be thanking me. For not knowing I was supposed to get naked with you. Otherwise I would have let you freeze."

Grant shook his head, but he was smiling, too.

"I brought you something," Luther said. He set the sack on the bed within reach.

Adam used his un-IVed hand to tentatively pull a box from the sack. "Pop-Tarts," he said, looking at the breakfast pastries. Brown Sugar and Cinnamon flavor.

"You don't remember?" Luther asked, mostly hiding his disappointment.

"No, sorry. But I like Pop-Tarts." Adam ran his finger around the top of the box where it was sealed, but didn't open it. "I'll be honest, Luther. There's a lot I don't remember."

"About that," Grant said. "I'd rather you didn't see Rachel until we get a statement from you. That's why I told JJ not to talk to you about what happened, either. It's confusing enough putting the pieces together without somebody else's recollections muddying the water. At least so far as the details go."

"I understand." Adam had been relieved when JJ hadn't spoken to him about it, beyond letting him know Rachel was okay.

"I've got Special Agent D'Antonio out in the hall," Grant said. "If you don't mind, we could start now."

"Okay."

Grant opened the door for a dark-haired man that Adam recognized as the man from the Command Center who'd asked him about Danny's disappearance. He wore a dark suit this time, but the small scar on his lip was unmistakable. He strode to Adam's bed and held out his hand. When Adam didn't respond, the man reached for him anyway.

"Please don't touch me," Adam said. The man's eyes narrowed, so Adam added, "I'm having a lot of sensitivity to touch. Something to do with the hypothermia."

"Of course," the agent said, and pulled a chair over next to Grant. Luther remained standing, arms crossed, and gave Adam the distinct impression that he was not a fan of the outsider.

Adam had difficulty focusing on words, but movement held his attention. He watched as Grant rotated his Sheriff's hat in his hands, *end* over *end* over *end* over *end*...

"Virgil Rutledge is in custody, but we've transferred him for a psychological evaluation. It might be a while before he's competent enough to understand the charges against him or assist with his own defense," Grant said.

Adam nodded, but only because Grant seemed to expect a response.

"Shovel seems like an odd choice of weapon, don't you think?" Agent D'Antonio asked.

Adam started at a sudden flash of metal on metal, of pain in his back. "He thought she was dead."

"What's that?" Grant asked, leaning in.

Adam blinked, waited for a patch of dizziness to pass. "He thought Rachel was dead. From the asthma attack. The shovel was to bury her."

Grant nodded. "That makes sense. JJ saw him gathering rocks before he attacked you. Maybe that was for a grave marker. He said something in custody—it was something Rachel remembered, too—about not wanting her to be alone. Do you know what that was about?"

"No," Adam said automatically. "Wait, there was something... Did he say that to JJ, or to me alone later?"

Adam closed his eyes, but it was just out of reach. There were images, images that didn't belong to him and he hoped remained lost, but also images of things he'd seen that night, or thought he'd seen... the girl that wasn't Rachel, for instance. And words that he'd dreamed... *the eyes of a prophet.*

Adam sensed movement and opened his eyes. D'Antonio was reaching for his hand again.

"I said don't touch me!"

The man lifted his hands in surrender. "You were gone there for a while, and I was just checking to see if you were okay."

Adam didn't apologize, just held D'Antonio's eyes until he looked away. Adam turned his attention to Grant, who appeared his usual unperturbed self.

"I'd look for where he left the rocks," Adam said. "If he didn't want her to be alone, he might have intended to bury Rachel next to Sarah Edmunds and Danny Carpenter."

"Jesus," Luther said, turning away and rubbing his hand over the back of his head. Grant didn't seem surprised, but then he'd been privy to a lot of things the other men in the room hadn't.

"I've heard of Danny Carpenter," D'Antonio said, "but who is Sarah Edmunds?"

"They're both missing children from twenty years ago," Grant said.

"What makes you think your father killed them?" D'Antonio asked.

His father. The man had clearly said it to push his buttons. Adam was starting to see why Luther didn't like him. "I can't explain it," Adam said, which, strictly speaking, was true. "I must have heard things and put them together. But there's so much I can't remember."

"Did you know before this week that he'd killed them? Maybe he told you in the past," D'Antonio suggested.

"I didn't even know my father was alive before this weekend," Adam snapped. "I hadn't seen him since my mother died."

"Adam," Grant cut in, "why don't we go through what you do remember. Let's start with when you and JJ left Jim's property."

Adam gave them a broad outline that, Grant said, confirmed what JJ had said. D'Antonio clenched his jaw, whether unhappy the two accounts meshed or that the Sheriff was sharing that they did, Adam wasn't sure.

"So your father attacked you. Ms. Tulley couldn't risk the shotgun with all of you bunched together, but you managed to subdue your father, and Ms. Tulley restrained him. Then what?" D'Antonio asked, taking over the questioning.

"We decided JJ should take Rachel on the ATV, I gave her my coat..." Adam paused. *And I gave Rachel everything else.* "And that's the last thing I remember."

"You don't remember anything that happened after Ms. Tulley left with the child?" D'Antonio sounded skeptical.

"No," Adam said.

"You ever come across a vehicle of any kind?"

Adam shook his head.

"I'm sure we'll find one soon. You said there was a cabin in the opposite direction, but you chose not to go there after Ms. Tulley left. So when we process that cabin, we're not going to find a sign of you having been there?" D'Antonio asked.

Grant silently handed Adam a cup of water with a straw. Adam flinched when their fingers touched, but gratefully sipped before answering. "We've been told there's a cabin, but I've never seen it myself and didn't know how far away it was. There's no way I would've made it. JJ probably told you, I couldn't even make it back to the ATV."

"But you knew about the overhang nearby," Grant said.

"Yes, I'd stumbled on it earlier when I found Rachel."

"When did you untie your father's hands?" D'Antonio asked.

"I didn't," Adam said, shocked. "Why would I?"

"Then how did he get his hands free?"

Adam was speechless. He remembered JJ tying Virgil's hands

behind his back. If the man had gotten free, why hadn't he run away?

"And if you were in such bad shape," Agent D'Antonio challenged, "how'd you manage to make a fire?"

Adam had to laugh. "I have no earthly idea. But when I get out of here, you can bet I'll be thanking Jim Henderson for teaching me how."

67

L ater that day, Adam was lying in his bed, thinking about not thinking, when JJ came into his room. She was in uniform—scrub pants in a solid blue and a top covered with cavorting monkeys.

"Aren't we spiffy?" Adam said, referring to the bug-eyed primates.

"They've got me filling in over in pediatrics today, so I dressed accordingly," JJ said, glancing automatically at his IV and the machine that monitored his heart. Apparently, hypothermia was not always kind to that important muscle's rhythms, but his seemed to be doing fine.

JJ drifted back toward the door, drawing out the words, "While I was over there, I ran into someone who wanted to say hi."

Otto entered the room, wheeling Rachel ahead of him. Otto looked as if he'd aged a decade in the past few days, while Rachel looked even younger, tinier in pale pink pajamas with ruffles at the neck and the cuffs of her pants, dark hair hanging loose over her shoulders. Her eyes were on her lap, and she fidgeted with the plastic ID band on her wrist.

"I don't know that you've ever been properly introduced. Adam, Rachel," JJ said, with hand flourishes.

Rachel blushed a little, and her head moved from side to side in the typical kid blend of embarrassment and shyness and mortification. Adam desperately wanted to see her eyes, eyes he'd first seen *through*, and then seen closed for far too long.

"Do you like Pop-Tarts?" Adam asked.

Rachel glanced up, rewarding him as he'd hoped with the sight of her big, blue eyes. Virgil's eyes had been pale and cold, like snow trapped in glacial ice. Rachel's were the blue of warm seas, filled with life.

"Mom doesn't let me eat Pop-Tarts," Rachel said.

Otto leaned over her wheelchair and put his hand on her shoulder. "I think we can make an exception, this once. It'll be our secret, yours and mine. *Just like this visit.*"

Otto raised his brows and met Adam's gaze with the last phrase. Presumably Dorothy wasn't ready to embrace the son of her daughter's kidnapper with open arms. Adam couldn't blame her. He suspected he hadn't done a whole lot for the Nicholson marriage, either. Still, he felt sure they'd be okay. Eventually.

Otto wheeled Rachel closer while JJ handed Adam the pastries. Adam hoped the girl couldn't see his hands shake as he tore open the box. He pulled out a two-pack and stared at the foil wrapper as if it were a padlocked gate without a key.

"Oh, no, you don't," JJ said, taking it and easily peeling the wrapper open at the top before offering the first one to Rachel. "I learned when we were kids never to let Adam open these. More often than not, they ended up on the sidewalk. I think he did it on purpose, so he wouldn't have to share. Because *I* don't eat food off the ground."

Adam grinned conspiratorially and whispered, "Five-second rule," earning a hint of a smile from the girl in return. His first bite of the pastry broke it in half, and a small chunk landed on his blanket. "Works in hospital beds, too," he said, tossing the renegade piece in his mouth.

Rachel relaxed into a full smile then. His heart nearly burst—*she's going to be okay*—but he maintained his goofy facade. Adam hoped that if he kept it casual, she'd become comfortable enough with him to say anything she needed to say. He and Rachel ate slowly, breaking off little bits of sugary goodness, while Otto and JJ talked in the background about things that were coming up in school for Rachel and JJ's daughter Evie.

Rachel was nearly finished when she asked, staring at the last bit of crust, "Did that man come talk to you?" She pointed at her lip where Agent D'Antonio had a scar, accidentally dropping her last bite on the floor in the process.

"Whoops," she said, and grinned.

"No five-second rule for hospital floors. Here—you want to finish mine?" Adam reached out with the final corner, but at the last second, when their hands were nearly touching, he panicked and dropped his on the floor, too.

JJ paused in her conversation with Otto to pick the food off the floor. "Geez, I can't take you guys anywhere."

"Sorry," Adam said, making a face and earning another Rachel smile. Then he picked up where Rachel had left off. "Yeah, that man came by and asked me questions. I guess he wouldn't let you sleep, either."

Rachel shook her head. JJ and Otto were both trying to feign disinterest, but watched her out of the corners of their eyes and uttered words to each other that made sounds but said nothing.

"I didn't tell him about everything," Rachel said in a soft voice, and Adam saw Otto stiffen.

"Like what?"

Rachel looked down at her lap again. "I didn't tell him about you being there sometimes. In my head."

Adam avoided looking at Otto while asking, "Is that all?"

Her voice dropped almost to a whisper. "And I didn't tell him about you helping me, when I was dead."

Otto's hand gripped the wheelchair, and his jaw clenched. JJ gave up any pretense of not listening and said, "Sweetie, you were never dead, just really sick."

"It felt like I was dead," Rachel said, bottom lip sticking out and trembling slightly.

"Rachel," Adam said, and waited for her to look up at him. "It's okay that you didn't tell the scar man about that stuff. He doesn't need to know. But you should talk to your parents about it."

She nodded, but hesitated, as if there were something still on her mind.

"What is it?" Adam asked.

"I was afraid they'd think I made it up. Or if they believed me, it might get you in trouble," she whispered.

"The people that love you, they'll believe you. And you should never keep secrets from them, because they're the ones that'll always help you. Always. Okay?"

"Okay," she said, with an expression that looked like she was trying to take a lot in, but not troubled.

Otto said they should be getting back before Dorothy got worried and wheeled Rachel out, but not before promising they would see him again.

"Hold on, and I'll be your escort," JJ said. She walked to Adam's bed, with the excuse of putting the box of pastries back on his nightstand.

"You know," she said, squeezing Adam's shoulder through his gown, "you might want to think about taking your own advice."

JJ's WORDS stuck with Adam. He'd been avoiding speaking with Iris, faking sleep when she entered his room, or pleading exhaustion at the first sign of conversation. He wasn't sure he was ready. Maybe she wasn't, either.

Still, the next time Iris came into his room, Adam found himself asking, "Have you seen him?"

"Who—your father?"

"Yes."

"No, I have not," she said, hanging her purse over the back of her chair before sitting.

"Are you going to?"

"I haven't decided."

Adam closed his eyes and let the stillness settle around him. He could feel Iris's presence next to him like... like a bowl of her warm soup.

"You know," she said, "raising you wasn't easy—the circumstances and all—but you have no idea how happy I was that you were normal."

Adam kept his eyes shut and let her talk.

"You never met your grandfather, but... well, there's no other way to put it. He was crazy. And not in a wear your pants backwards kind of way. He tried to hide it with religion, or maybe use religion to exorcise the crazy or make it okay, like it was spiritual somehow. So Lawrence Rutledge spoke in tongues and handled snakes, but that wasn't enough. Instead of keeping him in check, it made him spin out even further."

Adam opened his eyes and turned his head painfully toward her. He couldn't say why, but it seemed important to know. "Where'd he do it?"

Iris's expression was matter-of-fact as she said, "A bunch of them used to go to Dead Hollow. Said it was the Valley of Death."

A nurse came in to check something; Adam was too distracted by Iris's uncharacteristic disclosures to know or care what. He was also in too much pain to stay twisted around to have a face-to-face conversation with Iris. Instead, he consciously relaxed his shoulders and neck, his chest and ribs, trying to keep the muscle spasms at bay. His eyes drifted toward the bottom of the bed. The gray hospital blanket rose over his feet like a mountain covered in dirty snow.

The nurse finally left, and Iris continued, "Your grandfather was a scary man. And I told myself that kind of crazy had to skip a generation. But I knew better. I always knew your father wasn't right. From the time he was a little boy."

Adam stiffened. "What about my uncle?"

Adam could hear the smile in her voice as she answered. "Bo was a lot more like you. Easygoing, got along with everybody. He kept an eye on your dad, and your dad did better when he was around. But when Bo died..." Iris paused, and Adam caught movement from the corner of his eye as she fidgeted with a sweater button. "If your mother hadn't been dating your father at the time, we'd have lost him then. We almost did. But she convinced him to go somewhere. That's when we found out Virgil was schizophrenic."

"Were you surprised?"

"Yes and no. Your mother wasn't. Being diagnosable meant he was treatable, to some extent. Virgil didn't like taking the meds, but he did it for Charlotte. And, eventually, for you. But the meds weren't a cure. You hear people talk about friends that have 'split personalities,' when they don't know any better. I wouldn't say that about your father, but I would say there were days when I knew he wasn't right. It was like flipping a switch. Other days he'd seem fine. You never knew ahead of time which way he'd be, but you could tell within seconds of seeing him. Sort of a primal thing."

Adam remembered his father's eyes, and the wave of images washing over him. He shivered. Iris reached toward him, and Adam jerked his nearest hand away from her, wincing as he shoved it beneath the blanket.

"Easy. Just tucking you in." She gently pulled the bedding up to his shoulders and continued, as if nothing had happened. "A couple of months before your mother died, Virgil started to unravel. We weren't sure if the meds had stopped working, or if he was lying about taking them. He never harmed you or your mother, but he was convinced other people were trying to. And that it was his job to protect you."

Iris's words triggered something in Adam, the recognition of a vague fear that he realized he'd carried with him throughout his life. And yet, he also felt an intense sense of loss.

"Your mother and I were exploring options—inpatient options —to get him stabilized. And then the accident happened. With your mother gone, your father went fully psychotic, and I knew I could only save one of you. I chose you." Iris rubbed Adam's hand through the blanket. "I will always choose you."

68

Adam startled awake. He'd been dreaming—a nightmare of crashing metal and dark woods—but now he was in a dark room, and someone was watching him.

"It's okay, son. It's me." *Harlan.*

Adam blinked and shielded his eyes when the older man switched on the light next to the bed, then winced as he inadvertently tugged on his IV.

"You look like shit," Harlan said.

"You came here to tell me that?" Adam asked, raising the bed for company.

"No. I came here because you won't talk to Iris and JJ. Leastways, not about anything that matters. And I don't have a phone."

But Jim did. Harlan could have called from Jim's. Adam looked at the clock next to the bed. "It's almost midnight."

"I know. I had to be extra charming to the night nurse." Harlan waggled his eyebrows, but Adam wasn't biting. "Look, kid, hospitals aren't easy for me."

"Is that why you smell like a distillery?" Adam felt guilty as soon as the words left his mouth, but by then it was too late.

The corner of Harlan's mouth curled into an almost-smile.

"Yes, it is. It's the only way I can block out the majority of what passes through these kinds of places, and what gets left behind. Well, booze and these."

Harlan held up hands that still wore suede gloves that would have looked much less out of place outdoors. His eyes, nearly as dark as his brows, crinkled at the corners when he leaned close. There was only the slightest hint of bourbon on his breath. So what had Adam picked up on before? The slight flush in his face? That could be explained by the warmth of the room, and because, in addition to his gloves, Harlan was still wearing his coat and a John Deere cap. Was it something about Harlan's eyes, or how deliberately he'd pronounced his words?

"So I told you what I'm hiding from," Harlan said, in a voice that sounded perfectly normal. Adam thought he must be picking up on some other cue. "What about you, Adam? What are you hiding from?"

Adam turned his face away, wishing he could roll on his side to face the opposite wall. He really wasn't ready to deal with this, with his crazy, kidnapper father and everything else. If he could drive—and his car wasn't still in a ditch—he'd be on the interstate in an hour. Say his goodbyes to Iris and find the next soft-hearted bar owner willing to let him sleep next to the inventory.

"Don't worry. We don't need to talk about your dad yet," Harlan said.

Adam jerked his IV again when he twisted around with the intent of—what? Yelling at Harlan. Telling him to stay out of his head. Lot of good that would do.

"I'm not reading your mind—I promise. Just intuition, remember? And common sense. Obviously the man's going to be on your mind, after what you experienced, and what Iris told you. But he's not the only thing, is he? What is it you want to ask me?"

Adam shook his head. "Is anyone able to keep secrets from you?"

"You'd be surprised," Harlan said.

Adam had his own burst of intuition—*Iris*. Iris kept secrets from Harlan.

Harlan nodded as if Adam had spoken out loud.

If Harlan could trust him enough to allow him that peek, Adam supposed he could allow Harlan the same. "Okay, fine. When I did whatever I did up on the mountain..." Adam faltered.

"You mean, when you saved Rachel's life?" Adam nodded, and Harlan went on, "An incredible feat of stupidity, by the way. Like using your blood to put out a fire when there's a bucket of water handy. I wonder what the doctors made of you when you came in, if there were any symptoms that didn't add up. It's hard to tell what you did to your body physically, or how much they could do to fix it."

"You didn't feel it, did you?"

Harlan's mouth wrinkled in a kind of grimace as he tried to explain. "Well, I'd say I had an inkling of something."

"But I didn't drain you, too, did I?" Adam asked.

"No!" Harlan reached for Adam's hand. Adam jerked away, then relaxed when he felt the soft fabric of Harlan's glove instead of bare skin. "You are your mother's son. Through and through. You know that, don't you?"

Adam shook his head. "I never knew my mom."

"Both soft-hearted idiots, in the best possible way. Well, that's why you need to talk with Iris. Your father isn't the only one she can tell you about. And like I said, you don't have to talk about him until you're ready." Harlan released Adam's hand and leaned forward on one elbow on the bed, as if he were sitting at a bar. "Iris is waiting outside, by the way. She's hoping you can stay for a while. With her, here in Cold Springs. Not that she'll ever come out and ask directly."

Adam was tempted. Not that he'd come out and admit it, either. He might be his mother's son, but he had a lot of Iris in him, too. And then, there was the other thing.

"What other thing?" Harlan asked.

Adam wanted to be angry when Harlan read him like that,

except sometimes he needed it, too, needed someone to meet him half—or maybe more than half—way. "I'm afraid to touch anyone now," Adam whispered, as if it were a shameful secret.

"Why?" Harlan asked, pragmatic, as if it were the kind of confession he heard every day, one with no more significance than which brand of gasoline he preferred.

"Sometimes, it's because I'm afraid I'll... take something from them."

"You mean, you're afraid you'll drain JJ and Iris, the way you let Rachel drain you," Harlan translated.

Adam nodded.

"And what about the other times?" Harlan asked.

Adam thought of his father, of the images washing over him, and of his physical aversion to Agent D'Antonio. "Other times, I'm afraid of what they'll let me see."

Harlan sat up and rubbed his face with his hands, then let out a heavy exhale. "Next time, I'm bringing a flask. Listen, those are perfectly reasonable and understandable fears. You've got crazy shit going on, and you don't know how to control it. That's something I can help you with, if you stick around for a while. But in the meantime, I don't think you need to worry too much about the touch thing."

"Why not?"

"I told you before, this works different for everybody." Harlan leaned in and pointed a tan gloved finger at Adam. "But what you did... you almost died, Adam. Trust me, you came too goddamn close. And for most people, it takes a while to come back from something like that. Sort of like blowing a fuse. It may never come back at all. Or the touch thing could have just been something temporary you picked up from me."

"You think?" Adam asked, hopeful for the first time since he'd woken up.

Harlan grinned and pulled off a glove. "Care to find out? If you're as burned out as I think you are, you may be the only person I can shake hands with in the whole damned building."

Adam stretched out his right hand, the one that wouldn't make a proper fist or a proper handshake, but didn't have an IV in it. He felt the slightest tingle when Harlan gripped his hand. Harlan squeezed harder, and the tingle faded away until Adam was left with nothing but the sensation of the man's rough calluses.

"See, that wasn't so bad," Harlan said. He stood, releasing Adam's hand. Adam felt an instant of anxiety, until Harlan peeled his coat off and settled back into the chair. Harlan switched off the light, before slouching down in his chair and pulling his cap farther down over his eyes.

It was so quiet. Peaceful, even. Adam felt Harlan's hand brush his forehead, and his eyes drifted shut. Just before he sank into sleep, he heard Harlan's voice next to him.

"So what do you say, son? Is it finally time to stop running?"

"Yeah, okay," Adam mumbled. "For a little while."

"Good," Harlan said.

And then a woman's voice (Adam couldn't tell—was it Iris or JJ?) echoed, *Good*.

ACKNOWLEDGMENTS

You wouldn't be reading this series if it weren't for the fine folks at Sterling & Stone—thank you for the structure, the guidance, and most of all for the kick in the pants. Thanks also to my fellow Apprentices, especially the White Gloves, for the camaraderie and support and various sanity-saving hacks.

Continued thanks to Alida and Calee for their assistance in pushing a structurally sound and shiny manuscript across the finish line, and to Sandy and Paul for keeping me narratively honest and emotionally intact. Finally, a big thank you to the readers for sharing my stories and helping me do what I love.

Once we've moved on to different pastures (green or otherwise), many of us have ambivalent relationships with the places we've come from. For me, time and distance have softened the edges of my experience, and this book draws from what remains. In other words, it's a distillation—a moonshine of the mind, if you will—not a guidebook to West Virginia. If you do feel the urge to visit that lovely state, I recommend the fall, with the leaves as bright as a child's paper cutouts. And have some apple butter for me.

ABOUT THE AUTHOR

A recovering criminal attorney, Judy K. Walker writes from her home in Hawaii, where she is surrounded by husband, dogs, cat, and assorted geckos. Her life's journey may have taken her thousands of miles from her West Virginia origins, but she's thrilled to return to her roots in the *Dead Hollow Trilogy*. She also writes the Sydney Brennan Mysteries, a private investigator series set in Tallahassee, Florida, another of her stops along the way.

Many readers need an extra nudge to take a chance on an Indie Author because—let's face it—they're afraid one of my dogs barfed on the keyboard and I hit "Publish." If you enjoyed *Prodigal*, please consider leaving a quick review on your retailer or book review site of choice—just a few lines will do. Thank you!

You can learn more about Dead Hollow and connect with me online at:
www.judykwalker.com